Praise for Audrey Bellezza and Emily Harding's
"charming debut" (*Publishers Weekly*)

Emma of 83rd Street

"A glamorous romp that is heartfelt, steamy, and romantic . . . For fans of the movie *Clueless* and retellings of classics."

—*Library Journal*

"The best romantic comedy I've ever read."

—Lauren Layne, *New York Times* bestselling author of *Made in Manhattan*

"A compulsive page-turner with excellent slow-burn tension. An instant favorite!"

—Sarah Hogle, author of *You Deserve Each Other*

"The authors bring plenty of wit to this classic friends-to-lovers tale."

—*Publishers Weekly*

"Delightfully modern and compulsively readable, this made my *Clueless*-loving heart sing—a knockout debut!"

—. . . *ipped*

T0191005

"A delightful debut . . . sweeter than candy."

—Marilyn Simon Rothstein, author of
Husbands and Other Sharp Objects

"A great summer beach read . . . From its Lilly Pulitzer–colored cover to its Blair Waldorf–type protagonist, this book should be purchased immediately because it's going to ride off shelves like a vintage Jaguar with the top down."

—*Bookreporter*

"Austenites and rom-com fans rejoice: *Emma of 83rd Street* is witty, wonderful, and the best retelling of *Emma* since *Clueless*. I loved every minute of it."

—Sarvenaz Tash, coauthor of
Ghosting: A Love Story

"[A] fresh, utterly charming, feel-good retelling of an enduring classic. Whip-smart, pitch-perfect, and newly minted."

—Julie Valerie, author of
Holly Banks Full of Angst

"Bellezza and Harding balance introspection with a healthy dose of New York glitz . . . as with all Austen adaptations, the joy—and there's plenty of it—is definitely in the journey."

—*Shelf Awareness*

"Warm, sweet, and funny, *Emma of 83rd Street* is a fun take on a comforting classic and a fresh reminder of all the reasons we love romance."

—Genevieve Novak, author of *Crushing*

"[A] witty and romantic debut novel."

—*The Nerd Daily*

"A frothy city romp based on one of Austen's most delightfully fun stories. I couldn't have enjoyed this slice of NYC fantasy more."

—Ali Rosen, author of
Recipe for Second Chances

"A delicious wonder of a book . . . Bellezza and Harding effortlessly make this contemporary retelling of the classic Austen novel into a delightful romance filled with characters and a love story you'll definitely want to revisit."

—*Sheaf & Ink*

ALSO BY
AUDREY BELLEZZA AND EMILY HARDING

Emma of 83rd Street

Elizabeth
of
East Hampton

A NOVEL

AUDREY BELLEZZA
AND EMILY HARDING

G

GALLERY BOOKS

New York   London   Toronto   Sydney   New Delhi

G

Gallery Books
An Imprint of Simon & Schuster, LLC
1230 Avenue of the Americas
New York, NY 10020

This book is a work of fiction. Any references to historical events, real people, or real places are used fictitiously. Other names, characters, places, and events are products of the author's imagination, and any resemblance to actual events or places or persons, living or dead, is entirely coincidental.

Copyright © 2024 by Audrey Bellezza and Emily Harding

All rights reserved, including the right to reproduce this book or portions thereof in any form whatsoever. For information, address Gallery Books Subsidiary Rights Department, 1230 Avenue of the Americas, New York, NY 10020.

First Gallery Books trade paperback edition August 2024

GALLERY BOOKS and colophon are registered trademarks of Simon & Schuster, LLC

Simon & Schuster: Celebrating 100 Years of Publishing in 2024

For information about special discounts for bulk purchases, please contact Simon & Schuster Special Sales at 1-866-506-1949 or business@simonandschuster.com.

The Simon & Schuster Speakers Bureau can bring authors to your live event. For more information or to book an event, contact the Simon & Schuster Speakers Bureau at 1-866-248-3049 or visit our website at www.simonspeakers.com.

Manufactured in the United States of America

10 9 8 7 6 5 4 3 2 1

Library of Congress Cataloging-in-Publication Data

Names: Bellezza, Audrey, author. | Harding, Emily, author.
Title: Elizabeth of East Hampton : a novel / Audrey Bellezza & Emily Harding.
Description: First Gallery Books trade paperback edition. | New York : Gallery Books, 2024.
Identifiers: LCCN 2024002712 (print) | LCCN 2024002713 (ebook) | ISBN 9781668052556 (trade paperback) | ISBN 9781668052563 (ebook)
Subjects: LCGFT: Romance fiction. | Novels.
Classification: LCC PS3602.E6476 E45 2024 (print) | LCC PS3602.E6476 (ebook) | DDC 813/.6—dc23/eng/20240118
LC record available at https://lccn.loc.gov/2024002712
LC ebook record available at https://lccn.loc.gov/2024002713

ISBN 978-1-6680-5255-6
ISBN 978-1-6680-5256-3 (ebook)

To our fellow Austenites.
Thank you for loving love (and Jane) as much as we do.

MODERN EAST HAMPTON OCEANFRONT ESTATE

Available for Sale and/or Summer Lease

Just 100 miles east of downtown Manhattan, nestled behind a private gated entrance on one of the most desirable lanes in the Hamptons, this impeccably constructed 6,000 sq. ft. home is perfect for both escape and relaxation. The modern 5-bedroom beachfront estate sits on 2.5 acres+/- and features a heated pool, steam sauna, chef's kitchen, detached three-car garage, and imported Italian porcelain bathrooms throughout. The open-flow design concept—which comes fully furnished and includes a bespoke grand piano—boasts floor-to-ceiling windows overlooking the ocean, creating bright and airy spaces that seamlessly connect the interior to the natural beauty outside. A private path through the native grasses allows easy access to the beach. It's also ideal for entertaining, thanks to an expansive verandah off the kitchen and bucolic grounds with well-articulated landscaping. In addition, you'll be mere steps away from all the world-class shops, galleries, and restaurants that East Hampton Village has to offer.

Please contact Carrington Realty to schedule a private viewing today.

CHAPTER 1

The Atlantic Ocean hated her. It was the only feasible explanation.

Elizabeth Bennet stared out at the horizon, her surfboard bobbing lazily between her legs. The sunrise painted the clouds in grays and yellows and pinks, colors reflected in the endless expanse of water ahead. It would have been a perfect morning, really, except for one problem: the water was absolutely flat.

Lizzy squeezed her eyes shut and lifted her face to the sky, silently praying to whoever might be listening: *Come on. All I want is one wave. Just one, and I promise to go the rest of the summer without rolling my eyes at anybody. Please?*

A moment, then she peeked out at the water around her. Still flat as a pancake.

Well, that settled it. Mother Nature was a sadist.

It was no secret that the beach break off East Hampton was mediocre at best, especially this late in May. Yet somehow the waves had been fantastic over the past two weeks—something akin to a miracle. But today, the one day Lizzy really needed it, the ocean had flatlined.

It wasn't that the summers in East Hampton were awful, per se. Lizzy used to love them when she was younger and would steal muffins from the family bakery to eat amid the dunes on the beach. But as she grew older, she began to recognize how, for three months every year, their small village became something else entirely. Starting Memorial Day weekend, traffic clogged Montauk Highway all the way from the city to the eastern tip of Long Island. Manhattanites crowded the beaches, more intent on posting photos to social media than swimming. The local gossip mill consumed every family conversation, nourishing her mother more than anything they made at Bennet Bakery. It was the same every year.

And Lizzy could just about face it all—she really could—if she could just catch one last wave before summer officially began.

The ocean had other plans, apparently.

She pushed the wet strands of her long red hair away from her face and closed her eyes again, ready to offer the last twenty-one dollars in her savings account—maybe even a few of Bennet Bakery's popular sour cherry muffins—when a sharp ping pierced the silence. She glanced down at her wrist to where her old digital watch was blinking.

5:30 a.m.

Time to go to work.

For a half second, she debated ignoring it. Her dad was probably at the bakery already. He would turn on the ovens, put the cinnamon rolls in the proofer, take the scones out of the fridge, and—

The thought was cut short by a familiar pang of guilt. Wasn't this the whole reason she had put graduate school on hold a few months ago? So she could help out at the bakery while her dad recovered from his stroke and the rest of the family came up with a plan?

You mean the same family who hasn't been able to agree on a movie to watch together in over a decade? a small voice whispered in her head.

Lizzy frowned. It was true, long-term planning was not a Bennet strong suit.

She avoided that sobering train of thought—and the second round of guilt it introduced—to send one last glance out at the ocean ahead.

A minute passed, then a seagull bobbed by. It stared at her expectantly.

"What?" she asked.

It cawed at her.

"I know, I know." She sighed. "I'm going."

The bird looked doubtful.

To prove her point, she turned away and began paddling her board toward shore. That's when something in the periphery caught her eye. Just there, set back on the dark beach.

The lights were on at Marv's Lament.

Huh. Now, that was different.

While most of the houses neatly lining East Hampton's stretch of coastline were fun-house mirror versions of small shingle-sided cottages—bloated in size but still following the unwritten rules of Hamptons aesthetics—the house overlooking Georgica Beach near the end of Lily Pond Lane was a geometric amalgamation of steel and glass, all right angles and sharp lines.

The village dubbed it Marv's Lament over the fact that, despite a public petition that claimed it was an "eyesore" and "insulted the architectural integrity of the village," their mayor, Marvin Long, hadn't found a way to halt its construction. But just as quickly as the nickname had become ubiquitous, the house was mostly forgotten about, sitting dormant except for a few weekends in the summer. Even then, Lizzy couldn't remember who actually owned it. Some tech billionaire? A celebrity? She had no idea, and it never occurred to her to find out, especially after the house went on the market as a summer rental a few years ago. Thanks to its questionable design and a ridiculous price tag, it had been empty and dark ever since.

But not today.

Today every light was on, revealing the modern furniture sparsely placed throughout. As Lizzy emerged from the water and made her way past the wind-sculpted sand dunes peppered with beach grass to the parking lot, she could see a cleaning crew vacuuming around a long, low sofa, meticulously scouring the kitchen's marble countertops. They were still there after she threw her board into the bed of her old Chevy truck and changed from her wetsuit into a T-shirt and her favorite overalls.

Well, well, well, she thought as she slid onto the truck's cracked pleather driver's seat, turning on the heat as soon as the engine roared to life. *Someone finally rented Marv's Lament.* Maybe it was a person her own age, for once. Maybe even someone who knew how to surf. It would be a nice change of pace, exactly the kind of thing she needed after the past year.

Then she turned right out of the beach's parking lot and found a half dozen trucks parked along Lily Pond Lane in front of Marv's Lament, almost entirely blocking the road. The same cluster of cleaners and landscapers and delivery vans from the city that became pervasive every Memorial Day weekend.

She rolled her eyes and laughed to herself, maneuvering around the vehicles as "Fake ID" by the Anemic Boyfriends blared out of her truck's speakers. She should have known better. Hoping for summers out east to change was like hoping for her mother to start speaking at a decibel below screaming: impossible.

~

Bennet Bakery sat between the Mulford Credit Union and East Hampton Hardware in the center of East Hampton Village. Everyone called it "downtown," but really it was just the row of shops lining the corner of Main Street and Newtown Lane. When Lizzy was growing up, there had been more local businesses, but year by year they had been swallowed up by high-end boutiques and brands. Minny Conklin's salon, where Lizzy had gotten her first haircut, was now a gourmet food market. Barbara Long's bridal shop had been replaced by Gucci. Even the old library building was now a Chanel boutique. Bennet Bakery and its two neighbors were some of the last locally owned storefronts in the Village, a fact that had more to do with the building's inexplicably low rent than their profit margin.

Lizzy parked in her usual spot around the back, then gathered her still-damp hair into a bun on top of her head before getting out and entering through the kitchen door. Just like that, the morning's chill evaporated in a fog of heat and powdered sugar. Metal tray racks and bags of flour lined the warm yellow walls, while the smell of vanilla and yeast floated in the air. It hadn't changed much since the bakery opened forty-eight years ago, when her grandparents opened it with the last of their life savings. They had retired and moved to Florida before any of the Bennet sisters were born, leaving the business to Lizzy's dad.

She was fairly certain that nothing had been updated since. They still had her grandfather's original answering machine. The walls were still the same color as they were when Lizzy took her first steps across the red clay tile floors. They even had the same sign in the window, which her grandfather had painted himself.

Lizzy smiled. Every detail fit together like puzzle pieces in one fully formed memory. Remove any one detail and it just wouldn't be the same.

"Morning," she said to the broad back of the man who was pulling a tray out of the bread oven.

Mr. Bennet shifted, turning enough to peer over his shoulder at her. The hard line of his brow accentuated his frown, the fluorescent light above half illuminating his downturned mustache.

"Well?" he asked, his voice gruff.

"Mother Nature hates me," she said with a heavy sigh.

His mouth ticked up with a smile. It was still a bit lopsided on the right side—a subtle reminder of his stroke a few months before. "Or that low-pressure system moved off the coast."

She shrugged. "Tomato, tomahto."

"Right." He turned back to the oven. "Well, I need to start on those delivery invoices, so why don't you get going on the croissants."

Lizzy gave him a small salute, the same one they shared at the start of every shift since she was a teenager, and tied her apron over her overalls, kicking off their morning routine. It was the same every day. Every year.

Apparently, this summer wasn't going to be that different at all.

CHAPTER 2

Will Darcy loved flying. The freedom. The silence. Even the turbulence. It reminded him of being out in the ocean: the irregular bumps, the occasional pitch from side to side. A small nudge to his ego, reminding him how small he was.

Charlie Pierce, on the other hand, had turned green.

"Fuck." His friend mumbled from the seat across from him, eyes squeezed shut as the luxury helicopter angled to the left. "Fuck, fuck, fuck, fuck. Are we there yet?"

Will glanced out the window. From ten thousand feet, the ocean beneath looked serene. The white crests of the waves folded into the shore, while the sun sparkled off the deep blue waters.

"No."

Another bump and Charlie's grip on the leather armrests tightened. "Fuck."

Will leaned back and continued reading the biography he had started at the beginning of the flight. Now wasn't the time to remind Charlie that he had been warned about how rough the forty-five-minute ride from the city out to the Hamptons could be. Will should know—he'd made the trek to the far edge of Long

Island hundreds of times, spending almost every summer in nearby Montauk as a kid. Sure, a jet might have offered a smoother ride, but a helicopter didn't have anywhere close to the environmental impact. Despite the turbulence—and Charlie's weak stomach—it was the most efficient choice. And that was what this summer was all about: efficiency.

A few minutes—and half a chapter—later, the helicopter straightened out and began its descent into East Hampton Airport. The landing was fairly smooth, but when the wheels finally hit the ground, Charlie didn't move.

"Are we alive?" he asked, eyes still squeezed shut.

"Yes."

Charlie exhaled and ran his hands through his dark curly hair. "Thank God."

The blades slowed, and the loud rumble of the engine came to a stop just as the door to the helicopter opened. A cool breeze swept over them as they stepped out onto the tarmac. Will allowed himself a brief moment to enjoy it, tilting his head up to the sun and breathing in the familiar smell of salt and sand floating in the air.

"Welcome to East Hampton."

The cheerful voice broke his reverie, and Will turned to see a woman standing nearby, tablet in hand. It took him a minute to place her. She was a representative with the charter company; he had met her before a flight out to Montauk last summer. She had tried to give him her number, but he had declined. His rebuttal achieved the desired effect at the time, but today her gaze lingered a bit too long on his dark blond hair, his lips set in a grim line. And soon her smile gained a suggestive edge.

"It's nice to see you again, Mr. Darcy," she said.

Before he could answer, the cockpit door opened. The pilot had barely stepped out before Charlie pushed forward and embraced him in a rough hug. "Oh my God. You did it. Thank you."

"Yes, sir, not too bad," the pilot replied, patting Charlie on the back as if this happened all the time. "Just a few bumps at the end there."

The woman laughed, then brought her attention back to Will. "Do you two have plans while you're out here?"

He didn't bother to temper his frown as he answered, "Yes." Then he stepped forward and clamped his hand over Charlie's shoulder. "Let's go."

Will didn't look back as he started toward the car with Charlie trailing behind, enthusiastically thanking the crew again. The woman would probably share the story of him being rude, one that would likely evolve into something much worse the more people who heard it. And that was fine. He had learned a while ago that a momentary break in decorum was better than the slow breakdown of a relationship.

When they settled into the back seat of the black BMW sedan, Charlie grabbed his phone from his jacket pocket. He had turned it off during the flight—according to him, looking at a screen made him even more nauseous—so as soon as the screen illuminated, a flurry of text messages arrived with one long frenetic *PING*. The sound accentuated the caffeine headache beginning to throb at Will's temples.

He needed a cup of coffee.

"Everything all right?" Will asked as their car pulled out of the parking lot.

"One hundred percent," Charlie said with a nod. "Just a few texts from Annabelle and Vivienne."

From the sound of it, "a few" constituted well over a hundred. Even before the flight there had been nonstop messages from

Charlie's sisters, asking when he'd be there, what room Will preferred, even what temperature they'd like the pool.

Charlie hummed, scrolling through the latest litany of texts. "Sounds like the house is great. I just need to call the pool people about the heater . . . and get someone in to clean the windows on the second floor . . . and organize a different rental car . . ." Then his expression lightened. "But Annabelle says that she got Vivienne out of bed this morning, so that's a win, right?"

Will nodded and turned back to the window.

That was the real crux of this summer rental: Vivienne Pierce and her impending divorce. While Annabelle had the same entrepreneurial spirit as her brother—and a successful business to prove it—the older Pierce sister, Vivienne, had made her money the old-fashioned way: through marriage. Three years ago, she married Richard Leland III, the CEO of Hurst Petroleum. Will knew it was a mistake, not only because Hurst Petroleum was under continual investigation by the EPA, but because Richard was widely regarded across New York City as a philandering asshole. Sure enough, in March, Vivienne came home to find the locks changed on their Midtown penthouse and an email waiting from Richard's attorney, clarifying the terms of their prenup. Since then, it had been a war of attrition, so much so that Charlie had been desperate to get his sister out of the city and away from Page Six. At least for a little while.

Once the Pierces secured a house in East Hampton, it had been Charlie's suggestion to work out there remotely all summer. At first, Will had ignored the idea, assuming it was just another whim his friend would eventually forget. After all, they had enough to deal with over the next quarter. The two friends had founded Hampshire M&A after business school and had just celebrated the most profitable quarter in their six-year history. That trajectory needed to be maintained. There were deals still being negotiated—Blaxton Agriculture being the big one—contracts that had to be signed, and Will refused to let anything fall through the cracks, least of all because his business partner got distracted while on a three-month-long vacation.

Unfortunately, Charlie hadn't forgotten. But he had also done his due diligence, meticulously planning out the next few months so his remote presence would barely be noticed. He had even convinced Will to join him on the weekends, because apparently, Will needed to relax.

Will let his head fall back onto the leather headrest. All he needed right now was coffee.

PING.

Another text arrived.

"Oh." Charlie's eyebrows knitted together. "Vivienne wants us to find a bar to go to tonight. She says she wants to drink and 'revenge flirt.' Whatever that means."

Will began to massage his temples, willing his headache to abate.

PING.

"And Annabelle says the groceries haven't arrived yet."

PING.

"So fair warning, there's nothing for breakfast."

PING.

"No milk. No juice. And no coffee, so—"

"Tell her we're taking a detour," Will said.

As their car got closer to town, the sprawling fields surrounding the airport gave way to the main road and colonial homes dotting either side. They passed old South End Cemetery next to Town Pond, and the ancient windmill towering over them both. Each landmark elicited more adulation from Charlie. By the time they pulled up to the sidewalk along the village's main street, Will wasn't even surprised when Charlie gasped aloud at the sight of the grocery store.

"Man, even the franchises look adorable!" Charlie exclaimed as he got out, beaming at the Stop & Shop across the street. "Don't you love it?"

"It's great," Will replied, his voice a steady monotone.

Charlie laughed. "Try to contain your excitement, Will. You're embarrassing yourself."

Will had a biting remark ready, but he swallowed it down. After all, Charlie wore his heart on his sleeve at all times. Will almost envied him.

"Oh, come on," Charlie continued. "You're the one who insisted on flying us out here in that steel death pencil. You can at least pretend to enjoy it."

"Get me some coffee first." Will started forward again, past a boutique selling what appeared to be designer baby clothes.

His friend let out a satisfied sigh. "Well, I love it. Just what Vivienne needs, too. Sun and the beach, and once we get her out of the house, she can go shopping and maybe even meet someone. Then—"

"Focus, Charlie."

"Right, right." His friend gave a decisive nod. "Coffee."

They walked further down the block, past a row of luxury boutiques, until they reached a storefront with a sign in the window that read *Bennet Bakery*. More importantly, there was another one underneath it that read: *Coffee, $1*.

A bell above the door dinged when they entered. There was a long glass counter running the length of the room displaying a scattered selection of pastries and muffins, while baskets full of baguettes lined the top. They blocked the view of the register, so it wasn't until Will and Charlie were in the middle of the room that they noticed the man sitting behind it. He glanced up from his pile of paperwork, watching as Charlie took in the bakery's muted yellow walls and mismatched tables and chairs. Meanwhile, Will zeroed in on the coffeemaker behind the counter.

"I'll take a coffee," Will said, approaching the man. Then he called over to his friend. "Charlie?"

"Hm?" He snapped out of his reverie and turned. "Oh! Um, can you do a decaf flat white?"

The man stared at Charlie blankly.

Will took out his wallet. "Make that two coffees."

The man nodded, then turned to the coffeemaker and began filling two paper cups.

While Will waited, he looked down the row of baked goods under the glass. There was a small selection left—a few croissants, a couple of apple turnovers, some blueberry muffins. There was also an empty tray behind a small handwritten sign that read: *Try our famous sour cherry muffins!*

"Any more of the cherry muffins?" he asked.

The man leaned away from the coffeemaker and bellowed to the back room, "Any sour cherry left?"

Will followed the man's gaze, looking through the doorway at the end of the counter into the kitchen. It was only then that he noticed that someone else was there: a woman. Her back was to him, but Will could see she was in overalls, with a mess of red hair thrown up in a bun on the top of her head. He'd never seen hair like that, every shade of crimson and copper and rust. Pulled together, it almost looked like a flame.

"Nope!" the woman yelled over her shoulder without turning around. Then she turned to her left and disappeared from view.

"Nope," the man repeated, putting the two coffees on the counter. "Anything else?"

Will cleared his throat and brought his attention back to the pastries display. "We'll take those croissants, then. A half dozen blueberry muffins, too."

The man nodded and snapped open a white pastry box. "That all?"

Charlie snapped his fingers. "Oh! And a bar!"

The man paused. "A what?"

"Sorry," Charlie said, catching himself. "This is our first summer out here. We're renting a house on Georgica Beach. This modern one off—"

"Marv's Lament?"

Charlie blinked. "Excuse me?"

"Marv's Lament. That big glass house on Lily Pond Lane."

"That's us." Charlie laughed. "I didn't realize it had a name."

"Yup." The man grabbed the croissants from their tray. "Marv almost lost reelection over that eyesore."

Will's lips twitched as Charlie laughed again, albeit a bit more nervously. "Right. And Marv is . . ."

"The mayor."

"Ah." Charlie looked momentarily confused. "That's such a coincidence. The landlord told us that there had been a guy named Marv taking care of the house in the off-season, so I thought—"

"Same guy."

"Oh," Charlie said, then offered a warm smile. "Well, I'm Charlie Pierce. This is my friend Will."

The man nodded and then reached for the blueberry muffins. "Bob Bennet."

"It's nice to meet you, Bob," Charlie said. It looked like he was about to try to shake hands before noticing that Bob had the pastry box in one hand and two muffins in the other. "Right. So, like I said, we just got in and my sister's looking to go out tonight. Grab a drink. Can you recommend a place nearby?"

Bob leaned back and shouted toward the kitchen again. "Hey, kiddo!"

"Coming!" a woman's voice called back. There was shuffling, the sound of a metal tray sliding into a rack, then the redheaded woman appeared in the doorway. Her hair was still piled on top of her head, but a few wisps had escaped, skimming her cheeks as she adjusted the apron over her overalls. When she finally looked up, Will's attention snagged on her eyes. They were dark, so dark it was almost distracting.

"What's up?" she asked.

Bob motioned to Charlie and Will. "These guys want to go out tonight and are looking for a bar."

"Just a recommendation. If it's not too much trouble," Charlie added, his smile widening. He already had his phone out, ready to type the name in his Notes app.

She smiled back, leaning against the doorframe as she wiped her flour-covered hands on her apron. Whether she realized it was all over her cheeks and hair as well, Will had no idea.

"Well, there's that new place over by the golf club. I think it's called Almack's?" she said. "I haven't been there, but I hear it's nice. Everybody's been talking about all the palm trees they brought in, and I guess there's a martini—"

Will scoffed before he could stop himself. He knew the kind of bar she was describing: sleek, stylish, and filled with people looking to be seen. There were enough of those in the city; he didn't want to waste his time at one out here.

The woman's smile flattened. "Do you have a problem with palm trees?"

"Not at all!" Charlie interjected. "We love palm trees." He turned to Will, as if expecting his friend to affirm their shared love of tropical foliage.

Will chose not to. Instead, he brought his attention back to the woman's eyes. "We're looking for somewhere a bit more authentic."

She stared at him for a moment, then her smile returned a bit sharper than before. "Ohhh. You want somewhere *authentic*."

Will frowned while Charlie stood with his phone poised and ready, completely missing the sarcasm laced in the woman's tone.

"Well then, you should definitely check out Donato Lodge," she continued.

"Donato Lodge," Charlie repeated.

The woman nodded. "It's just about as authentic as you can get."

Bob coughed, though it sounded like a feeble attempt to disguise a laugh, and began ringing them up.

"Perfect!" Charlie said, typing out what Will could only assume was a verbatim transcription of the conversation so he could relay it to his sister later. "Thank you."

"Sure thing," the woman said to Charlie. She completely ignored Will.

He ignored her, too, handing Bob a twenty and waving off his change as he picked up his coffee.

"This has been great. Really great." Charlie slipped his phone back into his pocket so he could pick up the pastry box in one hand and his coffee in the other. "I'm sure we'll be in again soon."

Bob hummed, his attention already back on his paperwork. "Do you have Marv's number?"

"I think so." Charlie paused. "Why?"

"If you go out tonight and need a cab. Cheaper to call him than going through the app."

"Because Marv is . . ."

"The Uber driver in town, too."

"Of course. Right." Charlie nodded. "Well, thank you!" Then he turned and followed his friend out the door.

Outside, Will stopped on the sidewalk, taking a sip of his coffee as he watched the tall trees that lined Main Street sway lazily in the breeze. Just yesterday he had been in a three-hour-long board meeting, picking apart a prospective company's earnings report. But now, as the comforting smell of the salty ocean air enveloped him, it felt like he was in a different world. Despite how it had changed over the years, the Hamptons had a way of anchoring his emotions, calming any ruminating thoughts, like nothing else ever could.

The coffee helped, too.

Charlie stopped beside him and let out a satisfied sigh. "See, this is what I was talking about! Small town, nice people. I know we're here for Vivienne, but I think this might be exactly what I needed."

Will stole a glance over his shoulder. Through the front window, the bakery looked empty, with only the top of Bob's head visible behind the counter. No redhead in sight.

He turned away and took another sip of his coffee, enjoying the first moment of peace he'd had all day. "Me, too."

CHAPTER 3

At exactly 11:04 a.m., the ethereal sound of Stevie Nicks singing "Dreams" through the bakery's ancient speakers was interrupted by the distinctive voice of Mrs. Joanne Bennet.

"BOB!"

Lizzy winced, leaning back from the massive glob of sourdough she was shaping into loaves to peer through the kitchen doorway to the front room. The morning rush had abated hours ago. To be fair, it wasn't much of a rush. With the exception of that pretentious guy who hated palm trees, it had just been their regulars who ordered the same thing every Saturday morning. Now the front of Bennet Bakery was empty except for the woman maneuvering her way inside.

"Why do I have to do everything myself!?" Mrs. Bennet cried, struggling to fit through the front door with her pink tote bag on one arm and a life-sized pair of disembodied mannequin legs wearing iridescent zebra-print leggings under the other.

Lizzy turned to peer into the small office near the bakery's back door. "I think that's for you."

Mr. Bennet looked up from the bank statements on his desk to glare over the rim of his reading glasses at his daughter. Crumbs of a past donut dusted his mustache, accentuating his frown. Whether the look was due to the bakery's negligible profit margin or the arrival of his wife was unclear.

He stared at Lizzy. She stared back. And then, in unison, they each raised a single fist.

"Rock, paper, scissors, shoot!" they recited in unison.

Mr. Bennet threw scissors.

Lizzy threw paper.

Mr. Bennet barely cracked a smile as he turned back to his paperwork.

"We need to go back to flipping a coin," Lizzy mumbled as she wiped her hands on her apron and started toward the front room.

When Lizzy reached the doorway, Mrs. Bennet was just navigating around the glass countertop and heading toward her, a blur in bedazzled purple athleisure wear as she dropped her pink bag in a nearby chair. It missed, falling to the floor with a thud.

"Is he back there?" she demanded, stopping in front of her daughter.

Lizzy crossed her arms and leaned against the doorframe. "Dad? No, he took a job at this paper company in Scranton. Good benefits."

Mrs. Bennet rolled her eyes and pushed herself and her mannequin legs past her, through the kitchen, and into the back office.

"Why was my leggings display still sitting at home this morning when I told you— Bob Bennet, are you eating a donut?" her mother shrieked, the door slamming shut behind her.

For a moment, Lizzy debated whether she should go rescue her father, but then Lydia's voice cut through the air.

"Oh my God, it's so *early*."

It seemed the other Bennet sisters had arrived, too.

Lizzy turned back around and saw Jane first. The eldest Bennet sister was kneeling down to pick up their mother's tote bag where it lay upside down on the red tile floor. Her dark hair was in a ponytail, with a few wisps framing her heart-shaped face. It was hard for her sister to skew her angelic features into anything like disapproval, but she was trying her best as she replied, "It's eleven a.m., Lydia."

Lydia moaned as she landed in a chair at a nearby table, then promptly let her head collapse into her arms. Kitty sat down across from her, her attention on her phone. They were identical twins and for most of their life, it had been almost impossible to tell them apart. Then they both started at Suffolk County Community College two years ago. Within a few weeks, Kitty had joined the Future Business Leaders of America, while Lydia joined TikTok. Now, with both about to graduate next month with associate's degrees, they couldn't be more different: Lydia, with long hair like a silk curtain over her back and an oversized sweatshirt almost completely covering her small biker shorts, barely passed most of her classes. Meanwhile, Kitty—who looked like she was on her way to a board meeting with a short bob and perfectly pressed white button-up shirt—was already looking into bachelor's programs at SUNY.

"Eleven *is* early," Lydia whined into her sleeve.

"Not when you were supposed to be here at six," Kitty murmured, attention still on her screen.

Lydia picked her head up, eyes barely open. "Why are you yelling?"

"I'm not yelling."

"You're so loud," Lydia grumbled as she stood up again and shuffled around the counter, her Crocs making a dull scraping sound on the floor as she made a beeline to the coffee machine. "I don't even know why I have to work this weekend anyway. Do you even know how many parties are happening? This is child abuse."

Lizzy cocked her head to the side. "Bold claim from a twenty-one-year-old."

A rogue tube of lip gloss had rolled under a chair, and Jane stuffed it back into their mother's tote as she gave Lizzy a look. It was the look the two eldest Bennet sisters had honed over the past twenty-five years: a weary smile, a furrowed brow, a roll of the eyes. All a truncated version of the same conversation they had had a million times before:

Be nice, Jane would say.

I am being nice, Lizzy would reply.

Okay. Then be patient.

Jane, I don't think anyone could survive in this family without the patience of a saint.

Are you the saint in this scenario?

In the colloquial sense? Absolutely.

Jane smiled and shook her head.

"Like, the party last night was epic," Lydia continued, oblivious. "It was at this huge house in Sag Harbor, and there was just . . . so much rum."

Jane stood and placed the tote on a table, her eyebrows knitted together. "I thought you hated rum."

Lydia paused, the coffeepot in hand, as if this fact sounded familiar. "Do I hate rum?"

"You hate rum," Lizzy, Jane, and Kitty answered in unison.

Lydia scowled. "You're all so loud." Then she let out a tortured cry. "How am I supposed to get a cup of coffee if there's no cups for the coffee?"

Jane was already coming around the counter, picking up a sleeve of to-go coffee cups from below the register as she passed. Lizzy followed, taking the cups from her sister's hand before she could restock them. "You're not on the schedule today."

Jane smiled, trying to grab them back. "Neither are you."

"And where are all the sour cherry muffins?" Lydia moaned.

Lizzy ignored the question as she dodged Jane's reach, then handed the sleeve of cups to Lydia. "Here. Restock these."

Lydia offered another pout, and Lizzy was about to remind her that if she had bothered showing up for her shift, she would have known they sold out of sour cherry muffins hours ago, but then their mother's voice pierced the air again.

"It's not going to take up the whole bakery! I just need a little space up front for a small display. You won't even notice it." She emerged from the back office and marched through the kitchen, the mannequin legs still cradled under her arm. Mr. Bennet followed behind her, though there was no evidence he was actually listening to his wife. He was still studying his paperwork as he stopped in the doorway.

Mrs. Bennet walked to the front of the bakery, lifting the mannequin legs onto the table by the window. "We'll put it right here. That way, even if she doesn't come in, she'll see it when she walks by, you know?"

Lizzy watched, amused. "And who is 'she'?"

Mrs. Bennet's eyes lit up, realizing she had stumbled into a rare moment when she had her family's attention.

"Oh, you haven't heard?" She abandoned the leggings to waltz into the center of the room. "Well, Donna called me last night with some *very* interesting news."

Lizzy leaned across the glass counter and rested her chin in her hand. She knew what was coming. Her mother wielded gossip the way the Dutch masters wielded a paintbrush.

"You know that house near the end of Lily Pond Lane?" Mrs. Bennet said. "The enormous glass one that's been empty for ages?"

"Marv's Lament?" Kitty ventured.

Mrs. Bennet continued as if she hadn't heard. "You know, Marv's Lament! Well, someone rented it! A rich businesswoman from Manhattan. And you'll never guess what she made her money in!" Mrs. Bennet paused to not-so-subtly motion down to her bedazzled purple leggings as she waited for an answer.

"Charades?" Lizzy offered.

Mrs. Bennet rolled her eyes. "No, *fashion*. Her name is Annabelle something or other, and she owns a chain of boutiques that's worth millions!"

Kitty's head popped up from her phone. "You mean Annabelle Pierce? I just saw a piece about her on *Bloomberg*! She expanded her mom's clothing store in Denver to over two hundred locations across the country and she's only like thirty-two or something. She's brilliant. God, do you think she'd be willing to look over my business plan? Maybe I could even—"

"And she's coming here for the whole summer!" Mrs. Bennet cut her off. "Can you believe it? Just when I've started to break into the fashion business myself. It's kismet!"

Lydia yawned as she ripped open a sugar packet. "So what? Rich women from New York are like a dime a dozen here."

"Oh really?" Mrs. Bennet said, turning to glare at her youngest daughter, even as a sly grin pulled at her lips. "And how many of those rich women bring their single brother with them?"

This made Lydia perk up enough to abandon her coffee. "Brother?"

Mrs. Bennet nodded, biting her bottom lip. "The real estate agent who brokered the deal is friends with Donna's neighbor's sister, and she said this Annabelle woman was looking for a place for the whole summer for her, her sister, and her brother. Her single, *rich* brother. At least, that's what Donna said. Supposedly there's some other man coming in on the weekends, too, a friend of the brother or something."

Lydia's expression flattened. "So he's gay."

Mrs. Bennet shot her a look. "He's not gay."

"To be fair, he could be gay," Lizzy said, barely holding back a smile.

Her mother waved her off. "If he was gay, he'd go to Fire Island."

Kitty looked as if she was going to object, but Mrs. Bennet barreled on.

"Anyway, according to Donna, they're all supposed to arrive today, but no one has seen them yet." She turned back to her husband. "So?"

There was a long moment before Mr. Bennet looked up from the bills in his hand. "What?"

Mrs. Bennet gestured wildly to the door. "Has Annabelle Pierce come in yet!"

"I didn't see anybody named Annabelle." His attention went back to the bills. "But two guys from the city stopped in a little while ago."

All eyes turned to him.

"Two . . . men?" Mrs. Bennet took a step toward her husband. "Did you get their names?"

He paused, deigning to give the query a moment's consideration. Meanwhile, Lizzy and Jane shared another look. They both knew their father probably remembered, but toying with his wife's nerves was one of the few joys Mr. Bennet had these days. They let him savor it. "One of them was named Charlie something. Powell? Prince?"

"Pierce!" Mrs. Bennet practically screamed.

"Yeah. That was it."

Mrs. Bennet let out a strangled cry as Kitty and Lydia eagerly leaned toward him.

"What did they say?" Kitty asked.

"Were they hot?" Lydia probed.

"Girls, focus!" their mother said, recovering. Then she turned back to her husband. "Tell me everything."

Mr. Bennet's frown returned. "It's a bakery, Joanne. They came in, bought some muffins, and got some coffee. Then they asked where they could grab a drink tonight and Lizzy told them to go to Donato Lodge."

Mrs. Bennet's mouth fell open in horror as she turned to her second oldest daughter. "You sent them to the *Lodge*?"

Lizzy cringed. When she'd recommended the Lodge to the palm tree hater, it had almost been a joke, a small payback for a man who obviously needed to be knocked down a few pegs. She hadn't thought her mother would offer a critique. After all, she didn't seem to mind that her daughters spent almost every Saturday night there. Of course, that was usually in the off-season, when their town was dead and the bar was only ever half-full with locals imbibing warm beer and Tater Tots. Summer changed its DNA, when tourists clogged the dance floor, making it feel like a Disneyland version of a dive bar.

"They said they wanted someplace authentic," Lizzy replied with a shrug.

Lydia snorted out a laugh.

"Okay, you know what? This is fine," Mrs. Bennet said almost to herself. "Completely fine. We can work with this."

Jane sighed, betraying a half second of exasperation, which, for a woman who spent most weekdays teaching a room full of six-year-olds, was colossal. "Mom, can we not spend another summer trying to sell—"

"Come on, ladies! It's Lux Leggings time!"

There was a collective groan across the bakery.

The only other thing as consistent as gossip in East Hampton

Village was their mother's dedication to a new multilevel marketing business every summer. By May, Mrs. Bennet would latch on to one that inevitably took over their entire basement for the season, and then, like clockwork, it would be abandoned by September. Last year it was Porto-Pockets, detachable pockets that could be stuck to any dress with Velcro. The year before had been the Shimmer Scrunchie, a hair accessory that featured solar-powered LED lights. Now their mother had decided the best way to succeed was by starting her own MLM from the ground up. So, after weeks of YouTube sewing tutorials and hundreds of yards of fabric strewn around the house, she was ready to bring her brainchild to market: Lux Leggings, the world's only leggings with a built-in belt (patent pending).

Lydia frowned as her mother turned the disembodied mannequin legs so their zebra-print Lycra hips were angled toward the door. "You think this lady is going to want to buy your leggings?"

"You better hope so, or all five of you will be stuck working at the bakery until the end of time," Mrs. Bennet quipped.

The comment lodged in Lizzy's chest, heavy and sharp and too close to the truth. She had dreamed of leaving East Hampton since childhood, staying up past her bedtime to read countless breaking news stories about the world beyond her bedroom walls. Then, in twelfth grade, a hurricane tore through the Hamptons and she wrote about the town's lack of preparedness for her school newspaper. The article was so explosive it was picked up by *New York* Magazine and almost got Marv impeached. But more importantly, it gave Lizzy a purpose: she wanted to be a journalist.

Six years and countless online classes squeezed in between her shifts at the bakery later, she earned her bachelor's from SUNY. And maybe if she had wanted to stay in the Hamptons, covering stories close to home, that would have been enough. But she didn't want to stay here. She was going to travel the world, covering issues that mattered to millions of people. And to do that, she needed her master's. She had spent weeks perfecting her application to Columbia's School of Journalism before finally sending it in. It was a long shot—she hadn't even told her family—but then, on a mundane morning in March, she received her acceptance email. For a brief, shining moment, it felt like everything was finally falling into place. Like all the hard work and monotony had counted for something. Then, two days later, before she'd even figured out how to tell her parents, she walked into the bakery to find her father on the floor of the kitchen.

The stroke had been so severe that the paramedics said if they had arrived five minutes later, he would have died. And even though Mr. Bennet was out of the hospital after two weeks, claiming he would be back to his old self in no time, his doctor said recovery could take a year, if not more. Suddenly, Lizzy's plan to spend the summer getting ready to start school in the fall was usurped by the need to keep the family business afloat. Columbia let her defer for a semester—space permitting—but she didn't know if it was long enough. Her sisters did what they could, but none of them knew how to run the bakery the way she did. Even now, Lizzy realized, they hadn't all bothered to show up. "Where's Mary?"

Lydia waved her hand indiscriminately in the air. "I think she's still tied to that tree on the North Shore for PETA."

"It's a Green Justice protest," Kitty murmured, eyes back on her phone.

"Can we focus, please?" Mrs. Bennet clapped her hands, bringing the conversation back to herself. "I need you all to think big picture, m'kay? You girls show up to the Lodge tonight all wearing Lux Leggings. Annabelle comes in, sees them, and the seed will be planted. She'll compliment you—of course—then she'll ask where you bought them. She'll tell her friends, they'll all post about them online. Orders will come flying in! Then this Annabelle woman will see everyone wearing the leggings she discovered, and she'll want to invest! And that brother of hers? Supposedly he works in mergers and acquisitions! He literally *buys* companies! You can bet he'll take an interest, too. What else does he have to spend his money on? It's like my mother always said: 'A single man in possession of a good fortune, must be in want of—'"

"Zebra-print leggings with an adjustable waistband?" Lizzy said, offering her mother an overly sweet smile.

"Well, he's definitely not looking for a twenty-five-year-old with a mess of split ends and overalls." Then Mrs. Bennet clicked her tongue in disappointment as she seemed to finally take in the pile of red hair on top of her daughter's head. "Honestly, Lizzy. Did you even try that deep-conditioning mask I left in the bathroom?"

"I'm going with an organic seaweed treatment," Lizzy said, fluffing her topknot and pretending to fix her flyaways. "You just take bits of seaweed you find floating by and grab them, which is actually really hard to do because they're so slippery—"

Mrs. Bennet huffed and picked up her tote from where Jane had placed it. "I'm leaving. Bob! No more donuts! You have an appointment with your neurologist next week. Lizzy! I don't want him eating any more donuts." She didn't wait for Lizzy's reply, just turned to Lydia. "And I need you at home for inventory. We should narrow down the options for tonight."

Lydia rolled her eyes. "But it's eleven a.m. On *Saturday*."

"Exactly. We have to get going," Mrs. Bennet replied, her tote over her shoulder as she started for the door. "God, I haven't even gone through the new bedazzled collection yet. You can help me with that, Jane."

"Actually, I have to head to the school today and get the classroom ready for—"

"You can do that after," their mother continued, undaunted. "Okay, I think that's it. Now where's Kitty? Kitty!"

Kitty looked up, brows pinched. "I'm right here."

"Well, why didn't you say so?" Their mother didn't wait for an answer, just threw open the front door and ushered the women through. "I'm not waiting around all day, ladies! Come on!"

There was a flurry of goodbyes, a sympathetic look from Jane to Lizzy, and a final moan from Lydia before the door closed behind them with a ring of its tinny bell.

And just like that, the bakery was quiet again, with only Fleetwood Mac's *Rumours* still playing overhead.

CHAPTER 4

When Bob Bennet had mentioned that locals called Charlie's house Marv's Lament, Will hadn't given it much thought. But after their car left the bakery and made its way down Lily Pond Lane, past the long line of multimillion-dollar wood-shingled estates tucked safely behind manicured privet hedgerows, it all made sense.

The house, which loomed over the end of a long driveway, was a steel-and-glass monstrosity, rising up from the manicured lawn like a half-finished construction site.

"Here we are!" Charlie announced like a kid showing off a shiny new toy.

He leapt out but Will took his time, collecting his jacket and putting his sunglasses on before emerging. The white gravel stones of the driveway crunched loudly with each step as he walked to where Charlie was gaping up at the angular facade.

On paper, the house checked every box: expansive grounds, obligatory swimming pool, private beachfront access, too many windows to count, and a flat slat roof with overhangs that seemed to be miraculously suspended by God himself. In person, it was about as far from the Hamptons as you could get. And nothing Will would have picked himself.

Thankfully, he hadn't been forced to. Even though Will had spent every summer of his childhood just twenty minutes further up the coast at his family's beach house in Montauk—and was now spending too much time renovating it—he had little interest in helping Charlie and his sisters navigate the Hamptons real estate market. When they asked, he simply passed along his aunt's information. Birdie Carrington had made a name for herself in real estate out east, building one of the most prestigious agencies on Long Island. Will knew she would salivate at the chance to find the Pierces the perfect beachfront rental, and sure enough, just three weeks after Annabelle contacted her, she had the Pierces signing a three-month lease before Charlie had even seen a picture.

"Wow, it's . . . big," Charlie said, his hands on his hips. Billowing hydrangeas framed the path up to the looming front door, but they did nothing to soften the structure's hard lines. "But beautiful. It's beautiful, right?"

Will glared up at it. He usually didn't mince words, but in the interest of time, he made an exception.

"Let's find your sisters."

That was the only prompting Charlie needed. He bounded up the front steps while Will followed behind.

"Annabelle? Viv?" Charlie called out as he opened the front door.

The foyer was cavernous, but it was merely a hint of the space beyond: an enormous sunken living room with a grand piano and a sprawling chef's kitchen on the left. As Will walked forward, staff—cleaning crews carrying sheets and towels up a wide staircase, movers lifting a long white sofa across the living room—buzzed around him.

None of it distracted from the panoramic views of the beach just a few yards away, though. Sunlight reflected off the ocean onto every surface in the place through the building's glass walls. Will stopped at the sliding doors that were open to the pool, filling the space with the smell of salt and sand.

"Took you long enough," Annabelle announced, appearing from a nearby hallway. Her brown hair was up in her signature ponytail to showcase what Will could only assume were new honey-colored highlights. A long beach dress hung loosely over her thin frame. "I thought the whole point of flying was to get here faster." Before either of them could reply, her attention snagged on the group of movers in the living room. "The sofa is fine. We need to move the piano to the corner!"

The men set the sofa down and moved to roll the piano to the far corner of the room. Will frowned. The piano was just about the only thing he liked about the place. Now it was almost completely hidden. Then again, that was probably the point. Will was sure none of the Pierce family even knew how to play.

"God, I'm exhausted," Annabelle huffed, throwing herself down in an oversized armchair. "The cleaning crew was supposed to be done hours ago, and did you see the car those people from the rental company left? It's last year's model. Obviously, they're coming by to replace it this afternoon. And then, there's Vivienne."

"Is she here?" Charlie asked.

Annabelle sighed and pointed over her shoulder toward the verandah just beyond the sliding doors.

There was a row of lounge chairs lined up alongside the pool, all empty except for the one furthest to the right. Will couldn't see her face from under the wide-brimmed sun hat but recognized the slim body tented under an enormous pink kaftan.

"Hi, Viv," Charlie called out.

The woman didn't turn around, just lifted a well-manicured hand to offer a listless wave.

Charlie held up the white pastry box. "Want a muffin?"

There was a sound of disgust as her hand fell limply to her side.

"She seems . . . good," Will murmured.

"Oh, fantastic," Annabelle said sarcastically, draping her long legs casually over the arm of the chair. "She found out Richard took a date to the ballet's gala last night, so she's spent the whole morning mainlining mimosas."

"I can hear you, you know," Vivienne yelled without moving a muscle.

Charlie smiled through a grimace. "Well, at least she's outside."

"That's only because they haven't made up all the beds yet," Annabelle said. "Speaking of which, we're taking the two suites downstairs. You two are upstairs, in the bedrooms on either end of the hall."

Charlie clapped his hands together again, as if the motion recharged his enthusiasm. "Sounds great!"

"What do you think of the house, Will?" Annabelle asked, a smile now on her face as she waved her hand in the air. "Aren't you glad you came out?"

Will tried not to frown again. The reason he'd finally accepted Charlie's invitation to stay on the weekends wasn't the house, or even to relax. It was nice to catch up with the Pierces, of course, but it also meant Will could ensure Charlie remained on task with work. The fact that he could use the time to also check in on the renovations of his own house in Montauk was an added bonus. There were roofers and plumbers to coordinate, electricians and carpenters to hire . . . even the thought of it gave him a headache. He should have ordered a second cup of coffee from that bakery.

"It's . . . big," he finally replied.

"And beautiful!" Charlie quickly added. "Really gorgeous. And yes, really . . . huge." He paused, looking around. "I mean, I love it, but do we need something this big?"

"Of course we do! Even if Will is only here on weekends, the rest of us are here all summer. We need enough distance from Vivienne so when she gets arrested for stalking her ex-husband online, we can all claim plausible deniability."

From the lounge chair, Vivienne raised her hand again, this time to give her sister the finger.

Annabelle ignored her. "Besides, we need the space for entertaining. You'll want to invite friends out at some point, right? I'm already thinking of throwing a party on the Fourth. Supposedly there's a fantastic fireworks display right out there over the water."

"Perfect. I love it." Charlie smiled broadly, strolling over to the windows. "And that view of the beach! Did you see it, Will?"

"Yes," he responded flatly.

"It's private, too," Annabelle added, smiling smugly.

Will paused, frowning down at her. "The beaches out here are public."

Annabelle's red nails batted away the words. "Technically, yes, but not many people wander down this far. Supposedly a few surfers in the morning, but the real estate agent said they're usually gone by the time we get up, thank God."

Will wanted to challenge her again, ask what was wrong with a few surfers, people who were likely locals and enjoying a beach that was theirs, anyway. But then Charlie interrupted.

"Oh! We found a bar for tonight!" he exclaimed. "A local recommended it. Supposed to be very authentic."

Annabelle's lips pinched, like she was mentally cataloging all the possible definitions of the word, while across the verandah, Vivienne finally perked up.

"Do they have alcohol?" she called out.

Charlie blinked. "It's a bar, Viv."

She seemed to consider, then turned back to face the water. "I'm in."

"Fine," Annabelle replied. "But if my shoes stick to the floor, we're leaving."

Charlie's smile broadened as he turned to Will. "What about you?"

Will wanted to say no, that this bar was probably god-awful and the woman with the dark eyes and fiery red hair knew as much. But it had been a challenge. And as he thought about it, he found himself wanting to meet it. He was practically a local himself—and although he had nothing to prove, there was nothing he hated more than someone thinking he was something he wasn't. "Let's leave by nine."

CHAPTER 5

At precisely seven p.m. Lizzy pulled her old pickup truck into her parents' driveway on Surrey Lane. The sun was still peeking over the evergreens surrounding their yard, casting a soft orange glow off the wood-shingle siding of the Bennet home: a modest two-story saltbox house that hadn't changed all that much over the last twenty years. When the Bennet sisters were young, it had barely been big enough for their family of seven. Now, with all five girls grown up and still living at home, its meager 1,700 square feet felt like it could explode at any moment.

As if on cue, Lizzy's phone pinged in the front pocket of her overalls. She took it out to find the text chain with her sisters on the glowing screen.

THE BUTTER FACES

LYDIA

I found a pic of Charlie Pierce! Sooooo hot

JANE

Are you stalking him now?

LYDIA

Google image search isn't stalking

KITTY

Oadsy buot amoeik sudoiur

JANE

???

MARY

She's typing with oven mitts on.

JANE

Oh. Okay, just finishing up at school—be home soon!

LYDIA

But what time are we leaving???

Lizzy put the phone back in her bag and brought her hand up to the ignition, letting her fingers hover over the keys while she enjoyed a few more precious moments before facing the inevitable chaos inside. She had closed up the bakery at five, flipping off the electric *Open* sign and ignoring the ringing phone, letting their ancient answering machine field calls from would-be customers so she could prep the kitchen for the following morning. By six she was locking up the back door, dropping her bag in the back of her truck, and getting behind the wheel.

She didn't go straight home, though. She never did. Despite the bakery being only five minutes from the Bennet house, Lizzy always found a way to extend the drive to almost an hour. Her rusted maroon Chevy truck would ramble down Main Street, past the old Gardiner Windmill to Dunemere Lane, where the scattering of colonial buildings slowly disappeared behind the tangled branches of oak trees that lined the road. As those fell away and the sand traps for the Hunsford golf course swallowed up the landscape on either side, she'd take a right, winding around Hook Pond and parking along the beach to watch the tide come in, mentally giving pointers to the surfers dotting the break line. It wasn't until the light began to shift, and she had gotten at least three texts from her mother asking where she was, that she knew it was time to head home.

Lizzy waited for the last few notes of Beach House's "Superstar" to fade from the stereo before turning the key, cutting the ignition. Through the house's front bay windows, she could view the figures of her sisters and her mother moving in and out of the living room, the blue glow of the television silhouetting them against the curtains. She couldn't see her father in there, but that wasn't a surprise. She knew exactly where he was.

For the past twenty years, the eyesore Bob Bennet called his sailboat sat permanently and unapologetically landlocked on their lawn, the last remnant of his dream to sail around the world. When he was Lizzy's age, he had been working for his dad at the bakery, too, saving up to join a crew for the Newport Bermuda Race with the plan to eventually climb the ranks of international offshore racing. But then his parents retired, leaving the business to him. Not long after, Mrs. Bennet got pregnant with Jane. And slowly, the dream faded until there was nothing left but an old boat parked next to the garage.

A light flickered in its cabin as Lizzy got out of the truck. The red paint along the hull had probably been vibrant a few decades ago, but now it was faded and peeling. The only part of the boat that remained pristine was the name of the vessel, *Calcifer*, which was perfectly scripted in brilliant gold across the starboard bow.

Lizzy stopped in front of the ladder that led up to the deck. She could hear the familiar muted voices of NPR from above.

"Permission to board?" she called out.

"Granted," her father answered.

Lizzy pulled herself up, then navigated around the perennial mess of ropes and sails to the steep metal stairs that led below deck. The cramped cabin was barely big enough for the V-shaped sleeping berth at the far end, let alone the galley kitchen here at the bottom of the steps. Yet somehow her father had wedged himself under the small sink, his toolbox beside him.

"I thought you fixed the generator?" she asked, eyeing the battery-powered lantern on the table, the cabin's only source of light.

"I'll get to it," he murmured, grabbing a nearby wrench. "First I need to get this filter working."

"And then you'll be set to hit the open seas?" The two had had this conversation a thousand times. He promised every summer he would have the boat ready, but inevitably there was always one more repair standing in his way.

He chuckled. "Right."

She smiled, but it faltered as he sat up, wincing and massaging his temples.

Her heart dropped and she leaned forward, ready to move. "Are you okay?"

"Just a headache." He made a vague motion toward the house. "Your mom found my stash of beer in the garage and was out here yelling at me about it."

"But—"

"It's fine, kiddo. Stop worrying."

She studied his strained expression. His salt-and-pepper hair and smile lines that peppered his tan skin revealed his age. It was becoming harder and harder to remember the larger-than-life dad from her childhood who used to carry her on his shoulders at the beach and who helped her and her sisters dig holes in the sand to reach the center of the earth.

He caught her expression and sighed. "Why don't you go inside and grab some food?"

"Okay." She reluctantly nodded. "Want me to bring you anything?"

He made another gruff sound as he set the wrench down and picked up his pliers. "No. Your mother won't let me put salt on anything anyway. I'm good."

She gave him a small salute and started up the metal steps to the deck.

∽

"Shut up!"

Lydia's voice rattled the house before Lizzy was even through the front door.

There was a familiar wall of sounds and smells to welcome her. The clatter of pots and pans and glasses. The smell of sugar and butter wafting through the air . . . and burning. Yes, something was definitely burning.

Lizzy left her bag by the door and wandered from the small foyer into the living room, which opened up to the kitchen just beyond. Lydia was curled up on one end of the couch, her phone to her ear as she filed her nails while an episode of *Love Is Blind* played on the TV.

"That is insane. So insane," she squealed. "What did you say?"

Behind her, Mrs. Bennet flitted from the refrigerator to where her wineglass was on the countertop, refilling it with her trademark pinot grigio and ice—a staple for the summer months—while Kitty tried to move around her. Mary was there, too, her short blue pixie cut bent over the kitchen table as she folded a pile of pamphlets. She was only a year older than the twins, and looked a lot more like them than she would ever admit. Maybe that was why she seemed to work so hard to distance herself from the fact, both physically and philosophically. Right now that meant wearing a small *No Nature, No Future* T-shirt and a recently acquired septum piercing.

"Somebody turned off my timer!" Kitty wailed as she opened the oven. She pulled out a muffin tray that was almost entirely black.

Mary ignored her, not looking up from her pamphlets as she asked, "Does anyone know where that leftover red paint is from Christmas?"

The question wasn't directed at anyone in particular. They never were. Trying to get answers in the Bennet household was a bit like fishing: you had to just throw a line out and wait for someone to tug.

This time, it was Lizzy.

"The one from the Santa Claus decorations?" she asked, reaching into a nearby cabinet for a bowl.

"Yeah."

"It's in the garage. Benjamin Moore, Hot Tamale."

Mary nodded, as much of a thank-you as anyone could expect.

Kitty cradled her tray of charred baked goods, looking for a place to set them, while their mother took a sip of her wine. Her own cell phone was wedged between her shoulder and chin, and the conversation seemed to require so much attention that she barely noticed Lizzy's arrival.

"Okay, Donna. Let's go over it again. You buy a box of Lux Leggings from me, which you go out and sell yourself," Mrs. Bennet said into her phone, her voice sweet as honey as she waved Kitty away from her corner of the kitchen. Lizzy maneuvered around them both as she headed to the pantry and grabbed a box of cereal. "Then you recruit other people to buy boxes of leggings from you to sell, then share the profits with me. Got it?"

Kitty finally settled at the butcher block island, setting her muffin tin next to where Lizzy was pouring Frosted Flakes into her bowl.

"They're ruined," Kitty moaned.

"Oh my *God*, that's amazing!" Lydia yelled into her phone from the sofa.

"Did someone move my vegan glue?" Mary seethed, looking around the table.

"No, Donna, it is not a pyramid scheme!" Mrs. Bennet exclaimed.

"What were you going for this time?" Lizzy asked Kitty, eyeing the blackened muffin tray.

Kitty sighed. "Paprika popovers."

Lizzy nodded sympathetically. While the Bennet sisters had all practically grown up in the bakery, Kitty was the only one who seemingly hadn't inherited the baking gene. Unfortunately, she was also the only one who seemed to have any real business sense.

Lizzy added milk to her cereal and gave Kitty an encouraging smile. "Next time you'll nail it." Then she took her cereal bowl and a spoon and headed out of the room.

As she passed the couch, Lydia's head popped up, ignoring her call for a brief moment to ask, "What time are we leaving?"

"Wow, I've never seen you so eager to spend Saturday night at the Lodge," Lizzy said, working to convey her sarcasm around a mouthful of cereal. "Looking to stalk this Charlie guy or do you just have a hankering for Tater Tots?"

Lydia rolled her eyes.

"Oh!" Kitty perked up. "I'm in, too! I want to see if Annabelle Pierce is really here."

"I have to go and pass out some pamphlets," Mary added from the kitchen table.

Lizzy sighed. "Fine. We'll head out when Jane gets home."

Mrs. Bennet snapped her fingers, the universal Bennet sign to shut up, and the sisters complied, with Lizzy disappearing upstairs as her mother returned to her call.

Lizzy was lying in her usual spot—the flat bit of roof just outside her open window—with her empty cereal bowl beside her and was halfway through chapter 18 of *The Court of the Serpent King* when she heard Jane's familiar knock on her bedroom door.

She dog-eared her page, then copied the same knock against the windowsill. Their lifelong cue.

Jane entered quietly, closing the door behind her, and walked across the small room lined with travel posters, dodging clothes strewn across the floor, until she reached the open window.

"God, I'm exhausted," she said with a groan as she climbed through and landed beside Lizzy. "Do you know how hard it is to get Play-Doh out of carpet?"

"No, but now you have to tell me," Lizzy said.

"Hours. Those first graders really rub it in there."

"You live life in the fast lane, Jane."

"Always," her sister said with a smile. "What did you do today?"

"Sourdough proofing."

"Whoa." Jane laughed softly to herself.

"Do I know how to have a good time, or what?"

"Slow down already."

"I'm out of control," Lizzy said through her grin, letting her gaze wander up to the stars overhead.

Jane nodded to the book sitting between them. "Well? What do you think of Lord Magnus Beaumont?"

Lizzy sighed dramatically. "Six foot five, black hair and green eyes. Yes, he has a weird fascination with reptiles, but I think I could change him."

"I knew you'd love him. Now hurry up and finish so I can give you the sequel."

"Are there dragons?"

"*So* many dragons."

Lizzy laughed. Ever since they'd stolen a copy of *Outlander* from the bakery's lost and found in middle school, the two sisters had been trading romance books back and forth. But while Lizzy usually liked more straightforward rom-coms, Jane had slowly gotten her hooked on romantasy. It wasn't a surprise—her sister had always loved fantasy and science fiction, so much so that she was bullied relentlessly through grade school. It surprised most people who met her now, but that was only because they weren't privy to those years when Jane hid her acne and braces behind the stacks at Atomic Comics. As much as she had grown into her looks, Lizzy knew that Jane still saw herself as that awkward teenager who wrote *Lord of the Rings* fan fiction in her spare time.

"Speaking of dragons, you might want to avoid Mom before she makes you wear a pair of her leggings to the Lodge tonight," Lizzy said.

In the darkness beside her, Jane groaned. "Are we really doing the Lodge tonight?"

"It's Saturday. Of course we're doing the Lodge tonight."

"But what if we run into those guys who came by the bakery today?"

"Trust me, those two are going to take one look at the Lodge, and then turn right back around."

Jane seemed to think about it. "I don't know. I should really get started on my lesson plan for next week, and—"

"Stay holed up in your room again, binging *Doctor Who?*"

Jane pursed her lips. "I'm not watching *Doctor Who.*"

"No?"

"No. The new season of *Rings of Power* is streaming."

Lizzy rolled her eyes. "Come on. I know it's going to be crowded and awful, but it's better than hanging out here all night."

"Maybe I *like* hanging out here all night," Jane replied in that voice she usually reserved for her students.

Lizzy didn't argue, mostly because she knew it was the truth. Their childhood had been defined by a mutual need to escape from their small town and their even smaller house. But while Lizzy had tried to get out into the world and never look back, Jane was an introvert and preferred to disappear into her favorite books.

After a moment, Jane sighed. "Okay, I'll go. But only because I'm craving Tater Tots."

"That might actually be the only legitimate reason to go to the Lodge."

Jane laughed, and as it faded, she rested her head on her sister's shoulder. A rare moment of peace extended then, quiet and calm, and they both knew enough to soak it in, because only a minute later, it was shattered by Lydia's voice bellowing up from downstairs.

"LIZZY! ARE YOU DRIVING US OR WHAT?"

CHAPTER 6

It was a truth universally acknowledged that Donato Lodge was awful. But that was part of the appeal. From the lingering smell of room temperature beer to the stained burgundy carpet only partially hidden by the dim overhead lights, it was the unassuming second home for much of East Hampton.

The Bennet sisters arrived through the narrow front hallway just before nine. Framed photos of all the up-and-coming bands that the bar's owner, Hank Donato, was sure would make it one day lined the walls. Alongside them were posters advertising Hank's magnum opus, HamptonFest: a three-day-long festival that would surely transform East Hampton into a musical mecca. Unfortunately, after years of promises, the town was still waiting for the event to actually happen.

Lydia entered the bar first, her chin high as if she were holding court. Her dark hair was wavy and wild at her shoulders, and her tanned skin was covered with a gold shimmer powder that made her hazel eyes sparkle. Despite their mother's demands, she wasn't wearing a pair of Lux Leggings. Neither was Kitty, who had only added a navy sweater tied around her shoulders, while Mary was still wearing her T-shirt and jeans, although now she donned an

Our Planet, Our Rules button and a huge pile of *Save Gretna Island!* pamphlets under her arm. Lizzy had only swapped out her overalls for a pair of jeans.

Jane wasn't so lucky. While the rest of the sisters were only too happy to ignore their mother's pleas for self-promotion, Jane could never bring herself to do it, so she entered the bar wearing a pair of yellow-and-pink leopard-print leggings with gemstones embroidered on the seams.

As soon as they walked in, Mary disappeared into the crowd to hand out her pamphlets, while Lydia and Kitty headed straight to the end of the long bar near the front entrance to see everyone who came or left that evening. Jane and Lizzy followed them, but only because there were a few empty stools nearby and Hank's daughter and bartender, Piper, was already there pouring them drinks.

"What'd we miss?" Lizzy asked as she landed on one of the stools. Jane sat down beside her.

"Nothing so far," Piper replied, sliding a beer in front of Lizzy and a glass of white wine in front of Jane. Piper's curly chestnut hair was in a loose bun, and she donned the same dimpled smile she'd had since middle school. And while Lizzy knew her friend was happy to see them, she was also aware that Piper's current grin probably had more to do with the fact that she had just returned from visiting her girlfriend in Boston than the bar's clientele. "Here Comes the Sandman just finished their soundcheck."

"Here Comes the Sandman?" Jane asked, looking almost concerned.

"They're a Beatles/Metallica cover band." Piper nodded to the nearby stage. "My dad's expecting it to get crowded tonight, so he wants them to start soon."

"The cidiots are coming," Lizzy whispered solemnly as she took a sip of her beer.

Piper laughed, as much at the sentiment as at the old nickname for the "city idiots" from New York who invaded their town every summer. It looked like Jane wanted to laugh as well, but she was fighting it as she shook her head.

"Those cidiots keep the lights on, you know," Jane said.

"Which also happens to be the reason I can't stay late tonight," Lizzy replied. "I have to be at the bakery extra early tomorrow."

Piper threw her friend a skeptical look. She was all too familiar with Lizzy's work schedule, mostly because it meant that their time off was always diametrically opposed. "Seriously?"

"Seriously. And don't try to butter me up with free food, either."

"Too late." Piper grabbed a basket of freshly fried Tater Tots from the kitchen window behind her and placed it in between Lizzy and Jane. While the Lodge was objectively awful, their culinary skills with a deep fryer were anything but.

"Well, it won't work. I've got to be up by five to prep for the farmers market and I need my beauty sleep," Lizzy replied, pretending to fix the mess of hair still piled on top of her head. "Obviously."

"Boo," Piper deadpanned, pushing the basket of Tater Tots toward Jane. Lizzy reached over and pulled it back again.

"Why don't I do it?" Jane offered. "I was already going to meet you there later, so I could get up early and deal with all the prep."

"Nope," Lizzy retorted. "You're not technically on the schedule until school's out."

"But you always—"

Lizzy interrupted her with a sigh. "I'm sorry, Jane, but Bennet Bakery has a very strict HR policy."

Jane shook her head even as she smiled at Piper. "Please talk some sense into her."

"Oh, I learned that was a losing battle in second grade," Piper replied. Then she turned back to Lizzy. "Seriously, though, if you want to stick around, I'm sure your dad can handle it. He's pretty much recovered at this point, right?"

It was a question that had been nagging Lizzy for a while. Only a couple of weeks ago, she had been so confident in her father's recovery that she had drafted an email to Columbia, promising that she would honor her deferment and enroll in January, if they had space available. But the next day, he woke up lethargic and spent the rest of the day at the hospital. Every step forward felt precarious, leaving everything else in limbo, including her email.

Lizzy didn't know how to quantify that for Piper, though, especially since Columbia was still a secret—even from her oldest friend. So instead, she tossed another Tater Tot in her mouth and shrugged.

Piper frowned but before she could press Lizzy further, something on the other side of the room caught her eye.

"Oh Lord," Piper groaned. "Is Mary handing out pamphlets protesting HamptonFest again?"

Lizzy and Jane followed their friend's gaze to Mary's spiky blue hair in the far corner. She was gesticulating wildly to a group of people waiting in line for the bathroom.

"Maybe she just really has to pee?" Jane volunteered.

Piper shook her head. "She better hope my dad doesn't see her. He has a potential partner from the city coming in this weekend, and if Mary makes a scene, he'll ban her from the bar again."

Lizzy hid her smile behind another sip of her beer. For the past few years, the Lodge had hosted a steady stream of potential partners coming by to talk with Hank about HamptonFest. And ever since he announced plans to hold the prospective festival on Gretna Island, a small island off the North Shore that also happened to be the home of the endangered forester field slug, Mary had been trying to thwart him. It was why she had been banned from the Lodge the past two summers and, like clockwork, this year looked like it would be no exception.

"Someone has to think of the slugs, Piper," Lizzy said gravely. Piper just rolled her eyes.

As the band entered the stage and began playing the opening chords of what sounded like a heavy metal version of "I Want to Hold Your Hand," Lydia did a turn around the room with Kitty in tow, and then, with fresh looks of disappointment on their faces, they made their way over to Jane and Lizzy at the bar.

"I can't believe I wore my new Prada top and there aren't even any hot guys here," Lydia huffed, landing on the stool beside Lizzy.

"What are men to beer and Tater Tots?" Lizzy said wistfully, raising her pint glass as if it were a liquid oblation.

Jane laughed.

Kitty looked up from her phone to eye Lydia's shirt. "How did you even afford that?"

Lydia smiled smugly. "Remember Danny?"

"No."

"Yes you do. That insurance guy with the Bentley from that white party?"

"Oh, right." Kitty nodded. "So?"

Lydia waggled her eyebrows.

Kitty didn't look impressed. "Are you serious?"

"He knows I'm an influencer who's trying to build my impressions on TikTok and said he'd write it off as a business expense."

"I thought you said he worked in insurance," Jane said, her brow furrowed.

Lydia shrugged one shoulder. "He does. He's like an adjuster or investigator or something."

"With an unlimited credit line, apparently," Kitty murmured, looking back down at her glowing screen.

Lydia ignored her, taking a careful sip of her drink through a small pink straw, keeping her red lipstick intact. "It's all about building my brand. And if my brand position is luxury, I need content that speaks to my target audience. Not fried food and guys I've known since kindergarten."

"So . . . no to the Tater Tots, then," Piper said.

Lydia threw her a glare, then popped one from the basket into her mouth.

Lizzy smiled as she turned to do her own audit of the room. She would never admit it, but she understood Lydia's frustration. Lizzy recognized almost everyone there. The bar was full of regulars, the same familiar faces who had populated their social circle since birth.

But just as soon as the thought entered her head, Lydia's unmistakable squeal cut through the air.

"Oh my God, they're *here*," she whispered, though the volume was anything but low.

Lizzy followed her sister's gaze to the door, where four people now stood, surveying the room.

She knew those cidiots. Well, the men at least. She immediately recognized Charlie Pierce with his mess of brown curls and wide smile. And next to him was the palm tree hater. He stood a bit taller than Charlie, with thick blond hair and a white shirt unbuttoned just enough to give the impression that he was relaxed. His posture told a different story, though. His broad shoulders were tense and his back was straight, while his blue eyes scanned the bar with a distinct look of disapproval.

The two women at their sides had to be sisters—they looked almost identical with their glossy brown hair falling at their shoulders, and coordinating linen dresses, long and perfectly pressed. The only difference was that the slightly shorter woman was wearing sunglasses and looked absolutely miserable.

"That's her!" Kitty gasped, barely managing to keep her voice at a whisper.

Jane's eyebrows were knit together as she craned to look. "Who's her?"

"Annabelle Pierce! Remember, Mom was talking about her? She took over her mom's boutique in Denver five years ago and grew it to over two hundred international locations. She's incredible," Kitty said, narrowing her eyes on the group. "That must be her sister in the sunglasses. And her brother there with the curly dark hair."

"Okay, but who's the blond guy?" Lydia murmured, nodding to the palm tree hater, who was still giving the room a contemptuous look. His veneer wasn't as polished as the others', but it somehow signaled even more refinement, if that were possible. The sharp line of his jaw was camouflaged by stubble, and his hair was long, as if he'd missed his last five or six haircuts. Lizzy couldn't help but notice that it was also that distinct shade of blond that would probably lighten after just a few days in the sun, the way it probably had every summer since he was young. She could almost imagine it, with his skin bronzed just enough to make those blue eyes glow—

She stopped herself, turning back to her beer and taking a deep sip. She had never allowed herself to become collateral damage in some wealthy tourist's pursuit of summer distraction, and she wasn't about to start with someone like that.

"Who is he?" Kitty asked no one in particular as she watched the foursome approach the other end of the bar.

"The 'not-boyfriend' friend," Lizzy replied, popping another Tater Tot in her mouth.

Jane laughed softly, while Piper went over to take their order.

"Well, we're obviously going to fall in love and run away

together, so I should probably introduce myself," Lydia said, re-adjusting her crop top. "How do I look?"

Lizzy cocked her head to the side. "Like an influencer with at least . . . two dozen followers."

Lydia stuck her tongue out at her, then flipped her long hair over her shoulder and started toward the group.

Even before Lydia reached them, Lizzy could see that both men had captured the attention of everyone within a twenty-foot radius. And while the two Pierce sisters surveyed the room with bored expressions, Charlie Pierce leaned against the bar, smiling brightly as he chatted with Piper, completely oblivious to the attention from the room. The other man, however, seemed desperate to escape it—an underwear model pissed off to be stuck in a J.Crew catalog. Either that, or he was silently plotting murder.

The bar was too loud to hear the conversation when Lydia finally reached them, but Lizzy still watched like it was a pantomime: how her sister tossed her hair from one shoulder to another as she started talking to the tall blond, how he glanced down blankly when she touched his arm and appeared to say something that she found amusing, because she closed her eyes and laughed. Then how her coy expression turned to a sneer when she opened her eyes again and found he had turned away from her completely. Lizzy bit back her smile. If Lydia had been in love with the palm tree hater for the past five minutes, it only took her another five minutes to fall decidedly out.

"What a prick," Lydia hissed as she returned and collapsed on the stool next to Lizzy.

Jane looked toward the other end of the bar again. "The one talking to Piper seems nice."

"Oh, Charlie?" Lydia replied like they were already friends.

"He's fine. I'm talking about the tall, hot one. Like, he sent back his *beer*. Who does that?"

"A man who doesn't appreciate warm beer," Lizzy said, taking another sip of her own.

"Whatever," her sister huffed. "Blond guys aren't my type anyway."

"What about Chris Hemsworth?" Kitty asked.

Lydia waved her off.

"And Austin Butler?"

She rolled her eyes.

"And Charlie Hunnam? And—"

"We're going to dance," Lydia said, grabbing Kitty's hand and leading her closer to the stage.

Despite the band's disjointed mash-up of "Master of Puppets" and "Strawberry Fields," the dance floor was packed. It was almost enough to forget about the newcomers altogether . . . until Lizzy turned to order more Tater Tots and noticed one of the men's attention focused squarely on the sister beside her.

"Um, Jane?" Lizzy said, turning around slowly so as not to be conspicuous.

Jane glanced over at her. "Hm?"

"That Charlie guy is staring at you."

Her sister's eyes grew wide. "What?"

"Don't look—"

But it was too late. Jane had already straightened her back, straining above the heads around them to see. As soon as she did, she sank back down, cheeks aflame. "Ohmygod."

Lizzy laughed. "I told you not to look."

Jane brought her hands up to cover her face as if it would hide her. "He saw me!"

"Of course he did. He's staring."

"But *why* is he staring?"

Lizzy pushed her half-empty pint glass out of the way and rested her elbow on the bar. "Sorry to break it to you, Jane, but you're gorgeous."

Jane's hands fell back to her lap as she shot her sister a doubtful look. "I haven't washed my hair in three days and I'm wearing Mom's leggings and my TARDIS earrings."

"Maybe he loves *Doctor Who* accessories."

"Or maybe he just feels sorry for—"

"Hello," a deep, jovial voice cut her off.

Lizzy and Jane turned at the same time to see Charlie Pierce standing before them, a wide smile on his full lips, and his eyes fixed solely on Jane. His curly brown hair was mussed, but in the adorable way that implied he had been running his hand through it all day. His clothes were casual, too, though his linen shirt and khakis were as perfectly pressed as his sisters' outfits. The palm tree hater loomed beside him.

"Hi," Jane said, matching his smile.

"Sorry, I hope you don't mind me—"

"Not at all, I—"

"It's just that I saw you—"

"Me, too."

Then they both laughed.

Lizzy watched in awe. It was like having a front seat to a real-life rom-com. Meanwhile, the blond man at Charlie's side looked on with a confused frown, as if the two of them had suddenly started speaking in tongues.

Charlie was oblivious, though, holding out his hand to Jane. "I'm Charlie Pierce. And this is my friend Will Darcy."

Jane took Charlie's hand and shook it gently. "I'm Jane. This is my sister Elizabeth."

Lizzy waved her off. "It's just Lizzy."

Charlie didn't even look at her, his eyes were still locked with Jane's. "It's a pleasure."

At that moment, Lizzy half expected the band to break into a moving pop-rock ballad and the entire scene to go into slow motion. As if the stars had aligned and everything that had ever happened had led Jane and Charlie to this moment.

Then his friend cut in.

"You work at the bakery."

His deep voice was startling, and Lizzy looked over to find him—Will, was it?—now glaring at her. His blue eyes were intense as he studied her with what looked like concern. Or was it annoyance? She couldn't tell.

In any case, she forced a smile. "I'm surprised you remember."

His harsh gaze moved to the bun on top of her head. "You were covered in flour."

Lizzy tilted her head for a moment, considering him, then almost laughed. Was he serious?

"It was powdered sugar, actually," she replied, throwing a Tater Tot in her mouth.

He stared back.

"Oh my gosh!" Charlie turned, eyes wide like he had only just noticed her. "That's right! Bennet Bakery! You recommended this place!"

"I did," Lizzy said proudly.

"Well, it's perfect. Thank you. And who would have thought I'd see a fellow *Doctor Who* fan out in the wild, too," Charlie said, then made a slight motion as if he was about to reach for the TARDIS dangling from Jane's left ear, but stopped himself. Then he cleared his throat and nodded to Jane's bedazzled legs. "And those pants! They're very . . . shiny."

"Oh. Thanks," Jane said, looking down as if she had only just remembered she was wearing them. "My mom forces all of us to wear them at some point."

A touch of confusion entered Charlie's expression. "I'm sorry?"

"It's just . . . my mom designs them. And then she makes me and Lizzy and our other sisters wear them to spread the word, so . . ."

Jane's voice trailed off, but Charlie didn't seem to mind. "It's a good idea. You look stunning."

Jane let out a soft laugh, and Lizzy's heart swelled.

"How many sisters do you have?" he continued.

"There's five of us."

"Wow." Charlie's eyes widened. "How do you keep track?"

Jane laughed again, but it faded quickly as her gaze went to her lap. The introverted side of her was beginning to take hold, but Lizzy refused to let it ruin the moment.

"Oh, that's easy," Lizzy said, pointing down the bar at her two sisters in the middle of the dance floor. "Lydia and Kitty are identical twins, but you can tell them apart because Lydia usually has her phone out recording herself, while Kitty looks like she's preparing a run for Congress. And that short blue pixie cut over there is Mary." She pointed to Mary's head bobbing through the crowd by the door. "She's saving the world and has the literature to prove it. Then there's Jane. She's easy to remember because she's the most beautiful, and also the nicest."

Jane rolled her eyes as her cheeks flushed.

"What about you?" Will's voice cut through the moment.

Lizzy blinked, turning to him again. His voice was rough, with an unhewn edge that felt coarse in her ear. Maybe that's why it sent an odd shiver down her spine.

"I guess I'm just the redhead," she answered with a shrug. She tried to add levity to her voice, to make the statement sound less pathetic than it really was. But while Charlie chuckled, his friend just maintained her gaze, as if he saw right through her.

Whatever. She brought her attention back to the rest of the group. "What are you doing in East Hampton, Charlie?"

"My sisters and I rented a house for the summer. We wanted to get away from the city to relax and spend some time together." It was an excuse Lizzy had heard a hundred times before, but the way Charlie said it—equal parts sincere and self-deprecating—made her realize it was the first time she had ever believed it. "Will's just coming out on the weekends to make sure we actually do some work while I'm here."

Lizzy smiled. "And what do you do for work?"

"We run a mergers and acquisitions firm in the city. I mean, we run it together. Mainly deal with finding emerging sustainable technologies and pair them up with larger firms. To be honest, it's just an excuse for me to spend all my time researching green tech. I know that sounds boring but—"

"Not at all!" Jane said, perking up. "I just mean, it's not boring. Science, that is."

Charlie's eyes lit up. "Are you a scientist?"

"No, I teach first grade at East Hampton Elementary. I love it, but it's nothing like saving the world or—"

"She's amazing," Lizzy interrupted before her sister could say anything else self-deprecating. "You've never heard so many six-year-olds bring up mitochondria in casual conversation."

Charlie laughed. Will's expression remained flat.

Lizzy continued, "She's also the one that keeps our mom and the rest of us from burning our house down on a daily basis."

"You still live at home?" Will asked. It sounded more like an accusation than a question.

Lizzy bristled, but worked to maintain her smile as she replied,

"Yup. We would move out, but all these Manhattanites keep summering out here and jacking up the real estate prices."

She said it jokingly, though there was a bite under her words. She hid it well, though, enough that Jane smiled and Charlie laughed again. But Will's expression remained unchanged, like he knew it wasn't the full truth.

And he would be right. Sure, rentals were expensive, but between her and Jane, they could likely afford something nearby, maybe up in Sag Harbor or Springs. God knows they had talked about it enough. With Kitty and Lydia still living at home while they attended community college, and Mary moving down to the basement after she graduated last year, the house had never felt more claustrophobic. But moving out only to stay nearby would mean settling, admitting to herself that her delay in starting grad school was more permanent. That those dreams of getting out into the world were only ever going to be that. Dreams that would slowly fade with every flick of the light switch on the bakery's *Open* sign.

Will didn't deserve to know that much about her, though. He hadn't earned it. So Lizzy just stared right back at him and took a long sip of her drink.

After a moment, he finally turned away. She did the same.

The band kicked off with a song they called "Fade to Blackbird," and Lizzy cheered and clapped as the guitar licks alternated between ear-splitting and trippy. When she turned back around a few minutes later to get Jane's opinion, she found her still in close conversation with Charlie.

Will, on the other hand, had disappeared.

Thank God, Lizzy thought, taking another swig of her beer.

One song led into another, and she soon forgot about Will Darcy. She laughed and cheered and even managed to drag Mary into the center of the room to dance to a mash-up of "I Want to Hold Your Hand" and "Seek and Destroy." But when she finally found herself back at the bar, sweaty and tired and demanding ice water from Piper, she saw Charlie's phone light up with a text from where he had placed it on the polished wood.

WILL

She doesn't need my pity.

Lizzy stared down at the words. It could have been about anyone, she knew that. Still, she couldn't help but recall how Will had looked at her and Jane earlier, as if he were cataloging every mannerism, every flaw. What if he was referring to Jane here, trying to somehow convince his friend that she wasn't good enough, or—

Jane's laugh interrupted her thought. "You're right. It's like I tell my students: always try to be nice, but never fail to be kind."

"'Twice Upon a Time'!" Charlie replied, lighting up, "Peter Capaldi!"

She nodded. "It's one of my favorite *Doctor Who* quotes."

"It's the best!"

The knot in Lizzy's chest dissolved. Regardless of Will's text, she had nothing to worry about.

"Hey," Piper's voice broke through the noise. She was placing a glass of ice water in front of Lizzy even as she said, "I thought you had to get your beauty sleep."

Lizzy grabbed the glass as she rolled her eyes. "I'm going."

As she took a deep sip, Charlie's phone buzzed again. He reached over and read the incoming text, then quickly typed out a response before abandoning the phone on the bar to turn back to Jane. Her legs were crossed, and she was absentmindedly playing with the ends of her long dark hair. Charlie watched, entranced.

Yeah, he was a goner. But then, by the look on Jane's face, she was, too.

Lizzy set her glass down next to Charlie's phone, which was still lit up. When Lizzy stole a glance, his entire text conversation took up the screen.

CHARLIE

Where are you? Jane's sister is still at the bar and not talking to anyone . . .

WILL

She doesn't need my pity.

CHARLIE

Oh, come on.

She's gorgeous.

WILL

She's a mess.

Lizzy stared at the words until the phone went black again. Well, at least the message wasn't about her sister. Still, the revelation left a sting of embarrassment in her chest. It dissolved quickly, though, and all she could do was laugh to herself. The night had left no doubt that Will Darcy was an asshole. But he was right about one thing: she didn't need his pity.

Lizzy dug in her pocket and pulled out her car keys, then gave them to Piper. "Give these to Jane when she comes up for air, okay?"

"How are you getting home?"

Lizzy shrugged. "I'll walk."

Piper shook her head, like she should have known.

Lizzy slid off her stool and weaved through the crowd toward the back exit, or—as it was affectionately called by regulars—the Irish Goodbye Door. It opened out onto a small porch that no one ever used, with stairs that led down to the gravel parking lot, making it the perfect means of escape for those looking to avoid notice.

Sure enough, the porch was empty as she walked out. The door shut behind her, muffling the music inside, so she stopped to close her eyes and enjoy the sudden stillness. The walk back to her house wasn't too long, and she congratulated herself for being the only Bennet sensible enough to wear sneakers tonight. Another Saturday night on the books.

Then she opened her eyes and noticed someone standing in the shadows just a few feet away.

Will Darcy.

"Crap," she whispered under breath. It was dark, so his harsh features were lost in the shadows, but his phone was in his hand and the screen was illuminated as if he had just been typing another text message. But now his attention was on Lizzy.

She didn't blink. In fact, she refused to look away at all.

"Leaving?" he finally asked.

"Yup," she said, adding a slight edge to the word. "Hiding?"

"No." Then a frustrated sigh, as if he had been caught out. "Is it always so chaotic in there?"

"You said you wanted authentic," she replied. "The chaos is part of its charm."

He threw her a sardonic glare. "Charm?"

"Yeah." She shrugged one shoulder. "I guess some people don't mind a mess."

Lizzy didn't wait for him to reply, just gave him a sharp smile before turning on her heel and starting down the wooden steps to the parking lot.

The same bright stars shined down from the night sky as she walked home, passing the same storefronts, the same line of luxury cars parked along the street. It was true, nothing really changed in East Hampton. But at least Lizzy could take comfort in the fact that she would never have to see that asshole again.

CHAPTER 7

The bar was a wall of sound when Will reentered. Laughter and shouting and off-key singing all melded together over deafening guitar chords that sounded suspiciously like "Yellow Submarine."

He ignored them as he navigated his way through the packed room. Or, at least, he tried to ignore them. What usually came so easy—that ability to shore up his defenses, put a mental barricade between himself and the outside world—suddenly felt flimsy and weak, making him only too aware of just how uncomfortable he really was.

It was that woman's fault. He didn't like crowded spaces and forced social interactions, but he usually had it under control. Then Elizabeth Bennet appeared. He had recognized that red hair immediately and said something before he could stop himself. Maybe that was what annoyed her—that or the flour comment—but regardless, she bit back.

Some people don't mind a mess.

The words echoed through his head as his gaze slid to Vivienne and Annabelle. They were still at the same table in the back, although Vivienne's head was now resting in her arms next to an empty martini glass. Beside her, Annabelle appeared to be in physical pain listening to the band.

It was time to find Charlie and call it a night,

Will continued his survey of the bar until he found him. Charlie was still standing beside Jane, leaning down to hear something she was saying. Impossible, considering how loud the fucking music was, but that didn't seem to deter him.

Here we go again. Will thought he would at least have a week or two before Charlie fell headfirst into another relationship. What was the percentage he read in the *Wall Street Journal* the other day, 70 percent of couples break up before they make it to a year? For someone who was obsessed with facts and statistics, it was mind-boggling that Charlie chose to ignore that one. The man loved falling in love, and while that fact had been endearing in college, it was now like catnip to women who were more concerned with his net worth than his emotions. Of course, each relationship ended in the same predictable way, with Charlie giving too much only to have his heart broken, while Will ran interference, taking care of the mess left behind and picking his friend back up again.

And while this woman seemed perfectly lovely, Will didn't have the bandwidth to fix another one of Charlie's heartbreaks. They both needed to stay focused this summer.

Charlie caught sight of Will and motioned him over, his smile broadening across his face.

"You finally decided to join us!" Charlie exclaimed, raising his glass like this deserved a toast.

Will offered him a tight nod. Then he turned to Jane. "Your sister left."

She blinked, as if the comment caught her off guard. Then he realized it probably had. "Lydia or Kit—"

"Elizabeth."

Her expression relaxed and she nodded. "Piper told me. She has to work in the morning, so she headed home."

Then she took a sip of her wine, like that answer was sufficient. Like it was fine that her sister just disappeared into the darkness all by herself.

"She walked." Will's voice was loud enough to be heard over the music, so the words came out almost like a shout.

Jane offered him a reassuring smile. "It's okay. We live nearby; you don't have to worry about her."

"I wasn't," he murmured. He didn't bother to consider whether that was true until the words had already left his mouth.

"Sorry?" she asked, leaning forward to hear him over the music. She laughed sweetly. "I can barely hear a thing. It's not usually this crazy here."

Charlie shrugged one shoulder as he practically yelled, "I don't mind!"

Elizabeth's words echoed through Will's head again.

Some people don't mind a mess.

There's no way she could have seen the text message. No chance in hell that Charlie would have shown it to her. It was just a coincidence.

Then Will's gaze slid over the bar, to where Charlie's phone lay face up. The screen illuminated with a notification—one that could be read by anyone standing there. Like a redhead who'd been sitting at the stool in front of it just a few moments ago.

Well, shit.

He wasn't embarrassed. After all, he hadn't said anything that wasn't true. Still, something hot and uncomfortable flared in his chest as he turned to Charlie.

"We should get going."

"Are you kidding? The band hasn't even finished their set!" he exclaimed.

Will leaned closer. "And Vivienne is barely conscious."

Charlie's smile flattened as he craned his neck to look toward the other side of the room. "Fuck."

Goodbyes were quick, and to Jane's credit, she didn't seem to mind. Will couldn't make out their words, but while Charlie was verbose, the eldest Bennet sister seemed happy to just smile and nod. She didn't even look up from her drink as they walked to the door.

Will thought that was it. But the ten-minute drive home was one long soliloquy from Charlie about the beautiful Jane Bennet.

"Did I tell you that Tom Baker is her favorite Doctor?" Charlie asked, his voice echoing through the sharp angles of the house as their foursome entered the dark foyer.

"Yes," Will replied flatly, continuing forward into the living room.

Charlie followed him, undaunted. "She even has all the 'Pyramids of Mars' episodes on DVD. Those are impossible to find! She said she would let me borrow them, but I think I might invite her over for a whole *Doctor Who* marathon, you know? She hasn't seen 'Planet of Giants,' and I think—"

"Sounds great, Charlie," Annabelle interrupted as she walked past him on her way to the kitchen. "Just don't get attached."

Charlie paused by the towering windows on the far side of the room, completely dark now except for the faint outline of the clouds against the black sky. "What does that mean?"

"Oh please," Annabelle said with a roll of her eyes. "You can't be that naive." She didn't even look at him as she said it, just opened the refrigerator and took out some water.

Charlie's hands went to his hips. "I guess I am, because I have no idea what you're talking about."

Annabelle already had the bottle of water to her lips, so Vivienne piped up from where she had landed on the sofa, arm flung over her face. "She's probably just after your money, Charlie."

Charlie's brow furrowed as he looked from his sisters to Will, then back to his sisters. "Oh, come on. She doesn't know I have money."

Annabelle put her bottle of water on the counter. "Does she know you work in mergers and acquisitions?"

"Yes."

"And that we rented this house for the whole summer?"

"So?"

Across the room, Vivienne laughed so hard it turned into a snort.

Annabelle tossed him an incredulous eye roll before taking another sip of water. "She knows you have money, Charlie."

Neither of his sisters was privy to the way that Charlie's expression dimmed, how his brow creased in an unfamiliar way and his gaze dropped to the floor. Will was tempted to soften the blow, but he also recognized the hard truth there. The one Charlie needed to hear.

After a moment, Charlie lifted his head, his attention now on Will. "What do you think?"

Will considered. Yes, he could tell Charlie what he really thought. And with anyone else, he wouldn't hesitate. But Charlie wasn't just anyone. Since they'd met freshman year at Columbia, he had been like a brother, and, considering Will was an only child, that meant a lot. When Will's parents had died a few years ago, it started to mean even more. He wouldn't sacrifice Charlie's excitement on the altar of honesty. Instead, he simply said, "She smiles too much."

Charlie's pensive expression melted away as he shook his head and chuckled. "You're a dick."

The corner of Will's mouth teased a grin before falling flat again.

"On that note," Annabelle said, rolling her eyes, "I'm going to bed. Come on, Viv."

She abandoned her water on the counter and walked over to the sofa. Vivienne was sprawled across it, her long dress wrapped around her legs and one sandal hanging off her foot.

"I'm not tired," she whined, her eyes closed.

Annabelle grabbed the arm lying over her sister's eyes and pulled. "Then just lie in bed and research companies that can send Richard an anonymous box of dog shit."

Vivienne seemed to think about it for a minute, then sighed. "Okay." She stood slowly and, Vivienne leaning on Annabelle, they both disappeared down the hall.

"I'm going to bed, too," Charlie said, stretching his arms up over his head. "You all set?"

Will scratched his jaw, looking over to the towering windows that revealed darkness where the ocean should be. "Yeah. Going to stay up for a while."

Charlie bobbed his head and started toward the stairs but paused at the foot. "You think Jane is nice, right?" he asked, turning just enough to look over his shoulder at his friend.

Will nodded. "I do."

"And gorgeous?"

"Very."

"Her sister is really pretty, too."

Will stared at him.

Charlie smiled. "Maybe the four of us could go out, like a double date. Wouldn't that be great? We could get—"

Will turned and started toward the kitchen. "Good night, Charlie."

He heard Charlie laughing to himself as he ascended the

stairs, but Will ignored it, his attention on the refrigerator. He had volunteered to drive tonight, so after two sips of that warm swill they served at the bar, he'd stuck with water. Now, as he grabbed a cold beer from the shelf, the drink felt well-earned. He twisted off the cap and took a deep sip as he walked to the doors that led out to the verandah.

They slid open easily, letting in a rush of ocean air, flush with salt and brine. He walked to the edge of the verandah, where the slate stone tiles met the craggy beach grass, and closed his eyes, listening to the steady rhythm of rolling waves breaking on the shore.

He needed this. Despite how much the Hamptons had changed over the years, how its unrefined edges had been polished and honed, nothing could take away the calm of the beach, the ocean, the wind. Even in the stillness it felt raw and untamed. He had come to rely on that feeling of peace mixed in with something unpredictable and wild. If he wouldn't have it this summer in Montauk, then East Hampton would have to do.

An image of red hair and dark eyes flashed in his mind, of powdered sugar and a smirk, but he ignored it and took another sip of his beer. Why should he fixate on something that didn't matter? It was a moment and it was in the past. By tomorrow, Elizabeth Bennet wouldn't even remember him.

CHAPTER 8

"Will Darcy did *not* say that." Jane was staring at her sister over a basket of baguettes, mouth agape.

Lizzy set a tray of zucchini muffins down on the long folding table under their small white pop-up tent at the farmers market, squinting against the morning sun. "Technically, you're right. He texted it."

Behind her, Kitty snorted out a laugh from the top of the ladder where she was hanging American flag decorations from the tent's metal frame.

The East Hampton Farmers Market was a Sunday tradition, and this Memorial Day weekend was no different. The field outside the Village Hall was a flurry of activity as locals set up their wares. Bennet Bakery had one of the smaller stands—just a table lined with muffins and breads and pastries—so while they were almost done setting up at nine a.m., others were still erecting their tents and hauling their goods from the nearby parking lot. Still, the smell of cherry muffins and sourdough bread was already mixing with cotton candy and hot dogs and citronella candles.

"Maybe he was talking about someone else," Jane said, positioning a pile of napkins near the register.

Lizzy laughed, turning around to grab another tray of muffins. "I'm not sure that makes it any better."

"But Will is Charlie's best friend," Jane said, shaking her head. "Charlie wouldn't be friends with someone who would say something like that."

"Oh, he *wouldn't*?" Lizzy paused, resting the tray against her hip so she could wag her eyebrows at Jane. "Anything else about Charlie Pierce that you care to share?"

Jane's cheeks flushed. "I don't know what you're talking about."

"Are you sure? Because you've been smiling at those sticky buns for a disturbing amount of time."

"Stop it."

"And you're blushing."

"I am not."

"And I heard you humming," Kitty added from the ladder.

Lizzy smiled even as she feigned a gasp. "She's right. You were humming. Woodland creatures could join us at any moment. And then—"

"Fine!" Jane dropped the pile of napkins and took a deep breath. "He's . . . nice. Okay?"

Lizzy's smile fell. "Nice?"

"Yes. Nice."

"That's it?"

Jane nodded once.

"Nice." Kitty looked like she was trying very hard to think of something else to say.

"Did you get his number?" Lizzy asked, desperate for at least this crumb. There's no way she would have left the bar if she hadn't assumed they would at least exchange contact information.

Jane's eyes widened. "I'm not going to ask for a guy's number."

Lizzy groaned, her head falling forward. Her older sister was hopeless, and she was about to tell her so when Mary appeared in front of their table. Her thin frame was tented in a T-shirt emblazoned with the words *Plastic Kills*, and she had a large piece of canvas folded under her arm. "I need scissors."

Kitty climbed down from the ladder and handed her the pair she had been using.

"Does Green Justice have a booth today?" Jane asked encouragingly.

"Not exactly," she answered, pocketing the scissors. Then she started to turn away.

"How about some sustenance on your quest to destroy capitalism?" Lizzy asked, biting back a smile.

Mary considered, then grabbed a zucchini muffin.

By the time the sisters finished setting up, people were already filtering into the lopsided circle of tables and tents that constituted the weekly farmers market. As soon as anyone passed the old paint-peeled Village Hall, they would immediately see the Bennet Bakery stand between Vicki Lyon's organic soaps and Marv's homemade pickle cotton candy. They had been in the same spot for the last ten years.

"All right," Kitty said, clapping her hands together like they were in a boardroom. "The table is all set, so is the register. But I still think Dad needs to talk to Marv about moving us closer to the produce tables. Market research says that over 66 percent of people buy fruit and vegetables from farmers markets, and I think—"

"Pace yourself, Kitkat," Lizzy said, pulling *The Court of the Serpent King* from her bag and settling in to where the page was dog-eared at chapter 25. Her sister had been making the same point ever since she took that Principles of Marketing class last year. "We can't get too busy; I have a book to finish."

Kitty rolled her eyes as if Lizzy were joking. "All right, I'm heading home. Call if you two need anything."

Lizzy didn't look up as she waved goodbye.

Within an hour, the market was seeing a steady flow of weekenders and locals alike, all meandering around the different tents. Only a few people stopped at the bakery's table, so Lizzy stayed engrossed in her book while Jane rang up any purchases.

It was only when she got to chapter 28 and Lord Magnus Beaumont had finally thrown his true love Adrianna over his shoulder and stormed up to his bedroom that Lizzy looked up. She always felt a bit self-conscious when she was reading in public and stumbled upon a particularly racy bit of a book. Although, to be fair, she hadn't particularly *stumbled*, since she had been waiting precisely 270 pages for this moment. Still, as she looked around the market, she couldn't shake the feeling that everyone was watching her, that they knew exactly what was about to happen in Lord Magnus's chambers.

Then her eyes snagged on a man on the other side of the field. His back was to her, so all she could see was his black hair, his broad shoulders. He seemed to be interested in the HamptonFest table, with Hank Donato standing next to him, talking and gesturing around the market. The man seemed to be listening intently, nodding as he slowly turned around.

Ohmygod. It was Lord Magnus.

Okay, not really. But it might as well have been. He had the same dark hair, deep green eyes. And his smile was electric, like it was lit up by some internal force. Then he cocked his head ever so slightly, as if he somehow knew someone was watching him, and turned those green eyes to her.

Oh. *Oh.* Lizzy was definitely not hallucinating. Not only was he real—he was staring right at her. And she was suddenly aware that her Guns N' Roses vintage *Appetite for Destruction* T-shirt had seen better days.

Her brain scrambled, synapses trying desperately to connect, to figure out what to do next, but then her view was gone, blocked by someone stepping into her line of sight. A tall, blond someone who needed a haircut and personality transplant.

Lizzy's expression fell.

It was Will Darcy.

He was standing just a foot or so away from their table, surveying the farmers market with a look that lived somewhere between derision and boredom, and she found the heat in her core now felt more like annoyance. She was about to lean forward and tell him that if he really had to stand there and brood, to please do it three feet to the left, when Charlie appeared at his side.

"Hello!" He beamed.

Jane spun around from where she was taking inventory of the mocha chip muffins. The motion was so fast Lizzy thought she would fall over into the nearby ginger peach scones. "Charlie! Hi!"

Charlie's smile broadened, and it was another minute before he noticed Lizzy there, too, sitting behind the table. "Oh, Lizzy! Good to see you! Will, look! It's Lizzy!"

Will only glanced at her before letting his gaze continue across the crowd.

Lizzy was almost grateful for the excuse to ignore him, waving at Charlie as if his friend wasn't there at all. "How are you, Charlie?"

"I'm great! Better now," he said warmly.

Jane blushed. "I . . . I didn't expect you to stop by."

"Well, you told me I had to try your muffins, so here I am!"

Lizzy couldn't stop the laugh that bubbled up. She coughed,

trying to disguise it, but she apparently didn't do a very good job because when she looked up again, Will was glaring at her.

"So what do you have?" Charlie continued, oblivious.

Jane began to walk him through the litany of flavors. "Well, there's lemon poppy seed and blueberry and zucchini. And my favorite: sour cherry."

She picked one up and handed it to him. He didn't hesitate in taking a bite, crumbs dusting his chin as his eyes rolled closed.

Lizzy knew that look, the moment when the flavor hitting a customer's taste buds exceeded their expectations. It happened the first time she'd tried one of their sour cherry muffins, too. No one could remember which Bennet came up with the recipe—her father claimed it was his invention, while Jane insisted it was her mistake after she used almond extract instead of vanilla—but either way, they were so popular they practically kept the lights on.

"You have good taste," he said, still chewing. "This is incredible."

"Oh, it's not just me. It's everyone's favorite," Jane said, tugging a strand of dark hair behind her ear.

"Will, you have to try this," Charlie said to his friend, then turned back to Jane. "Can I get one more?"

Jane opened her mouth to answer, but Lizzy beat her to it, leaning forward in her chair and blocking the sign that identified the long row of sour cherry muffins. "Sorry, that was the last one."

Will watched the motion, pointedly looking between her and the baked goods she was doing a poor job of hiding. She offered him another plastic smile.

"Oh, too bad." Charlie clasped his friend on the shoulder. "You're missing out, Will."

"We can only hope he survives the hardship," Lizzy said with a painfully manufactured sigh.

Jane laughed so loud and so nervously that everyone turned to look at her, including a few people passing by.

"How much do I owe you?" Charlie asked, nodding to what was left of his muffin.

"Don't worry, it's on the house," Lizzy said.

"I insist." He reached into his pocket and handed her a five-dollar bill. "And don't worry about change. This muffin is worth at least double that." Then he took another bite.

Lizzy smiled, slipping the money into the cash box before turning to her sister. "Jane, have you volunteered to show Charlie around the farmers market yet?"

Her sister blanched, mouth falling open. "Oh ... I ... I'm sure Charlie has other things to do ..."

"I would love that," Charlie said, ignoring the fact that she was tripping over her words. "If you'd like that, I mean."

"Sure. Yes ... okay," Jane said, a deep flush crawling up her neck as she turned around, awkwardly looking for her tote bag before realizing it was still over her shoulder. Then she finally looked up to meet his gaze again. "Ready?"

They stared at each other, and for a moment Lizzy wasn't sure if Charlie would wait for Jane to walk around the table or if he would just lean across it and kiss her. But finally he said, "You lead the way." Jane smiled. Then she stepped around the table, and together they made their way into the crowd.

It was finally happening—Jane was falling for someone. Her last date had been two years ago, and Lizzy had started thinking her sister was embracing celibacy. Now she wanted to jump up and celebrate, high-five someone or at least share a thumbs-up. But as she looked around, she realized there was no one to share her excitement with. Well, not no one. The blond palm tree hater who had unceremoniously blocked her view a few minutes before was still there. He was staring down at the line of sour cherry muffins separating them, and she was fairly certain it would be impossible for him to muster excitement over anything.

So instead of trying, she delved back into her book. She was just getting to the part where Lord Magnus was about to tear off Adrianna's dragon-skin corset when Will's voice finally broke the silence.

"It's a shame."

Oh God. Was Will Darcy making small talk? Lizzy hated small talk. Especially when Adrianna was running her fingers through Lord Magnus's dark hair.

She glanced up at him, hand over her eyes to shield them from the sun.

"About the cherry muffins," he said.

Lizzy waited for him to continue. When he didn't, she offered him a tight smile and returned to her book.

"You were out of them the other day, too," he finally said. "When Charlie and I stopped by the bakery."

"Oh, that's what you're talking about," she replied, not taking her eyes off the page. "I didn't know if you had a question or if you were looking for me to support your astute observation."

"Then you should have asked me to clarify."

She sighed. "It's okay. Once I realized I didn't really care either way, ignoring you altogether seemed like the best option."

His eyes narrowed on her, like someone looking at an instruction manual written in a foreign language. "I see."

She offered him another smile. "Feel free to ignore me, too. I won't be offended."

"All right."

Then he reached over and grabbed one of the sour cherry muffins.

Lizzy's mouth was agape in equal parts shock and horror as Will maintained eye contact, his blue eyes locked on hers, and took a huge bite. It was like a challenge, as if he expected her to admit the lie, to apologize.

Well, he obviously didn't know Lizzy. She would rather go over and eat a whole serving of Marv's pickle cotton candy. So she snapped her mouth shut and just lifted her chin as she watched the line of his jaw move as he chewed, the way his throat bobbed when he finally swallowed.

They were still staring at each other when an angry chant began on the other end of the field.

"THAT'S BULLSHIT! GET OFF IT! OUR ISLAND'S NOT FOR PROFIT!"

A small group of protesters appeared in the crowd, with Mary at the front, holding a canvas banner that read: *Save Gretna Island.* They were marching toward Hank Donato and his HamptonFest table.

Oh God.

Lizzy didn't have time to cringe before Mary threw the first liquid-filled balloon. Where she grabbed it from, Lizzy had no idea. All she knew was that it hit the HamptonFest banner with a thunderous crack, exploding on contact and sending red paint in every direction. It was followed by more, each in quick succession, until the entire table was covered in Benjamin Moore's Hot Tamale.

People were running in every direction, yelling for them to stop, screaming for really no reason at all other than the fact that they had been standing too close and now looked as if they were extras in a Quentin Tarantino movie.

When Lizzy looked back at Will, he was watching Mary with his holier-than-thou glare in place.

"That's one of your sisters, right?" he asked.

She frowned. "Yup."

He watched for another minute, and Lizzy could almost feel the judgment radiating from him.

"She's got good aim," he finally replied, tossing a five-dollar bill onto the table. Then he took another bite of his muffin and turned toward the parking lot.

She narrowed her eyes at him, mentally cataloging a dozen biting retorts. But in the end, she decided to keep her mouth shut and just watch him disappear from view. She'd save them for next time.

CHAPTER 9

Apart from Mary being escorted from the farmers market by police and Hank filing a restraining order against her, the next few weeks in the Bennet household were fairly uneventful. Lydia spent almost every night out at a different party, Kitty toiled away on her top secret business plan, and Mary continued to add to her climate change manifesto. Meanwhile, Lizzy spent all her time at the bakery. She had to. While business was negligible during the fall and winter months, summer held the best chance for profit.

The only real change to the Bennet dynamic was Jane's sudden absence from it. As the school year at East Hampton Elementary wrapped up, it wasn't unusual for the eldest Bennet daughter to spend more time at home, but now her days were filled with walks on the beach with Charlie, tours of the Gardner Windmill with Charlie, dinners and lunches and endless coffees with Charlie.

Lizzy couldn't be happier for her, even though there was an inevitable issue ahead. Every summer, Jane picked up extra shifts at the bakery. She never missed one—she even showed up to help with others. But that was before she met Charlie, back when she had nothing better to do. And despite the extra strain it would inevitably put on Lizzy's schedule, it would be up to her to convince Jane that she *should* be doing better things.

Such as spending the last Friday in June getting ready for a date rather than nailing plywood to the bakery's front window.

"Hold it straight or I'm going to put this nail through my hand," Mr. Bennet grumbled.

Lizzy rolled her eyes, even as she lifted her side of the wooden sheet up a few inches.

A tropical storm was barreling up the eastern seaboard, set to hit East Hampton that night. There was usually at least one every year, and they knew how to prepare. It was the same routine they followed for years, a fact Lizzy was reminded of when she dragged the large piece of plywood used to protect the front window up from the basement and found it still had *ONE DIRECTION 4EVER* scrawled on one side, right where she'd written it twelve years ago.

"I thought you were supposed to replace these after every storm," she said.

"They're fine," Mr. Bennet said, waving her off. He pounded in another nail, then stepped back to observe his work. "All right, I think that's it. Let's go ahead and close up so we can get out of here."

"You sure? What about those outstanding invoices? We have to pay those before the end of the day."

He nodded. "I got it, kiddo."

She hesitated. Did he?

"I got it," he repeated, giving her a look from under his brow like he could read her mind. "You reel in the awning, and don't forget to take off the crank wand."

She gave him a small salute and was rewarded with a crooked smile before he disappeared inside.

A gust of wind sent strands of her red hair dancing across her face as she spun the hand crank for the awning. The blue-and-white-striped canopy slowly retracted, groaning with each turn. Did she want to think about how much this early closure was going to cost them? How one lost afternoon during their busiest time of year could set them back weeks? Or the financial hit the bakery would take if this tropical storm left any damage in its wake? No, not really. Lizzy already knew the worry would eventually come. For now, she wanted to focus on the fact that it was Friday, the impending storm was sending six-foot waves crashing onto the beach, and her surfboard was waiting in the flatbed of her truck.

Then Hank Donato's voice called out behind her. "Lizzy!"

Lizzy closed her eyes, fortifying her patience. It wasn't that she didn't like Hank Donato—if anything, Piper's father was more like family than anything else. It was just that he loved to talk and also had an uncanny ability to misread all social cues.

That's why Lizzy took a deep breath before donning a smile and turning around to face him. "Hi, Hank."

Sure enough, there he was, standing just a few feet away on the sidewalk. His belly was a bit rounder than it had been when Lizzy was a child, but otherwise he looked just about the same, thanks to what she could only assume was a monthly application of dark brown hair dye. She had seen photos of him in his youth, when he lived in the city and wore ripped jeans and T-shirts, but those had long been replaced with khakis and polo shirts.

But Hank wasn't alone. There was someone else standing beside him, a tall someone with dark hair, green eyes . . .

"Lord Magnus," Lizzy blurted out before she could stop herself.

Hank's forehead wrinkled with confusion even as his companion's mouth curved up into a smile.

"Sorry," Lizzy continued, squeezing her eyes together for a

moment before turning her attention back to Hank. "Um. How are you?"

"Good! I'm good!" His smile faltered slightly. "Mary's not working today, is she?"

"Nope."

His smile returned, even brighter than before. "Good! That's great. Yes, well, I see you're getting ready for the storm. We have the windows at the Lodge shuttered up, too, but I'm not worried. Maybe some flooding by the beach, but that's to be expected, isn't it?"

Silence as he stared at her, as if waiting for a reply. Then his companion cleared his throat.

"Oh! Of course. Lizzy Bennet! This is Tristan Cole. He's come on board to help get HamptonFest off the ground."

The memory of Piper's comments from a few weeks ago, about how her father was expecting a potential new partner to come by the Lodge, and the image of the two men at the farmers market the following day, clicked into place in Lizzy's mind.

"Oh right. I think Piper mentioned something," Lizzy said, turning to Tristan. "You're from the city."

"Not exactly," he replied, his head cocking to the side. "I live in the city now, but I'm from Long Island."

"Where on Long Island?"

His mouth quirked up in a smile. "Queens."

She couldn't help but smile back. "That's the city."

"Not to people from the city."

She almost laughed. He wasn't wrong.

"Tristan is a party and events promoter, has some incredible connections," Hank said with a satisfied nod. "After I convinced Marv to give HamptonFest a line in the town budget, Tristan here reached out and, let me tell you, he has some huge ideas. Really huge. I've hired him as a consultant to help grease a few wheels. He even has a plan to get those permits for Gretna Island so we can build a more permanent setup. Can you imagine? It's going to be huge!"

"Huge, you say?" Lizzy said, unable to help her teasing tone.

Tristan mirrored it back. "No. Really huge."

They stared at each other, each biting back their own grin, as Hank laughed. "Exactly!"

"It's nice to meet you, Lizzy," Tristan said, extending his hand.

She took it, letting his long fingers envelop hers for a moment longer than she probably should have. "You, too."

"Like I said, huge ideas," Hank continued. "We're making the rounds, seeing if there are some opportunities for synergy. We have so many locals who have always wanted to get in on the ground floor of something like this."

Tristan nodded as if he endorsed every word Hank was saying, even as he snuck a sly glance at Lizzy. Something in his gaze seemed brazen, and suddenly she felt a rush of warmth to her cheeks. Was she . . . blushing?

"I was thinking Tristan should meet your dad," Hank said, oblivious. "Walk him through the whole proposal and see the big picture. Is he around?"

"You just missed him." It was a blatant lie, but Lizzy was also under strict instructions to deflect as many of Hank's visits as possible.

"Well, I could walk you through it," Tristan said. His voice was deep and warm.

"Oh!" Hank's eyes lit up. "Even better!"

"What do you say?" Tristan nodded down the street. "Want to grab a coffee before the storm sets in? I could give you a quick rundown of the project."

Lizzy hesitated. She knew better than to get involved, but as Tristan's full mouth ticked up in a playful grin, she convinced herself that she could at least listen. After all, she didn't want to be rude. "Sure."

Hank clapped. "Synergy!"

And then there was a loud ping, a text message alert from Lizzy's back pocket. For a moment she debated ignoring it, but another rang out seconds later.

"Could you excuse me for a minute?" she asked, then turned around and pulled her phone out.

A message from Jane illuminated the screen.

JANE

> Hey! Dad just called and said you're closing early. Any chance you can drive me to Charlie's?

JANE

> Just wondering!

LIZZY

> I thought you were borrowing Mom's car so you could leave Charlie's before the weather got bad?

JANE

> She says she can't spare it.

Lizzy blinked down at her phone. No, that couldn't be right. Their mother rarely drove anywhere except to the bakery or Donna's. How could she not spare it? But then Lizzy remembered who they were talking about. Nothing was beyond the realm of possibility where Joanne Bennet was concerned.

LIZZY

What's her excuse?

JANE

She said she has errands? She offered to drop me off herself, though, so she could officially meet the Pierces . . . not sure I'm ready for that yet.

JANE

No worries if you can't!

I can call Marv!

LIZZY

Wait right there. I'll be home in 5.

She turned back to Tristan. "Sorry, minor emergency at home. Rain check?"

"Of course," he said. He bowed his head and when he brought it back up again, another cheeky grin was on his lips. "I'm looking forward to it."

Hank clapped his hands proudly again. "Synergy!"

"I can't believe she wouldn't just let you have the car," Lizzy murmured, gripping the wheel of her truck tightly as she turned it down Lily Pond Lane.

Jane sighed as she checked her makeup in the visor's cracked mirror again. "It's not a big deal. I could've called Marv."

"Marv doesn't drive in the rain, Jane."

"Oh. Right." Jane blinked, then snapped the visor back up again. "Well, it all worked out. Worst-case scenario I had to walk, and you do it all the time."

"Not right before a hurricane."

"It's not a hurricane. It's a tropical storm."

Lizzy rolled her eyes. "I'll make sure to remind you of that when you drown in the middle of Main Street."

When they reached the break in the hedges near the end of the lane, Lizzy turned down the long drive toward the house while Jane began fidgeting with the frayed string at the bottom of her bag. By the time she threw the truck into park outside the front door, Lizzy thought she might unravel the entire thing.

"Ready?" she asked carefully.

Jane nodded, her wide eyes locked on the house.

"Do you want me to walk you up?" Lizzy asked.

Jane shook her head as a weary smile tugged at her mouth. "I can handle it from here."

"I know, but I can just say hi."

"Lizzy."

"Let them know about the storm. What to do if the roads close. Or—"

"Lizzy," Jane repeated, resting a hand on Lizzy's arm. "It's fine. Really."

Lizzy knew that tone. It was the one Jane reserved for when Lizzy was trying to control too much. When she needed to let go just a little bit.

"Okay," she replied.

Jane nodded. "Okay."

But then she didn't move.

Lizzy's eyes narrowed on her. "What's wrong?"

"It's nothing, just . . . I've been hanging out with Charlie all month, but I haven't really spent much time with his sisters." Jane kept her eyes glued on the looming house, her bottom lip trapped between her teeth.

"And?"

"What if they decide they don't like me?"

Lizzy let a small smile turn up her lips. "I don't think that's possible."

"I'm serious, Lizzy. What if—"

"I'm serious, too," Lizzy replied. "You're kind and thoughtful and you have no idea how gorgeous you are, which is a little annoying, if I'm honest, but it's not enough for them not to like you."

Jane didn't look convinced.

"But more importantly, who cares if they don't like you?" Lizzy continued, her voice softer. "Charlie likes you. As long as he's there, how bad can it be?"

"Right." Jane seemed to consider. "And if it is bad?"

"Then I promise to come save you so we can live the rest of our lives in an old mansion, where we'll collect cats and hide from the outside world until they make a documentary about us."

Jane fought her smile as she pretended to look exasperated. "Are you describing *Grey Gardens* again?"

"Of course not," Lizzy replied. "They were mother and daughter. We're sisters. Totally different."

Jane laughed, then leaned across the truck's console to give her sister a hug. "Love you."

"Love you, too," Lizzy whispered. "Now, go in there and blow Charlie away with your extensive knowledge of damasks."

Jane groaned as she pulled away and opened the car door. "They're called Daleks."

"That's what I said!" Lizzy yelled just before the door slammed shut behind her sister. Then she watched through the windshield as Jane threw her bag over her shoulder and started up the front steps to the door.

Jane was halfway there when Lizzy's phone rang in the pocket of her overalls. She grabbed it and found her mom's photo on the screen.

"Hello, Mom," she answered.

"Did you drive your sister to Charlie's?" Mrs. Bennet replied in greeting.

Lizzy sighed. "Yes, I drove her. Is that a problem?"

Mrs. Bennet tutted, as if the sound were the epitome of disgruntlement.

"Where are you right now?" Lizzy continued.

"Me? Oh, I'm . . . shopping. Grocery shopping. And errands. I'm very busy."

Lizzy could clearly hear Donna Donato in the background, which meant she was actually at Donna's and probably on her second round of margaritas. The sound of a blender coming to life a moment later only confirmed it.

"Mom."

"What?"

"Did you tell Jane she couldn't have your car just so she'd have to ask you for a ride? And then you could invite yourself in and meet Charlie?"

"I don't know what you're talking about," she replied defiantly. Then she added, "Charlie doesn't even own one store. Annabelle owns *hundreds*."

Lizzy closed her eyes. "I appreciate your dedication to the success of Lux Leggings, Mom, but the storm is set to hit us in just a few hours. Jane could get stuck here. Charlie's car isn't four-wheel drive. If it rains more than three inches, Lily Pond Lane will flood, and then she'll be stuck."

"Well then, I guess we'll kill two birds with one stone, won't we?"

"What are you talking—" Even as the words left Lizzy's mouth, her brain made the connection, recognizing the signature Joanne Bennet plot just under the surface. "Oh my God."

Mrs. Bennet hummed, barely disguising her self-satisfaction.

"Mom."

"Hm?"

"Please tell me you're not purposely stranding your daughter at a stranger's house during a hurricane."

"It's not a hurricane. It's a tropical storm."

Lizzy frowned. "I'm concerned that the only thing you find wrong about that statement is the category of the impending storm."

Another tut. "Stop being so dramatic."

"What if it's worse than expected? Then she's stuck—"

A tittering laugh filled the line. "Trust me, everything will work out. Just you wait."

"Mom—"

"Lizzy, your sister is so introverted she's almost a hermit. Now, you have your way of dealing with that and I have mine. M'kay?"

There was a peal of thunder in the distance as Lizzy watched her sister disappear inside the front door. Maybe it wouldn't be so bad, she rationalized. After all, the storm might already have been downgraded to a tropical depression. By the time it arrived, they would probably see a little rain and that would be it. She had nothing to worry about.

CHAPTER 10

Will couldn't remember a storm that bad in years.

He tugged a gray T-shirt over his head as he descended the glass-and-steel staircase. Charlie's house was still quiet, with the watery morning light only just beginning to bleed through the wall of glass on the far side of the room. The storm had passed, but the lingering clouds left a sobering reminder behind.

Normally, Will would have canceled his weekend trip out east and ridden out the storm alone at his apartment in the city. But thanks to a series of construction delays, the Montauk house was still without a roof, so he knew he had to take matters into his own hands. He flew out yesterday morning, landing just before they began to cancel flights. By the time he had finished ensuring his house could withstand the beating, he drove down the coast to East Hampton, arriving just before Montauk Highway flooded and made the journey impossible.

When he got there, Will had been surprised to find Jane Bennet in the living room, sitting alongside the Pierces as they all watched a meteorologist motioning to a radar covered almost entirely in red. Soon every road that led to the house was closed, which meant

Jane was stuck there for the night. But while Charlie couldn't have been happier about the situation, Jane seemed hesitant. Not that Will thought she would have been overjoyed, but there was a reluctance there that nagged at him.

Then the power went out.

Will found some candles in a kitchen drawer, while Vivienne and Annabelle found two bottles of wine. They downed them over the course of an hour, singing every top forty song they'd downloaded on Spotify between swigs. Thankfully, by ten o'clock both their phones had died.

"Oh, my phone is almost out of battery, too," Jane had said, staring at her glowing screen.

Vivienne's head popped up from the sofa. "What if all our phones die?" she asked, her words slurred. "What if we're stuck here . . . forever?"

Will took that as his cue. He stood up, ready to excuse himself to the blessed solitude of his room upstairs, when Charlie piped in from where he sat with Jane by the fireplace.

"We should get Lizzy's number before Jane's phone dies, don't you think, Will?" he asked.

Will paused. "Why do we need Jane's sister's number?"

"In case of an emergency."

"An emergency," Will repeated flatly. Charlie may have been one of the most brilliant minds in green tech, but when it came to scheming, he was about as subtle as a jackhammer.

"Yeah," his friend said nonchalantly. "We could start a group text or something. For safety. Or . . . for going out and doing other things. Maybe."

"She's free most nights," Jane offered brightly.

Great. Charlie'd gotten the sister involved in this, too.

"Like . . . Friday or Saturday nights," Charlie added.

Will narrowed his eyes at both of them, then turned without answering. He headed to the fridge, suddenly parched, and grabbed the pitcher of Annabelle's cucumber water to pour himself a glass. He headed upstairs shortly after, with Annabelle and Vivienne passed out on the sofa, and Charlie and Jane still sitting close by the fireplace.

Now the gray morning light revealed that the living room was empty.

Coffee. Will needed coffee. His bare feet padded along the marble floor to the kitchen where the coffeemaker blinked 12:00. Apparently the power had come on at some point. Will pressed the on button and listened to the coffeemaker spurt and start slowly brewing.

When it was done, he took his cup and made his way to the wall of windows facing the beach. Usually the sun was so bright in this house that it practically blinded him, but today, gray clouds blanketed the sky, silhouetting seagulls making lazy loops across it.

He unlocked the sliding door and walked out onto the verandah, where the teak furniture was surprisingly intact. There was a slight chill in the summer air, mixed with the usual smell of seaweed and salt. The Hamptons had endured their share of hurricanes and forced evacuations over the years, but Will still marveled at the way it always fell back into its own rhythm afterward.

There was shuffling behind him then. He glanced over his shoulder to see Vivienne on her way to the kitchen, Annabelle in tow.

"I'm never drinking again," Vivienne moaned. "Please tell me the power is back on. If I can't have a latte, I'm going to cry."

"I think you'll survive, Viv," Annabelle murmured.

A pit of dread formed in Will's chest. As much as he loved Charlie's sisters, he had learned years ago they were better in small doses. And definitely not first thing in the morning.

There was a commotion in the kitchen as the sisters raided the refrigerator, but Will continued forward across the verandah and down the narrow path to the beach. The cool sand was still wet, and he could feel the bottoms of his sweatpants getting damp as his feet sank into it, but he didn't care. He just took a sip of his coffee. The bitterness bit at his tongue as he watched the massive swells crash on the beach over and over again.

I should have brought my board, he mused, hypnotized by the long line of the beach break. Yes, surfing right after a storm wasn't the smartest idea—urban runoff made for more risks than he was used to taking—but even he couldn't deny that today was the perfect day for it. Just the waves and the wind. No distractions.

Then something in the periphery caught his eye.

One lone surfer had decided to tempt fate and battle the ocean. They were winning, too. For several minutes, he watched from the beach, clocking them as they sliced through the water, caught a wave and rode toward shore.

Then they turned around and paddled back out to do it all again.

After a few minutes, the surfer was almost directly in front of Charlie's house. They swerved, riding another monster wave onto the beach just a few yards from where Will stood watching.

Once in shallow waters, they picked up their board and dragged it up onto the sand. While Will couldn't see their face thanks to their wetsuit's hood, he could see now that it was a woman. Her dark purple wetsuit clung to her body like a second skin.

Then she turned, pulling the hood down and shaking out her hair just as the sun peeked out from behind the clouds. Her wet, red hair.

His coffee hovered at his lips as his pulse stumbled. It was Elizabeth Bennet. Dripping wet and walking straight toward him, like he should be expecting her.

"Hi," she said, stopping just a few feet away.

"What are you doing?" he asked before he could stop himself.

Her head tipped to the side as she stared up at him, her chest rising and falling with each fast breath. "Quantum physics. Obviously."

He frowned. "You shouldn't be surfing in this."

Her eyebrows bobbed up. "Excuse me?"

"You shouldn't surf after a storm. The water pollution levels—"

"I know about urban runoff, Will," she said, then motioned down her body. "Hence the full suit."

He glanced down at the purple neoprene and immediately noticed a tear in it along her left thigh.

"There's a hole in it."

She looked down, as if noticing it for the first time, and shrugged. "I have glue at home."

"Doesn't do you much good in this situation."

"Neither does unsolicited criticism." Her tone was clipped as she narrowed her eyes on him. "Anything else you care to comment on?"

He took a sip of his coffee. "Give me ten minutes. I just woke up."

Her dark eyes flared like she might smile. He'd thought he would see it at the farmers market a few weeks ago, when he grabbed that muffin despite her lie, and he had been disappointed when she hadn't. Now he waited, surprised by the knot of anticipation tightening in his chest.

Then Vivienne's voice wailed from back up on the verandah.

"Charlie! The cushions are soaking wet!"

Lizzy craned to look up toward the house. "Did everyone survive the storm?"

"Yes."

"My sister, too?"

He nodded.

"Can I see her?" she asked, as if the follow-up should have been obvious. To be fair, it probably was.

"If she's up."

"Not being held against her will, then?"

"If you were worried, you should have called."

"I did. Her phone went straight to voicemail."

"So you went surfing instead."

"And now, here I am," she said with a sharp smile he knew was artificial. "Waiting to see her."

She was staring up at him, her dark eyes expectant, as if challenging him to keep this volley going. And he was surprised to find he wanted to. But then Annabelle's voice cut through the air.

"Just flip them over, Viv! It's fine!"

Will frowned, then nodded toward the house. "Come on."

Lizzy followed him, leaving her board in the sand at the foot of the path that led up to the verandah.

Annabelle and Vivienne had apparently found a solution to the wet cushions, each now lounging on a separate chaise. Despite the overcast skies, Vivienne was wearing sunglasses along with a black kaftan. Next to her, Annabelle was in a matching gray pajama set. The sisters were in conversation, but that halted the minute they saw Will appear with Lizzy at his side.

"Did you just come from the ocean?" Annabelle asked, looking back and forth from the beach to Lizzy.

Vivienne snorted out a laugh.

To her credit, Lizzy just smiled. "Just Main Beach. The roads down here are still closed, but I wanted to check on Jane."

"Right," Annabelle replied, though she didn't sound totally convinced.

With that, the sliding doors opened again.

"Lizzy?" Jane appeared on the verandah, a smile quickly overwhelming the confusion on her face. "What are you doing here?"

"She emerged from the ocean, apparently," Vivienne murmured.

Jane laughed softly, as if she had somehow missed the hidden jab in Vivienne's tone. "Lizzy has never been able to pass up a storm surge."

"Not true," Lizzy said. "I promised to come save you, remember? The surf was just an added bonus."

Jane laughed again, but something about Lizzy's comment still sat heavy in Will's chest. Had he missed something? Did Jane need saving? The night before had seemed benign enough, but then again, Jane was hard to read. If it was awful, he wasn't sure he would have been able to tell.

Charlie himself appeared then, yawning and smiling as he ran a hand through his well-tousled hair. It took him a moment to notice Lizzy, but when he did, his eyes lit up. "Lizzy! Hey! Will, Lizzy's here!"

Will didn't reply, just braced himself for the inevitable.

"This is great! Wow. We were just talking about you last night! Weren't we, Will?" Then Charlie noticed Lizzy's wetsuit. "Are the roads open? Did you drive or . . . swim?"

"Ah, no, not exactly," she replied, still smiling, though it was beginning to look weary. "The storm kicked up the waves, so I surfed down from Main Beach."

"You surf?" Charlie's eyebrows shot skyward. "What a coincidence! Will surfs, too! Don't you, Will?"

Will only stared at him.

"He's got a whole stack of boards at his place. Wetsuits, too," Charlie continued undaunted. "And his favorite movie is *Point Break*!"

Jesus. That was not Will's favorite movie by any means, but he didn't have the energy to correct Charlie.

"Wow," Lizzy said, completely failing to dampen her sarcasm as she turned to Will. "*Point Break*, huh?"

He met her gaze. He was expecting that same patronizing look she had given him before, an invitation to continue their volley. But now, there was a hint of amusement, too.

"So, you're like, a *real* surfer," she continued.

"Something like that," he replied, his tone noncommittal.

"Lizzy, you should take Will out one of these mornings," Jane offered, even as the words came out like they had been thoroughly rehearsed. "Show him the best spots. Or waves. Maybe."

Lizzy laughed. "I'm sure Will has better things to do on the weekend that don't require waking up before dawn."

"You go out that early?" Will asked before he could stop himself.

She shrugged. "Yeah, most mornings."

"Alone?"

Her expression turned sardonic. "Is there something wrong with that?"

"It's dangerous."

"Only if you don't know what you're doing."

"And do you?"

Her eyes flared again. He was becoming familiar with that look. The way her lips turned up ahead of the retort, how her back straightened ever so slightly, like her impending words had sharpened it. He was learning that it was inevitable. And surprisingly beautiful.

He quashed the thought as quickly as it had appeared.

"Lizzy's been surfing since she found our dad's old board in the garage when she was six," Jane said. She turned to her sister. "He taught you for a while, didn't he?"

Lizzy nodded, her smile now authentic. It left an odd pit in Will's stomach. He filled it with the last dregs from his mug.

"That's crazy!" Charlie said. "Will's dad taught him, too. Didn't he, Will? Starting when you were about that age, right? You even said that when you were younger, you both—"

"Does anyone want coffee?" Will interrupted. It was abrupt enough that all eyes turned to him, but he didn't care. He barely shared personal details about his parents with his friends, let alone strangers. The fact that the Bennet sisters didn't fit neatly into either category left him feeling even more off-balance.

"Oh, sorry, I should have offered that! I'm the worst host," Charlie said, already moving toward the door. "Who wants coffee? Water?"

"Can you get me some of that water in the fridge?" Annabelle asked, barely moving her body. "The one with the mint, not the cucumber."

"I want the one with the cucumber," Vivienne added.

"Right. Got it," he said with a decisive nod. "Lizzy?"

"No, that's okay," she replied. "I can't stay long. I just wanted to check on Jane before my mom freaked out and called the Coast Guard."

"Oh God, I forgot to call her last night," Jane said with a groan. "My phone died and I don't even think I tried to charge it."

"That's okay! You can use my phone. It's inside. And then Will and Lizzy can catch up!" Charlie said, nodding his head toward the sliding door. Then his gaze darted between Lizzy and Will before returning to Jane, waiting for her to pick up on his not-so-subtle hint.

Jane's eyes widened in recognition. "Yes. Good idea. I'll call her. Inside. Lizzy, while I'm gone, you can tell Will about your . . . surfboard. And . . . things."

Then they both disappeared into the kitchen.

A moment passed before Vivienne's head turned lethargically toward her sister. "Have I seen *Point Break*?"

Annabelle hummed as if already bored. "I don't know, Viv."

"Who's in it?"

"Keanu, I think."

Vivienne seemed to consider. "Is it that one that's on TV all the time?"

Annabelle stared at her sister blankly.

"The one where he's the cop . . ." Vivienne continued.

Nothing.

"On the bus . . ."

Jesus. This was painful.

"And the guy blows up . . ."

"That's *Speed*," Will and Lizzy answered in unison.

Will turned to Lizzy just as she turned to him, eyebrows pinched together.

"Right." Vivienne nodded, too deep in thought to notice. "Richard loved that movie."

Annabelle groaned as if she already knew where this was going. "Oh God."

The words were barely out of her mouth before Vivienne was on her feet, heading back inside. "I'll be right back."

"Can we hold off on cyberstalking your ex-husband until after breakfast, please?" Annabelle said, following close behind.

The sliding door closed behind them, leaving Will and Lizzy alone on the verandah. Silence descended, broken only by the steady roar of the waves on the beach.

Lizzy turned to watch them, and it allowed Will a moment to study her face. She was striking, really. Her eyes were impossibly large, separated by the dramatic slope of her nose, an elegant curve from her forehead down to her full lips. It would have made for an intimidating profile if not for the way her nose scrunched up when she squinted.

She turned back to face him. "So. *Point Break*?"

His gaze darted away from her as he cleared his throat. "That's Charlie's favorite movie, not mine."

"Ah," she said, nodding. "Does Charlie surf?"

"No," he replied. He should have left it at that, but found himself adding, "But when we were in college and he found out I did, he made us watch it. I hadn't seen it before, and I think he assumes I loved it as much as he did."

Lizzy blinked. "Are you telling me you've surfed your whole life but didn't see *Point Break* until college?"

"Yes."

He expected some of the confusion to dissipate from her expression, but it held steady as Lizzy tilted her head. "Will, I'm going to be honest, that's the craziest thing I've ever heard. And I regularly listened to my mother pitch a Velcro pockets business."

"I'm sorry?"

"Porto-Pockets." She motioned vaguely in front of her, as if it helped illustrate her point. "They were these detachable pockets. With Velcro. It was a whole thing."

"I thought she did leggings."

"She does." Lizzy sighed. "When it comes to business ideas, Joanne Bennet doesn't discriminate."

"So that's where the bakery came from."

"No. That's my grandparents' business. They retired and left it to my dad. If it was up to my mom, they would have sold it ages ago, but there's not that big a market for family-run businesses running on dial-up and a dream."

"You still use dial-up?"

She laughed to herself. "No, not really. But I'm the only one with the Wi-Fi password, so if I ever leave, they'll be completely cut off from the outside world. Especially because no one except me knows how to use the phone or the answering machine."

Will frowned. He had totally lost the thread of the conversation, but he slowly realized he didn't care. He wanted to keep her talking, find out what else might come out with the right prompt.

Unfortunately, he was thwarted by the sliding doors opening again. Charlie reappeared, followed by Jane. She was holding her phone in front of her, and had a look on her face that Will could only interpret as pained.

"Okay, Mom, I'll tell them," Jane said to her video call, then turned to Charlie. "My mom says thank—"

"Thank you so much!" Mrs. Bennet crooned, her voice echoing out from the phone. "We were *so* worried, what with the storm and the roads! You should see the bakery; it's a mess!"

"Of course!" Charlie said, popping up behind Jane and giving a big wave. "I'm just happy I got to steal a few more hours with her."

"You're so sweet," she replied. "But don't worry, I can come pick her up! The roads aren't totally clear yet, but I'm sure my minivan can make it through."

"Or she can stay!" Charlie said. "I don't mind."

"Oh, you should stay, Jane!" Mrs. Bennet concurred. "That house is just *so* gorgeous. Not that I've ever been invited inside, but I've heard stories! Maybe someday . . ."

Lizzy's head fell forward, her wet red hair hiding her face.

"Why not next weekend?" Charlie offered. "We're throwing a big party for the Fourth of July. You should all come! I have your number in my phone now, so I'll send you the invite."

Shit. Will watched the scene unfold with abject horror. He knew Charlie was falling hard, but he hadn't expected him to embrace the entire family. This would only make the inevitable fallout worse.

"Oh, how wonderful!" Mrs. Bennet cried. "We would love that. I can't tell you—"

"Why don't I just drive Jane home?" Lizzy piped in.

Charlie's expression dimmed a bit, even as Jane's brightened.

"Lizzy?" Mrs. Bennet said, her voice louder, as if she had gotten closer to her phone. "I thought you were surfing?"

"I was," she called out. "But I'm just parked up at Main Beach. It's a walk, but I'm sure Jane won't mind."

"What about your board?" Will asked.

She shrugged. "I can carry it."

"Okay, Mom. We got it figured out." Jane gave the screen a tight smile. "See you soon!" She quickly hung up and handed the phone back to Charlie as the smile fell. "I'm so sorry."

"Why? This is great!" he replied, threading an arm around her waist. "I can't wait to meet your mom. We'll have so much fun."

"Right." Jane nodded, though she didn't look convinced. "Okay, well, I guess we should get going."

"You don't have to," Charlie said hopefully. "Stay. Lizzy, too! We could all hang out. Maybe play charades? Or a card game? Or—"

Will was about to tell Charlie to leave it alone, but then he caught the look shared between Jane and Lizzy. It was too quick to decipher, but it was enough that Lizzy stepped forward with an apologetic smile. "Unfortunately, I've got to steal her away. The bakery's basement took some water damage last night, so it's all-hands-on-deck."

"Oh, okay," Charlie said. "Well, I can walk down with you, if you want?"

Jane nodded and quickly grabbed her bag from inside before saying a gracious thank-you to Will. Then she and Charlie began walking down the path to the beach.

It looked like Lizzy would follow them, but then she stopped in front of Will. "Thanks for taking such good care of Jane."

"Of course," he replied. Suddenly, muscle memory kicked in, and he stuck out his hand like he was saying goodbye to one of his investors.

She stared down at it for a long moment.

Damn it. He thought she would laugh, even walk away, but instead a smirk teased her lips as she finally reached out and shook it, her skin warm against his.

"Always a pleasure, Will."

Before he could reply, she released his hand and started down the path to the beach to catch up with Charlie and Jane. Will watched her go, then turned around and went back inside. Annabelle and Vivienne were bickering, but he ignored them, the same way he ignored the memory of wild red hair and torn purple neoprene. Instead, he focused on brewing another cup of coffee, then picked up his book and headed upstairs, determined to relax.

Ten minutes later, he was sitting on the balcony off his bedroom just as he intended. But his coffee was cold. His book hadn't been opened. And all he could think about was the fact that he could still feel the warmth of Lizzy's hand against his palm.

CHAPTER 11

"This place looks like something out of a horror movie," Lydia murmured.

Lizzy wanted to tell her sister she was being melodramatic, but as she looked around the basement of Bennet Bakery, she had to admit that Lydia wasn't too far off. It was bad enough that two inches of murky water covered the ground, seeping into the bags of flour they had stored along the walls, but the power was still out, so the entire mess was lit only by their flashlights and a few battery-powered lanterns from their dad's boat.

"An extreme weather event caused by the ravages of global warming *is* a real-life horror movie," Mary said from where she stood perched on the stairs, arms crossed over her chest.

"Thanks for the perspective, Mary." Lizzy pushed a strand of red hair away from her sweat-soaked brow. In addition to being flooded, the basement felt like a sauna.

To be fair, it could have been much worse. A tree fell down on the Prada boutique around the corner and, ironically, the Brazilian blowout salon across the street had its windows literally blown out, so hairbrushes and bottles of leave-in conditioner littered the sidewalk.

But unlike so many other shops downtown, this wasn't the Bennet Bakery's first storm. Lizzy and her father had prepped the space just as they had a dozen times before. It should have worked. But they hadn't taken into account that the hardware store next door would forget to close the window to their basement, which also happened to share a wall with theirs.

Now it was noon, and while all the other shops had cleaned up and were open for business, the bakery was closed. Mr. Bennet was on hold with the insurance company at home, so Lizzy had been tasked with assessing the damage, along with Mary and Lydia. Meanwhile, Kitty and Jane were helping their mother dry out three hundred pairs of leggings that had until that morning been stored in the basement's far corner.

Lizzy looked down at the water sloshing around her rain boots. The numbers were already starting to tally in her head: 108 pounds of flour, 82 pounds of sugar, 27 pounds of yeast . . . then there was everything in the refrigerator. With the power out, they'd have to throw away the butter and eggs and milk . . . she almost choked as the math began to add up.

Even with insurance, it could be weeks before they saw any reimbursement. In the meantime, if they wanted to get Bennet Bakery back up and running, they would need to put thousands on credit cards, which would mean calling to beg for their limit to be raised again.

She let out a deep breath. If they hadn't already been at a breaking point, there was no doubt they were now.

"So . . ." Lydia said, poking at a sodden cardboard box nearby. "When you got to Charlie's this morning, what was everyone wearing?"

Lizzy blinked up at her. "What?"

"Like, was Jane in her clothes, or did it look like she borrowed Charlie's?"

"Why does that matter?"

"Because I'm trying to figure out if they slept together or, like, *slept* together." Lydia waggled her eyebrows.

"Why don't you ask her," Mary said bluntly.

"I did, but she's not giving me anything, so I need some clues. Was she wearing his T-shirt? Maybe a robe?"

Huh. Lizzy hadn't thought to look at anyone's clothing when she strolled up from the beach unannounced. In fact, she couldn't even remember what anyone had been wearing.

Well, that wasn't completely true. She remembered what Will Darcy was wearing. Black sweatpants that hung low on his hips, a gray T-shirt that was just on the right side of tight. His blond hair had been a mess, sticking out in every direction as he sipped his coffee, watching her walk toward him on the beach, like he was expecting her.

Lizzy shook her head, jostling the thought away. Maybe that urban runoff from this morning was affecting her brain.

"I think we have bigger things to worry about right now, Lydia," she said, leaning down to fish a submerged bag of walnuts from the floor.

"I don't know. Jane finally getting laid seems like a pretty big thing."

"And so is the industrial-sized fridge that's been without power for twelve hours." Lizzy handed her an empty trash bag. "You two go in there and start throwing stuff out. I need to go upstairs to the fuse box and turn off the main."

Lydia rolled her eyes. "Why would you turn off the power if we already don't have power?"

"Because I don't want to die in a pool of standing water when it finally comes back on."

Lydia huffed but didn't argue.

The bakery was dark when Lizzy emerged from the basement. She had propped open the front door earlier with the hopes of airing out the stale smell and bringing in some sunshine, but the plywood was still nailed up over the windows and clouds still lingered in the sky, so the room was filled with an eerie half-light. It sent shadows across the room, and Lizzy was so busy ignoring them that she almost missed the tall man standing in the doorway.

"Hello."

Lizzy jumped and let out a strangled shout. The man stilled, then took a step forward, his head of dark hair suddenly visible.

"You okay?"

Lord Magnus. Her stomach did an odd flop, but she ignored it, ready to offer a reply. Before she could open her mouth, though, Lydia and Mary appeared behind her.

"What's wrong with . . . oh." Lydia's tone changed the minute she saw Tristan. "Hello there."

The man's smile broadened a bit. "Hi."

"I'm Lydia," she said, somehow making her name sound suggestive.

Tristan walked forward, offering her his hand. "Tristan Cole."

Lydia took it, smiling wide.

Then he extended his hand to Mary. She didn't move, only stared at him from over Lizzy's shoulder. "I know who you are."

He nodded, unfazed.

"Tristan . . . what are you doing here?" Lizzy asked. Why was her voice so high?

"I drove out this morning. Hank wants us to check on Gretna Island. If there's any storm damage, we could use it to help get our permits for HamptonFest through," he replied. "And since I was in the neighborhood, I thought I'd see how you weathered everything."

Mary's lips curled into a sharp smile. "I guess capitalism never sleeps, huh?"

Tristan didn't seem offended. He just chuckled as if she had somehow complimented him. "It's a good thing I don't mind staying up all night."

Lydia's eyes widened, like she had stumbled upon a unicorn. "Wow."

"So, how bad is it?" Tristan continued, his gaze traveling down to Lizzy's rain boots.

"Oh, it's fine." Lizzy pushed some hair away from her face, suddenly much more aware of her sodden overalls and old Stone Roses T-shirt. "Just the basement. And some electrical work. And our fridge."

"Do you need any help? I could pitch in."

Lydia made a strangled sound, something between a laugh and a prayer to heaven.

"No, we've got it under control," Lizzy said, forcing a smile. "Thanks, though."

"Sure," he replied. It was that tone again, like he had read some hidden subtext in the conversation. Then he took a step back toward the door. "Well, when you're done, I was going to head over to Donato Lodge tonight. Apparently they didn't have any damage, so Hank's throwing a 'Survived the Storm' party. Maybe I'll see you there?"

Lizzy opened her mouth to answer, but Lydia beat her to it again.

"Oh, you definitely will," she purred.

"See you tonight, then," he replied with a smile.

Lizzy's cheeks flushed as she watched him saunter through the door and out of view.

"Parasite," Mary murmured.

⟳

Donato Lodge was already bursting when they arrived later that night. With Mary still banned and Kitty at home working on her business plan, it was just Lizzy, Jane, and Lydia who faced the thumping beats of tonight's band. The dance floor was packed, but thankfully the bar wasn't as mobbed, so Lizzy and Jane found seats, while Lydia disappeared into the crowd.

"You're late!" Piper exclaimed from behind the bar, already placing their usual drinks in front of them.

"You're lucky we made it at all," Lizzy moaned.

"The basement at the bakery flooded," Jane explained.

Piper winced. "Is it bad?"

Lizzy pushed a few strands of wet hair from her face. She had taken a long shower when she got home and washed her hair twice, but she felt like she could still use another one. "Well, I just spent the past eight hours covered in flour and rainwater. Possibly raw sewage. So it's not great."

"We saved Mom's leggings, though," Jane said, her voice heavy with forced optimism. "And Dad thinks we should be back up and running in a couple of days."

Lizzy took a sip of her beer to avoid offering her own opinion, which was that they'd be closed longer than that. But those realities could wait until tomorrow. For right now, she had beer and Tater Tots and a very intense guitar solo being performed onstage.

She turned to stare at the band, which seemed to include guitars, drums, bagpipes, and a lead singer dressed in a football jersey and oversized sunglasses.

"What's going on up there exactly?"

Piper pointed to a poster behind her emblazoned with the word *Korndogg.*

Jane looked confused, while Lizzy asked, "Do I want to know?"

"Korn meets Snoop Dogg."

Lizzy laughed, but the sound was lost in the music. She was about to ask her friend how her dad found these acts, but stopped when she suddenly felt someone looming at her side. She turned and found Tristan there, smiling down at her.

"Hello there," he said. His gaze slid down her old Duran Duran T-shirt to her jeans and back up again as a wry grin pulled at one corner of his mouth.

She smiled back. "Hi."

"I was starting to think I missed you."

"I don't think you can miss someone you've only met twice."

"Then I'm glad we made it three times."

She laughed again, not so much at his words but at the fact that her cheeks heated with them, leaving her feeling flushed, off-balance. God, blushing twice in one day? What was going on?

"Tristan! I'm glad my dad finally got you to stop by!" Piper announced, practically leaning over the entire width of the bar to insert herself between them. "Do you two know each other?"

"Her sister threw a paint-filled balloon at me a few weeks ago," Tristan said with a smile.

Lizzy rolled her eyes playfully. "To be fair, I think you were just collateral damage."

"Nothing a long, hot shower couldn't fix," he replied.

Jane instantly melted, a smile on her lips. "Hi, I'm Lizzy's sister Jane."

"Tristan," he said, taking her hand.

"It's nice to meet you."

"My dad won't shut up about you," Piper said, her chin resting in her hand. "I haven't seen him this excited about HamptonFest since he came up with the idea. You've set the bar high."

"Well, I hope I exceed your expectations."

Piper smiled dreamily.

Lizzy wasn't sure she had ever seen Piper swoon over a man before, especially since she'd been in a serious long-distance relationship with her girlfriend, Sasha, for the past three years, but right now it looked like she was pretty close.

Over a basket of fresh Tater Tots, the three of them listened as Tristan talked about his plans for the inaugural HamptonFest next summer, how everyone from Bono to Beyoncé was just a DM away. He had stories of partying with Leo, attending Art Basel with the painter Max Betrug—his contacts were seemingly endless.

He was in the middle of detailing his plan to get the permits required for Gretna Island when something at the front of the bar caught Jane's eye and she lit up. They all turned to see Charlie and Will enter. Charlie's eyes scanned the room, and when he found Jane's, he lit up, too. Will noticed their group at the same time, his gaze lingering on Lizzy before landing on Tristan. Something fiery and raw flashed across his expression, but then it was gone, replaced by his usual frown as he leaned over to whisper something to Charlie.

Tristan turned, swallowing down the rest of his beer. His expression was altered, too, but Lizzy had a hard time reading it. Still, she knew enough that whatever passed between him and Will wasn't good.

"Want to go grab some fresh air?" she asked him.

A bit of relief softened his features, and he nodded. "I'd like that."

Lizzy grabbed her beer and another one for Tristan, then dragged him away from the bar before the two other men arrived. They avoided the dance floor, weaving their way around the crowd until they reached the Irish Goodbye Door.

116 | AUDREY BELLEZZA & EMILY HARDING

The air outside was humid and thick, so the music seemed to still vibrate around them even after the door closed. It helped fill the silence as she took a sip of her beer and leaned back against the building's shingle siding.

Tristan settled across from her by the railing of the small porch.

"So," he said.

She smiled. "So."

"Are those two guys friends of yours?"

"Which one, specifically."

"Will Darcy."

"No," she said, shaking her head once. "Not a friend."

He nodded and took a sip of his drink.

It suddenly felt like a game, extracting information from each other without making it too obvious.

"Is he a friend of yours?" she asked.

A moment, then he sighed. "He used to be."

"Used to be?"

"We were friends in high school."

Lizzy didn't even try to mask her shock. "Really?"

"All four years."

"Wow."

"Is that surprising?"

"No. I just assumed he emerged from a lab, fully formed and void of all human emotion."

Tristan chuckled. It was a deep sound, and Lizzy enjoyed how it cleared away some of the clouds that had settled over him. "No. He grew up in the city. Upper West Side. You know, old money."

"Old money?"

Tristan's easy smile faltered, and his gaze dropped to his feet. "Yeah. *Very* old."

"What happened?"

He looked up. "What do you mean?"

"Well, you're clearly not friends anymore," she said, nodding to the door that led back into the bar.

"Right," Tristan said, his wry grin returning. "Sorry to disappoint you, but it's not very original. He has money and I don't."

Lizzy blinked. "Are you serious?"

He took a sip of his drink before shrugging.

Lizzy opened her mouth again, ready to argue the opposite, but she couldn't. She knew all too well how social standing worked for people in the upper echelons of society, how the numbers in your bank account mattered more than your character. It was a lesson imbibed from birth out here.

His gaze shifted to the darkness beyond the porch, as if taking a moment to remember. "My dad was head of maintenance at this private school in the city. Really prestigious. In a normal world I could never afford to go, but thanks to my dad's job, I attended for free. It was great, don't get me wrong, but it put a target on my back, too. Will didn't seem to care, though. We became friends. It was the first time I didn't feel like I was . . . less. It was the best four years of my life." Tristan paused. "Then we graduated, and Will went to Columbia."

Lizzy blinked. She hadn't known Will went to Columbia. The information left an odd weight in her belly, another connection to a man she didn't want any connection with at all.

"What did you do?" she asked.

"I got into a bunch of schools but tuition was just too high, and I couldn't make it work. If I saved for a few years, really buckled down, maybe I could do it, but that required a job that paid well. I knew Will's family ran an investment firm in the city, so I reached out. He agreed to help but warned me that it would probably be tough. His dad came through, though. Took me under his wing.

Suddenly I had a good job, was making good money at entry level, even without a degree. I learned a lot."

"And then?"

Tristan let out a long breath. "Will's parents died. Horrible car accident. It was like my world got turned upside down. Will obviously took over for the estate, and one of the first orders of business was to get me fired."

Lizzy was struck dumb for a moment. "No."

Tristan nodded once, his gaze locked with his pint glass as he tipped it back and forth.

"But . . . why?"

Another shrug. "He never reached out to explain. To be honest, I wasn't surprised. His dad had always wanted him to join his company, but Will took a different track. So the fact that I was on the path his father had always wanted him to follow . . ."

The realization hit Lizzy hard. "He was jealous."

"I don't know. Maybe."

Lizzy was stunned. Will Darcy wasn't exactly her favorite person, but sabotaging someone's career? A person he had called a friend? They had to construct an all-new level of asshole for that.

"I'm sorry," Tristan said, shaking his head.

"What do you have to be sorry for? He should be the one apologizing."

"Yeah, but I don't want to get in the middle of whatever's going on between you two."

Lizzy's nose scrunched up. "There's nothing going on between me and Will Darcy."

Tristan smiled like he wasn't convinced. "Are you sure? I saw the way he looked at you in there."

"You mean the barely concealed loathing? I'm pretty sure he gives that look to everyone."

He chuckled as he pushed off the porch railing to start toward her. "Interesting."

"Not really," she said with a shrug. "It's like you said. He has money and I don't."

Tristan stopped in front of her, studying her face before raising his beer to clink against hers. "Well, cheers to that."

She bit back a smile. "Cheers."

Lizzy had no idea how much time passed. She had been too busy listening to Tristan talk about his plans, where he had hoped to be and how he had to work twice as hard for it now. She was so entranced that she almost missed the sound of cheering erupt from inside, the telltale sign that the band had finished their set.

Her heart dropped. "What time is it?"

Tristan pulled out his phone. "Almost midnight."

"Crap," she murmured. "I should head home."

"Everything okay?"

"Yeah, I just have to be at work early. The repair guy's coming by to fix the fridge, then I have a whole pantry's worth of supplies to replace . . ." She let out a deep sigh and pushed her hair from her face.

"Do you want a ride?"

She shook her head. "No, it's all right; I live close by. I'm used to walking."

He nodded. "Okay."

Neither of them moved. In the stillness, Lizzy was suddenly aware of just how close they were standing, the intensity of his stare.

Then, slowly, Tristan leaned forward, just enough for his mouth to hover over hers. Her brain was still registering the move when his hand came up to cradle her jaw, tilting her head just so, and forcing her eyes to meet his.

Oh, she had missed this. Tristan hadn't even kissed her yet, but the warmth and the comfort of another body so close to hers was enough to send a steady hum through her bloodstream. Suddenly she couldn't remember why she hadn't hooked up with anyone in months. A travesty that needed to be remedied at the earliest convenience.

But then the Irish Goodbye Door opened, and the boisterous sounds of the bar cut through the haze around them.

That's when Will Darcy emerged.

He didn't see Lizzy and Tristan immediately, just walked out and stopped on the porch. He took a deep breath, letting his head fall back so the lights in the parking lot highlighted his profile. The arch of his nose, the severe line of his brow.

Tristan cleared his throat.

Will's attention snapped to them. His body was like stone as he took in the scene: Lizzy pressed up against the side of the building, Tristan's body caging her in. There was no doubt what was happening. Still, Will did a slow audit, as if trying to decipher the details, until his gaze finally came up to meet Lizzy's. His blue eyes were partially hidden under the shadow of his brow, but it didn't matter. She could see them locked on her, clear and hard.

"Hello, Will," Tristan said. "Can we help you with something?"

Will looked over to Tristan. Whatever had been burning behind his expression went out. A moment passed, then he turned, walking down the steps and into the parking lot.

Lizzy's heart was racing, and she didn't know why. Who cared if Will Darcy caught her with a guy? If anything, she should have enjoyed the look on his face. Still, her skin had cooled as she let out a shaky breath.

"I should get going."

Tristan's attention returned to her, seemingly unfazed. "Are you sure?"

She nodded.

"All right," Tristan murmured, but he didn't move. "What are you doing next weekend?"

"Working," she said, then remembered what day it would be. "Oh, and going to this big Fourth of July party on the beach here. I would invite you, but it's being hosted by one of Will's friends, and that probably means he'll be there, so . . ."

She let the words hang, knowing she didn't have to explain further.

"Right," he said, smiling to himself. "What are you doing after?"

"After the party?" She let out a dry laugh. "Probably going to bed. Why?"

"I have a thing in the city that day, but I'm driving back out here after. We should get together when I get in. Grab a drink or something."

Oh. *Oh.* Lizzy knew exactly what "or something" meant, and she was not the least bit opposed to it.

"Sure," she said with a shrug, as if her pulse wasn't currently tripping through her veins.

"Cool. I'll text you when I'm heading out." He reached back and pulled his phone from his pocket. "What's your number?"

She rattled it off and he typed away on his screen. A moment later, her phone pinged in her back pocket.

"And now you have mine," he said.

She bit back a smile. "So I do."

He sighed, letting his head fall forward like he had to take a moment to collect himself. "You really don't want to come back inside? I can give you a ride later. To your place, or you can come hang out at mine. I have a hotel room tonight in Bridgehampton."

"Oh." Her skin felt hot again, and a forgotten part of her wanted to say yes, wanted to jump into the passenger seat of his car and just go. But then another part of her roared to life, one that tugged on her attention. And she hated how it looked a lot like Will Darcy.

"Not sure that will make an early start tomorrow any easier," she said with a smile.

"No. But I promise it will be more fun."

She laughed softly but left the suggestion untouched. "I'll see you next weekend."

"I'm looking forward to it."

He shot her one last grin, then turned toward the door and disappeared back inside.

CHAPTER 12

"Have you heard from him since last weekend?" Jane asked, catching Lizzy's eye in the bathroom mirror. The double vanity upstairs at the Bennet house was somehow accommodating all five sisters as they got ready for Charlie's Fourth of July party. While Lizzy and Jane did their best to touch up their makeup on one side, Lydia and Kitty were fighting over counter space on the other. In the center, Mary brushed her teeth.

Lizzy tried to appear nonchalant, ignoring the flush in her cheeks as she finished applying her eyeliner. "Not yet. But he said he'd text today when he was leaving the city."

"Who?" Kitty asked, focused on her reflection as she redid her center part.

"Tristan Cole. The guy Lizzy climbed at Donato's last week," Lydia said, putting the finishing touches on her cheek contour.

Mary spat a wad of toothpaste into the pink ceramic sink. "The capitalist."

"I didn't *climb* him," Lizzy said, shooting Lydia a sharp glare. "We didn't even kiss."

"Right," Lydia replied sarcastically. "You went outside to discuss the environmental impact of Hank's wannabe Coachella."

Mary paused. "You did?"

Lizzy shook her head. "No."

Mary frowned and left the bathroom.

"So then, what's the plan?" Jane asked Lizzy, forcing the conversation back on track.

"Tristan suggested we meet up after the party."

Jane raised her eyebrow. "That's kind of late for a date, don't you think?"

Lizzy gave her sister a placating smile. "That's why it's not a date."

"Whatever," Lydia said. "I don't care what's going on with you two, as long as it doesn't stop me from going to that party of his."

Lizzy paused. "What party?"

A smug grin curled up Lydia's lips. "Oh, he didn't tell you? Apparently, he has an amazing place in the city and throws huge parties with all these celebrities and professional athletes. People he's worked with, I guess. He promised to invite all of us."

"When did he promise that?"

"At the Lodge," Lydia said, shrugging. "You shouldn't have left so early."

Lizzy scowled at her.

"HURRY UP, LADIES!" Mrs. Bennet yelled from downstairs, hitting a decibel that seemed to resonate through the walls. "OR I'M LEAVING WITHOUT YOU!"

Kitty's brow furrowed as she looked at Lizzy. "Aren't you driving?"

Lizzy nodded, then focused on her reflection. When the official invitation arrived for the party, it described the dress code as "resort casual," but after a week of research, she still had no idea what that meant. Her blue slip dress paired with her combat boots were probably nowhere near the ballpark but it was the nicest thing in her closet, and left her freckled shoulders exposed. Her hair was loose, falling around them in orange and crimson waves, and her dark eyes were accentuated by a slight cat eye. Whatever the dress code, Lizzy had to admit, she looked good. Over the past year, she'd barely had time to put on mascara, let alone wear anything other than her same small collection of band T-shirts and overalls. She hadn't realized how much she had needed this refined view, so she took a moment to appreciate it, to finally—

"LET'S GO!"

Lizzy sighed. Never mind.

"You heard the woman," she said, and began to shoo her sisters out of the bathroom.

"I'm not done with my lipstick!" Lydia moaned.

One by one they abandoned their tasks, disappearing out the door and down the stairs. Just as Lizzy was about to follow, Jane grabbed her hand, holding her back for a moment.

"Are you sure I look okay?" she said, her voice low again. "Is this dress too short? Maybe I should go try on—"

"Jane." Lizzy cut her off with a smile. Her sister looked even more gorgeous than usual. Despite the fact that she barely had any makeup on, her red lip tint made her large eyes pop, and the square neckline of her cream-colored linen dress highlighted her long neck. If Charlie wasn't already head-over-heels in love with her, he would be after tonight. "You looked amazing in all fifty outfits you tried on. You picked this one because you love it, right? That's what matters."

Her sister nodded, even though there was still a line of worry between her perfect eyebrows.

Before they could discuss further, Mrs. Bennet's voice rattled the house again.

"THAT'S IT! I'M LEAVING!" Then, a moment later: "WHERE ARE THE CAR KEYS?"

~

Lizzy didn't know what she expected from Charlie's Fourth of July party, but it was definitely not this.

The driveway down to Marv's Lament was lined with hundreds of small lanterns, each with its own candle inside, while every tree had at least a dozen white paper globes hanging from its branches. The house itself was illuminated by uplights hidden in the hydrangea bushes along the front, making the steel and glass look even more severe against the dark sky.

It was a slow approach thanks to the line of cars ahead of them, and by the time Lizzy pulled their parents' old minivan up to the front door, Mrs. Bennet was swooning.

"Oh, it's gorgeous!" she exclaimed from the passenger seat. "Just stunning!"

Lizzy was tempted to remind her mother that this was the same house she called "an abomination" just a couple of years ago, but she bit her tongue.

A valet opened the driver's-side door, then the back to let Jane, Lydia, and Kitty pile out. Lizzy almost laughed as she handed over her keys, along with her *I Got Crabs at Mike's!* key chain, to the valet. To his credit, he didn't even crack a smile as he climbed into the driver's seat just as a Bentley Continental pulled up behind them.

The house's front doors were propped open, the inside ceiling decorated with the same paper lanterns as were on the trees outside. Beyond them, the sliding glass doors along the far wall were open to the pool, where it looked like the entire population of East Hampton had congregated.

"Just breathtaking!" Mrs. Bennet's voice rang through the foyer. She was wearing her latest creation, the Disco Lux Leggings, which meant both of her rhinestone-covered legs reflected spots of light across the floor as she navigated all of them out to the verandah.

Outside, the party was already in full swing. There was a burst of color at every turn, from the glowing dance floor stretching over the pool to the cascade of fairy lights hanging from the roof of the house. Lizzy was sure she was missing a thousand details, but with so many people suddenly so close, she gave up trying to notice.

"I'm going to go find Donna," Mrs. Bennet said, barely looking at her daughters as she surveyed the crowd. "You girls mingle. And remember: I have the valet ticket, so nobody even *think* about leaving early."

Then she disappeared toward the bar, leaving them on the threshold to gape at the scene in front of them.

The Pierce Party, as it had begun to be called by locals, had been the most exclusive invite in town a few weeks ago. But after Charlie invited the Bennets, Mrs. Bennet began inviting anyone she ran into. But they weren't the only guests. Amid the locals, there were tall, elegant women in impossibly white linen dresses, and gorgeous men in various shades of khakis paired with navy blazers. A *Town & Country* photoshoot dropped in the middle of this year's county fair.

And then there was Will Darcy, standing near the edge of the crowd.

The last time Lizzy had seen him on this verandah, he had been in a T-shirt and sweatpants, but now he wore a linen button-down with the sleeves rolled up, revealing his tanned arms, and a pair of jeans that hung low on his hips.

So that's resort casual, she thought.

He looked good, and she hated that he looked good. In fact, she hated that she had any reaction to him at all. He silently judged everyone around him, he actively sabotaged his friend's career with seemingly no remorse . . . he was an asshole.

She scowled, even as she stole another glance at him. His blue eyes were locked on hers now, and his gaze was so intense that her heart stuttered, sending her pulse tripping through her veins. She hated that, too.

Was he mad at her? Judging her for what he'd seen outside the Lodge the other night? His expression gave nothing away, but she also couldn't attribute anger to it. There was something else there, something just under the surface that felt like a challenge.

She ignored it as she reached into her small bag and pulled out her phone. Holding it close so her sisters wouldn't see, she opened Tristan's contact information and typed out a message.

LIZZY

> Your former best friend is giving me a death stare and I need saving

> See you soon xo

She smiled and pressed send just as her sisters pulled her attention back to their small group.

"How do I look?" Kitty asked.

"Like you're about to audit somebody," Lydia said, eyeing her sister's pencil skirt and cardigan.

Kitty blanched. "It's resort casual!"

"It's lovely," Jane assured her. "You look beautiful."

"Professional?" Kitty asked.

"Very professional."

Lizzy paused. "Why do you want to look professional?"

"Annabelle Pierce is over there, and I'm going to pick her brain about a business idea I've been working on."

She disappeared into the crowd before Lizzy could stop her.

"This. Is. Amazing," Lydia said, pulling her phone out of her bag, ready to record.

"Put away your phone, Lydia," Lizzy said.

"Why? You just had yours out."

"Yes, but the invite said no photos," she explained.

Lydia scoffed. "I'm not taking photos. This is *video*."

"Just be discreet," Jane chimed in. "Annabelle doesn't want anything to do with the party showing up online. I guess if Vivienne's ex sees her spending any money, his lawyer could start making a fuss about alimony."

Lizzy shot her sister a wry grin. "I didn't realize you were spending every spare moment with the whole Pierce family now."

Jane looked away, but Lizzy could still see her sister blush. "We don't spend *that* much time together."

"Whatever helps you sleep at night," Lizzy said, patting Jane's hand. "Or, you know, doesn't."

Jane's rouged cheeks turned bright red as a laugh burst out of her.

"Lizzy!" Piper's voice rang out over the music. A moment later, their friend emerged from the dance floor, unsteady in her heels as she threw an arm around Lizzy's shoulder. She had an unnaturally blue drink in her hand, topped with a pink paper umbrella.

"Hey!" Lizzy replied, working to maintain her balance as her friend leaned against her. "What are you drinking?"

"I have no idea, but it's delicious. And strong." Piper took a deep sip from the small straw. "Very strong."

Lizzy laughed.

The DJ transitioned to "The Tide Is High" by Blondie, and there was a collective cheer across the verandah. One voice rose above the rest, though, a shrill cry that made Lizzy cringe.

"Oh my God!" Mrs. Bennet screamed from somewhere in the crowd. "I *love* this song! Donna! Remember this song?"

Lizzy turned to Lydia. "Can you go make sure she doesn't fall off the dance floor and into the pool?"

"Nope." Lydia waltzed away. "I'm working. I need some content for the weekend, and this place is perfect!"

Lizzy let her head fall back in frustration. Tonight was shaping up to be exhausting.

"I'll go check on your mom," Piper said.

"Are you sure?" Jane asked.

Piper nodded, the small straw still in her mouth. "Gives me a good excuse to steal that drink out of my mom's hand. She has absolutely zero tolerance."

With that, Piper sucked up the last dregs of her drink, handed the empty glass to a passing waiter, then started forward to the dance floor.

"And then there were two," Lizzy said with a sigh, leaning into Jane's side.

Her sister rested her cheek against Lizzy's red hair. "Has Tristan texted?"

"Not yet." Lizzy didn't point out that she had already texted him and he hadn't replied yet.

"He will," Jane said with an encouraging smile. "It might not have been an official date, but he wouldn't just stand you up. Right?"

Lizzy nodded, even though she wasn't entirely sure. Yes, Tristan had been the one to suggest getting together, but he hadn't exactly committed to coming. Even now, she didn't feel hurt, only a growing hole inside where disappointment should have been. The same hole that seemed to materialize when she'd deferred her acceptance to Columbia.

She shook the thought loose and turned back to her sister. Tonight wasn't about her. At least, not anymore.

"What about Charlie?"

Jane sighed. Lizzy knew her sister wasn't done prodding about Tristan, but she also knew that Charlie was probably the only topic that could delay that conversation until later.

"I haven't seen him yet."

"Well, he's got to be here somewhere. It's his house." Lizzy craned her neck up to look over the crowd.

Her gaze found Charlie on the other side of the pool's illuminated dance floor. He had caught sight of them, too, though it took less than a second for Lizzy to realize that it wasn't so much the two of them that held his attention, but Jane. His omnipresent smile somehow grew even wider, while his expression . . . Something in Lizzy's heart ached at the way his eyes softened, how his chest rose slowly and fell with a deep breath, like there was relief mixed in with his happiness. As if, despite the music and drinks and impending fireworks, this moment was what tonight had always been about.

She wondered if anyone would ever look at her like that.

Before she could squash the thought, Charlie was weaving through the crowd toward them.

"You made it," he said, stopping within a few inches of Jane. The words were said in one long exhale of breath.

"You invited me," her sister replied.

"I did, didn't I?" It looked like he was trying to tamp down his grin, but it was a losing battle.

Lizzy bit back her own smile and melted into the crowd before Charlie had time to realize that he had completely ignored her. She didn't want to be a third wheel. Not that they would have noticed anyway—they were caught in each other's orbit, and Lizzy almost wondered if the whole house burned down right now, whether either of them would even notice.

Once she found her way to the other side of the dance floor, Lizzy pulled her phone from her bag again. No new text messages. She told herself to lock her screen and just have faith that Tristan would text. Unfortunately, she had never been good at waiting, which was why she typed out another quick message.

LIZZY

Hey! Party in full swing. Have you left the city yet?

She pressed send before she could think better of it.

The DJ transitioned seamlessly from song to song as Lizzy wandered through the party, chatting with familiar faces and bobbing her head to the beat. A waiter walked by with a tray of various cocktails, and she grabbed one with a yellow umbrella, walking to a quieter corner of the party and taking a small sip. It was bitingly sweet and she cringed, just as a deep voice spoke from behind her.

"Hello, Elizabeth."

She turned to glance over her shoulder. Will Darcy stood near the edge of the yard, half-hidden in the shadows. Had he just been skulking around the perimeter all night?

"Hello," she replied.

The party was a cacophony of sound, but somehow she could

still feel the weight of the silence between them. She wanted to walk away—they had exchanged pleasantries, so there was nothing keeping her here. Still, she didn't move. Neither did he.

"Hiding again?" she finally asked.

"Debating it." A moment passed before he asked, "What about you?"

"What about me?"

"Are you leaving again?"

"I'm an East Hampton native, remember?" she replied with a plastic smile. "I laugh in the face of linen button-downs and disdain."

He almost looked amused. His mouth was still a grim line across his face, but something in his eyes seemed to dance. Then he nodded to her glass. "What about rum and cocktail umbrellas?"

She rolled her eyes. "Well, this isn't exactly a Hamptons staple."

"None of this is," he murmured. "It's the same party, just in a different place."

As much as Lizzy hated to admit it, she knew exactly what he meant. The party was beautiful and fun, but it was a bit like this house: impressive but impersonal, devoid of everything that made the Hamptons so special. They could have been anywhere in the world having the same drinks, listening to the same music. And tomorrow it would all go away again, leaving everyone with the same memories.

"If you hate it so much, why do you keep coming out here?" she asked.

The hard edge of his expression faltered. "What do you mean?"

"You come out here all the time, but you never seem to be enjoying yourself."

He stared at her for a moment. "How do you know I'm not enjoying myself?"

The words hit low in her belly. Maybe it was because his voice was so deep, but she had heard deep voices before. No, his had an added layer, one that seemed to add physical weight to each syllable, like they were deliberately shaped on his tongue before being uttered.

Then Lydia's shrill laugh cut through the air, snapping Lizzy's attention back to the dance floor. Her sister was flanked by two men in the middle of the crowd. She had her phone held above her head, angling it down as she smiled up at it. "Hey, lovelies! Lydia here. Come with me as I celebrate the Fourth in the Hamptons!"

Lizzy cringed. "Oh my God."

"What?" Will asked.

She turned to find him still watching her, his brow knitted together.

She offered a half-hearted smile. "Haven't you ever been embarrassed by your family before?"

He glanced over to the dance floor, like he was noticing Lydia for the first time, and frowned. Then he brought his attention back to Lizzy. "No."

Her smile fell as the heat of embarrassment rose in her cheeks. "Right."

She didn't bother excusing herself, just started forward, trying to escape the feel of his gaze on her back as she maneuvered through the throngs of partygoers toward her sister.

"Lydia!" she yelled.

Lydia ignored her, and Lizzy could only watch helplessly as she laughed and continued talking to the camera.

Oh God. The night was quickly getting out of control.

Knowing her sister was a lost cause, Lizzy gave up and headed toward the bar. Just as the bartender delivered her another drink, this one with a giant piece of pineapple on the rim, her phone pinged in her bag.

Tristan.

Her heart tripped as she reached for it, eager to see the glowing screen.

JANE

Hey! Charlie and I are going down to the beach to watch the fireworks. Want to come?

Disappointment landed heavy in her chest.

LIZZY

That's okay

But have fun!

She pressed send, then scrolled back to her texts to Tristan. There was still no reply, but she did notice something written beneath the messages: Read 8:21 p.m.

He had seen her texts over an hour ago and still hadn't written her back.

Lizzy looked up to survey the crowd. Mrs. Bennet and Donna were stationed next to the DJ booth, swinging their hips to the beat. The rhinestones on her mother's leggings were almost blinding in the iridescent lights of the floor below her, and Lizzy could see other dancers pointing and snickering. Just beyond her, Kitty was standing beside Annabelle, talking animatedly while Annabelle listened, an unreadable expression on her face. Then Lydia's laughter erupted from the dance floor again, and Lizzy turned just as her sister was hoisted into the air by the two men, grinning widely at her phone as they did so.

"THIS IS THE BEST NIGHT OF MY LIFE!" she cackled.

For a moment, Lizzy considered marching up to her again and telling her to control herself. But she was too tired to do anything but turn around and head straight through the house to the front door.

The driveway was empty when Lizzy walked out, not that she was surprised. All the guests had arrived, and the fireworks would be going off soon. She could slip away unnoticed—go home, crawl into bed, and forget this night ever happened.

"Where are you going?"

Will's voice came from behind her, deep and gravelly. She hated how she recognized it, how it hit some hidden part in her chest that she wasn't even aware of before him.

For a long moment, she didn't move. Maybe if she stalled long enough, he would go away. Or, better yet, maybe she'd just imagined his voice so when she turned around she would find only an empty doorway.

But when she did look over her shoulder, there he was. His gaze was expectant, like the statement required a complicated answer.

Unfortunately for him, she didn't have one. "Home."

"The valet can get your car."

The valet. It rolled off his tongue so easily, like he discussed valets as often as Lizzy did muffins.

She shook her head. Why was she even here? This was a different world, and she didn't belong in it.

"Don't worry about it. My sisters will grab it later. I can walk," she said.

"You're not walking home."

"Really? Because I'm pretty sure I am."

She didn't wait for a reply, just turned and started forward. Yes, it was rude, but no more than he usually was. Besides, she knew he would inevitably turn around and disappear inside whether she was polite or not, leaving the appropriate level of disapproval in his wake.

Except she didn't hear any movement from behind her. Then his voice rumbled to life again.

"I'll give you a ride."

She stopped. She must be imagining things, because she could have sworn Will Darcy just offered to drive her home. But when she turned, she found him still glaring at her from a few feet away.

"Why?" she asked.

The grimace deepened into a frown. "Why what?"

"Why are you offering me a ride?"

"Why aren't you taking it?"

"Because I walk home all the time. It's no big deal."

"It's after dark in a town that barely has working streetlights."

She crossed her arms over her chest. "Did Charlie force you to come out here and do this?"

His expression changed again. It was slight—to anyone else it would just look like he was still frowning at her—but she could see a softening of the edges into something like confusion. Or maybe it was offense.

"You think Charlie made me come out here?"

"Why else would you?"

A muscle ticked in his jaw as he stared at her. It almost looked like he had something to say but was forcing himself to hold it back. Like the words tasted sour on his tongue.

She sighed. "Listen, I appreciate the offer, but I don't want a ride. I want to go home." She was too tired for this, and her exhaustion made her voice waver.

Another shift in his expression. She hated how she was already an expert in his looks, on how the subtle movements of his brow and jaw and mouth could convey a whole series of emotions. Right now it was the line between his eyebrows. It had deepened, like he was concerned. There was a hint of anger there, too, ready to be called up if needed.

"What happened?" His voice somehow sounded even gruffer than before.

She blinked. "Nothing happened. I'm fine."

He didn't move. It was like he could see right through her and already knew the truth. Her heart stuttered as the thought suddenly hit her: if she had unwittingly become an expert on his expressions, maybe he had become one on hers. He could tell when she was lying, when she was exhausted and so overwhelmed with disappointment and regret that she wanted to scream.

"Did Tristan do something?" he finally asked. Some sharp emotion tinged his deep voice.

She narrowed her eyes at him. "First of all, that's none of your business. Second, even if he had, the last person I would want help from right now is you."

Something flared in his eyes. "And why's that?"

"Because I've heard about how you help people, and I'm not sure I'm that masochistic."

That one hurt. She wished she hadn't said it, but there was no other way to interpret the sting in his eyes.

She should apologize. Or at least tell him what she thought of how he had treated Tristan. Give her words some context. But just as quickly as the hurt had come, it was gone, shuttered behind a cold glare and hard frown.

So instead she said, "Good night, Will."

She turned on her heel and started walking again, the gravel crunching under her combat boots as she made her way down the long driveway. Behind her, she heard Will curse, but his footsteps retreated in the opposite direction. Probably back inside, she thought. Sure enough, within a few seconds they faded altogether. It should have been a relief—she *wanted* to feel relief—but instead an odd disappointment swelled inside her, threatening to swallow her up, and she knew she had to keep moving to stop herself from collapsing.

Lizzy had just reached the end of the drive when headlights flared behind her. A car was approaching, its tires rolling along the gravel slowly to maintain its distance. She moved further to the side of the drive, but the car didn't pass. And when she reached the street and turned right, it did the same.

No. There's no way . . .

She glanced over her shoulder. Sure enough, there was Will Darcy, behind the wheel of Charlie's BMW, following about ten feet behind.

Whatever regret she felt about what she'd said evaporated. What part of "I'm fine" did he not understand? Did he think that if he followed long enough, she'd finally concede and let him drive her home?

Absolutely fucking not.

Chin raised, she continued forward, her long shadow preceding her as she marched down Lily Pond Lane with a BMW sedan in tow. He could follow her home. He could follow her to the end of the earth. But she was never getting in that car.

BOOM.

An explosion of light erupted in the sky above. Yellows and reds sparkled, then fizzled out, replaced a moment later by another *BOOM* and a shower of electric blues and greens.

The fireworks illuminated the road, saturating the trees and grass in a rainbow of color. It was beautiful, something that Lizzy would have normally stopped to watch. If it was anyone else in the car behind her, she would have even made a joke about the ridiculousness of the situation, shared a laugh before enjoying the view. But it wasn't just anyone.

It was Will Darcy.

Technicolor explosion after Technicolor explosion filled the sky as Lizzy walked down Lily Pond Lane, then up Ocean Avenue all the way into town. Even in her boots, her feet hurt by the time her house came into sight. But her steps didn't falter as she finally turned down the driveway, past her father's boat, and up the steps to the porch.

Will turned down the driveway, too, so the headlights lit up the front door. Lizzy would never admit that it made it much easier to find the spare key under the mat. And she would never tell a soul that she looked back at the car before unlocking the dead bolt.

Or that, despite all the anger and frustration still smoldering in her chest, her heart tripped when she found his gaze locked on her until she disappeared inside.

"Stubborn asshole," she murmured, then slammed the door behind her.

CHAPTER 13

"Stubborn as shit," Will cursed as he sped down the dark street, wondering how the hell anyone could find their way home on these back roads during the day, let alone someone on their own in the middle of the night.

It would have taken them two minutes to drive the distance. Maybe less. But Elizabeth Bennet insisted on walking for forty-five fucking minutes instead.

Why was he the only one watching out for this woman? Where was her family? It was maddening. He had never known anyone in his entire life who seemed so cavalier about their own personal safety. Didn't she realize the reason so many true crime podcasts existed was because those crimes actually happened?

He cursed under his breath again.

The car windows were down, and he was hit with the smell of cool salt air mixed with the lingering scent of smoke from tonight's fireworks. He hated feeling out of control. He spent most of his adult life working to avoid it. Problems were always carefully managed, potential issues swiftly mitigated. All to avoid this, a wild panic that clawed deep in his chest, the fear that if he lost that grasp, someone would get hurt.

This was the danger in paying Elizabeth Bennet too much attention, he thought, gripping the steering wheel harder. She wasn't his problem to fix, especially now that she and Tristan Cole were . . . friends? Together? He shook his head. It didn't matter. None of it did.

Cars still lined Lily Pond Lane when he returned, and the gate to the driveway was wide open. He hardly knew anyone at the party and wondered again how Charlie and his sisters had allowed it to get so out of control.

He stalked through the front door, past the few guests lounging on the couches. At the top of the stairs, Will threw open his bedroom door and slammed it shut, finally letting out a long breath.

After a minute his pulse slowed, and he made his way to the balcony doors. His room was on the quieter side of the house, so when he walked outside, all he could hear was the dull thump of the bass mingling with the waves crashing in the distance. He took another deep breath, willing his body to finally relax. Then he paused. There was someone out there with him.

He turned, and as his eyes adjusted to the darkness, he realized it was Charlie, slumped against the wall with an unopened bottle of tequila in his hand.

"What are you doing?" Will asked.

"Debating if I should pick up an old habit," Charlie mumbled.

Charlie had never been a heavy drinker—he could barely get through two beers without passing out. The only time Will had seen him touch tequila was in college after he broke up with his high school girlfriend. After two shots, Charlie spent the rest of the night with his head over the toilet.

"Where's Jane?" Will asked.

"Downstairs."

"So why are you up here?"

"I needed some space."

Will leaned against the railing, waiting for him to continue. After a long moment, Charlie finally did. "I told her I loved her."

Will tried not to react, steeling his expression so as not to give away the fact that he had predicted this course of events the second they'd met Jane Bennet. The only real question now was how bad the inevitable fallout would be.

"And?"

"She left," Charlie said quietly, staring up at the dark sky.

Will blinked. "What?"

"We were sitting on the beach, talking. I told her I wanted to take her away for a weekend, someplace romantic. In my head, that was where I was going to tell her I loved her. Make it special, you know? Then the fireworks started and it was perfect. So I said it, right then. I said I love you and she just . . . stared at me. Then she stood up, said she had to go to the bathroom, and left."

A bit of tension released from Will's muscles. This was new. He had expected that Charlie's proclamations of love would be returned, followed by the usual requests for support, ones that would quickly evolve from emotional to financial. But this . . . this was a surprise. Almost a relief.

"I know what you're thinking, Will," Charlie continued. "But I promise you, I have never felt like this about anyone. Not even close."

"All right. Then what do you need?"

"I don't know," Charlie replied. Somewhere on the other side of the yard, the DJ switched tracks and the bassline became deeper, more frenetic. Charlie groaned, his head falling forward. "I need to think, and I can't do it here."

Will nodded. "I'll get rid of the DJ. Shut down the party."

"No, I mean *here*. East Hampton. If she doesn't feel the same way, I can't . . ." Charlie looked up at him. "What should I do?"

Will knew what his friend was really asking: *Help me out of this mess.*

Like most people in his life, Charlie was all too aware of Will's unique ability to compartmentalize almost every situation and see things clearly and objectively. Remaining in control at all times was a trait that defined him; an innate skill that had been honed after his parents' death. It was why the people he loved relied on him to fix problems that anyone else would find too overwhelming. He had done it for Charlie before, and he was ready and willing to do it again.

"You said it yourself. You need space," Will stated. "We'll head back to the city tomorrow."

Charlie exhaled, the tension in his brows subsiding. "I just need a couple of weeks."

Will nodded, even as his mind rebuffed the idea. Charlie had fallen hard for Jane Bennet. It would take him a lot longer than a couple of weeks to get over it.

"Thanks, Will," Charlie continued.

Will didn't reply, just gave him a heavy pat on the shoulder.

He wouldn't admit it to Charlie, but they both needed to get out of East Hampton. All the distractions were pulling at them like the ocean's riptide. If Will wanted to remain in control, they needed space. Getting back to the city was the first step. Now he just had to find a reason to keep them there.

Will woke up early the next morning thankful the house was finally quiet. In the hours that followed his conversation with Charlie, his mind had been on overdrive. By the time he woke up, he had formulated a plan. Will got out of bed and grabbed his phone, scrolling down until he found the contact he needed. After a few rings, he heard a familiar voice on the other end.

"It's six a.m.," George Knightley said in greeting.

"It's Will."

"Yeah, you don't have to say that each time you call. Your name pops up. There's even a lame picture." There was the sound of shuffling, then George sighed. "You know, some people sleep in the day after a big holiday."

"You're up, though."

"Now I am. Everything okay?"

"Fine. How's the city?"

George laughed. "Too hot. But you and I both know you're not calling for a weather report."

Will released a deep breath. "I think we're falling behind on the Wentworth deal. If we want this next stage to go through before Q4, we need to work out the logistics."

"Are you worried about something?"

"No."

"Why don't I believe you?"

Will frowned. "There are a lot of moving parts on this one. And considering we hammered out the deal that put Freddie on the board at Blaxton Agriculture in the first place, it's in our best interest to make the first acquisition he recommends foolproof."

George sighed. "All right. I'll talk to Freddie about flying out from LA. Let's plan for an in-person meeting midweek."

"Great. Call me when you have something in the books."

Will hung up and released a relieved sigh. Part one of the "get over Jane Bennet" plan was complete.

CHAPTER 14

Lizzy was on the roof outside her bedroom window, halfway through her new book, *The Sword of Sin and Sorrow*, when she heard the rest of her family get home from Charlie's. She tried to ignore the drunken giggles and yelling coming from downstairs, but after restarting the same paragraph four times, she realized it was hopeless.

She dog-eared the page and rested the book on her stomach, listening to the muffled conversations and arguments happening beyond her bedroom. Closing the window might offer her a reprieve, but that would mean getting up and disturbing the rare peace she found out here. Besides, she knew she'd have a visitor soon who would do it for her anyway.

Sure enough, she heard the familiar knock a few moments later. Lizzy copied it against the windowsill, and then Jane appeared in her doorway.

"I didn't know if you'd still be awake," she said, making her way to the open window. She stepped through, then scooted over to her usual spot beside Lizzy.

They both stared up at the dark sky, ignoring the sounds of

Lydia bounding upstairs, yelling down to Kitty about profile views. Once Lydia's bedroom door slammed shut, Jane nodded to the book still resting on Lizzy's stomach.

"What do you think?" she asked.

Lizzy sighed dramatically. "Well, they just made it to the inn where there's only one room available and that room only has one bed, so we'll have to wait and see."

Jane laughed softly. The sound faded and was soon replaced by the chirping of crickets in the trees and muffled conversations still happening inside the house.

"How was the rest of the party?" Lizzy asked, staring up at the stars.

"Good."

A lopsided grin pulled at her lips as she turned to look at Jane. "Couldn't have been that good if you're home right now."

Her sister's profile was a silhouette against the darkness, but Lizzy could still see her smile falter.

"What is it?" Lizzy asked, suddenly concerned.

Jane released a long breath. "We were on the beach, and Charlie said he wanted to take me away on a romantic weekend. He was asking me if I've ever been to Paris or Rome just as the fireworks started and it was all so perfect . . ." Her voice stuttered, then came back in a whisper. "Then he told me he loved me."

Lizzy sat up with a jolt. "Oh my God. That's amazing!"

Jane nodded slowly. "Yeah. It's amazing."

"Okay . . . why don't I believe you?"

Her sister finally turned to her, her eyes lined with tears. "I didn't say it back."

An ache shot through Lizzy's chest as she reached over and took Jane's hand, squeezing it gently. "That's okay. You're not obligated to love him just because he loves you."

"But that's the thing. I *do*." Jane's voice was suddenly earnest, almost panicked. "And I wanted to say it back. He was looking at me, and the words were right there. I was just . . ." She swallowed, waiting a moment. "I didn't expect it. I just froze, Lizzy. And then . . ." Jane hesitated for what seemed like an eternity, then covered her eyes with her hands. "I panicked and told him I had to pee and ran back into the house!"

Oh God.

"I'm sure he understands, Jane," Lizzy said after a moment. "It's a big step. You were just caught off guard." After all, Lizzy thought to herself, this was Jane's first serious relationship. Maybe . . . her first real relationship. A little grace was important.

"I know," Jane replied, then gave her a watery smile. "But the look on Charlie's face tonight when I didn't say anything . . . then I left him there . . ." Jane shook her head, small, jerky movements. "I feel so awful."

"So call him and tell him now."

"Right." Jane threw her sister a cynical expression even as a small smile teased her lips. "Just call him up and say 'Hey, sorry I left you hanging earlier, but I love you, too!'"

"Why not?"

Jane let out a soft laugh. "I'm not sure that's the grand gesture that's going to fix this."

"So make it a grand gesture," Lizzy said, nudging her sister with her shoulder. "Plan something super romantic, and then tell him."

"Just . . . tell him?"

"Wait until he's completely entranced by how you tie your shoes or something equally erotic, then say, 'I'm totally and completely in love with you,'" Lizzy mimicked Jane's light and airy voice, then dissolved into laughter.

"I do not sound like that!" Jane said, trying to maintain some level of indignation in her voice, even though she was laughing now, too.

"Yes you do. But don't worry, he's ten times worse."

Jane let her laughter fade before she looked back up at the stars.

"It doesn't have to be a grand gesture, Jane," Lizzy added after a moment. "But if you want it to be, then let's make it happen."

Jane nodded, though there was still a line of worry between her eyebrows. It was like she was trying to convince herself, too. Another moment passed, then she spoke again. "What about you?"

"What about me?" Lizzy asked.

"You and Tristan."

"There is no me and Tristan."

Her sister's face fell. "No text?"

"Nope."

"Is that why you left early?"

Lizzy shrugged. "I was just bored."

"So bored you walked home?" Jane asked, skeptical.

"It's not that far."

"Lizzy. Charlie's is a lot further away than the Lodge."

"Well, if it makes you feel better, I wasn't alone."

Jane blinked. "Someone walked you home?"

"Technically, he didn't *walk*."

"I'm very confused right now."

You're not the only one, Lizzy thought. Then she scowled. "Will followed me home in his car. Or Charlie's car. He was in somebody's car."

"Will . . . Darcy?"

Lizzy nodded.

Jane shook her head slightly, as if it would help organize her thoughts. "Why didn't he just drive you?"

"Oh, trust me, he tried. Even after I explained to him *numerous* times that I didn't want a ride and I was fine to walk. Then he still went and got in his car and drove behind me at like five miles per hour the entire way."

"Really? How long did that take?"

Lizzy thought for a second. "Probably like forty-five minutes."

Jane's eyes widened.

"It's not like I asked him to!" Lizzy continued, suddenly feeling defensive. "Did Charlie put him up to it or something?"

"Doesn't sound like he had to."

Lizzy scrunched up her nose. "What's that supposed to mean?"

"Maybe Will was genuinely concerned about you."

The memory of Will's face as he stared at her on the front drive, how it changed from annoyance to concern so quickly. How his deep voice softened as he asked, *Are you okay?*

But Lizzy pushed the thought away. "Or he's a control freak."

"Or he's a good person."

Tristan's full account of Will's moral code was right there on the tip of her tongue, but Lizzy swallowed it down. Telling Jane would mean dissecting it, looking too closely at its motivations, at the men involved. And the last thing she wanted to do was linger too long on the memory of Will Darcy.

"Or he's a serial killer and I just narrowly escaped death."

"Or he *likes* you."

Something in Lizzy's stomach tumbled. She ignored it. "I know you and Charlie have been trying to get us together, but it's not happening. The guy can't stand me."

"Isn't that how all the classic love stories start?"

"This isn't a classic love story, Jane," Lizzy groaned. "No one is wandering over the moors at dawn to propose. This is a guy who has never smiled in his life and wears oxford shirts to the Lodge. He's probably a psychopath."

Jane sighed, leaning her head on Lizzy's shoulder. "I can't see Charlie being best friends with a psychopath."

Lizzy rested her cheek against the top of Jane's head. "Whatever. It never would've worked anyway."

"Why not?"

"You know I never get invested in a love story where the main love interest is blond. That's romance novel 101."

Jane's shoulders shook as she laughed. "You're awful."

Lizzy shrugged her free shoulder even as she smiled. It wasn't a lie. But as she stared out at the darkness, at the stars and the dark wisps of clouds overhead, she let herself wonder if it wasn't exactly the truth, either.

CHAPTER 15

For the first time in years, Will Darcy had to consider that he may have made a mistake.

Charlie stood at the front of the crowded conference room at Knightley Capital, his face drawn and his energy low as he tapped his computer key, advancing to the next slide of his presentation. He didn't look up from his screen as he read the copy verbatim to the nearly catatonic group surrounding the long table.

Usually, presentations were where he shone. Give Charlie Pierce a fresh batch of analytical data on bioethics or solar power and he could wax poetic for hours. Not only that, but his enthusiasm was contagious. People who entered his meetings with no interest in green tech left with their eyes bright and phones out, anxious to schedule the next meeting.

That's how it usually went, anyway. But ever since they returned to the city from East Hampton a week ago, it had been a different story.

"And as you can see from this graph . . ." Charlie motioned listlessly to the screen behind him. "By utilizing recent advancements in spatial genomics, Blaxton can acquire technologies around epigenome plasticity in plants to further diversify their hydroponics portfolio."

Will grimaced. He wasn't in the habit of making mistakes. In fact, he could probably count on one hand the number of times he had made one in his adult life. That's not to say he was perfect. Far from it. But he was careful. Emotions didn't enter the equation; rationality was all that mattered. It was why he had encouraged Charlie to leave East Hampton, why he spent the past week convincing him not to go back. It was the only rational decision. Or so he'd thought.

"This brings us to the projected growth in transcriptional dynamics over the next five years . . ."

Maybe it wasn't so bad. A bit dry, sure. And very monotone. But not *bad*, per se.

Charlie advanced to the next slide in his presentation. "Now, let's go over these numbers one by one."

A collective groan rumbled through the room.

Will's eyes wandered across the table to the only other two people he trusted to assess the situation.

Freddie sat with his shirtsleeves rolled up, watching Charlie with a look of morbid curiosity. Next to him, George leaned back in his chair, his brow furrowed.

Then Freddie turned to Will, cocked an eyebrow and mouthed, *Who died?*

Will frowned. *Well, shit.*

～

Will arrived at Ford's Cafe early and was halfway through his beer before George and Freddie walked in. They made their way over to Will's booth in the back, ordering a couple of beers of their own before sliding into their seats across from him.

"Well, that was fun," Freddie said, unbuttoning his suit jacket.

"If we want this viable by Q4, these discussions have to happen now," Will said defensively. "You both know that."

Freddie smiled before leaning his elbows on the table. "Yeah, but have you heard the saying, 'this meeting could have been an email'?"

Will ignored him, but he still felt a muscle in his jaw tick.

George chuckled as the waitress dropped off their beers. "So where's Charlie now?"

"Still at the office."

"Painting his nails black and listening to Joy Division?" Freddie asked.

Will's brow creased. "What?"

George sent him a sharp glare. "Come on, Will. In the past week you doubled our workload for the rest of the summer. Then Charlie shows up today like he just put down the family dog. What's going on?"

"Nothing is going on."

George was unconvinced. "Is this about a woman?"

"God, no," Will responded quickly. "It's about Charlie."

The two men stared blankly.

Will took another sip of his beer then added, "And a woman."

George released a sigh, as if he had known all along. Then Will realized that was probably true. Sometimes he forgot that George had known Charlie almost as long as he had. "All right. What happened?"

"We have another Cassidy Berger situation on our hands," Will replied.

"Who's Cassidy Berger?" Freddie asked, obviously confused.

"Charlie's ex from a few years ago," George explained. "Nice enough woman, but it was clear that she was more interested in Charlie's earning potential than his personality."

"Clear to everyone but Charlie," Will added.

George nodded. "It set off a bit of a pattern."

Freddie turned back to Will. "So who's the new Cassidy Berger?"

"A woman he met in East Hampton. Jane Bennet. She's a local."

"And how much is he out this time?" George asked.

Will paused. As much as he had been able to predict the outcome of Jane and Charlie's relationship, he rarely let himself consider how all the other usual factors were missing.

"Money wasn't the issue."

George's brow furrowed, like he was mentally reviewing the conversation to find where he'd missed a step.

Meanwhile, Freddie leaned forward. "Then what was the issue?"

"Charlie fell for her. She didn't feel the same way."

Something in Freddie's eyes suddenly dimmed, his usual wry grin faltering slightly.

Beside him, George shifted his weight, like he was still working it out in his head. "So she didn't want anything from him? A car? An apartment?"

Will shook his head.

"And he didn't promise her anything in the future?"

"No."

"So . . . you just didn't like her."

"I didn't say that." Will groaned, running a hand down his face. "Why the hell are we still talking about this?"

George shrugged. "Because this doesn't sound like a Cassidy Berger–type relationship, just a normal, run-of-the-mill relationship."

"Whatever it was, it's over. He just needs some time and distance, and he'll get over it."

Freddie let out a dry laugh. "Good luck with that."

The comment was unusually biting, and Will wondered if Freddie didn't have some personal experience in that department.

"So he's not heading out east again?" George asked.

"No. He's staying in the city. His sisters are moving out of the house in East Hampton this week and going to Palm Springs for a while."

"What happens to the house?" Freddie asked.

"My aunt handled the rental, so she's already working on sub-letting it." Will nodded to him. "Why, are you interested?"

Freddie's expression became sardonic. "I said I want to move back east, but not that far east."

The rest of lunch passed as it usually did, with the three of them talking specifics of the upcoming deal, interesting leads for others. Freddie was still contemplating a move back to the city and complained that the real estate market in lower Manhattan was worse than Malibu. George tried to sell him on the Upper East Side, which inevitably led to discussing his girlfriend Emma's aversion to moving in with him.

Will listened to it all, trying to ignore the itch in his brain, the thought that kept trying to snag his attention. It wasn't until they had paid the bill and put Freddie in a car bound for JFK that he figured out a name for it.

Doubt. Yet another feeling Will hadn't felt in years. But here it was, roaring to life in his chest, making him feel jittery. He thought he'd made the right choice keeping Charlie away from East Hampton. But now it felt more like a mantra to justify a bad decision. One that barely masked his ulterior motive, the one he was only beginning to realize himself: he had needed to escape a Bennet woman, too.

The thought stuck with him as they walked uptown. They reached George's office first, though Will barely noticed.

"Let me know about that call next week," George said over his shoulder as he turned toward the entrance.

Will nodded absently.

His friend stopped. "What?"

A moment passed as Will considered. "Can I ask you a question?"

"I'm already concerned."

Will glared at him, then continued, "Am I overbearing?"

"Ah, so it's a trick question," George said with a smile.

"I'm serious."

The gravity in Will's voice seemed to settle in then, and his friend's expression became serious. "I've known you since college, Will. I've watched you build your company in record time and save your friends from some awful situations while you were at it. You did that by stepping in and taking charge of whatever room you entered. And, yeah, that can be overbearing, but that's not a negative."

"No?"

"No. Because you're always right. It's one of your worst traits."

Will was surprised by the smile at the corner of his lips. "Right."

George chuckled. "Seriously, Will. You always put everybody else first. And, yeah, you might not be smooth about it, but it always comes from a good place. We all know that, including Charlie."

He nodded. "Okay."

"So you're not heading out to the Hamptons again, either?"

Will paused. "Why?"

"I was just wondering what was going on with the house."

"I told you. Birdie is looking to sublet it."

"No, your house," George clarified. "If she's out there dealing with Charlie's, I assume she's still trying to convince you to sell the Montauk house."

He was right. Birdie was eager to put their family home in Montauk on the market. Years of less-than-subtle hints and over-the-top offers had punctuated almost every conversation with her. Now, with the renovations almost complete, he was sure her efforts would double.

Will sighed. "I'm heading out there next month, so if she mentions it, I'll let you know."

"Want some company?"

Will gave him a quizzical look. "You want to come out to Montauk?"

George shrugged. "I haven't been out there in ages. And I'd love to see what you've done with the place."

Will stared at him, waiting.

"And Emma is scheduled to work every weekend in August and I have nothing else to do."

"I knew it," Will said, shaking his head.

"Hey, do you want help with Birdie or not?"

Will frowned. Birdie flirted with George every time Will brought him to a family event. Luckily, George didn't seem to mind. And, considering everything else on Will's plate, a distracted Birdie was probably a good thing.

"Fine," he said, already turning to continue down the sidewalk, leaving George behind. "I'll have Jenna send you the details."

CHAPTER 16

For Jane and Lizzy, having a friend whose dad owned a bar had its advantages. They had never been carded, entire tabs mysteriously disappeared at the end of a Saturday night, and on weekday afternoons, when the bakery was closed and the forecast threatened rain, the Lodge was the perfect place to catch up without too many interruptions.

On this particular day, before the doors officially opened and a James Taylor/Taylor Swift cover band took the stage, Piper Donato was able to relax with them at the end of the bar, though muscle memory dictated that she still serve her friends drinks and Tater Tots.

"All right, so let me get this straight," she said to Lizzy. "Tristan said he was heading out here on the Fourth and was going to text you about getting together, but then he didn't."

Lizzy nodded as she took a sip of her beer. It had been a week since Charlie's party, which meant it had been over two weeks since she and Tristan had shared that moment outside Donato's. Not that she was counting.

"And you haven't heard anything from him since."

"Nope."

Piper hummed as she seemed to consider. "Have you tried texting him again?"

"You mean after he left me on read over a week ago?" Lizzy asked, her voice dripping with sarcasm.

"Maybe he's been working. It sounds like he's really busy," Jane said, then turned to Piper. "Your dad was saying all the Hampton-Fest planning was really kicking off, right?"

Piper picked up the cue. "Totally! He's barely sat down over the past few weeks." Then she nodded decisively to Lizzy. "I think you should text him again. Give him another shot."

Lizzy was ready to argue, but . . . why not? Jane was probably right; Tristan was busy. He might have completely forgotten about her texts. He deserved the benefit of the doubt, at least.

She pulled out her phone and typed out a quick hello, pressing send before Piper or Jane could critique.

Then she placed her phone on the bar and they all stared at it, waiting.

After a long minute of silence, Jane offered an encouraging smile. "If he's really busy at work, he probably doesn't even have time to look at his phone."

Lizzy almost laughed. "That sounds like the adult equivalent of the dog ate my homework."

Jane's expression fell just as Lizzy realized her mistake.

Her sister had barely heard from Charlie since the Fourth of July party. There had been a few phone calls, a handful of texts, but Jane never disclosed what was discussed other than the fact that Charlie was in the city working on a big project. All Lizzy knew for sure was that Marv's Lament was now dark, and the local gossip mill was convinced none of the Pierces were coming back. Lizzy, on the other hand, was not.

"Charlie's totally different, though," Lizzy continued, waving her hand indiscriminately in the air. "He spent every second he was in East Hampton with you. And he wanted to take you away on a romantic weekend. He even programmed Mom's number into his phone."

Piper nodded solemnly. "That's love."

"Exactly. He may have gotten his ego bruised, but he'll come back."

Jane sighed, pushing her dark hair away from her face. "And if he doesn't?"

"Then we fall back on our original plan," Lizzy said patiently. "A derelict mansion and two dozen cats."

Her sister fought a smile as she sent Lizzy an exasperated look. "I think we're approaching the age where *Grey Gardens* references stop being funny."

"And start being aspirational?"

Piper rolled her eyes at both of them. "You two are ridiculous."

"Don't worry, you can come visit us," Lizzy said, popping a Tater Tot in her mouth. "You just have to learn to like cats. And the occasional raccoon."

Piper shook her head, stealing Lizzy's pint glass and refilling it. "Stop. The odds of a guy ghosting either of you are close to impossible, so if it somehow happens to both of you in the same week, I'm officially renouncing any and all belief in true love."

Lizzy smiled, resting her chin in her hand. "And how does Sasha feel about that?"

"I just promised to take her out to Montauk for a romantic weekend next month, so it could definitely get dicey."

Lizzy laughed. Piper's girlfriend, Sasha, was one of her favorite people in the world, and she regularly begged Piper to have her move down from Boston. She was about to ask when she would be in town, when an idea suddenly struck her.

"Oh!" Lizzy perked up and turned to her sister. "Charlie wanted to take you away for a weekend, right? Why don't you book a place in Montauk and surprise him?"

Piper's forehead knitted with confusion. "Who's booking what now?"

"Jane needs a grand gesture to show Charlie how much she cares about him, so we've been brainstorming," Lizzy explained.

Jane sighed. "That's not a grand gesture, Lizzy. He was talking about Paris. Montauk is only twenty minutes away."

"Who cares? It's still *away*," Lizzy replied.

"You can get a good deal after Labor Day, too," Piper said, leaning her elbows on the bar. "They're practically giving rooms away in the off-season."

"And you have so many vacation days saved up, Jane," Lizzy added. "You can use a few to take a long weekend in September, right? It's perfect!"

Jane bit her lip as she seemed to think about it, then nodded. "Okay. I'll check it out when we get home."

A bit of the weight in Lizzy's chest lifted. It felt like a huge win, and she was about to celebrate it when she remembered what had brought them to the idea in the first place.

"Wait, rewind," she said, turning to Piper. "When were you going to tell us that Sasha is coming down next month?"

Their friend bit back a smile. "Okay, remember how I've always wanted to get my master's in psychology but never had the money?"

Lizzy's eyebrows pinched together. "Yeah?"

"Well, I applied to Boston University, and I got in! Sasha and I are celebrating before classes start."

Jane jumped off her stool, clapping. "Piper! That's incredible!"

"I know! I wouldn't be able to afford it except that I got a massive scholarship. And since I'll be moving in with Sasha, my living expenses will be close to nothing. It's finally happening!" Piper said. Then she saw Lizzy's face and she became pensive. "Are you mad?"

"No, I just . . ." Lizzy paused, trying to school her expression. "I didn't even know you applied."

"I didn't tell anyone except Sasha. I didn't want to have to deal with all the questions from everybody if it didn't work out, you know?"

Lizzy wanted to say no, that she had no idea what she was talking about, but that would be a lie. She had done the exact same thing with Columbia. Except Piper was putting her plan into action, while Lizzy's remained stagnant. Suddenly, her frustration crumbled, and a new, unfamiliar ache replaced it.

"Well, that's great," Lizzy said. She hoped her thin smile was convincing. "Congratulations."

Piper waved her off. "Don't get too excited. I could still fail out and end up back here shilling drinks and free advice until I'm eighty."

Lizzy sighed. "Pipes, you were our valedictorian."

"That doesn't matter when you're writing a two-hundred-page dissertation and—"

Lizzy's phone began vibrating across the bar. She reached for it, quickly flipping it over to see the screen illuminated with a text message from Tristan in the center.

"Is it Tristan?" Piper said, craning her neck to see. "What does it say?"

Lizzy picked it up before either Piper or Jane could see the message.

TRISTAN

> Hey! Crazy with work. Maybe we can grab a drink next time I'm in town.

"He says he's been really busy with work," she finally said.

"Well, that's good, right?" Jane said. The manufactured levity in her voice was painfully obvious.

Lizzy nodded. "And he says we should grab a drink next time he's out here."

"I knew it!" Piper exclaimed. "And then there's the party at his place in September. You're going to that, right?"

Lizzy didn't have the courage to admit she hadn't been invited. He hadn't even mentioned it. So instead, she just said, "Right."

"It's all working out," Piper said, raising her glass of water. "To Boston. To Montauk. And to . . . HamptonFest!"

Jane laughed. Lizzy tried to as well. She really did. But she couldn't help feeling that the ground was beginning to erode around her feet. The world was washing out to sea and leaving her behind.

CHAPTER 17

August was proverbial hell. The heat wave that hit East Hampton made it feel quite literal—temperatures averaged over ninety-five degrees for eighteen days straight, and the asphalt on Main Street was actually melting—but for Lizzy, her misery had more to do with the monotony that permeated each day. The same routine at work every morning, the same people at the Lodge every night.

It didn't help that her mother and Donna Donato held court at the table by the bakery's front window almost every day, either.

"Oh, you're terrible, Joanne!" Donna cackled.

At the counter, Lizzy tried to ignore them, focusing instead on her book.

"I'm serious, Donna. If he gets Bon Jovi, I'll just die. Right there in the middle of HamptonFest. Dead," her mother said.

Lizzy glanced over at her watch. Just twenty-seven minutes until Kitty took over her shift and she could go home to nap. Less than a half hour to cover the register, to ignore how her jean shorts and the Cure T-shirt stuck to her body thanks to their feeble air conditioner. She could do this. Piece of cake.

"No, but seriously, what about that Tristan Cole?" her mother continued in her worst stage whisper. "If he says he knows Jon Bon Jovi, can you even imagine who else will be there?"

Lizzy groaned. Maybe not.

"Well, he apparently invited a few people to this big party at his apartment in the city in a few weeks, so maybe we'll find out," Donna said, punctuating it with a tittering laugh.

"Lizzy!" Mrs. Bennet yelled as if her daughter wasn't leaning against the counter five feet away. "You're close to Tristan Cole, aren't you? Are you going to this party?"

Nope, Lizzy wanted to say. *In fact, he hasn't even bothered to follow up about the meet-up we were supposed to have last month.* But she didn't say that. She just offered a long sigh as she closed her book and pretended to be in deep thought.

"I'll have to check my diary. It's so hard to keep up with all the social engagements these days . . ."

Her mother frowned. "I'll take that as a no."

Lizzy gave her a saccharine smile just as Donna's phone rang.

"Oh! It's Barb!" she squealed.

"Answer it!" Mrs. Bennet replied.

Lizzy picked up her book again. This was usually the way it went. As the afternoons slowly passed, the two women would be drip-fed the latest news around town, either over the phone or by a well-timed passerby. Lizzy had gotten so good at tuning it out, she didn't even notice when Donna hung up, or listen to her mother's demands for a full recap. The only thing that stopped her cold, forcing her to abandon chapter 30, was when she heard Donna say two words: Marv's Lament.

Lizzy's head snapped up.

"Barb said there's two cars, but she didn't recognize them."

"Was Charlie there?" her mother whispered.

Donna tutted. "She didn't waltz up and find out, Joanne!

She could only walk by so many times! But she said there were definitely people inside."

Lizzy froze. While Jane held out hope that Charlie would eventually return to East Hampton, there hadn't been any sign of life at Marv's Lament in weeks. The entire town knew the Pierces had rented it for the whole summer, so the question of what happened had been swirling ever since, enough that Lizzy had started staying home from the Lodge with Jane on Saturdays just to ensure her sister avoided overhearing any of the gossip.

And now, suddenly, Charlie was back?

Anger roared to life in her chest as she reached down and grabbed her bag.

"Tell Dad I had to go," Lizzy said, already walking around the counter toward the door.

Her mother barely looked over as she waved Lizzy away so she could continue her conversation with Donna uninterrupted.

Lizzy's emotions ran the full gamut on the short drive from the bakery to Lily Pond Lane. While she wanted to believe this was all a misunderstanding, she wasn't as forgiving as Jane. No matter the reason, there was no excuse for how unceremoniously Charlie had left, how much he had hurt her sister. And now he was back without even letting her know?

It would have been easier if Charlie had come with built-in red flags. If Lizzy had had even an inkling that this was what he was going to do, she could have been ready, she could have protected Jane. He was probably used to falling in love, but this was all new to her sister. How could he not realize that?

The cars Donna mentioned were waiting when Lizzy turned down the long driveway toward Marv's Lament, a sleek black Mercedes sedan and an Audi SUV. She pulled her truck into the spot between them, her mind racing in so many directions that she was barely aware of turning off the engine and marching to the front door. It was slightly ajar, allowing the sounds of a classical piano melody to float outside. She slowly pushed the door open, careful not to make a sound.

The grand piano that had been hidden in a corner only a few weeks ago was set in the middle of the room now, the rest of the furniture moved out of the way so it alone was framed by the tall windows. A sweeping melody reverberated from the instrument, chords and scales rising and falling with such intensity it made her heart swell. And there, sitting in front of the black-and-white keys with his back to her, was Will Darcy.

At first, she didn't recognize him. She was too distracted by the music, how it brought life to every sterile corner of the cold room. It was haunting. Ethereal and hypnotic.

Then he leaned back ever so slightly, and she froze in place.

There was no denying that blond hair, the distinct line of his jaw. The sleeves of his button-down shirt were pulled up to reveal tanned forearms as he leaned over the keys, his fingers dancing across them with confident ease. It was an odd juxtaposition, this man who was always so austere, so cold, yet now sitting here so casually, lost in this piece of music that . . . well, was the most beautiful thing she'd ever heard.

But Lizzy shouldn't be hearing it. She shouldn't be standing here at all. It suddenly felt like she had stumbled onto something illicit and that she needed to retreat. The music masked her steps as she moved toward the door. She would go back outside and ring the bell, pretend that this moment had never happened, and—

Her shin hit the massive coffee table, and an awful screech of wood-scratching-floor rang out. The music stopped and Will turned around to face her.

"Shit," she hissed, heat rising to her cheeks.

"Elizabeth?" he asked like he wasn't sure himself.

He got up slowly, his expression unreadable. The more he stared at her, unblinking and seemingly unfazed by her unexpected visit, the more she couldn't look away.

"I didn't mean to interrupt," she finally blurted out.

"You didn't."

She scoffed, but the sound came out like a nervous laugh. "I think running into a piece of furniture in the middle of Mozart is the definition of interrupting, actually."

He turned to close the top of the piano. "It was Mendelssohn."

She blinked. "What?"

"It was Mendelssohn's *Hebrides* overture."

"Ah," she said and swallowed. "So . . . not Mozart."

He shook his head slowly. "No."

She wanted to tell him that whatever it was, she loved it. That it somehow sounded like the sea: the rolling waves, the crashing surf, the exhilaration, and the quiet moments, too. But that felt like an admission, like she would be giving away a part of herself with the disclosure. So she cleared her throat to fill the silence and give herself a moment to remember why she was here in the first place. "Is Charlie here?"

"No, he's not."

As soon as he spoke, there was the sound of footsteps upstairs.

"Then who's that?"

"Do you think I'm lying?"

"I wouldn't put it past you."

Will's eyes narrowed at her, betraying a moment of offense. "It's my aunt. She's putting the house back on the market."

"What do you mean?"

"Which part wasn't clear?" Will asked—with concern or annoyance, she never could tell.

"All of it." She took a step toward him. "Charlie said he rented this house for the summer. Now he's gone and you're here. Can you blame me for being confused?"

He opened his mouth, but before he could answer, a voice called out from behind them.

"Will, sweetheart, I hope that wasn't you playing the piano. I told you it's *ornamental*."

Lizzy turned to find a woman at the top of the long staircase. She looked to be older than her mother, but by how much there was no way to tell. Her face was frozen, her skin pulled tight across her features, and her shoulder-length blond hair—which was so pale it could have easily been white—skimmed the shoulders of her cream-colored blouse. She sighed as she descended, taking each step with ease in her heels, and a tall and incredibly handsome, dark-haired man followed behind her.

"I'm telling you, George, it's kismet! You're out at the Montauk house with Will the same weekend we're putting this place back on the market?" she said to him as she descended. "It's just too perfect. And it would only be a monthlong sublet, so you don't have to worry about a long-term commitment. I think—" The woman finally noticed Lizzy, and frowned as she took in her worn T-shirt and overalls. Then she waved a hand at her, the motion sending the gold charms on her bracelet clattering together. "You'll have to wait outside, dear. I told the agency we didn't want any cleaners here until five, and—"

"Birdie," Will cut her off, his tone firm and so much colder than it had been only a few moments before. "This is my friend Elizabeth Bennet."

Lizzy's eyes snapped to him. There were a lot of words she assumed Will Darcy would use to describe her, but "friend" was nowhere on the list.

If he noticed her surprise, he didn't let on, only continued with introductions. "Elizabeth, this is my aunt, Birdie Carrington. She's helping us sublease the house." Then he nodded to the man beside her. "And this is George Knightley."

George smiled, taking a step forward as he held out his hand. "Elizabeth Bennet, is it?"

Lizzy shook his hand and smiled back. "Lizzy."

His smile widened with the revelation. "Nice to meet you."

"I didn't realize Will had friends still out here for the summer," Birdie said. "Are you here for the weekend or . . ." She let the words hang there, waiting for Lizzy to pick them up with some adequate answer.

"I live out here," she replied. "My family owns Bennet Bakery on Main."

"Of course. I thought the name sounded familiar." Birdie nodded, a smug smile on her lips as if she had known all along. "I think I might have stopped in once on my way out to visit Montauk. Just lovely. Do you remember, Will?"

"No," he answered absently. He was glaring at George, who was still smiling at Lizzy.

What the hell is going on?

"Sorry, I just came by to see if I could catch Charlie. Is he here?" she asked.

Birdie let out a little laugh. "No, he's safe and sound in the city."

It should have been benign, an offhand comment that would be forgotten just as soon as it was said. But Lizzy sensed the biting edge to her words.

"I didn't realize East Hampton was so dangerous," she said, her voice full of manufactured good humor.

"Well, you never can tell, can you?" Birdie replied, tapping a finger to her nose.

Lizzy forced a laugh, even as she gave a pointed look to Will. He just stared back.

"Lizzy," George said, breaking the sudden tension. "What are you up to tonight?"

Plotting murder, she wanted to say. But instead she turned to the man standing opposite her and smiled. "Nothing much."

"Then you should come to dinner with us. The club is nearby, right, Will?"

A muscle in Will's jaw ticked as he stared at his friend. It was like he had been asked to swallow glass.

"Yes, Hunsford Country Club. Have you been there before?" Birdie interjected, though she didn't wait for Lizzy to answer before continuing. "They just redid the dining room last season. Of course, we have a reservation and I'm not sure they can accommodate a plus-one. Especially a nonmember."

It was the same tone she had used at the top of the stairs. The one used countless times by cidiots who visited the bakery every summer. An admonition disguised as a pleasantry.

"I'm not a member, and neither is Will. I'm sure it's fine," George said, turning his warm smile to Lizzy. "What do you say?"

She ran through all the reasons why the answer was a big fat no.

She only had four more chapters left in her book.

She hated that exclusive club with a passion.

Dinner with Will Darcy would be a nightmare.

But then she caught the look on Will's face. He was staring at her from under the hard line of his brow, a look that seemed to be trying to communicate exactly the same thoughts.

And suddenly, the idea that Will didn't want her there was exactly the reason for her to go. If she got answers about what had happened with Charlie, even better.

"Sure," she said with a shrug. "What time?"

Birdie's smile deflated slightly, while George's broadened. "The reservation was for eight o'clock. Right, Will?"

"Right," he murmured.

"Great," Lizzy replied. "I'll see you there."

Then she turned and headed straight out the front door.

CHAPTER 18

Tonight would be an exercise in self-restraint. Or masochism. Will hadn't decided which.

The Hunsford Country Club was a hulking structure that echoed the formality of an English estate except for its shingled exterior. It sat within view of the ocean, flanked by a manicured golf course on one side and sand dunes on the other. Normally, when Will was wrangled into joining his aunt for dinner here, he took solace in the fact that the dining room faced the Atlantic. He could claim a seat that faced the large windows and stare out at the waves while Birdie dominated the conversation for the next two hours.

But that wouldn't work tonight. Because the only person who could possibly distract him from that view had just pulled into the parking lot.

"Is that her?" his aunt asked, somehow infusing her voice with both disappointment and surprise from where she stood on the club's threshold, glaring at Lizzy's rusted Chevy pickup.

Will nodded.

"Let's get seated," George said, already guiding Birdie inside. "I'm sure Will can show Lizzy to the table. Right, Will?"

Will glared at him as George smiled and disappeared through the front doors.

Lizzy Bennet's old truck rattled to a stop at the valet podium, its engine dying with a groan. The door creaked open and she stepped out, handing her keys to the valet with a smile. It dropped from her lips as soon as she saw Will waiting for her at the door.

He had half expected her to blow them off. It was one thing to test him in the foyer of Charlie's house, where it felt like battle lines had been drawn directly into the marble floor. But it was another to spend an evening at a country club full of blue bloods on the beach. Yet here she was, hair down and walking toward him in a denim skirt that was frayed along her thighs, a pair of combat boots, and a tight green top that revealed the soft dip of where her collarbones met.

So, it would be self-restraint, then.

She stopped a few feet in front of him. Her head tilted to the side, like she needed to examine him from a different angle. It caused a few strands of red hair to drift across her cheek.

"Are you waiting for me?" she asked.

"Yes."

"Why?"

"Because it's the polite thing to do."

"Ah," she said, nodding as if this thought hadn't occurred to her. "I thought you might be running interference."

He blinked. "I'm sorry?"

"That you're here to convince me not to go in."

"Why would I do that?"

"Because I fully intend on revealing all your worst habits."

"Such as?"

She gave him a tight smile. "We'll start with your sparkling personality and just go from there."

He stared down at her. She looked gorgeous right now, but not in any way that was familiar. Elizabeth Bennet was an objectively beautiful woman, there was no denying that, but her confidence was what truly set her apart. It didn't rely on how she looked or what she wore; it was a surety that made everything else superfluous.

"I am not afraid of you," he finally replied.

He didn't mean for the words to come out so low, so suggestive, but her dark eyes still flared. Then they narrowed on him, like she had caught herself and a retort was already taking form on her tongue. A hot spike hit his pulse in anticipation.

Birdie's voice cut through the air behind him. "Will, sweetheart, what's taking you so long? Our reservation is for *eight*."

He glanced over his shoulder to see his aunt standing in the club's threshold, tapping a finger against her wrist before disappearing inside again.

"Don't worry," Lizzy said, her voice suddenly low and husky as she walked ahead toward the door. "My courage always rises with every attempt to intimidate me."

His jaw clenched. *Shit*.

The main lobby of the club led straight to the dining room just beyond. The maître d' led them through the half-empty space, serpentining his way around the other patrons, to their usual spot by the window. Birdie and George were already seated at the table his aunt always reserved, mainly because it offered the best view of both the water and the rest of the dining room.

Birdie was seated beside George, leaving the two chairs opposite free. George stood as they arrived, and Will half expected him to offer Lizzy his seat. She would probably take it, too, as it would be the furthest she could get from Will without moving to an entirely different table. Before she could consider it, Will pulled out the chair beside his, and nodded to her. She stared at him for a moment, then, to his surprise, she took it.

"Yes, perfect. Elizabeth, you sit there, and Will, you sit across from me," Birdie said, snapping her fingers at her nephew.

Lizzy's arm brushed against Will's as she sat. He tried to ignore it as he took his seat beside her and picked up his menu. He didn't tear his eyes away from it until the waiter appeared, listing the specials while Will pretended to listen. Then he vaguely remembered ordering a beer. Lizzy might have ordered one, too, but he couldn't be sure. All he knew was that the smell of vanilla lingered in the air between them, so potent he wanted to lean toward her, find out if it was the scent of her hair or her skin.

"I'm so sorry, Elizabeth," Birdie said, leaning across the table to give Lizzy an exaggerated frown. "Will really should have told you about the dress code. I hope you're not too uncomfortable. No one will mind about the denim, I promise."

Lizzy's back was straight as she placed her napkin on her lap. Then Will watched a small, audacious smile curl up the corners of her full lips. "Well, that's a relief."

He looked away, clearing his throat.

"So how do you two know each other again?" George asked.

"That's a good question," Lizzy said. Her voice was light, like a breath, but there was a rough edge to it. Always that rough edge. Like its softness had been worn down by salt water. "Will's friend Charlie is dating my sister. Or *was* dating her. I'm having trouble keeping track. Do you have any insight on that, Will?"

She turned to him, her dark eyes locked on his, all fire and rage. *Shit*. He didn't have an answer; he never thought he would be in a position where he'd have to provide one.

"Oh, I just *adore* Charlie," Birdie crooned, oblivious. "He is such a darling. You three were just inseparable when you were at Columbia."

Lizzy's sharp smile fell.

"And his sister Annabelle, what a powerhouse. And such exceptional taste. I showed her that house and she signed the lease in twenty minutes. She just knew," Birdie continued. "It's too bad they had to leave the Hamptons early. How is Charlie doing, by the way?"

Lizzy's eyes widened. Will could almost feel her questions forming as he answered, "Fine."

"That's good. I worry about him." Birdie sighed dramatically. "Maybe he should join his sisters in Palm Springs. I hear that's where Annabelle took their other sister to help her get over that nasty divorce."

Lizzy leaned forward. "Why would Charlie—"

"Annabelle reminds me a lot of myself, you know," Birdie interrupted, as if she hadn't heard Lizzy at all. "I had just started Carrington Realty all on my own, you see, and within a year I had been on the cover of *Realtor Magazine* and done an interview on CNBC. I was almost a judge on *Shark Tank*! I had to turn them down, of course. My business was my top priority and it required just so much of my attention."

The waiter returned with their drinks, and Will took a deep sip of his beer. It was going to be a long night.

"Lizzy, you said your last name was Bennet, right? Do you have a sister named Jane?" George asked. He was barely biting back a smile that told Will his friend knew exactly what he was doing.

Lizzy blinked, like she was as surprised by him remembering her surname as she was about him knowing about her sister. "Yes. My older sister."

George smiled warmly. "How many sisters do you have?"

"Four."

"Lucky you. I'm stuck with just one brother."

Lizzy laughed. The sound was soft and warm, and Will hated the stab of jealousy that hit his chest at not being its recipient.

"Will is an only child," Birdie interjected, her expression suddenly somber. "Which is why I'm so glad you boys all found one another. Especially after . . . well . . . you know what happened. Suffice to say, it was tragic."

Will tensed as an uncomfortable hush fell over the table. He barely talked about his parents' deaths with anyone, and he hated how Birdie would bring it up, alluding to it but never giving it any proper attention.

"You three have always looked out for one another," she said, patting George's hand. "There's such value in friendships that stand the test of time. I like to think I would have stayed in touch with all my college girlfriends, but it's just not the same for professional women. There are so many demands on us. Not that I'm complaining, of course. It's such a blessing to be able to do what I do, but I have to admit," she continued, turning to Lizzy, "I'm jealous of you being able to just work at your family bakery and never having to think about it."

Beside him, Lizzy's body went tense. Birdie had hit a nerve, but before he could discover what it was, George interceded.

"Did you always want to be part of the family's business?" he asked.

Lizzy's attention moved to him. He smiled at her encouragingly. Will took a deep sip of his beer.

"No," she replied. "I've worked there since I was little, but I went to school to be a journalist. I wanted to travel and cover foreign affairs."

Will paused. "A journalist?"

Her forehead furrowed when she noticed his expression. "Is that surprising?"

"No. I just had no idea you had . . ."

"Aspirations?" she said, her tone biting.

Will opened his mouth to reply, to challenge her assumption, but then his aunt was speaking again.

"Oh, I always fancied myself a bit of a writer. You should see my bio on my website. I even came up with our slogan, you know. 'Carrington Realty—we care a ton.' Catchy, right?"

Birdie continued with her monologue as the waiter reappeared and took their food order. Once he left, and Will had requested one of the specials he was sure he wouldn't touch, the conversation flowed on. Birdie dominated it as always, but George was a good foil, asking questions about her business and her latest closings. Will tried to listen, but Lizzy's proximity occupied too much of his attention. Even after the food arrived and their meal was finished, he couldn't recall what he had eaten.

Once their plates were cleared, Birdie turned a smug grin to George.

"So, what do you think of Charlie's house, George? It's stunning, isn't it? And Lily Pond Lane is *very* desirable."

"It is," George answered, taking a sip of his wine. He was nothing if not polite, but Will could see how carefully his friend was choosing his words.

Birdie, on the other hand, didn't notice. "I knew you'd love it. It's the perfect Hamptons summer house."

"It's too bad the summer is almost over," George replied diplomatically.

She waved him off. "Oh, that doesn't matter. It's the kind of place you can show off year-round, maybe do some holiday enter-taining. I really think you and your girlfriend would be extremely happy there."

George nodded even as he said, "When I'm in the market, I'll keep it in mind."

"Who knows if it will be available then?" Birdie sighed. "It's one of the most exclusive addresses in the Hamptons. A house like that doesn't stay on the market for long, George."

"It might, though," Lizzy said.

Birdie's head whipped around to face her. "Excuse me?"

"Oh." Lizzy looked between her and George, as if she was surprised anyone had heard her. "It's just that Marv's Lament has been on the market for a while."

"Marv's Lament?" Birdie asked, her lip almost curling.

"Charlie's house. Or, former house. What's going on with that, exactly?"

Birdie waved off the question with her red nails. "The only reason it hasn't found a new occupant is because the market has been in flux. It's set to hit its stride in the next few months." Then she turned to Will. "Speaking of which, we have to talk about the Montauk house before you go. I'm getting calls, so I need you to let me know when we're putting it on the market."

Lizzy's attention snapped to Will.

"You have a house in Montauk?" she asked.

He nodded once. Then he adjusted his sleeve, avoiding her eyes.

George turned to Will, his brow furrowed. "I didn't think you were actually going to sell that place."

"It only makes sense," Birdie said, clasping her hands together so her red nails overlapped one another. "That house is gorgeous, but when does Will have time to go out there? And there's just so much land, it deserves to be developed so other people can enjoy it, too. Right off the cliffs at the very end of the island. Just beautiful!"

She sighed, like the listing was already written in her mind. Then Will remembered that it probably was.

That's when he noticed that Lizzy's gaze was still on him.

He was having a hard time reading her expression. There had been doubt there just a few moments ago, but now it almost seemed like she was surprised. As if the idea of him having any connection out east was beyond her comprehension.

"If you have a place in Montauk, why were you always at Charlie's?" she finally asked.

"My house out there was being renovated." He didn't want to give his aunt more of an opening to discuss it, but as Birdie drummed her fingernails on the white tablecloth, he knew it was already too late.

"It cost an absolute fortune, too," Birdie said, as if she was footing the bill. "I will never understand why you insisted on doing all that—the land sells itself! Homes out there are as rare as hen's teeth and go for top dollar with or without a new roof. In fact, I had an agent who had a listing nearby last summer that was half the size and it went for over fifteen million dollars."

"That is . . . a lot of money," Lizzy said.

Will took another sip of his beer.

"Exactly," Birdie said with a nod. "It's the smart choice."

A moment, then Lizzy looked over at Will.

"Do you want to sell it?" she asked.

The question stopped him. Her dark eyes were narrowed, but they had lost the fire that had threatened to scorch him earlier. She was studying him, like his expression might give away more than any possible answer.

No one had asked him that. Not since the topic came up shortly after his parents' deaths five years ago. There had been dozens of other questions: What are you going to do with Montauk? Did your father really leave it just to you? And then the inevitable pressure from Birdie herself, wanting to know his plans, persuading him that it was too much of a burden for him to maintain on his own. But the question of whether he actually wanted to sell had never come up.

Not until right now.

"Of course he wants to," Birdie replied with a plastic smile. "It's time to let it go. Yes, the property is lovely, but can you imagine a five-star resort out there?" She sighed again, then turned to Lizzy. "I'm sure you understand. As a native Hamptonite."

Lizzy's nose scrunched up slightly, as if the term left a bad smell in its wake.

Birdie's smile faltered. "Am I wrong?"

"Sorry," Lizzy said. "I just don't know anyone out here who calls themselves a Hamptonite."

"Oh, is Hamptonian the correct term?" Birdy said, laughing again. "Or Hamptoner?"

"We just don't really call it the Hamptons."

"But it's where you live." Birdy said it slowly, as if Lizzy needed help understanding.

Lizzy smiled at her. Will could tell it was forced, as if she was struggling to maintain her patience.

"No. The Hamptons is where you visit. The rest of us live on Long Island."

Birdie's lips pursed. "I appreciate your perspective, Elizabeth, but let me assure you, as a professional who has made a name for herself in real estate, you live in the Hamptons. Now, you might not be in a financial position to enjoy all that it entails, but that could change with just a bit of hard work and ambition."

Silence. Will's eyes narrowed on his aunt. Birdie Carrington presented herself as an aging socialite so perfectly—all cotton sweaters and starched shirts—that he forgot how her advice sometimes barely concealed her venom.

George looked equally as angry, though it was balanced with a concerned look to Lizzy.

Will leaned forward, working to keep his tone measured. "Birdie, that was—"

"Very true," Lizzy said, interrupting him. Then she removed the napkin from her lap and stood up. "It's getting late and I have to work in the morning, so I hope you'll excuse me."

She was already turning away when Will followed suit. "I'll walk you out."

They were silent as they made their way out of the dining room, through the lobby to the club's front doors. The sound of the ocean rolling nearby welcomed them when they emerged outside, and crickets filled the silence as they waited for the valet to get her truck.

It was another long moment before he stole a glance at her face. The light from the streetlamps filtered down through the trees, and the shadows of the branches danced across her skin. Her tight expression.

"I apologize for my aunt," he finally said. "She shouldn't have said that."

"Said what, exactly?"

"About why you work at the bakery. Your ambition. All of it."

"She wasn't exactly wrong."

He frowned. "Of course she was."

She let out a bitter laugh. "And how would you know that?"

"Because you don't decide to be a foreign affairs journalist just so you can stay in one place forever."

She stared at him for a long moment. Then she turned away,

watching as her truck appeared from the parking lot, driving slowly toward them.

"Whatever. It doesn't matter."

His brow furrowed. "Why the hell not?"

She shrugged one shoulder. "Just a mess. Remember?"

Shit. He had almost forgotten that text he sent to Charlie. "I'm sorry. You weren't supposed to see that and—"

"You don't have to apologize." Her voice sounded tired, and there was an unconvincing smile now on her lips.

"Yes. I do."

He wanted to say more, but before he could find the words, the valet pulled up with her truck and handed her the keys. She climbed into the driver's seat. "Have a good night, Will. And if you see Charlie, tell him my sister says hi."

Then she slammed the door shut.

She didn't look at Will as she started the ignition, and it was too dark to see if she stole a glance in her rearview mirror as she disappeared down the long drive toward the road. But he still watched her go, staring into the darkness until the red glow of her taillights disappeared.

"Well, that was brutal," George's deep voice interrupted a moment later. Will turned just as his friend sauntered out the club's front doors, his hands in his pockets. "Where's your date?"

Will glowered at him. "She's not my date."

This detail didn't seem to derail George's line of inquiry; he simply waited for Will to answer.

Will sighed, then nodded to the long drive. "She just left."

George nodded. "Birdie is inside chatting with some client she ran into, but said she'd be out soon."

Will didn't reply, just returned his gaze to where Lizzy's car had faded into the darkness.

George walked forward and stopped at Will's side. "So what do you want to do?"

Will knew what he meant. They had only planned to stay out here through today. A helicopter was already waiting at the airport to take them back to the city.

"Let me go talk to Birdie and we can head out," Will finally said.

"You sure?"

"Why wouldn't I be?"

George's head cocked to the side, as if he was mulling something over. "Remember when I escaped to LA last year to spearhead the Wentworth deal?"

Will nodded.

"You told me I should go, but only if it was about the deal. If I was using it as an excuse to run away from my problems—"

"You mean Emma," Will inserted.

George ignored the footnote as he continued, "—then work was only going to be a distraction. And you were right. I needed to admit my feelings for her and stop running away."

"Your point?"

"No point. Just an observation," George said with a self-satisfied sigh as he turned to stare at the same spot in the distance that had held Will's attention a moment before.

Will glared at him. "I liked you better when you weren't so smug."

George laughed.

Another minute passed before Will cleared his throat. "You go ahead. I think I'm going to stick around for another day or two. Check on a couple of things out in Montauk."

"Right. Makes sense," George said as he pulled out the valet ticket from his pocket. "I guess I'll see you back in the city, then." Then he threw his friend another smile. "And tell Lizzy I said hello."

CHAPTER 19

"Okay, tell me what you think of this one," Kitty said, leaning across the bakery's counter to hand Lizzy a small piece of oddly colored pastry.

Lizzy hesitated. "Is it supposed to be that green?"

Her sister nodded eagerly.

They had both been there for hours while the latest summer rainstorm raged outside, keeping almost all customers away. Kitty's laptop was open on the counter beside her and she had been back and forth to the kitchen so many times, Lizzy had almost asked what she was up to, but she was too busy trying to forget the night before. Still, the memory managed to pop up at the most inopportune moments, making her cringe. God, had she really endured an entire evening with Will Darcy and his insufferable aunt and not come away with one new bit of information about Charlie?

"Go ahead. Try it," Kitty said, eyeing the seaweed-colored blob in Lizzy's palm. "It's matcha and almond butter."

Lizzy braced herself as she took a bite. She had barely closed her mouth before she gagged.

Kitty's expression deflated. "That bad?"

"Are those ginger crystals in the icing?" Lizzy asked, forcing herself to swallow.

"I was experimenting."

"With muffin flavors?"

"No. With cakes," Kitty said.

"But we don't sell cakes."

"That's the point," Kitty replied, eyes lighting up again. "Last year, cake sales represented twenty-five percent of the bakery market in the U.S. alone, and we don't sell any! Just muffins and breads and the same old, same old. We're missing an entire revenue stream."

Lizzy discreetly threw the rest of the cake in the bin beneath the register. "Have you talked to Dad about any of this?"

"Not yet."

"Why not?"

"Because I've been busy."

"Working on your top secret business plan?" Lizzy asked, smiling.

"It's not top secret," Kitty replied, even as she closed her laptop. "I just want my ideas to be perfect and organized before I show anyone. Besides, Dad only listens to you when it comes to the bakery."

"That's not true," Lizzy said. "You suggested those new recyclable cups for the coffee."

Kitty rolled her eyes. "Cups? Spare me. This place might as well be yours."

Lizzy tried to brush off the comment, but it snagged someplace deep in her chest. Suddenly Birdie's words from the night before roared back to life.

I'm jealous of you being able to just work at your family bakery and never having to think about it.

It had hurt, not only because she said it out loud, but that she was right. Lizzy never had to think about it, and neither did anyone else. Everyone took for granted that she was the Bennet sister who would take all of this over, so much so, they had started to assume it was what she wanted.

Except that wasn't true. Will hadn't.

You don't decide to be a foreign affairs journalist just so you can stay in one place forever.

Lizzy had wanted to answer him, to say he was right, even though she hated to admit it. But it felt too honest. She had already revealed too much as it was. She wasn't sure now if the regret was much better.

"What's wrong?" Kitty asked.

Lizzy paused. "What do you mean?"

"You have that weird wrinkle between your eyebrows," she said, pointing to Lizzy's face. "You only have that when you're stressed about something."

"I'm not stressed, and I have no wrinkles," Lizzy replied, batting her hand away. She hoped it sounded convincing.

Apparently it didn't, because Kitty's expression turned stricken. "Is it that bad?"

Lizzy knew what she meant. Bennet Bakery looked like it was back to its former pre–tropical storm glory, but they hadn't truly recovered. "There's still a lot of damage. And the insurance company is pushing back on a lot of the claims, so we don't have the funds to cover some expenses. And with the summer ending soon . . ." Lizzy shrugged.

"It's going to be okay, though, right? I mean, we have insurance, so . . ."

Her sister's voice trailed off, but the question was there in the silence. *Is the bakery going to survive this?* Lizzy had been asking herself the same question every day since she'd deferred her enrollment to Columbia to help keep it afloat. Yes, her father looked better than he had in those weeks following his stroke, but it was hard to tell if it was a full recovery, let alone if a full recovery was possible. And even if it was, would it be enough? Would anything? Lizzy almost wanted to laugh.

Kitty's expression stopped her. Despite the fact that it was like a second home to them, no one in the Bennet family thought of the bakery as more than a source of income. At least, that's what Lizzy had always assumed. But now, as Kitty's face grew more anxious with each moment of silence that passed, she wondered if that assessment was true.

Lizzy forced a smile. "It's going to be okay, Kitty. I promise."

The words felt hollow, but it didn't matter. Kitty didn't seem to notice as she relaxed.

"Why don't you leave early?" Lizzy offered. "No one else is coming in with all this rain. You can take the truck. I'll lock up and have Piper pick me up before her shift."

Kitty's eyes lit up. "Are you sure?"

"Yeah. Just flip off the open sign on your way out."

Her sister didn't have to be told twice. She grabbed her bag and laptop, then maneuvered her way around the counter toward the kitchen. A moment later, Lizzy heard the back door slam shut, and then silence.

The rain made a steady cadence on the roof above as Lizzy made her way to the kitchen, too, and began cleaning up the mess her sister had left in her wake. Sealing up the bag of flour, wiping down the cutting boards, sorting the tins. There was a rhythm to it, one that calmed her mind for the first time all day.

Then the bell above the front door rang out through the bakery. *Damn it.*

"Sorry, we're closed," Lizzy said as she stuck her head out the kitchen doorway.

Will Darcy was standing in the middle of the room, taking

off the hood of his black rain jacket, which only made his blue eyes more vibrant.

"Hi," she said, her gaze darting behind him to see who else was there. But the threshold was empty. "We're closed."

"You mentioned that," he replied, unzipping his rain jacket and folding it over one of the nearby chairs. How his navy blue T-shirt and jeans managed to stay completely dry made no sense.

"Right, well, hopefully you remember where the door is, too," she said, hiding the sting of the words behind a plastic smile.

He didn't reply, just stood there, staring at her.

I don't have time for this, she thought. She grabbed a few pie boxes from the counter and carried them through the door to the kitchen.

Her heart was thundering in her chest as she dropped the boxes on the long steel island. God, what was wrong with her? All she had to do was finish cleaning up the kitchen and eventually he would leave.

With newfound resolve, she turned around, only to slam into a tall, broad figure looming over her.

She yelped only a second before realizing it was Will, standing there with the rest of the pie boxes from the front room in his hands.

"What the hell are you doing?" Lizzy asked.

He ignored her, placing the boxes down next to the others as he surveyed the empty kitchen. "You're here alone? Is that safe?"

"Why, are you worried about tall blond-haired men in raincoats coming in and harassing me?"

"I'm serious."

"Me, too," she said. "The kitchen is for employees. Customers belong out front."

"I thought you said you were closed."

"I am. I mean, I did. We are. I—" She closed her eyes to regain her composure. He was standing too close; she couldn't think straight. "You can leave now."

He didn't move. "I need to talk to you."

Her stomach flipped at his tone, the octave so low it felt almost intimate. "I'm pretty sure we covered everything last night, Will."

"We didn't."

She lifted her chin. "Oh really? Then what's the problem?"

The line of his brow hardened as he took a step toward her. "The problem is . . ."

His voice dropped off as his head fell forward and his hands went to his hips. The air felt charged, and she was suddenly aware that they were alone together in a windowless room with the smells of sweet baked bread lingering in the air.

He sighed, but it was another moment before he looked up, glaring at her from under his brow.

"You," he finally murmured.

She blinked. "What?"

"You distract me," he said, each syllable articulated so they felt sharp and heavy.

She narrowed her eyes on him. "Is this a joke?"

Confusion flashed across his face. "Excuse me?"

"I could have sworn you just went out of your way to come into my bakery while I'm working to tell me that *I* distract *you*."

A muscle in his jaw ticked as he stared at her. "Are you mocking me?"

There it was again. That tone. Warm and low, vibrating down to her core. She tried to ignore it as she crossed her arms over her chest. "Depends. Did you only come here to insult me?"

"No, of course not."

"Then why are you here?"

He cursed under his breath, closing his eyes for a moment like she was the one trying his patience. "I don't know."

"You don't know," she repeated slowly.

"Yes. And that's the problem," he said through gritted teeth. "You distract me so I can't think straight. I'm not even supposed to be here right now. I should be in the city, dealing with work, but instead I'm here. With you. There are a thousand other things I need to be thinking about every day, but all I think about is you."

The words felt like they were reverberating in the air, hitting some deep part of her chest so she felt them before her brain even processed what they were.

A moment passed, then her mouth fell open. "But . . . you hate me."

He stared at her from under the hard line of his brow. "I don't hate you."

She lifted her chin, determined not to look away as her breath hitched. "Well, I hate you."

She meant for the words to come out cold and biting, but her voice ended up breathless, almost like a whisper. He heard it, too, and his eyes darkened.

"I don't believe you," he said.

"I don't care."

His gaze traveled across her face, as if looking for another tell. Then he took a step forward. "Then tell me to leave again."

They were so close now that she could feel his breath on her cheeks. For a second she thought he would pull back, let her go. And a realization shuddered through her pulse: she didn't want him to.

"Don't tell me what to do," she whispered as her eyes darted to his mouth.

His blue eyes flared with something white-hot. She was about to speak again, more words already forming on her tongue, but his kiss cut her off, hungry and deep and clouding her mind before she could recall what she was even going to say. She didn't even try. The kiss was too good, too all-consuming. All she could focus on was the feel of his tongue sliding into her mouth, the smell of sandalwood and leather and salt overwhelming her senses as he pressed his body against hers.

His hand was cradling her jaw, angling her face as he deepened the kiss, and a guttural moan escaped her lips. She should have been embarrassed. She should have already pushed him away. But instead her arms found their way around his neck, pulling him closer.

The action made him groan, and suddenly he was lifting her up to sit on the steel table, slotting himself between her legs. He moved against her, holding her as she arched into him. Their bodies were flush as he moved his hand behind her head to grip her thick red hair. His other hand moved down her side, wrapping around her thigh so tightly she gasped and ran her fingers down his back. Suddenly, it was frenetic as they groped each other, every kiss more desperate than the one before.

"What are you doing to me?" he breathed against her lips.

Her head fell back, allowing his mouth to travel down her jaw to her neck. Something had snapped, and she no longer had control over her body. Her skin felt hot and alive, and it was so overwhelming that she almost didn't hear as he continued.

"I hate this," he murmured against the shell of her ear, his voice barely above a growl. "I hate how much I need this . . ."

The words rang in her head, cold and hard. His lips came up to meet hers again, but she leaned back, avoiding his kiss. "What did you just say?"

He blinked. "What?"

She pushed him away from her, and he allowed it, but only enough to open a few inches between them. "You just said you hate this."

He kept both hands splayed on the counter on either side of her hips as his brow furrowed. "No. I said I hate how much I need this."

"And you don't hear how insulting that is?"

"What, the fact that I hate feeling out of control?" His blue eyes narrowed and that muscle in his jaw twitched again. "That I'm so distracted by you that I can barely function? Do you think that's a choice?"

The words hit her chest, stealing her breath for a moment. She didn't want this, either, she knew that, but hearing it out loud felt like a deep cut where she was most vulnerable.

She let out a short, dry laugh. "Wow, Will. You really know how to make a girl feel special."

"I'm trying to be honest."

"God, I hate that," she said, shaking her head. "I hate when people say something cruel but dress it up as truth. Being honest doesn't excuse you for being a self-serving asshole, Will."

"Would you rather that I lied?"

"Isn't that what you've been doing anyway?"

He reeled back. "What the hell is that supposed to mean?"

"Where is Charlie?" she exclaimed, her arms flying out at her sides. "He tells Jane he loves her and then he just leaves? You're seriously going to keep pretending like you don't know what happened?"

Will frowned. "You want to know what happened? I'll tell you. Charlie follows a predictable pattern. He falls for someone, he gets hurt, and he looks to me to fix it. So I did. After what happened on the Fourth, he wanted to go back to the city. I made sure he stayed there. The further away he was from Jane, the faster he'd be able to move on. He was heartbroken."

"So was Jane!" Lizzy's voice rang through the kitchen, reverberating off the metal trays and cement walls. "And if he really loved her so much, he would have stuck around to realize that."

"He left because she didn't feel the same way."

Lizzy's mouth fell open. "Don't you dare blame my sister when leaving is all you people do."

He stilled. "What?"

"You, Charlie—all of you come out here looking for a change, but end up acting exactly the same way! You find a local who keeps you distracted for the summer so you don't have to think about how boring your lives are back in the city. Then September rolls around and you go back to those boring lives because none of this was real anyway, right? Just part of the vacation."

He leaned forward again, glaring at her from under his brow. "You don't know me."

"Oh, I know exactly who you are. You're the man who took time out of his day to come to my bakery to tell me I was an inconvenience. You're the man who promised to help his friend who had nothing, just to turn around and take it away the minute you felt like it."

Will's back straightened, and his hands went to his hips. "Excuse me?"

"Tristan Cole. Ring a bell? He told me everything."

"Tristan?" He looked genuinely shocked. "What the hell does he have to do with this?"

"He's working to get a music festival in East Hampton off the ground. Unless you decide to sabotage that, too?" She leaned forward, poking a finger at his chest. "Well, you might think all your money means you get to play with people like Tristan, but

I'm not fucking disposable, Will. Neither is my sister. And we're not interested in being tools used by people like you to work out your shit."

He gently pushed her finger down to her lap. "I think that's enough." His eyes were cold again, his expression blank. Whatever fire had been burning there only a few minutes before was gone. "Apologies for my lapse in judgment. It won't happen again."

She slid off the table and stood in front of him with her arms crossed over her chest. Her lips were raw, her mind was enraged, and there were tears ready to explode, but she refused to let him see it. "Good. Now get the hell out of my bakery."

He opened his mouth to speak, but shut it again, his jaw tightening. Then he turned and disappeared through the kitchen door. Lizzy stared at the empty space in front of her, listening to his footsteps, to the bell ring as the front door slammed shut behind him. Then she sank to the floor.

CHAPTER 20

The rain had finally stopped and it was almost dark by the time Will turned onto Old Montauk Highway. His car flew past the low trees and brush silhouetted against the darkening sky, weaving its way down to the cracked asphalt as the road's two lanes became an ambiguous one. He rolled down the windows, letting in the cold evening air. The sterile smell of the leather interior was lost in the overwhelming scent of ocean salt. God, he had missed this. He took a deep breath, and for the first time in an hour, felt his pulse begin to slow.

After leaving the bakery—and Elizabeth Bennet—behind, Will had debated going back to the city. But then his mind filled with a thousand obligations waiting for him there, and he could think of only one place he could go to get away from all of them.

The road ended abruptly and he turned right, down the private drive almost completely hidden by overgrown sumac trees and switchgrass. Despite knowing this journey by heart, he still turned on his headlights, dissolving the shadows left by the low branches on either side.

A slight curve to the left, a hard right, and then, there it was.

The scaffold that had surrounded the house for months had finally been dismantled last week, so the shingle siding, gray and weathered from years of exposure to sea air, made the house glow against the purple-and-orange sky. Two stories, with a sloped roof interrupted by a number of windows peeking out in all directions—one of which he'd broken when he tried to sneak out in eighth grade. Slate floors in the kitchen, with one loose tile in the far corner where his dad used to hide messages for him to find. A porch that wrapped around the back, facing the cliffside and the ocean beyond. It was a view he had loved since childhood, a permanent thing he assumed would be there forever.

It will be. Just not for you, a voice inside his head murmured.

He cut the engine and went inside.

The house was large—probably bigger than Charlie's rental—but deceptively so thanks to low ceilings and a maze of cozy rooms spread across both floors. Will dropped his keys on the small table by the front door and passed the beadboard-paneled walls lined with family photos on his way to the living room. It was spacious, with a hulking stone fireplace along the far wall and a piano in the opposite corner. In the center there was a worn leather sofa flanked by two armchairs. They had been red once, but thanks to years of use and sun, they had faded to a muted pink. Behind them was a bookcase, his destination. His father had kept his liquor on the top shelf—a joke that he repeated to anyone who would listen—but Will had never been a fan of whiskey or gin, so it had been neglected over the past few years.

But not now. Right now, Will needed scotch.

He reached up and grabbed the first bottle he could find and poured himself a glass, then took a deep sip.

The taste of smoke and peat filled his mouth, and he swallowed before he could think to spit it out. Jesus, how the hell did people drink this shit? Then a vision of Elizabeth flashed through his head again, the look she gave him right before she kicked him out of the bakery.

He downed the rest of his drink and poured himself another before taking the glass and the bottle outside to the back porch.

Red cedar trees crowded the yard, but there was still a clear view of the cliff's edge and the ocean below. It was dark now, too dark to see the waves, but he could hear them crashing along the beach. He was tempted to take his whiskey down the old wooden staircase to the water, but he could already feel the alcohol taking hold. If he went down now, he'd never find his way back up tonight, especially after the rain. So instead, he landed in one of the chairs situated on the porch and watched the branches of the trees sway against the dark sky.

He would miss this house. Birdie had been talking about selling it and the surrounding land for years, but suddenly the thought felt new and raw. He had always tried to control every element of life, to mitigate its ups and downs for everyone he loved. After his parents died, the desire had become all-consuming, so much so that it sometimes felt like pieces of himself were being broken off, limb by limb. But this house was more than a limb. It was the beating heart. The center of a life he had built himself around, that had built him. The last bits of his father, the last memories with his mother. All of it was here. Maybe that's why he had insisted on renovating it this summer, a way to delay the inevitable.

Do you want to sell it? Elizabeth's voice filled his head again.

He closed his eyes and let his head fall back. How could she do that? With one question, one look, everything else in his tightly controlled world fell away. She understood the core of this. She understood him.

No. She hated him. He had to remind himself of that before he let his mind wander.

And yet . . .

She had still kissed him back today. She had wanted him, and for a moment, a single fleeting moment, it had been perfect.

But then her voice rang through his head again.

Being honest doesn't excuse you for being a self-serving asshole, Will.

He took another sip of his drink and winced.

She was right; he was an asshole. And maybe it didn't matter that his version of self-serving only meant putting the ones he cared about first, because in the end, someone she cared about was still collateral damage.

But Tristan . . . that was another story. How had that asshole found his way into her life? Was he truly interested in her, or was he using her to get to him? Will shook his head. Did it even matter? Regardless of the reason, Tristan was there, spreading lies and further cementing Elizabeth's vitriol. Perhaps she even had real feelings for him. But if he was using her as a pawn in this . . .

Fuck it, Will thought, throwing back the rest of his drink.

If he couldn't defend himself on the first count, he sure as hell would lay out the facts about the second.

He pulled his cell phone from his pocket and took a moment to focus on the screen before opening his browser. The Bennet Bakery website looked like it was stuck in the early aughts, with two pages not even loading properly. But Will finally found the contact information on the bottom of the menu page.

It was the whiskey's fault that it took him four tries to tap the number. It was also the whiskey's fault that he didn't hesitate when his screen prompted him: *Do you want to call?*

He just tapped yes.

The phone rang three times before connecting. After a mechanical click, Lizzy's voice filled the line.

"Hi! You've reached Bennet Bakery. We're either busy or closed, but if you leave a message, we'll get back to you when we're not busy or closed. Thanks!"

He recognized her familiar tone, soft and uneven, like a cashmere sweater with a snag down the front. But it was different, too. Lighter somehow, and not just because she sounded slightly younger. It took him a moment to recognize why.

She was happy. The smile was evident in her voice, and at the end she even stifled a laugh. That was why it sounded so foreign—because she was never happy when she was talking to him.

It hurt, but the pain was usurped by a loud *BEEP*, the cue to start speaking.

"Hello, this message is for Elizabeth Bennet. Elizabeth, this is Will. Darcy. This is Will Darcy. I don't have your cell number or I would have called you directly. I also don't have an email address or I would have written to you. You really should have an email on your bakery's website, or at least a contact form."

Damn it. He was already messing this up.

He squeezed his eyes shut and powered on. "All that to say, my first choice wasn't a voicemail. But you said you were the only one who checks this, and I don't have any other way to contact you. I don't do social media, and regardless . . ." He stopped himself, focusing on the words he needed to say. "I'm not looking to relive what just happened. I'm over it, as I'm sure you are, too. But you leveled some serious accusations against me. And it's important that you know the truth."

He took a deep breath. "I don't know how you and Tristan know each other, and I know you will say it's none of my business, but I know him. I have known him since I was fifteen. We were best friends in high school. After graduation, I went to Columbia, but Tristan claimed he had to save up for tuition before applying to college, so I promised to help him find a job. I called my dad, and . . ." Will's hand bracketed his temples, massaging away the memory. "My dad liked Tristan. He wanted to help. So he gave him a position at his firm, he mentored him. Gave him access to clients most people only dream of . . ."

He swallowed and closed his eyes. "Then, a few years later, my parents were in California, driving through the mountains. It was late and snowing . . . and . . . they got in a car accident, and I lost them both."

He opened his eyes again and took a deep breath. "I took a leave of absence from work to help organize their estate. It was all so sudden; everything was a mess. So I took it all on. That's when I found the emails, the credit card statements, the loans . . ."

He stood up again and began pacing the deck.

"My father was a good man. And Tristan manipulated that. Made up stories about his family, his situation, even about me, to get money from my dad. Hundreds of thousands of dollars that he spent on vacations and clothes and God knows what. Then he didn't even come to my parents' funeral." Will stopped, taking a breath. "I confronted him afterward. And he just laughed it off. Like it was some sort of joke. He knew he hadn't technically broken the law, so there was nothing I could do. And he was right. But I still had my attorneys lock all my father's accounts, cancel his credit cards. If you don't believe me, I can have them contact you. The firm is Page, Lefroy, and Brandon. They have everything on file."

Will shook his head. "I don't know what he told you, but that is Tristan Cole. He is a liar and he uses people. And if you had bothered to ask me about any of this, I could have told you the truth in person. We could have avoided all—"

BEEP, the answering machine cut him off.

"Damn it!" he bellowed, his head falling back.

Then he turned back to his glowing screen and pressed the number again.

Three rings. A click.

"Hi! You've reached Bennet Bakery. We're either busy or closed, but if you leave a message, we'll get back to you when we're not busy or closed. Thanks!"

He glared down at his feet. "Hello, this message is for Elizabeth Bennet. Elizabeth, this is Will. My first message was cut off before I could finish, and I just wanted to say . . ."

His voice faded as he looked up. The branches were still swaying above his head, their leaves rustling together in a sound that seemed to mimic the beach break.

"I'm sorry if Tristan lied to you about me. And I'm sorry that I have to be the one to tell you." Another moment before he continued, "But I can't apologize for Charlie, or for finding a reason to keep him in New York after we left. He's been hurt before, and he didn't deserve that again. I'm just sorry if it hurt your sister. Or . . . you."

The leaves rolled above him. He closed his eyes and listened, breathing in the smell of salt and pine as his mind swayed from the whiskey.

"I hurt you, didn't I?" The words came at the same time as the realization. "And it doesn't matter that you kissed me back. I called you a mess. I said I hated how much I needed you. I've been so focused on controlling everything in my life, that you . . . this . . . I don't know what the hell I'm doing anymore." He let his head fall forward again. "I know we'll probably never see each other again. But I need you to know . . . you matter, Lizzy. You're not just the redhead. And you're not a mess. I wish I had told you that. I wish—"

BEEP, the answering machine cut him off again.

CHAPTER 21

The beach was quiet at five a.m. The soft predawn glow illuminated the skies, while the rising sun still hid behind the horizon. Lizzy was the only one crushing the surf this early and she was grateful for the solitude. She rode wave after wave, determined to get lost in her happy place. Last night's rain had left behind icy waters and near-perfect swells, and that was exactly what she needed to quiet her ruminating mind.

But every time she licked the salt water off her swollen lips, she couldn't help but remember Will Darcy and what he had said the night before.

. . . all I think about is you.

And then her mind would wander to what he had done. His grip in her hair, his kiss on her mouth, his body between her legs . . .

I hate how much I need this.

She shook her head, forcing the memory to the back of her mind as a wave sent from the heavens approached.

She paddled hard. But as she tried to stand, she lost her balance and the board shot out from beneath her as her tether pulled her under the surface for one chaotic moment. She let it happen just like she always did, staying calm while her body tumbled underneath the surface. Eventually there was a break in the surf, and she was able to pop up and take a cleansing breath of cool ocean air before the rough waters pulled her under again.

The Atlantic finally spat her out close to the beach and she found her footing. She stood up coughing and gasping for breath as she made her way to shore. She was a bit shaken, but okay. When she looked up to take stock of her surroundings, her eyes narrowed, furious that the one place she hoped would catch fire and crumble into the sea was right in front of her. Marv's Lament stood tall like an indestructible cement giant, as obnoxious as ever.

"Ah, screw you, too," she murmured.

The tide had unexpectedly pushed her down the coast, so the walk back to her car with her board would take forever. She'd barely have enough time to change out of her wetsuit before the bakery opened.

She stomped along the beach, her bare feet sinking into the wet sand, trying hard not to think of Will Darcy again. But the more she fought the impulse, the more pissed off she got. What was she even thinking last night? Apparently, she needed to get out more, because she clearly had no self-control, and being alone in a room with a hot guy made her fold like a deck chair.

The alarm on her watch went off just as she was loading her board into the flatbed of her truck. Thank God she had to work today. For the first time in ages, she was grateful for the bakery's tedious routine—the prep, the paperwork, the same predictable dilemmas and issues. She could get lost in it, forget what had happened the day before. And she could relish the fact that she never had to hear that deep voice ever again.

~

Lizzy stared at the wall of the bakery's office, eyes wide and phone in hand, as Will's voice murmured in her ear.

"*You're not just the redhead. And you're not a mess. I wish I had told you that. I wish—*" Then he was cut off by a sharp click.

The answering machine continued on to the next message— their neighbor Mrs. Stoll wanted to put in an order for blueberry muffins—but Lizzy wasn't listening. She could only focus on the blank wall ahead, as Will Darcy's voicemails played on repeat in her mind, echoing back over each other so the details were lost and all that was left was his gravelly voice and her own confusion.

"The timer went off on the . . ." Her father stalked into the office, pausing when he saw the expression on Lizzy's face. "The insurance company call again?"

She jumped, snapping out of her trance.

"What? No! It's nothing!" she replied with a bit too much eagerness.

His brow furrowed. "You sure?"

"It's just Mrs. Stoll. And muffins." Then she slapped the phone down and gave him a wide smile.

He obviously wasn't convinced, but he also didn't seem to care enough to prod her for the truth, either. "Scones are ready for an egg wash. I'll finish up the sourdough."

She nodded and stood, then quickly reached over and pressed delete on the answering machine before walking out into the kitchen.

Muscle memory got her through the morning. Meanwhile, her mind was reeling. Will's story was too convoluted and detailed not to be at least partially accurate, but which parts? Of the two men, who was to be believed?

Once the morning rush was over, she spent the rest of her shift doing the only thing she could think of: googling both Will and

Tristan to see if she could glean any information. In between customers and her father's requests, she scrolled through search results on her phone, combing through pictures. Tristan's name produced thousands of results, but oddly, there didn't seem to be any about his actual business acumen. Instead, there was a never-ending list of social media posts with pictures from different parties around New York, always with a different woman on his arm. Regardless of the truth, it was clear that he was no Lord Magnus. Not in the slightest.

Meanwhile, Will was harder to find. The first information to pop up was about his family, along with articles about their house in Montauk. A few recent articles mentioned his name alongside numerous charitable contributions large enough to make her eyes water. It was only when she stumbled upon his parents' obituary in the *New York Times* that guilt overwhelmed her curiosity and she put her phone away.

When she got home, she bypassed her mother in the kitchen and headed straight upstairs. She could hear Jane across the hall, but Lizzy didn't stop to say hello as she turned into her room and fell into her bed. She couldn't tell her sister what had happened with Will at the bakery, especially when it would only bring up the memory of Charlie. And the Tristan news . . . that felt dangerous, unwieldy.

So instead, she screamed into her pillow.

"Was work really that bad?"

Lizzy looked up to find Jane in the doorway. Her hair was pulled back in a long braid, and she was wearing the same oversized *Star Trek* T-shirt she'd had since grade school.

"No," Lizzy said, hauling her body up to sit on the edge of her bed.

"Just screaming into your pillow for fun, then."

"It's therapeutic. Like yoga or running into oncoming traffic."

Jane let out a soft laugh, but it was cut short by their mother yelling at Lydia downstairs.

Lizzy groaned, then motioned her sister toward the bedroom window. Jane nodded.

The evening air was warm as they crawled out onto the roof's black asphalt shingles. They laid out a blanket and Jane took one side while Lizzy took the other, sitting with her back against the house and letting the rays of the setting sun stroke her face.

"So," Jane said after a minute, "are you going to tell me what's wrong, or am I going to have to withhold my latest romance novel?"

Lizzy didn't reply.

"Are you sure?" Jane asked, leaning in with a smile. "It involves fairies. And a mating bond."

Lizzy laughed, but the sound came out low and wistful before it faded. She let the silence expand between them a moment longer before saying, "I got a weird message on the answering machine at work."

"From who?"

"Will Darcy."

Jane's face lit up. "Was he calling to ask you out?"

"No," Lizzy said. The fact that this wasn't too far away from the truth wasn't lost on her, but she still ignored it.

"Okay, then what did he want?"

The full litany of Will's confession was waiting on her tongue, but Lizzy swallowed it down, sticking to the one fact she needed to unpack. "He wanted to warn me about Tristan."

Jane's expression contorted with confusion. "Warn you?"

Lizzy let the story tumble out. Every detail that Will had revealed, every aspect it changed about Tristan's history. Saying it out loud only made her admit to herself how wrong she truly had been about Tristan. And Will, for that matter. She groaned and let her head fall into her hands.

Jane stared out at the treetops, stunned, before turning to look at her sister again. "Maybe it's all a big misunderstanding."

Lizzy shook her head. "Nope. In true Will Darcy fashion, he provided witnesses. An entire law firm, in fact."

"Wow." Jane's eyes grew wide as she considered. "I mean, I'm not Tristan's biggest fan after he broke your heart like that—"

"He didn't break my heart! We never even went on a date."

"—but I still thought he was a nice guy. He's helping Hank, and everyone seems to love him."

"I know." Lizzy gnawed on her bottom lip. "Should we say something to them?"

"I don't know. Will really only told you."

"Technically, he told the bakery."

"You know what I mean," Jane replied. "It's not public knowledge. We can't just go around town gossiping about it."

"True. Everyone would think I was making it up to be petty anyway." Lizzy groaned, letting her head fall back. "How is he so good at pretending to be a nice guy?"

"It's not *that* hard."

"Well, that's encouraging."

Jane laughed softly. "I just mean, being nice is easy. Anyone can pretend to be nice. But there's a difference between being nice and being kind."

"Which is?"

"Kindness takes effort. It can have rough edges and it can be impolite, but it's still genuine and good. But if you're nice . . ." Jane offered a shrug. "Well, you can be nice to someone and still stab them in the back, right? It just means when you do it, you might have a smile on your face."

Lizzy stared out over the rooftop, letting the words rattle in her brain until they settled in uncomfortable corners.

"I just don't get why Will called you now," Jane said after a minute. "The Tristan thing was so long ago, and Will hasn't been back out here in weeks."

Oh God.

"Well . . . that's not exactly true," Lizzy said.

"What do you mean?"

"I saw him a couple of days ago. At Marv's Lament."

Jane's brows pinched together, waiting for Lizzy to continue.

"I would have told you but . . . Charlie wasn't with him and . . ." She was so busy trying to police her words that they came out disjointed and jumbled.

"Then why was he there?" Jane asked.

Lizzy gnawed on her bottom lip before answering. "Because his aunt is helping them sublet the house."

It seemed to take a moment to sink in. Then Jane turned to look out at the horizon. The sun had fallen behind the neighboring houses, casting her profile in an array of yellows and pinks and grays. "Oh."

Lizzy opened her mouth to speak, then shut it again. She couldn't tell Jane the full extent of what Will had said. Jane would blame herself, and Lizzy refused to let that happen.

Another minute passed, then her sister's voice broke the silence. "I'm never going to see him again, am I?"

Jane sounded so small, so broken, and Lizzy's heart fell like a deadweight in her chest. "If Charlie really loves you, you will."

Jane nodded, looking back up at the darkening sky. "I've always thought that if you really love someone, nothing can stand in the way of it. You move mountains to make it work. But maybe, sometimes, love isn't enough. And that's okay."

A different kind of ache tightened Lizzy's chest. She had seen her sister heartbroken before, but this wasn't heartbreak; it was acquiescence. And she hated it.

"Besides, we always have that mansion with the cats waiting, right?" Jane continued, offering a watery smile.

Lizzy tried to match it. "Right."

Jane sighed. "In the meantime, how do you feel about Montauk?"

"Is there a vacant mansion you've got your eye on in Montauk?"

Jane let herself laugh softly. "No, but I do have a nonrefundable weekend booked at a motel on the beach next month."

Crap. How had Lizzy forgotten? She had helped Jane plan her weekend with Charlie, even split the motel reservation across their two credit cards. She groaned as her head fell forward.

"Oh, stop," Jane said. "It could be fun. You can surf; I can catch up on lesson plans. It'll be the perfect girls' getaway before we commit to something more permanent. And dilapidated."

Lizzy laughed, pushing a few errant strands of hair from her face. "I'll think about it."

Jane nodded, then rested her head on Lizzy's shoulder. "Good."

Another long moment passed. The cicadas had started to sing, blending with the muffled sound of the television downstairs.

Then Jane's soft voice finally spoke again. "So . . . how did Will look?"

Lizzy rolled her eyes. "Can we stop talking about Will Darcy, please?"

"If that's what you want."

Lizzy could hear the grin in her sister's voice. "I don't know what I want anymore," she replied.

The all-consuming anger she felt toward Will was fading, as his words, so raw and honest, replayed in her mind.

You matter, Lizzy . . . I wish I had told you that.

Maybe he was right. Maybe she did matter. But the fact that Will Darcy was the only person who might ever notice was a bitter pill to swallow.

After the sun had completely set and a chill settled into the air, the sisters headed back inside. Lizzy waited until she heard Jane close her bedroom door across the hall before she grabbed her laptop and went to sit on her bed. There was a long list of documents on her desktop: Numerous drafts of her application to Columbia. Information about GREs. Her acceptance letter. And there, just below it, the email outlining the terms of her deferment. She opened it, reading over the details again, how they were only allowing her to push back her enrollment for a semester, how it was contingent on whether a spot was available. And how she needed to confirm that she would be attending next spring by October 1, or she would forfeit the opportunity.

At the beginning of the summer, that date had seemed so far away, but now, with the season almost over, it felt like she had no time left at all.

How would she ensure that her father was well enough for her to leave before then? Or figure out what to do about the bakery, and make a plan to ensure that her family would be okay without her . . . ? It felt impossible.

Lizzy lay back on her bed. The same bed she'd inherited from Jane in high school. The walls still had the same pink paisley wallpaper, the same travel posters. Nothing had changed in years.

And maybe, she thought as she reached over and closed her computer, it was finally time to start accepting that.

CHAPTER 22

When Labor Day arrived in East Hampton, tradition dictated that locals congregate at Donato's for everyone's favorite holiday of the season: Get the Hell Outta Town Day. This year was no different.

"Good riddance!" Hank Donato bellowed from behind the bar, raising his pint to the window as a steady stream of Mercedes and Land Rovers crawled by, heading west. The rest of the bar cheered, and somewhere on the far side of the room, someone started an off-key rendition of "Na Na Hey Hey Kiss Him Goodbye."

None of them really minded the weekenders. If they were being honest, Lizzy knew most of them would say they might even miss them. Sure, it was nice to have their town back again, to be able to drive down Main Street in five minutes instead of twenty, and not to share the beach with a half dozen influencer photo shoots. But the end of season also meant that the locals' main source of income was gone. So many of their jobs, their businesses, existed because of the people who summered there every year. Now it would be a matter of hunkering down and surviving until next Memorial Day. Bennet Bakery was no different.

But today marked another milestone, too, one Lizzy hadn't dared say out loud: Charlie had never come back.

And neither had Will.

Not that she wanted him to. In fact, Lizzy had been plotting out what she would say to him if he did. How she would balance all these new emotions and still play it cool. But that chance never came. And now the summer was over. Temperatures were already dipping below sixty at night. Jane was getting ready to welcome a new class of first graders this week. The gossip mill was even whispering about how a team had already been hired to winterize Marv's Lament.

"Hello, Earth to Lizzy," Piper said, cutting off her train of thought.

"I'm listening," Lizzy said, her head lolling to one side as she turned to her friend standing behind the bar.

"Okay, what did I just say?"

"That you've come to your senses and decided not to abandon me for grad school next week?" Lizzy said, smiling brightly.

"Not even close. And today's Monday, so technically I'm leaving *this* week. My first class is on Thursday."

"Boo." Lizzy's chin fell into her hand.

Piper smiled. "Boston isn't that far. You can come up to visit me whenever you want. Sasha's apartment has a spare room."

"And be a third wheel on your new domestic bliss?" Lizzy replied, mock-condemnation in her voice. "I wouldn't dare."

"So what are you going to do?"

"Console myself with a second basket of Tater Tots," she replied, popping the last one from her current basket into her mouth.

Piper laughed and replaced the basket with a fresh one. Then an odd silence filled the space.

"You okay?" she finally asked.

Lizzy shrugged. "It's going to be weird not having you around."

"You survived when I was at Fordham for four years."

"Yeah, but you were just in the city and came back home every weekend. This feels like you're moving on and I'm just . . . here."

Piper watched her, then said slowly, "Want some advice?"

"Not really," Lizzy said, taking another sip of beer.

"You should start writing again. You're such a good writer, Lizzy, and last year you were talking about graduate school. I know it's been tough since the stroke, but your dad is doing so much better. And you've got Jane here to look out for him, and Kitty seems to be taking a serious interest in the bakery. You should start putting yourself first."

"It's not that simple."

"Why not?"

Lizzy pushed her hair out of her face, trying to organize her thoughts. Piper still didn't know about Columbia, the draft email just waiting to be sent. "Even if my dad is better, one small hiccup could force him to stay home. If I'm not here, that closes the bakery. That's the family's future in limbo, my parents' mortgage in jeopardy . . . even that storm in June almost ruined us."

Piper's eyes lit up. "Wait! I have an idea!"

Lizzy's brows knitted together. "What?"

"Your family should invest in HamptonFest!"

Oh God. "Piper—"

"No, this is brilliant, trust me. My dad already put in a load of money, and Tristan thinks that once the permits come through, we'll get double the return in just a couple of years of doing the festival. Imagine what that would mean for your parents if you did that with the profits from the bakery."

Lizzy sighed. "I don't know . . ."

"What's the issue?"

"Well . . . what about Tristan?"

Piper's expression contorted with confusion. "What about him?"

Tread carefully, Lizzy thought to herself. *Tread very carefully*.

"It's just . . . are you sure you can trust him? I mean, has anyone met these connections he supposedly has to help get HamptonFest off the ground? What do any of us really know about him?"

"Is this because he blew you off?"

"No," Lizzy said, trying to keep her tone even. "But I'm not sure anyone has really looked into this guy, and—"

Piper sighed. "Lizzy, I know he ghosted you, and that sucks. But you need to stop using other people as an excuse."

"That's not what I'm doing!"

"Then what are you doing?"

Lizzy leaned forward, ready to let the whole sordid story spew out. But it wasn't hers to tell. Besides, Hank had been planning HamptonFest for years and it had never come to fruition. If there was even a chance Tristan could finally make it happen, she couldn't ruin it. So she snapped her mouth shut and just shook her head. "Nothing, apparently."

Piper's expression fell. "Lizzy—"

"It's okay," Lizzy replied, sliding off her stool. "I'm going to head home. Call me later."

Lizzy darted through the crowd inside the Lodge and stepped out through the Irish Goodbye Door to find the line of luxury cars still stretched bumper-to-bumper along Montauk Highway. She followed the sidewalk as it snaked its way toward downtown, barely looking up from her Converse. She had done this walk so many times, she could probably do it blindfolded. Something she thought was a novelty, but right now felt like a life sentence.

At the Old Hook Windmill she turned left, passing the line of boutiques on her way down Main Street. She didn't want to go home right now and deal with her mother bemoaning another summer wasted on a failed business, or Lydia complaining about her follower count. Or Jane not complaining at all. So she headed to work.

"Hey."

The deep voice startled her and she stopped in the middle of the sidewalk. Tristan was in front of her, his tall frame leaning to one side, perfectly framed by a navy polo shirt and khakis. His hair was longer than it had been the last time she saw him, and he had it slicked back.

"What a coincidence," he purred. "I was just thinking about you."

The words were low and suggestive, but sounded hollow somehow. Like someone had turned on the lights in a dark room that had flaws in each corner.

She met his gaze. "Then you should have texted."

He manufactured a wince. "I know. I've just been so crazy with work. Hounding the right people about these permits, making sure we reach out to the right contacts . . ."

He let the words fade, as if anticipating Lizzy's acquiescence. She only stared back.

"Anyway," he finally continued, "I've been busy."

"Is that why you're here?" she asked. "Because of work?"

He nodded. "That, and there were a few events over the weekend. Have you ever been to the White Party?"

"Nope," she replied flatly.

"Well, it's incredible. You should definitely grab an invite next year." Then he cleared his throat. "I'm heading back into the city today but, if you're around, I'm having a big party in a couple of weeks."

Yeah, I know, she wanted to say. *Lydia won't stop talking about it*. But instead she feigned ignorance. "Really?"

He nodded. "You should come."

"I wish I could," Lizzy said, her voice flat. "But I'll be out of town with my sister. Girls' trip."

"Ah, that's too bad," he replied, as if it wasn't really that bad at all. "Well, we should still grab a drink sometime."

His head cocked to the side as a small smile ticked up the corners of his mouth. She knew that look. It was so obvious, she was embarrassed she hadn't seen it before. It was the look of a man trying to appear charming and vulnerable even though it went against his very nature. A wolf in sheep's clothing.

She offered her own sharp smile in return. "Have a safe trip back to the city, Tristan."

Then she started down the street again, waiting until she walked into the bakery to take her phone out and block his number.

Her shift at the bakery the next day drifted by in a haze. Muscle memory was the only thing getting her through, while her mind tried to dissect this feeling monopolizing her thoughts, a feeling altogether foreign and unwelcome.

It wasn't until just before closing, as she leaned over the counter finishing the last chapter of her latest book, *The City of Shadow and Smoke*, that she was shaken from her malaise. The main character, Lady Sonia Willowdean, learns that the king wasn't really her enemy; he had been in love with her all along. Suddenly, he slides a ring on her finger and whisks her away from her solitary life to join him in his castle hidden within a chain of caves.

Then her phone pinged from her back pocket.

She pulled it out to see a text waiting from Jane.

JANE

Hey! Don't kill me but I don't think I'm going to be able to make that trip out east in a couple of weeks.

They just scheduled Back to School night for that Monday so I can't take it off. 🙁

Lizzy dropped her phone back on the counter. She probably should have felt some sort of disappointment. Anger, annoyance, *something*. But all that flashed through Lizzy's mind was surrender. Jane was moving on with her life. Piper was gone, too. Even *The City of Shadow and Smoke*'s Lady Sonia was moving on to bigger and better things. Everyone was growing up and out and away. Everyone except her.

Was there a name for the feeling of anticipating loneliness? It wasn't here yet, but she could see it there on the horizon, approaching steadily every day. What had begun as a plan to stay home for a few months to help save the bakery was now becoming her entire future. Soon her sisters would move on with their lives, her mom with another multilevel marketing scheme. And Lizzy would still be here, sneaking chapters of romance novels between batches of sour cherry muffins.

Then, another ping from her phone.

JANE

But you should still go! It's all paid for! And you need a vacation. Please?

Lizzy let the text hang there for a moment. Then she let out a long breath and typed back:

LIZZY

You suck.

And then, a moment later:

LIZZY

Send me the info.

CHAPTER 23

Lizzy watched the ocean waves crash on the shore from her small balcony at the Ocean Surf Inn as she zipped up her wetsuit. The motel wasn't anything fancy, but it felt cozy and was in a prime location along Montauk's Ditch Plains Beach. Plus, the oceanfront views from her room were spectacular.

When Lizzy was nine, her Aunt Jean and Uncle Larry had come to visit from Syracuse and told their nieces a rumor that this strip of coastline was the best place on the whole eastern seaboard to go hunting for shells. They brought all five girls here for a weekend to confirm it, renting two rooms at the Ocean Surf Inn and helping them collect sand dollars, textured scallops, whelk spirals—all in perfect form.

Lizzy smiled at the memory, then snapped a picture of the Ocean Surf Inn sign and sent it to her sisters.

THE BUTTER FACES

LIZZY

They still have the same sign.

KITTY

Oh, I love that!

JANE

Have fun—maybe you'll meet a hot surfer!

LYDIA

You both need to pull back on the romance novel meet-cutes.

JANE

Never!

LYDIA

Whatever. Lizzy, be back for Tristan's party in NYC next Saturday!

LIZZY

Hard pass. Don't go to that, Lydia.

LYDIA

Too late. Already have THE BEST outfit.

MARY

You know what's too late? Fixing the ocean's co2 levels.

Good luck finding any good shells.

LIZZY

Thanks, Mary

JANE

> Not sure why you're still texting us when there's probably
> great waves today. Go!

Jane was right. There were already a few surfers out, and it wasn't even seven a.m. Lizzy got up and shut the sliding door, then grabbed her newly waxed board on her way out of the room.

She hustled down the sand of Ditch Plains Beach and into the ocean, diving under each crashing surf with her board until she could paddle out to deeper waters. There was an etiquette to the sport when so many surfers were out there in a lineup. The one closest to the peak got priority, so Lizzy patiently waited her turn.

It was worth the wait. Each ride was smoother and longer than the last. She got into a rhythm, a zone, and lost herself completely in the pure joy of every perfect ride and forgot to keep an eye on the shoreline. When she finally looked up, she found that she had been pushed east, well past Ditch Plains Beach.

She'd never been up this far before. The way the land and the rocks extended into the ocean felt like she had reached a stretch of undiscovered coastline. The walk back would be long and treacherous along the rocky beach, but she didn't care. It was beautiful. The sun was shining and she had the waves all to herself, so she rode one after another until she collapsed in the sand with a smile on her face.

That's when she caught sight of another surfer along the beach. She sat up and watched him expertly tackle the long swells, maneuvering his board with ease until he hit the shore and went back out again.

He was good. Really good.

Guess he'll be doing the same trek back to Ditch Plains, she mused.

She lay back down against the sand, looking up at the fast-moving clouds, willing the mid-September sun to dry her off. This weekend was exactly what she needed to clear her head. She was already starting to feel like her old self again. Focused. In control. Even . . . happy.

Grabbing her board, she untethered her ankle and stood up, ready for the long walk back to the motel. The other surfer had the same idea and was starting to head in her direction. Whoever he was, he was tall—even from this distance, she could tell that much. His wetsuit clung to his long legs, the top half zipped open and hanging low around his waist, exposing his bare chest and the hint of his board shorts at his hips. As he got closer, one of his hands moved to push his blond locks out of his eyes, and Lizzy froze.

It was Will Darcy.

The soft sand of the beach suddenly felt like cement, rooting her to the spot. Her mind screamed for her to flee, but her body refused to listen. All she could do was stand there, pulse thundering in her ears, waiting for the moment when—

"Elizabeth?" Darcy's voice rang out loudly over the crashing waves. He slowed when he approached, his eyes locked on hers.

Shit.

"Hello. Hi." She gave a little wave, her board slipping out of her grip and falling forward. She cursed and grabbed it before it hit the sand. Then she straightened again, brushing her hair out of her eyes even as the wind pushed it back. "Hey."

"What are you doing here?"

"I live here. I mean, not *here*. I'm surfing here. I don't live here. I'm just visiting. Here." She breathed in deeply to stop herself from rambling. But then her gaze found his again, darting from his hair to his eyes to his lips. The memory of those lips on hers was overpowering—his hand in her hair as he held her still, what he tasted like, how he kissed her like he needed her to breathe.

Shit shit shit.

Heat shot to her cheeks as she forced a smile and pointed a thumb over her shoulder. "Okay, well, good to see you."

Then she turned, her board under her arm, and started walking along the beach away from him.

She made it four steps before his voice called out behind her.

"You can't get back to Ditch Plains that way."

She stopped. She could feel his eyes on her back, sending her pulse into an uneven staccato as every impossible option swam in her head. She could try to maneuver the rocks, or maybe take her board back out and battle the tide. But then she realized that brought up another question.

"How were you going to get back?" she asked, finally turning around.

"I wasn't."

She stared at him, her nose scrunched up, and waited for him to continue.

"My house is just up there," he said, nodding to the wooden stairs leading up the bluff.

She blinked. *Oh . . . oh my God.* "Are you telling me I just washed up in front of your house? In Montauk?"

"It would appear so."

If there was a merciful God anywhere in the universe, Lizzy prayed he would open a crack in the earth right now just below her feet and swallow her up. Unfortunately, in the long moment that followed, there was only the steady lull of the waves at her feet and the cool breeze against her flushed cheeks. God was apparently busy.

This could not possibly get any worse, she thought.

"Come on." He nodded toward the stairs. "I'll drive you back."

Never mind, she thought. *This is worse.*

"No. It's okay," she said, waving a hand in front of her. "I'll just . . . figure it out."

He stared at her for a long moment. It was like he was waiting for her to realize she was out of options.

"How will you figure it out."

It wasn't even a question. Probably because he already knew she didn't have an answer.

That realization only made her more committed to coming up with one. Or at least lying to make it sound like she did. Because the truth was too mortifying. She'd traveled alone to Montauk to stake out his beach? Now she was the one who sounded like a psychopath.

"I'm staying with my aunt and uncle over at the Ocean Surf Inn," she lied, ignoring the fact that Aunt Jean and Uncle Larry hadn't visited in years. "They'll probably come looking for me soon."

He cocked his head to the side. "Oh really?"

"Yup." She nodded, a little too enthusiastically. "We're going to Mike's Crab Shack for lunch, and I think they made reservations, so . . ."

"I didn't know Mike's Crab Shack took reservations."

Crap. Mike's might have the best seafood on Long Island, but it was also just a one-room shack off Montauk Highway that used paper towels as napkins and picnic tables for seating. The chances of someone like Will Darcy even knowing about a place like that were minimal, though, so Lizzy lifted her chin defiantly. "Well, we're very loyal customers."

He considered her for a minute. "In that case, I'll give you a ride and save them the trip."

She shifted from one foot to the other, balancing her board under one arm as she weighed her options. "Are you sure?"

He nodded. Then his lip twitched, almost like he was suppressing a smile. "You can even get in the car this time."

Her mouth fell open just as he turned and started walking to the stairs.

CHAPTER 24

Elizabeth Bennet was in his car.

Part of Will's mind was still processing it, still prodding the fact to see if it was real. Even when she appeared on the beach, his first instinct was that she was a hallucination. He had been out in the freezing water too long and now his mind was playing tricks on him. But as she made her way closer, the details were too clear to be a dream: her red hair haphazardly thrown into a ponytail, her dark eyes startling against her pink cheeks . . .

His grip on the steering wheel tightened as he turned the car onto the main road. He had spent the past month trying to shake her, shake *this*, but the moment he saw that red hair against the ocean's varying shades of gray, it all fell away. An endeavor so futile that he suddenly couldn't remember why he had attempted it in the first place.

And now she was sitting next to him in the passenger seat of his F-150, the truck he left out at the Montauk house, dripping salt water all over his leather seats.

"Sorry," she murmured, pulling her arms around herself as if reading his mind. She was working so hard to avoid his gaze that it was amusing.

He almost pointed out that despite the leather seats and impressive dashboard, the truck was still filled with sand and the smell of salt and sun. It was well-used, and he wasn't precious about it. But he knew it would come out harsh, so he stayed silent. Then a tremor ran through her body and her shoulders seized up as if to stop it.

"Are you cold?" he asked.

He knew he should have grabbed her a towel from the house. But she had been so desperate to get away from him that he knew it wasn't worth trying. And to be fair, he had been just as desperate to make sure she saw his offer through. He hadn't even changed out of his threadbare T-shirt and old Columbia hoodie that he had thrown on over his board shorts at the beach. It wasn't ideal, but he also didn't want to leave her alone.

This felt like a stolen moment, like the universe had made a clerical error and he had to exploit it before the world corrected itself. He had left his board on the beach and carried hers up the stairs along the cliffside. She avoided the house, pretended she didn't even notice it there towering over the yard, and when he invited her inside to dry off, she declined. Still, he noticed how she studied the house's facade when she thought he wasn't looking, a brief but intense survey. Then she raised her chin and climbed into the passenger seat without a word.

She hugged her arms tighter around herself and shook her head. "It's fine."

No, it's not, he wanted to say. The heat was already on its maximum setting, though, so he reached forward and pressed the button for her seat warmer.

"Thanks," she murmured.

He nodded, waiting another minute before he spoke again. "What time is your reservation?"

Her eyebrows knitted together. "What?"

"Your lunch reservation. At Mike's."

"Oh. Right. Yes." She cleared her throat. "Soon."

"So . . . one?"

Her eyes darted down to the clock on the dashboard, then away again. "Yes. One."

He tamped down a smile. He knew for a fact that during the off-season, Mike's didn't open until four. Even then, they didn't take reservations. They barely had napkins. But he could also see the panic in Lizzy's wide eyes, and he didn't have the heart to call her out on it.

"Good. Wouldn't want you to be late. They might give your table away."

She smiled. It was brief, but he caught how her lips curled up despite how she tried to temper it.

It was a victory. A small one, but he took it.

Will forced himself to focus on the road again, navigating his way through town as "Captain Jack" by Billy Joel played softly on the radio. The truck was big, but she still felt close, too close. His head was swimming in the damp heat filling the car, and it took all his willpower to ignore how the wet strands of her red hair stuck to her neck, how her pink lips were slightly parted. How her thigh was just inches away from where his hand rested on the gear shift, fingers idly tapping to the music. But as the song swelled, he couldn't help his gaze wandering up her leg to the tear still there on her wetsuit.

"I thought you were going to get that fixed."

She turned to him, confused. Then he nodded down to her thigh.

"Oh." Then she lifted her chin. "Yeah. I'll glue it when I get back to the motel."

"That's too big for glue."

"Glue will work just fine."

"It needs a patch."

"Well, I don't have a patch. I have glue."

"Then let's get you a patch."

She let out an exasperated sigh. "Isn't it exhausting being right all the time?"

He ignored the comment, keeping his eyes on the road ahead, even as a familiar itch began under his skin, the same that crept up that day after the bakery. He stopped at the next intersection. But instead of turning left, he continued straight.

Her back straightened as she whipped her head around to glare at him. "My motel is off of Ditch Plains."

"I know."

"Then why are you heading in the opposite direction?"

"We're making a detour."

Her eyes narrowed on him. "If you're taking me out to a field somewhere to murder me, you should know that my aunt and uncle will worry if I'm not there in time."

"You will be."

"And not in pieces."

He bit back a smile. "I promise to be a gentleman."

She rolled her eyes and snorted out a laugh.

Jack's Surf Shop was just off Seaside Avenue, a shack that had looked like it was about to fall down for the last twenty years. It had started life as an old mobile home turned convenience store, but in the years that followed, the owner had added driftwood and old boards to the sides, so now it looked like it had been cobbled together over the generations. And in a way, Will supposed it had.

He parked his truck out front and was about to get out when Lizzy spoke. "Where are we?"

Will paused. "The sign is right there."

"Right, but *why* are we here?"

"Why do you think?"

She rolled her eyes again, and Will could see the reply already forming in her mind. He was almost looking forward to it. But then a shiver went down the length of her spine and he remembered why they were here.

"The sooner we're in, the sooner you're back to your aunt and uncle, and the sooner you can leave for lunch," he said before she could answer.

She seemed to consider, then turned and opened the car door, stepping out and slamming it shut behind her. He shook his head, biting back his grin, and followed.

Inside, the shop was as chaotic as the exterior promised it would be. Merchandise—colorful bikinis and towels and boards and wetsuits—hung from every available space, while faded photos of customers filled in the gaps. The place still smelled like it had when Will was a child, a distinct blend of coconuts from an array of sunscreens mixed with the slight tinge of neoprene.

Lizzy came to stand next to him, staring up at the layers of items surrounding them. He couldn't help but watch her from the corner of his eye as she surveyed the room. Her large, dark eyes divided by the delicate slope of her nose. Her flushed cheeks, full lips . . .

"Darcy!"

The sound of his name broke through the Beach Boys playing overhead. Will turned just as Ray Foglia emerged from the back, smiling and holding out his hand. "What's up, man? Forget something yesterday?"

Will shook his hand and smiled. "No, I'm all set. But my friend needs some help with her wetsuit."

He nodded to Lizzy. She was staring up at him and seemed dumbstruck for a moment but recovered quickly, turning to Ray. "I think he's talking about this," she said, motioning to the rip along her thigh.

"Oh, that's a good one." Ray turned to Lizzy and winked. "But definitely not the worst we've seen. You'll have to try harder next time."

Her apprehension seemed to melt away and she smiled. "I'll do my best."

"Glad to hear it." Ray nodded down to her wetsuit and then started toward the back again. "Let me borrow that for a few minutes and we'll have you on your way."

Lizzy's smile fell. "Oh. Right. Okay."

Her cheeks were already pink, but somehow reddened even more as she looked around for . . . what exactly, Will wasn't sure. A dressing room, an escape?

Then Will realized the problem. She might not be wearing anything underneath. *Shit.*

"We can come back another time," he said, low enough so only she could hear.

"No, no, it's okay. I'll just take this off and he can patch it, right? Easy peasy. No problemo." She forced out a laugh that was probably meant to sound nonchalant, but only added to the tension.

When her hand went around her back, flailing for the line connected to her zipper, he discreetly turned away. A few minutes later, he heard her throw the wetsuit over the counter to Ray. "Here you go."

"Give me five and you'll be good to go," he said, and disappeared into the back room.

Will turned around but wasn't prepared for what awaited him. Lizzy stood in a bikini, arms crossed tightly over her chest, the small scraps of fabric just enough to cover her while exposing the pale skin along her hips, the curve of her stomach . . .

This might have been a bad idea.

He reached around his back, pulling his hoodie over his head and handing it to her. "Here."

Her eyebrows pinched together. "No, I don't—"

"Lizzy," he said, his voice low and serious. "Take the sweatshirt."

Her mouth snapped shut but there was still a long pause before she reached out to take it. She slipped it over her head slowly, and while he expected to mourn the view of her bare skin, a new possessiveness took hold when he saw his sweatshirt draped over her, so big it fell to the middle of her thighs.

She hugged the sweatshirt to her body as she looked around the shop. "This place is amazing."

"It is," he said, looking away.

Her head tilted to the side as her gaze slid across the photos behind the register, and he studied her face. The line of her jaw seemed infinite, a graceful arch that never ended, merely fell out of view in her hairline.

He turned away from her, taking a deep breath, and willed his mind to find something else to fixate on.

"I can't believe I've never been here before," Lizzy continued, still surveying the store.

"Ray isn't exactly good at marketing."

Her nose scrunched up. "His name is Ray?"

Will nodded, pretending to see something interesting on the other side of the room.

"Then who's Jack?"

"No idea. I think Ray bought the place in the nineties and never got around to changing the sign."

She laughed. It was deep and rough, and it hit a chord low in his gut. "Reminds me of the bakery."

"How so?"

"There's about a million things that we need to update, but just never get around to. The computer, the bookkeeping system . . ." Then she shot him a wry half grin. "The answering machine."

He couldn't help the smile that spread across his face, and it didn't even occur to him to try. Not until he caught the look of confusion on her face.

"What?" he asked.

"I don't think I've ever seen you smile before. Now I've seen it twice in the last twenty minutes."

He almost argued. Then he realized she was probably right.

"Here we go!" Ray bellowed as he emerged from the backroom. "Good as new."

He laid the wetsuit flat on the counter, showing off where the hole had been, but which was now expertly mended beneath a patch. He'd even been able to match the purple neoprene.

"Wow," Lizzy said, eyes wide. "I'm impressed."

Ray laughed. "Don't be. Darcy probably could have done this himself in five minutes."

"Yeah, but it would have come with a ten-minute lecture on what I did wrong in the first place, and who has that sort of time?" Lizzy said with a dramatic sigh.

Ray laughed. "I like her, Darcy."

I do, too. He almost said it before he could stop himself.

Lizzy caught it in his expression, though. She studied his face for a moment, as if trying to decipher a code there that she may have missed before. When she didn't seem to find it, she turned back to Ray. "So, what do I owe you?"

"Nothing. It was my pleasure."

Her lips turned down. "No, I can't just take—"

He waved his hand at her, cutting her off. "I've been overcharging Darcy for years. One patch job is my way of making us even."

❧

The drive to the Ocean Surf Inn was quiet. Lizzy was still wearing Will's sweatshirt and had her wetsuit in her lap as she stared out the window. Even when he pulled into the motel's empty parking lot, she didn't move.

"Thanks for the ride," she said, turning to offer him a smile.

"Of course." He watched as she gathered up her wetsuit and gear, then got out to help her with her board. He lifted it out of the bed of the truck and handed it to her.

"Would you like to come over for dinner tonight?" he asked.

Damn it. The words escaped before even he had time to consider them. He wasn't sure why he had even asked; he was positive she would laugh at the suggestion before walking off.

But she didn't. Instead she just stared at him, a touch of confusion on her face. "What?"

"George is staying with me for the weekend. I'm sure he would love to see you again." He paused. "Your aunt and uncle are welcome, too, of course."

Her eyebrows pinched together, but she recovered quickly. "Oh. Right. Well, they're busy so . . . um, yeah."

She fumbled to put the board under her arm, to walk away. But once she made it to the curb, she turned around.

"But I can be there," she said.

He nodded. "Great. Come by around eight."

There was a long moment when the cacophony of sounds around them fell silent—the waves and the traffic and the seagulls overhead—and even longer before she finally turned and walked out of sight.

It was probably the last time he would ever see her. She might have accepted the invite, but it was likely done out of politeness. If Elizabeth Bennet actually showed up tonight, he would be blown away.

CHAPTER 25

Florence + the Machine ran through the truck's stereo, and Lizzy willed Ms. Welch to give her strength for the night ahead. The winding road from her motel to Will's Montauk home was eerily dark with only her headlights illuminating the way, the song "Free" blasting on her speakers.

The louder the music, the more it reduced her anxiety, so she cranked up the volume further. What was she even doing? She glanced down at her faded jeans and vintage Guns N' Roses concert T-shirt underneath her worn brown leather jacket. Her outfit wasn't too casual, was it? She hadn't brought anything nice with her on this trip—besides her wetsuit, all she had was a suitcase full of sweatpants, T-shirts, and bathing suits. She couldn't very well show up in purple neoprene.

After a quick shower to get the ocean and sand off, she'd let her hair dry naturally so it fell in loose waves around her face and shoulders. She'd thrown on some lip gloss and mascara she'd found in her purse and forgot she even owned. The biggest decision of the evening came when she had to choose between sneakers or flip-flops. She was annoyed she cared this much. What happened to the halcyon days of invites dictating "resort casual"?

It was pitch-black outside. Without her phone's GPS, she wasn't sure she would have turned from the paved highway to the unnamed dirt road that eventually led to a long gravel driveway. The homes in this area were legendary, hidden from view but well-known by locals. They were the first houses to be built this far east; luxurious spreads that had stood the test of time and the elements.

There was an Audi SUV parked next to Will's gray truck in the front drive. Lizzy pulled in next to it, taking a moment to repress the urge to bite her cuticles like she used to when she was younger. The bad habit had started when she was forced to do fast math for customers when the register broke at the bakery.

Lizzy finally got out of the car, brushing sand from the seat off her legs, then started toward the house. With its gray slate roof and wood shingled siding, it looked like it was part of the wilderness here, tucked within the overgrowth, growing and breathing along with the grass and the trees. When she reached the black-painted front door, Lizzy took a deep calming breath and knocked. And then she waited.

This was a stupid idea. Really stupid. But, she reasoned, she didn't have to stay long. Just a drink, and then—

Will opened the door. He was back in his usual attire, jeans and crisp white button-down, but for some reason, the view now made her pulse trip. Or maybe that was because of how his eyebrows raised when he saw her, like he was surprised she was there.

Crap. Had she gotten the time wrong or—

"You made it," he said.

"Am I late? I thought you said eight, but I didn't write it down or anything, so . . ."

"I said eight," he said. "I just wasn't sure you'd show up."

She rolled her eyes, even as her cheeks flushed. "Well, I didn't really have a choice. I had to return your—" Her voice stalled with the realization. "Oh my God. I left your hoodie at the motel. I'm sorry. I can go back and grab it—"

"Another time."

"Are you sure?"

"I'm sure."

He stepped to the side, enough that she could walk past him into the foyer, then closed the door behind her. But instead of leading her into the house, he just stood there for a moment. It was like he was debating something, like the words were there on the tip of his tongue. Before he could find a way to utter them, though, a woman rounded the corner.

"You realize it's polite to actually invite your guests into your house, don't you, Will?" the woman said, shooting him a sharp glare. Her dark hair was pulled back in a loose ponytail and her pink sweater fit impeccably, even as it was casually tucked into the front of her cream-colored skirt.

Oh God, Lizzy thought. She had been right. Her outfit was way too casual.

Then the woman's expression melted into a warm smile as she turned to Lizzy. "You must be Elizabeth."

Lizzy donned a smile, too—the one she reserved for customers that she hoped would buy the day-old scones at the bakery—and replied, "It's Lizzy."

"Lizzy! It's so lovely to meet you," the woman said, coming forward as if she was about to embrace her. "I'm Emma. I've heard—" Then she stopped short. "Is that an original Appetite for Destruction Tour T-shirt?"

Lizzy blinked, then looked down at her old, threadbare shirt. "Yeah. It was my mom's, actually."

Emma brought a perfectly manicured hand to her chest, as if she needed a moment to fully appreciate this information. "You're already one of my favorite people."

Lizzy's smile became genuine. This was not how she was expecting this conversation to go. "Are you a GNR fan?"

"Of course," Emma said, linking her arm with Lizzy's, leading her further into the house. "'Paradise City' is one of my go-to karaoke songs."

As Emma marched forward, Lizzy looked over her shoulder to see Will following, a slight grin still on his lips.

The interior of Will's home was like the inverse of Marv's Lament. Instead of modern and stark, everything about this house felt warm and inviting. The beadboard walls of the entryway were lined with mementos and framed photos. Along the hallway there were paintings of seascapes and gold-rimmed mirrors. Emma was still talking about the legacy of LA's '80s music scene as she led Lizzy past what looked like a library—complete with a ladder and so many books, they were spilling out of the navy blue built-in shelves—and into the kitchen.

George was standing at the massive island in the middle of the room, pulling takeout containers from a large paper bag. He paused as they entered, cocking an eyebrow at Emma. "Please tell me I didn't just hear a reference to Whisky a Go Go."

"Okay," Emma said, with a shrug. "You didn't just hear a reference to Whisky a Go Go."

He chuckled as he turned to Lizzy.

"Nice to see you again, Lizzy," he said. "I hope Emma's not forcing you to do karaoke with her yet."

Lizzy smiled. "Not yet."

"But the night is still young," Emma added sweetly, coming around the island to finish taking the food from the bag.

Lizzy laughed, but it was cut short as Will came up behind her.

His arm brushed against hers as he reached forward and pulled out a counter stool, sending a wave of goose bumps across her skin.

"Sit down," he said. "Can I get you a drink?"

"I'll just have a water," Lizzy said, working hard to keep her tone nonchalant. The last thing she needed right now was alcohol dulling her senses.

Will nodded and turned to the refrigerator. George made his way to Emma's side, whispering something in her ear, and she laughed. It felt intimate and sweet, and Lizzy darted her eyes away, letting herself look over the spread in front of her: a half dozen takeout containers brimming with calamari, lobster salad, crab cakes, french fries . . . and then something in her brain clicked.

"Is this from Mike's?" she blurted out.

Will appeared at her side again, nodding as he placed a glass of ice water in front of her. "You don't mind having it twice in one day, do you?"

Lizzy opened her mouth, but no words came out. Will was watching her, a look of amusement in his eyes, as if waiting for her to admit to her lie.

"Nope," she said, trying to make it sound nonchalant.

He smiled, leaning across the counter and popping a piece of calamari into his mouth.

Lizzy had never seen him so laid-back. He wasn't angry and brooding; he looked . . . comfortable, even happy. It was like running into your dentist or your fifth-grade teacher at the supermarket. It was hard for your brain to compute them in a new setting, and you're left wondering if you really knew them at all.

"All right, I think that's it," Emma said, arranging the boxes in a perfect semicircle.

George looked down at the array, his forehead furrowed. "Why do we have enough food to feed a dozen people?"

"I think you're vastly underestimating how hungry I am right now," Emma said, stealing a french fry before turning around to grab plates from the shelf behind her.

"I'm just impressed George got you to agree to order food from a place with 'shack' in the name," Will said, taking a long sip of his beer.

Emma turned back around with the plates and sighed dramatically. "It's called growth, Will. I highly recommend it."

He laughed, a sound so full and rich that Lizzy felt it in her chest. And for the first time in twenty-four hours, she allowed herself to relax. She leaned back in her chair and let her smile become easy as she turned to him.

"Thanks for inviting me tonight," she said, meaning it.

He maintained her gaze for a heavy beat, then replied, "Thanks for coming."

Then Emma gasped, and all eyes went to her as she smacked George's hand away from her plate. "Don't even think about it, Knightley. This lobster roll is *mine*."

Two hours later, the farmhouse table in the dining room was covered with the remnants of dinner, and Emma was sitting beside Lizzy, explaining her job as a modern art advisor and the intricacies of international art sales. Lizzy had to admit she'd never really cared about the art world before, but Emma's explanation was better than most shows on Bravo.

"... So *then* this guy tried to sell the piece in Europe, but someone must have sent the link to his ex-wife because she ended up calling literally every museum in London, Paris, and Madrid, telling them that the painting was hers until the divorce was finalized. It was such a mess!" she said, taking a long sip of her wine.

Across from them, George chuckled. "Sometimes I think you love the drama more than the actual art."

"Art *is* drama," Emma replied. "That's why I'm so good at my job." Then she turned back to Lizzy. "What about you? What do you do?"

She debated how to answer, if she could somehow make the bakery sound more exciting than it really was, but Will spoke first.

"Lizzy is a fantastic journalist."

Her attention snapped to him. He stared back, taking a sip of his beer.

"Are you serious?" Emma said, impressed. "That's amazing."

Lizzy rolled her eyes. "Writing a few articles in high school and college does not make me a journalist."

Will's expression turned sardonic. "You went to school for it."

"Undergrad, yes. But I still need my master's if I want to get into foreign affairs coverage."

"Have you applied anywhere?" George asked. "Will and I went to Columbia. We might know some people."

She smiled. "I got into Columbia, actually."

George's eyebrows shot up. "You got into Columbia's School of Journalism?"

She nodded while Emma batted her hand in the air.

"*Of course* she got into Columbia's School of Journalism," Emma said.

Will's attention was still on Lizzy, barely concealing his surprise. "When do you start?"

She let out a shaky sigh. "That's a good question." She took a deep breath and decided to just get it over with. "I should have started a few weeks ago, but my dad had a stroke in March, two days after I got the acceptance letter. I arrived at our family's bakery for my shift and found him. I . . ." Her voice faltered, then she shook her head. "I thought he was dead. The paramedics said if I had been five minutes later, he would have been. He was in the hospital for a couple of weeks after that. Even after he got out, he couldn't be on his feet for long, couldn't keep track of numbers. And I was the only one who knew how the bakery ran. How to fill orders, how to prep . . . everything. So I deferred for a semester, hoping to work out a plan. But right now there's still no plan, and I have just a couple of weeks to decide what I'm going to do, so . . ." Her voice trailed off and she shrugged.

Emma and George were quiet, frozen in place. But Lizzy barely noticed. She was too busy maintaining Will's gaze, watching as his hard brow softened.

"You're still a fantastic journalist, Lizzy. With or without Columbia," he finally said.

She smiled back.

After another moment, Emma broke the tension by turning to George and clapping her hands. "Okay! Knightley and I are going to clean up and make up some bowls of vanilla ice cream for dessert. Will, you should show Lizzy the view of the beach from up here. It's stunning!"

Will frowned. "There is no view. It's dark outside."

"It's not that dark," Emma said with a practiced smile.

"It's ten o'clock," he responded.

"That means moonlight. It's different with moonlight. See? Moonlight!" Emma said, pointing out the window and looking to her boyfriend for confirmation. George simply stared back at her with one eyebrow raised, like he wanted no part in her scheming.

Will turned to Lizzy. "Well?"

This morning, the suggestion of walking out into the darkness with Will Darcy would have elicited a hard no, but now, as he stared at her, his blue eyes expectant, she couldn't think of anything she wanted more.

So she smiled and shrugged one shoulder. "I don't mind moonlight."

CHAPTER 26

Will guided Lizzy out the back door to the porch, then made sure the door shut securely behind them so Emma couldn't eavesdrop. The less fuel for her scheming, the better.

"I'm sorry about that," Will murmured.

"Why? They're great," Lizzy responded, pulling her brown leather jacket around her tightly.

They walked out past a rectangular in-ground pool surrounded by low garden lights and made their way to the top of the bluff. Despite Emma's promises, there was no moon tonight—just dark skies, the sound of crashing waves, and a slight chill in the September air. Still, there was one thing worth sharing with her.

He turned, starting toward the long wooden shed on the other side of the lawn near the cliff's edge. "This way."

"Ah, I see," she said. "Middle of the night. No witnesses. The perfect crime scene."

His face contorted with confusion. "What?"

"I 'fall' to the rocks below," Lizzy began. "No one will see me because it's so dark and you, Will Darcy, certainly can't go down there to look for me. It's just too treacherous for your suede loafers. It's the perfect alibi. So you head back to the house, and after you've perfected your story, you call the police, knowing full well I didn't slip."

"That's . . . very dark," he said, his voice playful.

"That's nothing. You should see the plot of the last fantasy book my sister gave me," Lizzy said with a laugh, tucking a strand of her flaming red hair behind her ear.

He watched the motion, then looked away, clearing his throat. "Come on. There's something I want to show you," he said.

"Is it your collection of knives?"

"No." He shook his head with a half grin, then pointed to his right. "It's in the shed over there."

"You realize that doesn't sound any better, right?" Lizzy said back to him, then smiled. "I'll let you go first."

She followed him to the shed, which was near the top of the wood stairs they had climbed that afternoon. The weathered structure was a miniature unrenovated version of the main house, with shingle siding patinated by the ocean air.

Will opened the door. A thin string hung from the ceiling and he pulled it, lighting up the room. Its shiplap boards were painted white with decorative oars lining the walls, and about thirty surfboards he and his father had collected over the years placed carefully throughout the space. It looked like a mini surf shop inside, complete with a long table in the back for waxing and repairs.

"Oh, wow. This is incredible," Lizzy breathed as she entered, taking in the long line of boards and wetsuits. Then she paused. "Wait, what is that?" she asked, pointing to a small metal barrel on the floor with a hose sticking out the top.

"A portable shower."

Her eyes went wide as she turned to stare at him.

"With a water heater," he added with a lopsided grin.

"Are you serious?"

"My dad had a habit of picking up any gadget he could find, regardless of whether or not he needed it."

She smiled and kept exploring the small space, running her hand along an old wooden board sitting out as if it were still being worked on. Then a photograph on the wall snagged her attention. It was faded, but not enough that you couldn't see the blond woman in a sun hat with one arm wrapped around a tall man in the center. The man looked like a slightly older version of Will, except he had a huge smile on his face. Beside him was a small boy with a shock of white-blond hair, working to hold up a surfboard.

"Is this you and your parents?" Lizzy asked.

He nodded. "I think I'm about seven there."

A long silence followed before she asked, "How old were you when they passed?"

"Twenty-five," he replied.

She shook her head. "I can't even imagine."

"It was five years ago." The reply was automatic, what he usually said when people offered condolences. But even though it was years ago, the loss still felt raw, and he found himself continuing. "I think people assume that once you're an adult, losing your parents isn't as traumatic as it would be if you were a kid. But you're still their kid. And when they're gone, you still somehow feel like an orphan. It's hard. It probably always will be."

She stared at him for a moment, then turned to consider the photo again. "What were their names?"

"John and Claire."

She let out a long breath, bringing her gaze back to his. "I'm so sorry, Will."

It was the most he had spoken about his parents in a while. He tried to temper the emotion in his voice as he answered, "I need to apologize, too."

"For what?"

"Charlie's Fourth of July party." He took a moment, crossing his arms over his chest as he measured his words. "You asked me if I had ever been embarrassed by my family. I said no."

Her cheeks flushed as she rolled her eyes. "Oh God, we don't have to relive—"

"No. We do." He paused. He had to be careful, so very careful, to say exactly what he meant. To ensure his words didn't have any hidden sharp edges before he uttered them. "I wasn't saying that my family had never done anything to embarrass me. It's that I don't have the opportunity to be embarrassed by my family anymore. I'm an only child, so when they passed . . . it's only me now."

Every emotion that had been dancing on her face fell in a moment. "Will—"

"I knew my words stung. I saw it in your expression," he said, cutting her off. "But that wasn't my intention. What I meant was that you're lucky to have family to be embarrassed by."

A small smile curled her lips. "I'll remind you of that next time Joanne Bennet corners you with a business proposal."

He chuckled to himself.

Another moment passed, then she continued, "I have a question."

"Okay."

"How do you know I'm a fantastic journalist?"

Right.

"Because I read your articles," he admitted.

She looked genuinely shocked. "Which one?"

"All of them."

Her eyes widened. "All of them?"

He nodded. "I really enjoyed the one about the cleanliness of women's locker rooms across New York's public universities."

"Oh my God," she groaned, letting her face fall into her hands.

"And your op-ed from high school where you called your principal a puritanical hypocrite over a proposed book ban."

She laughed and lifted her gaze back to his. "But . . . why did you read them?"

"Because they matter," he added truthfully.

Silence stretched out between them then. She looked stunned, and suddenly it felt like there was an impending weight above them, that if they stayed here any longer, more would be said and he didn't want to press his luck.

"We should head back," he murmured.

"Oh," she replied. "Sure."

Will opened the door. Without thinking, he placed his hand against the small of Lizzy's back as he let her pass in front of him, feeling the soft leather of her jacket against his palm. It was an innocent gesture, but heat still flooded his veins, and once she found her footing on the grass outside, he removed it, turning off the light, then clenching his hand in a fist at his side to keep from reaching for her again as they walked back to the house.

"Oh! You're back!" Emma exclaimed when they entered the hall from the side porch off the living room. She was standing by the front door, a few overnight bags at her feet.

Will stopped. "Are you leaving?"

"First thing tomorrow morning," she replied brightly. "I have to get back. Work emergency."

"An art advisor emergency?" Will asked, suspicious.

"Yup! Right, Knightley?"

George was coming down the stairs, a bag over one shoulder and a scowl on his face.

"No comment," he murmured, throwing his leather duffel into the pile, then headed back toward the living room.

Emma seemed unfazed. "But you're staying for a few days, right, Will?" she asked. Her gaze darted to Lizzy, then back to him, as if working to psychically communicate her meaning.

He didn't reply. Emma and Charlie clearly went to the same school of subtlety.

Thankfully, Lizzy just looked amused.

"I should really get going, too," she said.

"You sure?" Will asked.

"It's getting late." She was already moving toward the front door. "It was nice meeting you, Emma. Tell George I said goodbye."

Will gave Emma a look, then opened the front door for Lizzy. "I'll walk you out."

Lizzy fished her keys from her pocket as they walked down the front steps, then followed Will to her pickup truck parked in the driveway.

"Are you going to be all right getting home?" Will asked. "I could drive you, or—"

"I'm fine," she said, stopping beside the driver's side of her truck. "A girl can only be escorted home so many times in one day."

He nodded. The atmosphere suddenly felt charged, like when they were leaving the shed, and it made it hard for him to think clearly.

"Elizabeth . . . Lizzy," he said quietly.

She paused with her hand on the driver's-side door.

"The waves will be good tomorrow," he offered. "You can park here and use the stairs down to the beach. Less crowded than in town."

A moment passed, and he realized he was holding his breath.

"I'll think about it," she said.

Neither of them moved. He should let her leave, because if she stayed for much longer, he wouldn't be able to stop himself from kissing her . . . and last time that had happened, she'd made it clear she wanted nothing to do with him. He needed to respect that.

"It's late," he said, leaning forward to open her car door. "You don't want your aunt and uncle to worry."

She cleared her throat. "Right, yes. I should go."

She slid into the driver's seat, fumbling with her keys as he leaned against the door. It took a minute, but she finally got them in the ignition and the engine roared to life. But she still didn't move to leave.

"Will?" she said, turning to look up at him.

"Yes?"

"I lied."

His brow furrowed. "About what?"

"I'm not really staying with my aunt and uncle. It's just me."

Will had already guessed as much, but the fact that she was offering him the truth stoked at something hot in his chest.

"That's all right," he replied. "I lied, too."

"You did?"

He let a grin tease his lips. "I'm not really a gentleman."

Her eyes widened and her cheeks flushed just before he closed the car door.

Will took a step back and watched as she finally maneuvered her truck down the drive, her taillights slowly disappearing in the darkness. Then he returned to the house and walked straight upstairs.

He could hear his two remaining houseguests in the living room as he ascended, George's serious voice followed by Emma's light laugh. He knew they were talking about him, but he didn't care, he needed space. He needed sleep. He needed to stop thinking about whether Elizabeth Bennet would show up on his beach tomorrow.

In his room, he collapsed into bed, ignoring the thoughts that rolled through his brain. But sleep was evasive. Even when it arrived, it came with dreams of Lizzy's red hair and husky laugh, of her moans and sighs, her bottom lip between his teeth.

He was licking along the column of her neck when his alarm went off at six. He lay there, staring up at the ceiling for a long minute. The house felt empty. George and Emma had left as promised. He was alone. As long as he lay there, the dreams stayed in his memory. The moment he stood up, the real world would invade again. One where last night could have been the end and he would have to live with that.

But he did get up. He shuffled to the bathroom and began brushing his teeth. And as he did, his eyes wandered to the window. Suddenly, all of the anxiety and worry and foreboding disappeared.

Lizzy's truck was parked in the front drive.

CHAPTER 27

Lizzy slipped behind Will's house before dawn, dodging the low tree branches and tiptoeing across the sprawling backyard past the surf shed. The wooden stairs creaked loudly as she made her way down to the beach, and she cursed under her breath, sure the entire eastern tip of Long Island would hear her. But then again, why should she care? Will had invited her to park there, to use his beach access. It wasn't a big deal. She repeated it in her mind even as her pulse stumbled in her veins.

The sea was quieter today, with a light breeze and gentler breaks, but it was still better than anywhere else nearby. As she dove in, the crisp waters felt like ice cubes down her body. She paddled out past the crashing waves to open water, determined not to pass up the swells that started small but had the potential to become spectacular.

Between rides, Lizzy floated on the undulating water, her board bobbing with the current. It really did feel like the end of the world out here. The ocean before her looked vast and never-ending, and she focused on it, determined not to think about the house on the bluff above her or the man inside who was probably still fast asleep. Nope. Not her.

Eventually, she stopped obsessively checking for a tall surfer in a black wetsuit on the beach. And that's right when he showed up, crashing through the surf toward the break just as she kicked out of a wave.

She straddled her board and watched him deftly maneuver his board over the icy crests, his wetsuit slick over his muscular body. He jerked his head sideways in an attempt to keep his blond locks from falling in front of his eyes. The movement was so small, so subtle, but her heart skipped a beat anyway. He looked like a fucking cover model for one of her dad's old surf magazines. There was no way he didn't realize how hot he was. He must.

She made a mental note to delete the memory of that body pressed up against hers at the bakery.

"You showed up," she said as he finally paddled over.

He nodded, angling his board to face her. His gaze flitted down her body. "How's the patch working out?"

"Well, I'm no longer freezing in this five-inch vicinity anymore, so I'll chalk that up to a win." Her fingers glided over the new purple neoprene high up on her thigh.

His eyes rested where her hand was, then roamed up to her face, like he was checking to see what else might be amiss. When he seemed content that she was in one piece, he looked to the horizon. "Well, if you need anything more, the shed has supplies. You can help yourself."

It was a kind offer. A month ago, she never could have imagined calling anything Will Darcy did kind. But since then he had moved from snob to decent human being, and she wasn't sure how to react. It was easier when she thought she hated him. Now, it felt like they were almost friends.

Then he started paddling away.

"Hey! Where are you going?" she asked.

He turned to look at her from over his shoulder. "I can surf by the sandspit over there. Give you space."

She blinked. The thought that he wouldn't surf with her hadn't even entered her mind. "Why don't you just stay here?"

He hesitated. "Are you sure?"

She shrugged. "As long as you don't steal my waves."

A small, unpracticed smile tugged at his lips. "Technically, they're my waves."

"Technically, it's a public beach."

He chuckled. "All right. Then what do you suggest?"

She scrunched up her nose, considering. "Rock, Paper, Scissors."

He blinked. "What?"

"You know, Rock—"

"I know the game. I just haven't played it since grade school."

"You clearly didn't grow up with four sisters and only one car. This is how all my family's problems are solved."

Another chuckle. Deep and low, so she felt it in her belly.

"Okay, then."

She smoothed back her wet hair, and lifted a hand. "Ready?"

"No cheating."

"How exactly would I—"

"You just admitted you've had years of practice. Maybe even entered tournaments. I could be getting hustled."

"You in or out?" she asked, trying to feign impatience, her board bobbing beneath her.

He frowned. "In."

"Okay. Rock, paper, scissors," she said as her fist hit her hand three times with each word. "Shoot!"

He looked confused for a moment but followed her lead.

"Paper beats rock," she said triumphantly, flourishing her flat hand. "I win."

She didn't stick around to see if he would challenge it, just sprint-paddled to the break as a glistening wave approached. She positioned her board and stood, fighting for balance, riding low, and managing to steer to shallow waters. It was a perfect ride.

She caught her breath and swam back out to where Will was straddling his board.

"That wasn't rock. I just had my hand in a fist," he said, his arms crossed over his broad chest.

She sighed dramatically. "Such a sore loser."

They spent the next hour falling into an easy rhythm. Lining up, yielding to whoever was closest to the peak, watching one take a ride while the other caught their breath. Lizzy's muscles burned hot while the cool water kept her temperature balanced; her entire body felt flushed. She loved it.

By lunchtime, the surf began to settle. They sat on their boards, watching the steady rhythm of the tide, waiting to see if it had anything left. Seagulls circled overhead, and the only sound was their boards hitting each other, pushing them close like the current had a mind of its own.

"It's odd," he started, then seemed to think better of it.

"What?" she asked.

"I'm usually so laser-focused out here," he said, staring out at the horizon. "It's me versus the ocean. It feels like a battle I'll never win but I need to keep fighting. Like I need it to remind myself where I fit in the world."

"What's weird about that?" she asked.

"I forgot how fun it can be."

His eyes met hers then, as if waiting for her to tell him he was crazy.

But he wasn't. Surfing was hard and scary, but it was also fun. When was the last time she had acknowledged that? Usually she wanted to work her muscles and body so hard that she could think of nothing else. She wanted to be alone instead of being pulled in a million directions. She wanted to escape. But sometimes, it was good to escape with another person.

That's when the realization struck her. *I needed this, too.*

"Why?" he asked.

Oh God. Had she said that last part out loud?

"There's just a lot going on," she said. "Stuff I need to figure out with the bakery. My dad. My sisters. But none of it is *my* stuff. I don't even have time for my stuff anymore. And the more I neglect it, the further away it gets." She let her eyes dart to the beach to avoid his gaze. But he still waited for her to continue. "I was supposed to start at Columbia a few weeks ago. If I hadn't deferred, I would probably be in class right now. It was all so close, but now it feels impossible. Like I was delusional for even thinking it could happen. And maybe that's just growing up, but it's still hard to let go. You know?"

He nodded, then said softly, "Yeah, I do."

She smiled, then turned to stare out at the horizon.

It was a long time before she noticed that her thigh was touching his, brushing back and forth against his leg as the current forced them closer. She knew she should move, start swimming to shore and head back to the motel. But she didn't want to. And for a second, she let herself be selfish.

"Hey," he finally said.

She looked over at him. His face looked calm under his wet hair, but his blue eyes were studying hers with a question.

"Are you hungry?"

She could eat.

⌇

Will didn't ask why Lizzy had a set of dry clothes already waiting in her car, and Lizzy was thankful as she disappeared into the guest room downstairs to change. It had felt presumptuous before she drove here, and even more so now. But not enough to stop her from shoving the clothes into the passenger seat that morning. When she emerged a few minutes later, Will was waiting in a pair of worn jeans hanging low on his hips and a faded sweater with the sleeves pushed up his forearms. She hadn't thought there was anything special about her jeans or the oversized cardigan covering her Smiths T-shirt, but he still stopped when she stepped into the foyer, staring at her for a long moment before clearing his throat and nodding toward the door.

Will insisted on driving, and Lizzy didn't argue, relaxing into the soft leather seats and letting the music fill the car as they drove up to Gosman's Dock. They ate lunch at a small stand near the water, sharing a selection of fried pickles and lobster salad and narrowly avoiding the seagulls swooping down to steal their fries. Afterward, when they piled back into the car and Lizzy was complaining she was so full that Will would have to roll her back into his house, it occurred to her that she was assuming she would be invited inside. He had only offered the beach to her to surf. There was no guarantee of anything else. Maybe he would pull up and say goodbye and that would be that.

By the time they turned down his long drive, she was trying to dissect her panic. The process was so distracting, she barely noticed as he parked and killed the engine, then walked to her side to open the passenger door.

"Want some ice cream?" he asked.

She was pretty sure that if she had some ice cream right now, she would burst. But she didn't care. She smiled at him and said, "Sure."

Ice cream led to sharing embarrassing stories from their child-hoods, which led to Will giving her a tour of the house, down every labyrinthine hallway until they found themselves back in the living room. She attempted to play the piano, he tried to teach her, until she finally claimed ownership of a new musical genre called "classical improv." At that point Will stood up and got a beer.

Lizzy didn't know what time it was when they found themselves on the porch, sprawled out on neighboring chaises. She took a sip of her beer and watched the branches of the red cedars sway in the darkness.

"I love these trees," she said.

He turned his head to look at her. "Yeah?"

She nodded. "I feel like all the trees out here get cut down, especially when they block the view of the water. As if they're not a part of the landscape, too."

A moment, then he shifted to look at the swaying branches. "I was obsessed with them growing up."

"Really?"

His throat bobbed, as if he were preparing what he was going to say. As if he was out of practice. "In high school, I found my dad's old 35mm Canon at our house in the city. I brought it out east that summer and spent hours trying to capture Montauk, hundreds of photos of the seagulls and waves and the lighthouse. But I always came back to these trees. They were somehow both integral and invisible. These permanent things that most people don't notice anymore." He paused. "Birdie wants me to cut them down, though."

"Why?"

"People want manicured lawns, neat property lines."

His voice was suddenly disconnected, cold. And something in her chest hurt so much she couldn't stop herself from whispering, "Why in the world are you selling this place?"

He didn't move for a moment. "Because sometimes what I want has to take a back seat to what's best."

"Best for who, though?"

He took a deep sip of his beer. "Birdie deserves this. It would set her business apart, and when my dad died, she was expecting this place."

"But he left it to you. Maybe he wanted you to keep it."

Will nodded. "Maybe. But I barely have time to come out here anymore."

"Really?" she said, rolling her eyes. "Because I distinctly remember you spending a lot of time at Charlie's this summer."

"Is that right?" He stared at her, his gaze so direct that she blushed and looked away.

"I'm just saying," she said. "It's your life. You're allowed to make your own choices."

He hummed. "So are you."

She scrunched up her nose. "What?"

"You should tell your dad about Columbia."

"That's complicated," she said. "It's not just about school. It would mean discussing the future of the bakery, his health . . ." She shook her head. "He doesn't even know I applied."

"But he knows you wanted to go."

"We talked about it, but that was months ago." She hesitated. "It doesn't matter now, anyway. The deadline to enroll next semester is October first."

"That's in a couple of weeks."

She sighed. "Exactly."

He was quiet for a beat. "What happens if you don't get back to them?"

"I'm no longer accepted," she said with a shrug. "Even if I send the letter in time, I'm not guaranteed a spot."

"Then you can reapply."

She threw him a wry look. "Are they really going to accept someone who already blew them off once?"

"Then you go somewhere else. The school doesn't make you a journalist, Lizzy. You do that."

She took another sip of beer.

"You should tell your dad," Will continued. "It doesn't matter if you end up going to Columbia. He would want to know."

She looked back over at the trees. Leaving East Hampton, the bakery, and going back to school felt so huge, so complicated that she didn't even know where to begin. But that one thing, that she could do. Maybe.

"It's getting late," she replied, setting her bottle down on the wood-planked porch. "I should head back to the motel soon."

He watched as she sat up. "Same time tomorrow?"

She turned to him. "Don't you have to get back for work or something?"

"I can take a few more days off. My name is on the building." He cocked his head to the side. "What about you?"

She shrugged, ignoring how her heart stuttered in her chest. "I can take a few days off. My name is on the building, too."

And then he laughed, the sound so deep that she felt it in her toes, and she couldn't help but smile.

CHAPTER 28

It became a daily ritual. Lizzy would wake before dawn, drive her truck up Montauk Highway to the gravel road that led to Will's house, then follow its narrow path through the switchgrass and oak trees of Amsterdam Beach State Park until she reached his private drive. They would spend the morning surfing, then stumble back to the house for lunch. By the time the sun set, she would be sitting beside him on his porch again, laughing and talking and praying that neither of them would notice the clock.

The first couple of mornings, she parked on the far side of the round driveway so she could offload her board and go directly down the stairs that led to the beach without having to walk too close to the house. She convinced herself that it made her less of a bother, that maybe he might not notice the rusty maroon truck parked next to his newer one.

That was easier than letting herself hope that he was waiting for her, insurance in case he didn't show up in the water a few minutes after her.

But he always did.

By Wednesday, he insisted she just keep her board there through the week, that it was easier.

By Friday, she could recognize the sound of his gait on the creaking wooden steps without having to turn around.

Saturday, though, the fear that he wouldn't show up was renewed. Lizzy eyed the dark clouds rolling above as she got out of her truck. The storm wasn't set to hit Long Island for a few hours, and between now and then the waves were sure to be epic. But they would also be dangerous.

As she grabbed her board from where it rested against the shed and navigated the stairs down the bluff, Lizzy was struck by the memory of that morning after the storm in June. When she had encountered Will on the beach on her way to see Jane, her own stupid anger and annoyance had clouded their interaction. Yet she could still recall his warning about the surf and a storm. It would make sense that his caution could extend to this storm, too, that he might deem it too risky—

"I'm not sure about those clouds," Will's deep voice called out.

When she reached the bottom of the stairs, she looked up and there he was, already on the beach. His wetsuit was pulled up his legs, but the rest hung around his waist, exposing his toned stomach, his strong arms.

"It's fine!" she said, darting her eyes toward the surf, the sky, anything other than his body.

He sighed. "All right. But the minute I hear thunder, we're out."

In her periphery she saw him pull his suit up and zip the back. A bit of tension released in her core then. This was fine. She was in control.

Then he turned around and flashed that rare smile, unpracticed and gorgeous, and she realized she had never felt more out of control in her life.

He held out a fist and waited for her to do the same.

"Rock, paper, scissors, shoot!"

❧

An hour later, Lizzy's muscles ached, her chest burned, and she couldn't shake the smile stretched across her face.

The waves were large and unruly, coming one after another and growing with each passing minute, ready to drag you under or give you the best ride of your life. It was perfect.

Her board bobbed between her legs as she watched Will line up and start paddling when a swell approached. It was big, already cresting by the time he popped up, the hard line of his body bending toward the water for balance.

They would probably have to call it a day soon, she thought. The clouds on the horizon were growing darker, and the wind was churning up the sea spray—even she had to admit it was getting too dangerous.

But today was Saturday. And tomorrow the weather would likely keep them out of the water all day. And ... well, that was the end, wasn't it? He would be leaving for the city, and she had to get back to her life in East Hampton. This, right now, could be all she got.

Or maybe not, a small voice whispered in her mind.

She shook the thought away, watching as he carved into the wave, the sea foam churning under his feet as he did a barrel turn to come at it again. Hope wasn't a plan. Yes, she could confidently call him her friend now, but that didn't negate anything he'd said in the message he left at the bakery. Whatever had happened between them, he was over it. Maybe it hadn't meant anything to begin with.

The wave mellowed, and Will dove back into the water, resurfacing a moment later and paddling toward her. His board pulled up alongside her own, so close that their legs brushed together. His breath was coming in quick and heavy gasps, and his blue eyes looked electric under the gray skies.

They both stared out at the horizon for a long minute. It wasn't awkward—if anything, she felt more comfortable in his silence than she did anywhere else—but still, it seemed like there was added gravity now, like they both knew there was something to say and now it was just a waiting game. She knew what she wanted to say. Or rather, what she wanted to ask: *Do you still have feelings for me? Because I think I have feelings for you.* But what was he waiting to say? What if she poured her heart out and all he had to tell her was what time he was planning to leave the next day?

No. She couldn't contemplate that. So, instead of honesty, she opted for the next best thing: avoidance.

"Taking a long break over here, Mr. Darcy," she said, forcing a wry smile.

He stared out at the ocean for another moment, then turned those blue eyes to her. "Just enjoying the view, Ms. Bennet."

Her pulse leapt and a hot flush coursed its way through every inch of her body almost simultaneously. *Get a grip, Lizzy.* She was ridiculous.

A peal of thunder in the distance just as she saw the growing peak of a wave approaching. It was huge and barreling toward them—the perfect diversion.

"It's mine!" she yelled.

Will's brow furrowed. "Elizab—"

The dull roar of the surf drowned him out as she paddled forward. She turned just as the wave met the tail of her board, pushing her as her arms cut through the water. Her arms burned at the pace until she finally popped up, leaning back to cut into the barrel. But there wasn't a barrel. As soon as she was up, the wave collapsed, throwing her into the air only to yank her back down again by her tether. The water swallowed her up then, pulling and pushing, and she couldn't tell which way was up.

Somewhere in her brain she remembered that this sort of thing had happened before; she knew what to do. But right now, her mind was blank. All she knew was that there wasn't any gravity, only freezing water dragging her down and her lungs burning in her chest.

Then there was something warm around her arm. Warm and firm and pulling her harder than the waves.

She broke through the surface, taking air in giant, desperate gasps as her feet found solid ground. But the warmth didn't leave her arm. In fact, it was all around her now, cocooning her as she coughed and wheezed.

"Lizzy!"

Oh. It was Will. The realization came to her slowly, as did the fact that his arms were around her, pressing her to his body as the water lapped at her waist. It felt so safe and warm, she closed her eyes and let her body go limp against him. *You saved my life*, she wanted to say. *Oh, and I absolutely have feelings for you.* But just as suddenly as he had pulled her to him, he yanked her away, gripping her shoulders to make sure her gaze was locked with his.

"What the hell were you thinking?" he roared, his blue eyes sharp and alive with panic. "You can't just paddle out into a wave like that! What would have happened if I wasn't here? What—"

She leaned into him before he could finish, bringing her lips to his to kiss him. She wasn't even aware that she was doing it. All she knew was that he was worried about her, that she mattered, and suddenly she couldn't remember why she hadn't done it days before.

He hesitated, his body tense.

No, no, don't pull away, she thought, wrapping her arms around his neck to keep him close.

Then he groaned and crushed her against his chest. His mouth was suddenly devouring hers, swallowing her moans while his hands tightened their grip. Somewhere in her mind, she was aware that the ocean was churning around their legs, that it had started raining, too. But none of it mattered. She was too lost in his warmth, his taste . . .

A crack of thunder split through the sky, making them both jump.

And just like that, the spell was broken. Will was frozen in place, his arms still around her, but looking down at her now like he'd committed a cardinal sin.

"Shit," he murmured.

Her brows knitted together as he released her and took a step back. Had she missed a step? Done something wrong? She couldn't tell. She didn't even know how to ask. And then, suddenly, she didn't have time to.

A flash of lightning lit up the sky, catching Will's attention. "The storm's here. We should head back."

She swallowed. "Okay."

They made their way out of the water, but she was barely aware of the steps, or the rain now falling steadily around them. Her brain was too busy trying to navigate a way out of this new awkwardness to pay attention to their journey up the stairs and to the house.

"I'm going to go upstairs and change," he murmured as they entered the foyer. Then he turned to her. "Are you okay?"

Was she okay? Absolutely not. But she was so lost as to what that meant that she could only nod dumbly.

He didn't seem to believe her, lingering another moment before he sighed and disappeared up the stairs.

Wait! she wanted to say. She was only just beginning to realize how much she had missed his arms around her body, his lips against hers. But now he seemed intent on forcing them back to that place they had existed in all week, the precarious limbo between friendship and so much more. And she wanted more. She needed it.

She hadn't moved when he returned a few minutes later. His wetsuit was gone, replaced by a pair of sweatpants and a black hooded sweatshirt.

His brow was furrowed as he stared at where she stood in the center of his foyer, her purple wetsuit dripping onto the floor. Then a flash of recognition as he seemed to realize his mistake. "Shit, your clothes are in your truck."

She blinked. Were they? She hadn't even gotten that far. All she knew was that she had to say something, anything, to fix this. "It's okay. I don't need—"

"No. I'll get them."

His hand was on the doorknob before she could reply, before she could say that she didn't care about clothes or wetsuits or . . .

"Stop!" she yelled as she reached out, grabbing his wrist.

He paused, turning enough to look down at her fingers.

"I'm a tool!" It came out before she could stop herself, and she winced. "I mean, I don't mind being a tool."

He didn't move. "Excuse me?"

She shook her head as she tried to organize her thoughts. "When you came to the bakery that day, after you kissed me, I told you I wouldn't be a tool you use to work out your issues . . . but I didn't mean it. Or maybe I did mean it, but that was only because I thought I hated you. I didn't even really know you, though. And now that I do . . ." She paused. "We're so similar, Will. We've both been so careful for so long and we hate feeling out of control. But I think that feeling might be exactly why we can't stay away from each other. It's why you said you hated needing me, but it's also why I didn't tell you that I needed you, too. I still do."

He didn't reply, only stared at her as a muscle in his jaw ticked.

Oh God. Had she completely misread the situation?

"I know I told you I never wanted anything to happen between us. And you told me in that voicemail that you were over it, but . . ." Her voice faded into silence.

He let out a long breath, his gaze hard as he stared down at her. "Do you really think I ever stopped needing you?"

She blinked. "But you said—"

"I lied."

His hand came up to push her wet hair from her face as his mouth descended to hers. The kiss was hungry and deep, their tongues clashing as he wrapped his arms around her, pressing her body so hard against his that she almost couldn't breathe.

The rational part of her brain knew they had to talk. There was a bigger discussion to have here, one that probably included things like expectations or something. But she couldn't consider anything like that right now. This already felt fragile, like it would fall apart all over again if either one of them stopped.

She tightened her grip around his shoulders and deepened the kiss. It was so overwhelming she barely registered when her body suddenly became weightless as he lifted her up and her legs slotted around his waist. He took a step forward toward the stairs, his mouth still on hers, desperate and wet, but then her hands found his hair, pulling at the strands, and it was like he couldn't hold himself back anymore. A deep, guttural sound left his throat, then he lowered them both to the floor, landing on his knees with her body still wrapped around him.

God, only a few hours ago she had been terrified of never knowing the feel of him against her skin again. But right now,

covered in salt water and sand, with the rain and the thunder outside punctuating every kiss, every touch, she couldn't comprehend
being anywhere else.

He held her weight on his thighs, her legs still around his hips as
her fingers dove down his back, yanking at his sweatshirt, clumsily
trying to remove the layers that separated them. He smiled against
her lips, then used one hand to pull it up over his head and throw it
across the room. Then his arms were around her again, his mouth
demanding hers, even as his hands found the wetsuit zipper on
her back and pulled it down, peeling it from her shoulders and
arms. He lowered her down on the soft rug as he roughly pulled
the soaking neoprene from her legs, hardly looking at her bare
skin before he was kissing her again, his arms caging her in as she
arched up, nipping at his mouth, his jaw, his neck. His hands were
everywhere, touching, holding, demanding, almost like he was as
lost in this as she was.

Then he stilled, his forehead resting against hers. "Shit."

"What?" she breathed.

"I don't . . . I don't have anything here."

"What are you talking about? You have everything here. You
even have that portable water thing in the shed."

His brow furrowed. "The shower?"

"Exactly."

That crooked grin. The one that looked unpracticed, like he was
still learning how to turn up the corners of his mouth. "I mean, I
don't have anything for this. It's been . . . a while."

Oh. *Oh.*

She arched up again, trying to catch his mouth as a stream
of consciousness escaped her lips. "It's okay . . . we don't need . . .
that . . . I'm fine . . . on the pill . . . we're good . . ."

His expression turned sardonic, though his smile didn't dim.

"What?" she asked.

"I think I just witnessed an incoherent Elizabeth Bennet."

"Shut up, Will."

He chuckled.

She rolled her eyes and tilted her head up, trying to close the gap between them. "Just . . . come here . . . down . . ."

"If I had known sex made you tongue-tied, I would have tried this ages ago."

"It's not the sex. It's you."

Will stilled.

It hadn't sounded like such a raw confession in her head, but as soon as the words left her lips, the air around them suddenly felt heavy.

A roll of thunder echoed through the house, fading into a second that was even louder than the first. Then Will leaned back to sit on his heels.

A chill shot down her spine, but it wasn't because of the wind whistling outside. It was his expression. He was staring at her, all humor gone as he studied every inch of her skin laid out before him, like he was memorizing every freckle. Finally, one hand came up to her stomach, then slowly drifted between her breasts, stopping at her sternum. Her breath caught in her throat. God, his hand was so big, spanning almost the entirety of her rib cage, the calloused fingertips holding her still while he conducted his audit. His lips were half-parted and his eyes so intense that she felt like she could ignite. Then his gaze came back up to meet hers.

There was no condescending look on his face, no arrogance or reproof. It was just Will. His face felt like a mirror of her own, like they were having some sort of unspoken confessional right there on the floor, a recognition of just how vulnerable they both were.

"It's almost too much, isn't it?" he murmured. "Needing someone like this. So distracted you can barely function . . ."

"Yes," Lizzy whispered back.

Then the corner of his mouth ticked up, that hint of a smile that was so familiar now, and he leaned down. His mouth met hers as his hands found the knots of her bikini top, then the bottoms, tearing them free. Then he pushed down his sweatpants.

She was becoming desperate, too, grabbing his arms, his hair. She needed him closer, she needed to feel everything . . .

But then he grasped her wrists, lifting them up and anchoring them together above her head with one hand.

"Always distracting me," he murmured against her lips.

She wanted to laugh, but it was swallowed in a gasp as he leaned forward, his body looming over hers, and she felt him hard between her legs.

"Lizzy . . ." Her name sounded like a plea, like he was asking permission beneath his growl.

So she answered, her voice breathless and demanding. "Yes."

He didn't hesitate, just pushed into her, a thrust that filled her up so fully that she gasped.

"God, you feel so good," he whispered into the shell of her ear as he pulled out. Then he pushed back in so achingly slowly, she thought she might die. "Tell me you feel it, too. Tell me . . ." His voice caught and then faded with a deep, molten moan as he slid in and out again.

She wanted to say a million different things, a million new truths, but managed only one: "Will."

It wasn't rushed now. Even as her muscles began to tighten, as she felt that delicious tension growing in her core, he didn't speed up. He just kept a steady pace and watched her face like it was a revelation. With one hand still gripping her wrists, the other came up to brush a few stray hairs from her sweat-lined forehead, and she turned into it, kissing his palm before he thrust into her again.

God, this didn't feel like a release anymore. It felt like they were building something, pouring foundation into something that could be substantial. Something that *should* be. Something real.

It was too much—too much emotion, too much feeling, too much *everything*—and she suddenly had to squeeze her eyes closed. Like if she could focus on his touch, the feel of him inside her, she could ignore everything else she saw in his gaze and pretend her heart wasn't bursting open, that he wasn't the one fusing it back together into something even stronger.

But then his rhythm slowed, and she felt his hand on her jaw, cradling it as his calloused thumb ran over her bottom lip.

"Don't stop," she whispered. "Don't you dare stop."

"Elizabeth."

It was a demand, and she opened her eyes, half expecting to see a challenge waiting in his gaze. But his expression was raw, stripped bare as he loomed over her, his body silhouetted by the gray light.

"Don't hide from me," he growled.

God, he saw right through her. And closing her eyes wasn't going to protect her from this. He knew that, too. So she finally gave up trying.

"Then don't stop," she breathed.

Hunger flared in his eyes and he leaned down to envelop her mouth with his as he thrust into her again.

I think I'm falling for you.

She repeated it in her mind, over and over until his pace became all-consuming and her senses took over. The heat and the sweat from his body. The feel of the carpet rubbing against her wrists where he held them above her head. And the sounds. He was whispering, swearing, and there were words on her tongue, too—*more . . . please . . . yes*—but before she could utter any of them, she felt a blinding, voltaic energy on the periphery, tightening every muscle.

He looked down to where their bodies met, like he could actually see it there, building beneath her skin. Then he brought his hand to the apex of her thighs and pressed down, like he knew exactly what she needed.

He was right. The pressure sent her over the edge and she came, an explosion of electricity surging in her core that ignited every nerve ending. Did she just scream? It didn't matter. Nothing mattered except this, the heat in her veins, his grip on her wrists, and that look—God, that look—as he watched her fall apart.

Then he let go of her wrists to wrap his hands around her hips, holding her in place as she reached up into his hair, roughly grabbing at the strands. His thrusts became wild and jagged then, and it was only a few seconds before he came, too, throwing his head back, whispering curses into the air.

For a long time there was no sound except the thunder, the rain, and their heavy, desperate breaths. His body bowed over hers as he wrapped his arms around her waist, hugging her close. She could feel his breath against her shoulder, the shell of his ear right there next to her lips.

I think I'm falling in love with you, she wanted to whisper. But she didn't.

CHAPTER 29

Will blinked open his eyes, the soft morning light peeking through the wood blinds and cascading into his bedroom where he slept. What the hell time was it anyway? He turned his head to the side and relief flooded his entire being. Elizabeth Bennet was there, sound asleep, with nothing on except his thousand-count Egyptian cotton sheets.

The details of yesterday came floating back to him in waves. How he'd pulled her from the ocean, how her skin felt warm and cold at the same time against his, and how she sounded when she came.

They had stumbled upstairs afterward, ready to fall into bed, but instead they found their way into the newly installed shower in his room, letting the glass walls fog with steam as they fought for space under the hot spray. She had tried to bat him out of the way to wash the soap from her face, but he stopped her, grabbing those wrists again and pushing her against the tile wall. Her face was still covered in suds, so she couldn't open her eyes, and he took advantage of it, watching her expression as his other hand ventured down between her legs, delving inside and setting a steady rhythm that sent her over the edge again.

If I had known sex made you tongue-tied, I would have tried this ages ago.

It's not the sex. It's you.

This wasn't one-sided anymore. At the very least, she didn't hate him.

The muted sun streamed in over her face, her hair a mess of vibrant crimson and gold curls falling around her, her small frame taking up half his bed. It hardly seemed real. He studied her perfectly upturned nose and high cheekbones, her lips almost as red as her hair. It was difficult to catch his breath; she was so damn beautiful.

Without waking her, he got up and padded quietly into the bathroom, turning on the shower again.

Shit, he thought as he turned his face up into the hot spray. He didn't know how to do this. He had no clue. Everything in his life fit into a neat box, and a serious relationship was the opposite of that. Why would he willingly throw himself into something messy and complicated, something guaranteed to uproot his orderly life with a high net return of heartache?

But this thing with Elizabeth Bennet had him questioning everything he'd meticulously constructed. Could he even imagine waking up without her now?

He turned off the water and grabbed a nearby towel, wrapping it around his hips. Then he brushed his wet hair back and took a deep inhale before he walked back into the bedroom. The bed was empty, a mess of sheets and pillows where Lizzy had been sleeping. His brow furrowed, but the confusion only lasted a moment before he heard clattering coming from downstairs—cabinets opening, metal hitting metal, and then a mumbled curse.

Lizzy had found the espresso machine.

He smiled to himself as he grabbed a pair of sweatpants and headed downstairs to find her.

Sure enough, through the living room to the kitchen doorway, there she was, struggling to dislodge the sump from the espresso machine. Her back was to him, so he leaned against the doorframe and took a minute to watch. Her mess of red hair was piled in a bun on top of her head, and it lolled side to side with every tug. She was wearing his Columbia University sweatshirt again, the one she had been trying to return to him all week. It barely fell to her mid-thigh, exposing the length of her bare legs, and he let himself wonder if she'd bothered to put anything on underneath. His cock twitched at the thought, all exhaustion and confusion forgotten as he fought the urge to come up behind her and kiss her neck.

"Come on, you little son of a bitch," she hissed, tearing Will from his train of thought.

"Did you break my espresso machine?" he murmured, his voice gravelly from sleep.

She whipped around, holding the now-free sump in her hand. Her dark eyes were wide with surprise, but she recovered quickly, raising her chin at him. "Depends. Do I need to break it to make a cup of coffee?"

He tried to maintain a serious expression around his lopsided grin as he walked to her, stopping just inches away.

They stared at each other for a moment, tension filling the cozy room. She ran her tongue over her full bottom lip at the same time that he bit his own. The old part of him wanted to talk. Sit down and hash out the last twenty-four hours, map out exactly what this was and where they were going. But this wasn't a business deal. This was Elizabeth Bennet. And as she looked up at him, eyes expectant, he realized there wasn't a rule book for this. He had to do this right, if she'd let him. Yes, there were details they needed to work out, but they had time—neither of them was leaving Montauk until that evening—so he would ease into it, step-by-step, for the both of them.

"Turn around," he said, walking forward to close the gap between them. "I'll show you."

She rolled her eyes but complied. "Why don't you just make us both a cup?"

"Because I want you to learn." He was pressed up against her back now, his arms bracketing her against the counter. There was a small mirror hanging above the espresso machine and he could see their reflection in the glass. "First, add the coffee grounds to the filter basket."

She sighed dramatically as she picked up the bag from the countertop and opened it. She was just about to pour them when he ghosted his lips down the side of her neck.

Her breath stuttered, and her movements became clumsy as she poured the grounds into the basket.

"Well done," he murmured into the shell of her ear. "Now, tamp them down."

She slowly reached for the metal tamper. As her fingers wrapped around it, his hand came up her hip, sliding up the edge of her sweatshirt to her bare skin. In the reflection he could see her eyes flutter closed.

"You're distracting me," she breathed.

He smiled to himself. "Well, now you know how it feels."

Her body stilled as his hand ventured up, resting on her sternum as his thumb moved back and forth just below her breast. "You were making us coffee, Elizabeth."

Her voice faltered with a breathless laugh. "I don't know if I can right now."

He leaned forward, his chest flush with her back. His mouth was at the shell of her ear as he maintained her gaze in the mirror. "Try."

She let out a soft gasp as his hand inched higher and his thumb grazed over the peak of her nipple.

"Will . . ." She let her head loll to the side, giving him better access to her neck. He growled his approval, sliding his mouth down from her jaw.

Somewhere in his mind the nagging anxiety tried to stay afloat, but it quickly drowned in the rush of her pulse under his lips. He pressed his hips harder against her, forcing her to feel how hard he was even now.

She let out a strangled moan, and suddenly he didn't care about coffee, or what was happening today or tomorrow or a week from now.

With one hand cradling her jaw, he reached down to find an elastic waistband—she was wearing underwear after all. But no matter. He pulled the thin material aside and ran his fingers against her.

"Oh my God . . ." Her voice was barely audible.

Her head fell back against his chest. The mirror reflected back her expression, a testament to everything he was making her feel, and the image ignited a live wire deep in his core.

Then a sharp ringing shattered through the air.

RING. RING. RING.

It was her phone.

They froze, listening until it finally fell silent, only to begin again a moment later. He wanted to tell her to ignore it, but he could see the concern on her face now, as if playing out the emergency that might be waiting on the other end.

"I should get that," she whispered.

"I'll wait," he murmured.

She slid out of his grasp to walk to her bag on the counter. Meanwhile, he gripped its surface, trying to get ahold of himself.

"Hey, Jane," Lizzy answered, a weary smile on her lips. But as she listened, it slowly dissolved. "What?"

The color drained from her face as her eyebrows knitted together. Something was wrong.

"Okay . . . Yes . . . Wait . . . I know . . . Okay . . . I'm leaving now. Tell everyone not to do *anything* until I get there," she said, and hung up.

"What is it?" he asked.

She didn't move. It was like she was in a trance, staring at the wall.

"Lizzy," he said, his voice a bit louder. That caught her attention. "What's wrong? Is it your dad?"

"No. He's fine. It's my sister. She's in trouble."

"Jane?"

"No." She turned and stared up at him for a moment, her eyes so wide and lost that it almost broke his heart. "Mary."

CHAPTER 30

When Lizzy finally walked into Bennet Bakery at noon, it was chaos. The bell above the door heralded her arrival, but no one seemed to notice. Lydia was behind the counter talking over Kitty, who was glued to her cell phone as she paced the length of the glass display case in her most sensible slacks. Jane was in the doorway to the kitchen attempting to calm her two sisters down, while also trying to placate their mother, whose wailing echoed from the back.

It had taken fifteen minutes to quiet everyone—their mother was still crying on the phone but had at least shut the office door—and another ten minutes for Jane to lay out exactly what had happened. Even then, Lizzy wasn't sure the details made any sense.

She leaned across the bakery's glass counter and closed her eyes, taking a deep, calming breath before saying, "Okay. Explain this to me one more time."

Jane stood across from her, biting her bottom lip. Her expression was grave, which alone would have been enough to make Lizzy panic, but right now she was too focused on trying to unravel the knot in her belly, to make sense of the insanity and ensure it wasn't as bad as she thought.

"Mary was arrested last night for crashing Tristan's party in the city and destroying a really expensive piece of art."

Never mind. It was as bad as she thought.

Lizzy looked back down at Jane's phone in her hand and pressed play again.

The video was a blur of color and light, a crowd of people in a sprawling apartment, moving in time with the blaring music. Suddenly, shouting erupted as a figure dressed in black stepped into frame, a can of spray paint in hand. Their face was covered, so Lizzy couldn't decipher who it was until they began to yell.

"This is for Gretna Island! Our home won't be exploited for profit!" Mary's distinct voice bellowed. Then she took the can of red spray paint and wrote GREEN JUSTICE FOR ALL across a huge modern art piece on the wall.

The video ended in chaos, people running and screaming as the image blurred, only to start again from the beginning, this time with an odd array of hearts flying up over the footage.

Oh God.

Lizzy handed the phone back to Jane. "Who posted this?"

"Who didn't," Lydia murmured.

"Everyone at the party recorded it," Kitty clarified. "There's like a dozen different videos from a dozen different angles."

"What was she doing at the party? Was she even invited?" Lizzy asked.

"It sounds like everyone in town was invited." Jane sighed. "But we all thought she was still doing that protest on the North Shore, so we didn't notice when she wasn't home yesterday morning. Then Donna called and said her niece sent her a link to the video . . ."

"So everyone's seen it," Lizzy said.

"Obviously," Lydia said, rolling her eyes. "Have you seen the views? She's up to like eight million."

"Nine," Kitty corrected her.

Lydia frowned with a look of self-pity. "So jealous."

Lizzy turned to her. "Why didn't you stop her?"

"Since when is that *my* responsibility?" Lydia replied.

"Didn't you go?"

Lydia almost looked insulted. "Yeah, for five minutes. Then I realized it was just a bunch of people looking for celebrities but, like, no *actual* celebrities."

Lizzy ignored her and focused on Jane. "Where's Dad?"

"He's on his way into the city. We don't know when she'll see a judge, but once she does, he should be able to get her out on bail."

For a moment, Lizzy was tempted to just walk out the door and drive back to Montauk. Crawl into Will's king-sized bed and sleep until this whole thing was over. But then the image of Will's face when she left flashed in her head, and she cringed.

Things happened between Jane's call and climbing into her truck, but Lizzy barely remembered them. There had been a mad grab for her clothes, a rush downstairs as she fielded texts from neighbors and friends. Will had been there, too, always just a step away to pick up the bikini top she'd dropped behind her, the shoes and surfing gear left in her wake. But he was altered, too—that severe line of his brow that had been omnipresent those first few weeks of the summer was back, and he was watching her like he was waiting for the right moment to speak.

That moment came outside, as she scrambled to throw her board and her bag into the bed of her truck.

"Elizabeth," he'd said from where he stood behind her.

But his voice only joined the jumbled mess in her head, everything too distorted by anger and worry and embarrassment. She had to get back to East Hampton, fix this mess before it got any worse and—

"Lizzy."

This time her name was hard. Clear. Two syllables that ran right down her spine.

She glanced over her shoulder to find him just a foot or so away, arms crossed over his chest, and that hard glare focused entirely on her.

"I have to go," she said, opening the driver's-side door. "If I don't leave now, everything's just going to—"

"Not before we talk."

She narrowed her eyes on him. "You want to discuss everything that's happened over the last few days *now*?"

"No. Jesus," he growled, head falling forward. It was like he had to get a handle on his frustration before he looked up again. "What do you need me to do?"

Crap. Of course that's what he meant. Her anger dissolved into guilt, but frustration and fear were still too overwhelming to give it its due.

"Nothing," she said, shaking her head. "This is on me."

"No, it's not."

"Yes, it is," she said. "We fix problems for the people we love, Will. That's what we do."

The line of his lips turned down to a frown. "Your parents could—"

"My parents could barely keep the bakery running after my dad's stroke. I did that," she blurted out, tears suddenly threatening the corners of her eyes. "Just like I got Jane over the worst heartbreak of her life. And I'll find a way to get Mary out of jail, too. I'll get Tristan out of our lives and out of East Hampton, and we can all just pretend this summer never happened!"

Something changed in his eyes then, a subtle darkening that made his expression unreadable. She wished she hadn't said it, or that she could explain that she didn't include him in that statement. That he was the only bright spot in any of this, but before she could open her mouth, he replied, "You can't do this on your own."

She let out a bitter laugh. "There you go with that brute honesty again."

"I'm not trying to be cruel," he said, his voice stern as he stepped forward to tower over her, one arm braced above her on the car, caging her in. "But this is too big."

"I've got it," she seethed. She was suddenly desperate to leave, to avoid the look in his eyes that was so dangerously close to pity she wanted to scream.

"There's probably more that you don't know, and—"

"I said I've got it."

"—you can't expect Tristan to—"

"I don't need you to solve my problems for me, Will!" she yelled. He stilled, watching her carefully as she took a deep breath, a feeble attempt to get her emotions back in check. "I don't want your help. Or your pity. I need you to let me go. Just . . . let me go."

A moment. Then, slowly, he lifted his hand from the car door and took a step back.

"Then I won't keep you."

She avoided his gaze as she climbed into the driver's seat and fumbled with the keys. When the engine finally roared to life, she pretended to check the gauges, buying herself another precious moment before she looked up at him again.

He was staring at her, his expression stern and cold. "Goodbye, Elizabeth."

She waited a beat, wanting to say something, anything to fix this. But nothing came.

"Bye, Will," she finally replied. It was all she could manage.

And then she shut the door and put the truck into gear, making the full loop of the drive around the front of the house before turning onto the gravel road. She hadn't even had the courage to look back. She hadn't even waved.

Lizzy squeezed her eyes shut, forcing the memory into the back of her mind. She couldn't let herself wallow right now. She had to focus.

"All right," she said, opening her eyes again to look at her remaining sisters. "We have to trust that Dad will get Mary out on bail. And if Tristan is pressing charges, the next step is finding an attorney. I know Marv passed the bar, but I think we need someone with actual experience in a courtroom. Jane, can you make some calls? And Lydia, can you calm Mom down and get her home? Kitty, you and I can man the bakery until Dad gets back, and then . . ." She looked up to find her sisters staring at her. "What?"

"There's something else," Jane said. Her voice had taken on an even softer tone, as if the real crux of this mess hadn't been reached yet.

Oh God. "Do I want to ask?"

"Tristan quit HamptonFest and now it's not happening!" Kitty blurted out. She turned her phone to show Lizzy her screen. "It's all over the *East Hampton Gazette*. *New York* Magazine even picked it up!"

"And DeuxMoi," Lydia said. "Word is they called Leo for a comment."

"But HamptonFest is Hank's idea. He doesn't need Tristan."

Jane winced. "No, but he paid a huge portion of the Hampton-Fest budget to Tristan. Part of it was a nonrefundable retainer fee. He was supposed to secure those permits, help line up talent . . . but apparently he hasn't actually delivered anything yet. Then he quit this morning, claiming hostile work environment. So now there's no money, no permits . . ."

Lizzy groaned. "And no HamptonFest."

Of course Tristan quit. This entire debacle probably gave him the perfect excuse to keep his paycheck, even though he hadn't done anything to earn it. Echoes of Will's voicemail came back to her about how Tristan had spun lie after lie to manipulate a small fortune from his father.

Lydia shook her head. "Asshole."

"I thought you said he was hot?" Kitty said skeptically.

"What, you think that's enough to get me to run off and marry the guy or something?" Lydia rolled her eyes. "Just because I think he's hot doesn't mean I can't also acknowledge that he's a dick. Look at how he treated Lizzy."

"Can we all focus, please?" Lizzy said, looking around the room.

"Focus on what?" Kitty said. "The fact that Mary is facing felony charges or the fact that Hank blames her for the collapse of HamptonFest and now everyone in town is boycotting the bakery?"

The realization was like a swift punch to the gut. Lizzy had thought it was bad before, but this . . . there was no coming back from this. Hank held a lot of sway, almost as much as Marv, and to get on his bad side was to face social ostracism.

Mrs. Bennet came flying out of the back room, her phone to her ear. "No one is picking up. None of the book club ladies. Not Barb or Nancy. Not even Donna!"

"It's okay," Lizzy said, working to keep her voice level. "Once Dad gets to the city, we'll know—"

"Oh, I already know!" Their mother dropped her phone onto the table between Kitty and Lydia, making them both jump. "I know everything. Your sister screwed us! Absolutely destroyed our lives!"

Lizzy was about to try to soothe her, assure her that they'd find a way to keep the bakery afloat, but then her mother continued.

"Weeks of work and preparation!" she cried. "I learned how to sew for this! I have a thousand ounces of rhinestones and two hundred yards of Lycra in the basement, and for what?"

Lizzy's jaw clenched. "Mom."

"While she's off trying to save the world, did she even think for one minute about all *my* hard work? My sweat and my tears and my *nerves*—"

"MOM," Lizzy repeated. "I'm pretty sure we have more important problems than your leggings."

"Oh really? You think so?" Mrs. Bennet's voice had hit a frantic octave, so her sarcastic tone came out wobbly and manic. "Well, maybe they're not important to you, but they're important to me. I had things in motion, and now"—the bakery phone began to ring in the office—"I'm left with nothing. Nothing! Did any of you think of that?"

"Mom," Jane said, her tone suddenly the same one she used in her classroom full of six-year-olds. In the back, the office phone was still ringing. "I know you think—"

"Don't tell me what I think!" Mrs. Bennet wailed.

The phone kept ringing, an incessant clangor that was shredding Lizzy's patience.

"Lydia," Lizzy said, turning to her sister. "Go see who that is."

"Why can't we just let the machine get—"

"Go." Lizzy rarely let her voice get so stern. Lydia's eyebrows bobbed up before she stomped off to the back office.

Lizzy brought her attention back to her mother. "We don't have time for this."

"Oh really? Would you rather we talk about tomorrow's bread orders? Or how many muffins we've sold today? Because I can

tell you right now that both are zero, Lizzy. Absolutely zero!"
Another cry.

Lydia's head popped out of the doorway to the back. "Lizzy?"

She ignored her. "I know it's bad, Mom. Which is why we need to focus on—"

"Don't tell me what to focus on!" her mother shrieked.

"Lizzy," Lydia called to her again.

"Do you want to see the order I just put in for zippers?" Her mother picked up her phone again, her acrylic nails tapping on the glass as she unlocked it. "Who's paying for that, Lizzy? Who?"

"Lizzy!" Lydia yelled.

Lizzy whipped around to glare at her sister. "What?"

"There's a call for you."

Lizzy stilled as her heart tumbled down to her stomach. Everyone she knew had her cell number. Everyone except Will.

"Who is it?" she asked.

Lydia shrugged. "I don't know. Some woman."

The disappointment was potent. She turned away, swallowing it down as she waved her sister away. "Take a message."

"She says it's important."

"So is this!" Lizzy said, her voice almost a shout. Then she let out a sigh, squeezing her eyes shut for a moment's reprieve before continuing. "Just take a message, okay? I'll call them back later."

Another eye roll, then Lydia disappeared into the back again.

"No one in this family cares," Mrs. Bennet moaned. "What about *me*?"

Lizzy wanted to argue. She wanted to tell her mother she'd just cut the best week of her life short to be here, that she'd put her dreams of becoming a journalist on hold for her family. But the fight had left her. She felt hollow, like all her emotions had been used up and she didn't have the strength to replenish them again.

She turned to Jane. "Take Mom home. Lydia and Kitty, too. I'll call Dad and close up here. We'll figure out next steps in the morning."

Jane paused, giving her sister that look they had shared since they were children, but now it was laced with concern, as if for a moment, she saw the full weight of what Lizzy carried with her every day. Then Mrs. Bennet wailed again and Jane sighed, ushering everyone out the door before she disappeared with them.

The next few hours were a fog. No one came in, and her calls to her dad went straight to voicemail. Despite the promise of no customers tomorrow, Lizzy still went through the motions of prepping the bread dough, filling the muffin trays, getting everything ready for tomorrow's usual five a.m. start.

She locked the doors at five p.m.

She was home by 5:10 p.m.

Her dad's sailboat was dark and empty as she walked by it on her way to the front door. She ignored the arguing and yelling inside the house as she marched up the stairs and into her room.

Once the door was closed, she emptied the contents of her Montauk bag on her bed. There were her books, her clothes. All her surfing supplies. But then she found what she was looking for: Will's hooded sweatshirt with *COLUMBIA* written across the front.

Then I won't keep you. His words rang in her head. It had sounded so final. A punctuation on their time together, one that ended it with a definitive period. But what did she expect? She had taken for granted that they had time to figure out what this was and where it was going. But now they were left with this truncated version of events, and no road map of where to go next.

That was her fault. She'd left without letting him know what she wanted. What she expected. God, she left without even getting his number.

Of course, she could get it. She could probably find a way to call him right now. But she didn't want his pity, or to become another problem he had to solve. She needed to fix this herself.

She slipped the sweatshirt over her head. It still smelled like him. Sandalwood and leather and salt. She burrowed her nose in it, closing her eyes and working to memorize each note. The smell would fade, she knew that. But for now, she could hold on to it. Even if only for a little while.

CHAPTER 31

Will had spent the past eight hours searching every inch of Manhattan, fueled only by pure rage and endless cups of coffee.

It shouldn't be this hard to find a prick like Tristan. The guy was a creature of habit and lived his life online. His location was tagged in every post. But there had been nothing in the past twenty-four hours. Now it was Monday, and Will couldn't ignore the feeling that time was slipping through his fingers. On his way back into the city yesterday, he'd had his lawyer call every police precinct in the city until they found Mary, only to learn that her first court appearance was Tuesday morning. The clock was ticking.

Will didn't panic. He prided himself on keeping his emotions in check regardless of the situation, but as he combed the city streets, visiting all of Tristan's favorite haunts—a high-end hotel on Grand and an underground VIP room in the Lower East Side, a rooftop bar on Thompson—he couldn't help the anger that burned in his chest. Mary had broken the law in spectacular fashion, but Will also knew there was no way Tristan was completely innocent, either.

And while he might not be able to prove it, he could at least make sure Lizzy's sister didn't carry all the blame.

Of course, Lizzy had told him in no uncertain terms that she didn't want his help, that she didn't need it. He could have listened, stayed in Montauk and away from this mess. But he would never forget the look on her face when she got that call. The worry and fear and dread that bled through her expression. It had only been there for a split second before she hid it away again, ready to tackle this problem for everyone. But even though he knew she'd try her damnedest, she couldn't fix this on her own.

But Will could. And if doing so meant she ended up hating him, so be it. He would find a way to apologize. To be happy with whatever she offered him in return, even if it was only scraps. Any piece of her would be enough. Because right now, he was starving.

Then his phone began to vibrate in his pocket.

"Hello?" he answered, turning down Spring Street.

"Any luck?" George asked.

"No," Will replied. He hadn't planned on telling his friend anything, but he'd happened to call right when Will was leaving Montauk.

"Did you try that old Chelsea hotel with the downstairs—".

"Yes, I've been there. I've been fucking everywhere." He stopped on the corner, taking a deep breath to keep his anger in check. "Have you found anything?"

Will had filled George in on Tristan's history with the Darcy family earlier. He hadn't wanted to, but he needed help scouring Tristan's social media accounts, looking for any clues as to where the man might be.

There was a commotion on the other line.

"Hold on a sec," George replied. Then he paused, and Will

could hear Emma in the background before his friend spoke again. "Emma needs Lizzy's number. She says it's about the Betrug."

"The what?" Will replied with annoyance.

"The Betrug?" George left the phone again for a moment, then came back. "From the video, she says."

Will had no idea what Emma was talking about, and he didn't have the patience to find out.

"Tell her to call the bakery."

"She did. Left a message yesterday, but she hasn't heard back from her yet. What's her cell number?"

"I don't have it."

George paused. "You're telling me you're in love with a woman who you have no means of actually contacting."

Will ignored the comment and started walking again, turning down Broadway. "Isn't that why social media exists?"

"What, you plan to express your feelings through DMs?"

Will shook his head. He didn't have time for this. "That's not the top priority at the moment, George."

His tone had a hard bite, and he knew George had picked up on it.

"Will—"

"I have to go. Text if you find anything."

Will hung up and shoved his phone in his back pocket. His gait wide and determined, he weaved along the sidewalks, passing New Yorkers heading home for the night or just starting out. The bright lights of the city made it seem early, but his cell read almost eleven p.m.

"Fuck," he cursed loudly, the sound buried in the dissonance of beeping cars that rang through downtown traffic. He picked up his pace.

He had made it down to Canal Street when his phone buzzed again. The screen illuminated with two text messages from George.

GEORGE KNIGHTLEY

New post. He's at the St. Clement Hotel on Nassau St.

GEORGE KNIGHTLEY

Go get that asshole.

~

Through the glimmering, low light of the luxury hotel bar, Will scanned the room.

The place was packed, but not too loud, with well-dressed Manhattanites and hotel guests lounging in velvet chairs while others socialized at the bar.

That's when he spotted Tristan sitting at a table in the corner, sipping a martini. His hair was slicked back and his black shirt was unbuttoned halfway down his chest so it gaped open as he draped an arm around the young woman seated beside him. Her friends flanked them on either side.

Will clenched his jaw and headed over.

It took a moment before Tristan noticed him looming over the table. His expression changed to one of recognition.

"Well, well, if it isn't my old friend Will Darcy." His forced smile was wide and insincere. "What a coincidence—"

"I've been looking for you."

"How flattering," Tristan said, then turned to the woman on his side and whispered something in her ear. She threw her head back and laughed before turning to her girlfriends nearby to share the secret. Then Tristan focused his attention back on Will. "What do you want?"

"You had a party recently," Will said.

"I have a lot of parties."

"But this one ended with a woman in jail."

Tristan shrugged. "That's what happens when you destroy someone's property, Will. Especially when that property is very expensive."

Will nodded, considering. "So, was this just another party that got out of control, or did the folks at this music festival in East Hampton finally realize you're full of shit?"

Tristan laughed. "Hey, I can't help it if some idiot with a bar decides to pay me without double-checking my references."

"So the plan was to keep taking the money until he caught on?"

"Give me some credit, Will. I was going to give him some suggestions. Make a few excuses. But that festival was never going to happen. It's not against the law if he wanted to pay me to eventually tell him that." The man gave a slight shrug. "It just so happens that this girl gave me the perfect excuse to quit without doing anything at all."

Will studied him again, looking for a glimmer of the boy he had been friends with so many years ago. "You need to drop the charges."

"And why the hell would I do that?"

"Because that woman is Elizabeth Bennet's sister."

It took a moment for recognition to cross Tristan's face. A moment for Will to realize that Lizzy was barely a memory to him. His hands became fists at his side.

"Oh, right. The redhead," Tristan finally said. Then he smiled. "I thought that might make you jealous."

Will clenched his jaw. "How much?"

Tristan sighed, as if bored. "What?"

"I'm offering to give you money to do nothing, Tristan." Will angled his head. "You remember how that works, right?"

The woman sitting beside Tristan giggled at something her friend said, leaned in to share it with Tristan, but he pushed her away as he stood. "Let me get this straight: you want to pay me off to get some random chick out of jail, just to impress her sister? There are easier ways to get pussy, Will. Trust me."

The room went blurry for a brief moment as rage coursed through Will's body. He had been friends with this man once. He had trusted him, even told his father to trust him, too. Tristan had fooled them all. "How much?"

Tristan watched him, as if waiting for the catch. Will only stared back.

"A hundred thousand," Tristan finally said.

"Done," Will said. "I want those charges dropped tonight. When they are, I'll instruct my lawyer to pay you the full amount. Then you're never going to step foot in East Hampton again. If you do, I will ruin you. Are we clear?"

"Crystal." Tristan smiled a little too brightly. A sad imitation of charming.

Before Will could think again, all the tension, all the hatred, all the regret for letting this man hurt the people he loved channeled into his right fist. Will's hand swung out and hit Tristan right in the nose, hard. Tristan fell backward, stumbling, causing everyone in the bar to stop and stare, snap a picture.

"What the fuck!" Tristan yelled as blood dripped onto his designer shirt. "What was that for?"

"The redhead," Will said, then headed toward the door. Tristan could clean up his own mess.

CHAPTER 32

Lizzy wasn't sure why she bothered opening the bakery on Tuesday. They had decided to close for the past couple of days, waiting for Mr. Bennet to return. But her father still wasn't back from the city yet, and there had been no word on Mary. The entire town was still ignoring them, too. A rational person probably would have kept the bakery doors locked today, maybe even used the free day as an excuse to spend a few hours in the surf.

But surfing only reminded her of Montauk. How she had stood on the brink of something real and terrifying and perfect, and then it had fallen apart. She wanted to blame Mary or Tristan, but in the end, it still came back to her. She was the one who'd insisted on facing this alone. She was the one who drove away.

Lizzy felt off-kilter, like someone had picked her up and set her back in a place that should be familiar, but everything was slightly askew. Not enough for anyone else to notice, but enough that nothing felt right.

So she did the only thing she could: she opened the bakery.

She walked through the back door at five a.m., flipped on the *Open* sign at eight, and by noon the Smiths were playing overhead, and Lizzy was leaning against the counter reading *Oracle of the Damned*, the new Susan Vernon romantasy she had been waiting to open for weeks. She was so lost in the heroine's attempted escape from her shape-shifting kidnapper that she missed the sound of the bell above the door. But then Donna appeared in front of the register, smiling so broadly a bit of her red lipstick stuck to her teeth.

"Hello, dear!" she said in a singsong tone that made every syllable feel like the prelude to a musical number.

Lizzy jumped, almost dropping her book as her body bolted upright.

Donna didn't wait for a reply as she barreled on. "I'll have our regular order, please. But no coffee."

Lizzy narrowed her eyes with the distinct feeling that she'd missed a step. "Okay . . ."

"I'm trying to cut down on my caffeine intake," Donna replied, her voice suddenly low with the weight of the apparent hardship. "I read a recent study that said caffeine can be linked to an increased risk of anxiety. Can you believe that?"

It was all so normal that Lizzy wondered if she had imagined the last forty-eight hours, or if she had somehow woken up in a parallel dimension. She went through the motions of putting together Donna's regular Tuesday order—four blueberry scones, two baguettes, and one loaf of banana bread—while Donna continued to pontificate on this week's new dietary challenge.

"I didn't think I'd see you today," Lizzy said when there was finally a brief lull in the monologue.

Donna's forehead creased. "Of course I came in. It's Tuesday. I always come in on Tuesday before book club."

"I just thought, with everything going on with Mary . . ." Lizzy said carefully, ". . . and Tristan?"

"Oh, *that*." Donna waved her hand in the air as if batting away Lizzy's concerns. "I'm just happy it all worked out."

"What worked out?"

"The whole Mary thing, obviously. I told Hank it was a misunderstanding, and sure enough, some law firm contacted him this morning about reimbursing Tristan's fee by the end of the week."

Lizzy blinked. "Tristan is giving back the money?"

"Apparently. In any case, cooler minds prevailed. Tristan must have realized it's not Hank's fault that Mary has issues."

Lizzy was struck dumb. Before she could find the words to ask Donna to elaborate, the woman was already distracted. "Oh! You still have sour cherry muffins! It's my lucky day. Can I grab a half dozen of those, too?"

Donna kept talking while Lizzy completed the order, waiting for another moment to glean as much information as she could. But Donna only babbled on, and Lizzy continued to listen, so confused she almost missed the faint sound of her cell phone ringing from the office. By the time it registered in her brain, the ringing stopped. Then it immediately started again.

Lizzy was tempted to just walk back and get it—Donna was so involved with counting out change that Lizzy doubted she would notice her absence. But then the woman pulled a penny from her wallet with a flourish.

"There you go!" Donna announced, dropping exactly $38.71 on the counter. "Thanks, Lizzy. Oh, and can you ask Jane if she can help with the haunted hayride again this year? We need her students to paint the side of the trailer to hide the logo for Larry's Lawn Service and make the whole thing look haunted. She can do that, right? Like a class project? Maybe I'll just call your mother. I need her to pick up some of the pumpkins for the carving contest anyway."

Donna was still talking as she walked out the door, balancing the cardboard box in one hand and pulling her phone out of her bag with the other. Meanwhile, Lizzy headed toward the back.

In the office, she pulled her bag out from under the desk. Her cell phone was ringing again, but by the time she found it at the bottom, hidden below a tube of sunscreen, it had fallen silent. The screen was still lit up, though, displaying the fact that she had eight missed calls and a litany of text messages from her sisters.

JANE

Did you disconnect the bakery phone?

KITTY

Is your phone on silent?

JANE

I'm at school until 3 but call me when you can!

KITTY

I can't believe you're missing this rn.

LYDIA

Bring home some sour cherry muffins im starving

Lizzy's heart began to race. What the hell was going on?

The familiar chaos of the Bennet house welcomed Lizzy when she walked in. Laughing and yelling, pots and pans clattering, all happening over the sound of the ancient air conditioner clattering away in the front window. It was so normal that Lizzy stood for a moment in the foyer, hesitant to break the odd spell.

Then Kitty poked her head around the corner and saw her. "Lizzy's home!"

Here we go, she thought.

Lizzy followed Kitty into the living room. Lydia was on her phone, deep in conversation on the sofa as Kitty landed beside her, listening intently to whatever her sister was saying. In the kitchen, Mrs. Bennet was filling a glass of wine with one hand and holding her phone to her ear with the other.

Lydia's head popped up when she saw the white cardboard box in Lizzy's hand. "Muffins!"

Lizzy deposited the box on her sister's lap as she stopped next to the couch. "What are you two doing?"

"Nothing," Kitty replied, even as her eyes went wide, a telltale admission of guilt. Lydia, on the other hand, had no such tell.

"Where are the scones?" she whined.

Lizzy was too tired to answer as she headed for the kitchen. Her mother was leaning against the counter, deep in conversation and oblivious to Lizzy's arrival. And behind her, at the kitchen table, was Mary, slathering a Pop-Tart with peanut butter. Scattered around her were piles of food wrappers—Oreos and Pringles and Sour Patch Kids.

"Oh my God," Lizzy said, rushing around the table and embracing Mary's blue pixie cut in a hug. "When did you get back?"

"A few minutes ago," Mary replied, her voice muffled by the sleeve of Lizzy's sweatshirt.

Lizzy released her and fell into a nearby chair. "And?"

Mary paused mid-chew. "And what?"

Lizzy's eyes widened. "Mary, you were in jail yesterday and now you're sitting at the kitchen table OD'ing on food with artificial preservatives in nonbiodegradable packaging."

She held up a half-empty bag of gummies. "These are going carbon neutral by 2030."

Lizzy sighed, pushing her hair away from her face. "What happened?"

"A miscarriage of justice."

"No, I mean, why aren't you still in jail? Did Dad post your bail?"

"No." Mary took another bite of her Pop-Tart. "Tristan dropped the charges."

Lizzy blinked. "Why would he do that?"

"Probably because I didn't do anything wrong."

"Mary, you destroyed an insanely expensive piece of art."

"Yeah, but he deserved it."

"Because he was securing the permits on Gretna Island for HamptonFest?"

Mary snorted out a laugh.

"Oh, please. He didn't even try to secure those permits. He got Hank to pay him to come out here all summer and 'consult' or whatever, but he was just living it up without doing anything."

"How do you know that?"

"Green Justice monitors all permit applications," Mary replied, as if the fact was obvious. Then she took another bite of her Pop-Tart. "Hank had been hounding the office about HamptonFest for the past three summers, but this year? Not one permit application. Not even a phone call."

Lizzy stilled as everything seemed to click into place in her brain. "Oh my God."

"I know," Mary said around her mouthful of food. "Capitalist pig."

"Why didn't you tell Hank?"

"He got a restraining order against me." Mary shrugged one shoulder. "Besides, I didn't want him to know and actually fix the issue. It's not like we *wanted* the permits to go through."

Lizzy shook her head. "If you were happy for Tristan to do nothing, then why crash his party and destroy that painting?"

"Didn't you ever hear him brag about the fact that he only flies on private jets?" Mary replied, disgusted. "Those cause fourteen times the pollution of commercial planes. He's a climate criminal."

Lizzy had assumed Mary's resentment toward Tristan had been because of the endangered island slugs; it hadn't even occurred to her that it would be about anything other than that.

"Mary, I swear to God, if I hear you say the words 'climate criminal' one more time!" her mother hissed, holding her hand over the phone as if it would mute her voice. Then she removed it and her pinched face transformed into a smile again. "Oh, Barb, I told you it was nothing, so it's not a surprise, you know?"

"Whatever," Mary said, standing up with her Pop-Tart in one hand and the jar of peanut butter in the other. "I'm going to my room."

∾

It was dark by the time Lizzy headed outside to the sailboat parked on the lawn. She had fixed as much as she could—now it was time for answers. Or at least commiseration.

Her father was sitting at the small table in the galley kitchen. His head was down, focused on a letter in his hand, so he didn't notice her until she was carefully navigating the narrow ladder down to the cabin.

"Hey."

He looked up. The hard line of his brow softened slightly. "Hey, kiddo."

She sat down on the bottom rung. "So."

"So," he repeated with a sigh. "Did you see Mary?"

Lizzy nodded. "She was eating everything in the pantry. I guess the NYPD doesn't offer a vegan menu in jail."

He chuckled, but it faded quickly.

She sighed, leaning back against the wall. "What happened?"

"Good question." He scratched at the stubble that had grown around his mustache. "It took a while to track down where she was being held. By the time I got to her this morning, they told us this Tristan guy had dropped all charges and she was free to go."

"You're sure?"

He didn't reply, just handed over the papers in his hand. The words *Affidavit of Non-Prosecution* were emblazoned on the top, followed by a long block of text that she could only skim. The words "right to counsel" and "State of New York" jumped out, along with Tristan's name and signature, and the capitalized statement: I DO NOT WISH TO PROSECUTE. Beside it, another signature from a law firm called Page, Lefroy, and Brandon LLP.

She stared down at it for a long moment. "But . . . why would he do that?"

"No idea. But I'm not going to argue. I guess that painting was worth over a million dollars, so it would have been a felony."

Lizzy's mouth fell open. "Are you serious?"

He nodded.

"But I don't get it. She admitted it. The video is everywhere."

"I guess he changed his mind. Which would explain why Hank got an email promising to have Tristan's entire fee returned this week, too."

Lizzy looked down at the papers again. None of it made sense. But she also didn't want to question it. They barely had enough money to cover the recent renovations to the bakery—she had no idea where they would have found the funds for a lawyer, and bail, and court . . .

She sighed, pushing her hair away from her face. "So, how long is she grounded?"

"Not sure I can get away with grounding a twenty-two-year-old. Besides, I can't blame her."

She shot him an incredulous look. "You can't?"

"Well, I can blame her for the felony," he said. "But I can't blame her for being passionate about something. She's doing what makes her happy."

"Criminal trespassing and destruction of property?" Lizzy groaned.

He chuckled again. "No. Following her heart. Not getting bogged down by everybody's expectations." He looked down, his gaze sliding over the floor of the boat. "Not all of us are that brave."

The words landed heavy in the small cabin, swallowed up only by the silence that followed.

"You're telling me Mary's your favorite?"

He smiled and stood up. "I'm going to bed. Bring in the lantern when you come in so the battery doesn't run out."

Lizzy didn't move as he climbed up onto the deck and down the ladder to the lawn. And it was another minute after she heard the front door close before she pulled her phone from her pocket. Before she opened her email and went into her drafts.

The email to Columbia's School of Journalism claiming her deferred spot for January was still sitting there, waiting.

If Mary could follow her heart, so could she. It was time.

She took a deep breath, closed her eyes, and pressed send.

CHAPTER 33

"All right, I think that's all of it," the disembodied voice said on the other end of the speakerphone. "The HamptonFest funds will be transferred tomorrow morning."

Will looked over the email on his computer screen again. His lawyer had sent it an hour ago, outlining the steps taken to repay Tristan's fee to Hank Donato. He didn't have the specific amount, but guessed it was around what Tristan had demanded to ensure Mary went free. If he was over . . . well, they could just consider it interest for the mess Tristan created.

"You're transferring anonymously, correct?" Will asked.

"Yes. Which will probably mean they'll think it's from Tristan. You're okay with that?"

"Yeah." Will frowned. "He hasn't been in touch, has he?"

A deep chuckle on the other line. "I think even Tristan is too smart for that."

Thank God. Will closed his laptop with a snap that echoed through his office. "I owe you, Christopher."

"That's why we have an accounts payable department."

Will smiled. "I'll talk to you later."

"Until then," his lawyer replied, and hung up.

Will leaned back in his chair and let out the first breath in what felt like hours.

It was done. The charges against Mary had been dropped. Tristan was gone. And the money he had been paid by HamptonFest was about to be back in the hands of the organizers. All was neatly settled, with Will's involvement reasonably concealed. It should have been a relief. He was good at making problems disappear, cleaning up other people's messes while no one was looking. It was a bit like slipping on a pair of old shoes, broken in and comfortable from years of use, so they almost felt like a second skin. He knew how to do this. He was good at it.

Still, relief was evasive.

There was no chance Lizzy would find out about his involvement. He would never want her to, especially since she would either be pissed or feel indebted. But he had been so busy fixing this he hadn't considered that, in order to keep his involvement concealed, he would need to lie about it when it was done.

But he couldn't lie to Lizzy. He felt gutted to even be considering it. So where did that leave him?

A beep from his desk phone stole his attention, signaling a call from his receptionist. He reached over and pressed the speaker button.

"Hi, Mr. Darcy," Jenna said nervously. "I have your aunt on hold? She says it's urgent."

Will scratched the stubble along his jaw, trying to curb his frustration. He had gotten her texts over the past few days, but barely read them. Something about scheduling a showing for the Montauk house. He couldn't contemplate that, not now.

"Take a message, please."

"I tried that, but she says she's already left three."

"Then let's make it four."

Jenna laughed. "I'll try."

Will hung up and stared at the wall again. He had to deal with his aunt, tell her about his concerns. But that could wait. Right now, there was one more problem he needed to fix. The thought had only just entered his head when there was a knock on his office door.

"You want the roast beef or the club?"

Will turned to find Charlie in the doorway, a bag from Lexington Deli in his hand.

"Club," he replied, ignoring the stab of anxiety in his chest. He wasn't hungry, but he wasn't about to send Charlie away, either. Not when he was exactly the person he'd been about to go looking for.

Will straightened in his chair just in time to catch the wrapped sandwich Charlie tossed his way. Then his friend sat down in the chair opposite the desk, grabbing his own from the plastic bag.

"Lexington Deli," Will said. "Bad day?"

Ever since they opened Hampshire M&A in this office six years ago, Lexington Deli had been their go-to on bad days. Whatever stress encroached on their work could easily be relieved by their extensive menu.

"No," Charlie replied. "Just a lot on my mind."

"Such as?"

Charlie unwrapped the brown paper from his sandwich before replying. "I know we talked about this, and I followed your advice to stay in New York, but I've been thinking. A lot. And yes, it's impractical and yes, I could be setting myself up to get my heart broken, but... I've decided to start looking for a house out in East Hampton."

Will blinked. "I'm sorry?"

"Not another summer rental. Something permanent." He fell back in the armchair, abandoning the sandwich on the side table. "I miss it, Will. I miss *her*."

Will let out a long breath. "Jane."

Charlie nodded solemnly. "I still love her. And I'm sure you have a thousand reasons why you think this is a bad idea but—"

"I don't think it's a bad idea."

His friend paused. "Really? Because ever since the Fourth—"

"I know," Will said, frowning. "And I have to talk to you about that."

His friend's expression blanched. "About what?"

Will laid out all the details in order, careful to leave out any emotion that might corrupt his rationale. He had to stick to the facts: his concerns about the Blaxton deal even before the summer started, his continued observation of Jane's apparent reticence, how Charlie's past relationships helped color his perceptions of the situation. How Will's only concern had been Charlie's happiness. But as he concluded, finally taking responsibility for keeping Charlie in the city for the rest of the summer, Will noted his friend's expression and realized perhaps leaving emotion out of it was the wrong choice.

"Why would you do that?" Charlie's voice was low and cold.

It was a good question. A few weeks ago, Will would have easily ascribed it to his concern over Charlie, but now, hindsight added clarity. There had been other factors in play—ones that hid behind his ego for too long—but that was before Montauk. Before every fortification around his heart had been laid to ruin at the feet of Elizabeth Bennet.

Yes, he had dragged Charlie away from East Hampton to protect his heart, but now, Will knew, he had been trying to protect his own, too.

"You're my friend and I didn't want you to get hurt. I was trying to help," Will finally said. "I know that's no excuse, but—"

"You're right. It is no excuse," Charlie said, his voice more urgent. "I love this woman, Will."

"But that doesn't guarantee anything," Will said, trying to curb the impatience in his voice. "What if it falls apart?"

"What if it doesn't?"

"But it could."

Charlie leaned forward, his expression softening. "But what if it doesn't? Yes, I could get my heart broken again. But what if it ends up being the best thing that's ever happened to me?"

What if. The words echoed in Will's head as he stared back. Then he sighed. "There's something else."

Charlie's brow furrowed. "Okay."

"Last week, when I canceled all those meetings to stay out in Montauk . . ."

"Yeah?"

"I was with a woman."

"Really? George mentioned that you met someone out in Montauk, but didn't really say anything else. So, what's her name?"

"Elizabeth Bennet."

Silence landed like a bomb in the center of the room.

There were only three times Will had seen Charlie Pierce truly angry. The first time was when the Denver Broncos lost the Super Bowl their freshman year of college. The second was after he found out they were remaking *Point Break*. The last time was two years ago when George remodeled his townhouse and didn't install a single solar panel. But now, as Charlie stared at him from under the hard line of his brow, Will realized he might have instigated number four.

"Elizabeth Bennet," Charlie repeated.

"Yes."

"Jane's sister."

Will grimaced at the harsh tinge in his friend's voice. "This wasn't something I planned, Charlie. Until recently, I thought she hated me. She still might. And I don't know—"

"So let me get this straight," Charlie said, interrupting him. "You convinced me that I was making the right choice by coming back to the city, that East Hampton was distracting me from the Blaxton deal. And then you go and cancel a dozen meetings about the Blaxton deal to spend a week with Jane's sister, who lives in East Hampton."

Will stared at him, eyes narrowing. *Damn it.* "Charlie—"

"You're unbelievable," Charlie said, standing up. "You're so worried about micromanaging everybody else's life that you don't even see it."

"See what?"

"You're a hypocrite, Will! You're not out here cleaning up everybody else's messes because you feel like it. You do it so you don't have to deal with your own shit! Well, news flash: life is messy and complicated. Even you can't fix that. So stop using everyone else's mess as an excuse to ignore your own!" Charlie said, hands flying out at his sides.

"Lizzy's not a mess, Charlie," Will said. But even as he said it, his text from that first night in East Hampton came back to him. "I'm in love with her."

His friend reeled back, his expression so livid that Will thought he might actually raise his voice, which he hadn't done since the *Point Break* revelation. "Does she know that?"

"No."

"So tell her!"

"It's not that simple, Charlie."

"Why the hell not?"

"I don't know if she feels the same way. And I don't have her number, so—"

Charlie's eyes went wide. "Are you serious? How the hell can you not—" Then he cut himself off and shook his head, letting out a short, dry laugh. "You know what? Fuck this. I'm not getting involved. This entire shitshow happened because you thought you had the right to fix other people's messes. So I'm bowing out. You want to clean up a mess, Will? Clean up your own. I'm going home."

Then he turned on his heel and walked out, slamming the door behind him.

The sound was still echoing through Will's office when the phone on his desk began to beep again. He sighed, then reached over to press the speaker button.

"What is it, Jenna?"

"I'm sorry, but it's your aunt again," Jenna said nervously. "She says she won't leave a message and will stay on hold until I can give her some new information."

You want to clean up a mess, Will? Clean up your own.

He stared at the wall, letting the words rush through his bloodstream again. Maybe it could be that simple. Maybe, for the first time, he should try.

"She wants new information?" He turned to the phone again. "Then tell her I'm not selling the Montauk house."

"But—"

"If she has a problem with that, she can call me tonight to discuss further."

"Yes, Mr. Darcy," Jenna said, her voice quiet.

He hung up, a new lightness on his shoulders. He hadn't realized how much the guilt and remorse had weighed on him, the dread of having to say goodbye to that house. But Lizzy was right; he didn't have to. He just had to say so.

The corner of his mouth ticked up in a grin. Here he was contemplating how he had saved her from her problems, and somehow, even in her absence, she had saved him from his own.

CHAPTER 34

"It's supposed to be a spider," Kitty said. She was standing beside Jane at the bakery counter, placing black-and-white candy circles on the cupcake's black frosting.

Lydia was draped over a nearby table, glaring at them. "It looks like a mold spore."

Jane sighed. "It's not a mold spore."

"It *should* be a mold spore," Mary murmured from the floor where she sat with paper towels and a squeegee, cleaning the glass display. It was one of the janitorial duties she had taken on as penance for her arrest. "Fungi are the backbone of the natural world."

Lizzy peered over the final pages of *The Oracle of the Damned* as Jane considered the cupcake again, her bottom lip now between her teeth.

"Maybe we should make a sign," Jane finally said.

Lizzy smiled. The conversation continued, sure to escalate to an argument that would inevitably fizzle out when something else grabbed their attention. It was a Bennet sister trait. But despite the bickering and laughing and rolling of eyes, Lizzy had to admit that it was nice not working a shift alone. In fact, as she watched her sisters navigate around one another, she realized it was the first time in ages that all five of them were there together. A small bit of life falling back into place.

A sense of normalcy had returned to the village, too. In one of her first journalism courses in undergrad, Lizzy had learned that news stories take about seven days to cycle in and out of people's minds until the next salacious story redirects everyone's attention. Thanks to a local teenager stealing a lobster ship and crashing it into the marina, HamptonFestgate—as it had started to become known—was forgotten after five. Now, a week later, East Hampton's news cycle had died down to a low rumble, and, like clockwork, Hank was back to discussing next year's plans for HamptonFest like nothing had happened at all.

"Are you okay?" Jane appeared beside Lizzy.

"I'm fine." Lizzy forced a smile. She wasn't, but she couldn't admit that. She had spent the past week working so hard to appear okay that she hadn't bothered to make it true. So instead, she kept pretending. Pretending not to be disappointed about how she hadn't heard from Columbia yet, or how embarrassed she was about the way she'd left Montauk and Will behind. So embarrassed, in fact, she hadn't even tried to find a way to contact him, to reach out and apologize. This is what happened when she didn't think things through and just reacted in the moment. Maybe she *was* a mess.

"How about some coffee," Jane said, already reaching for the sleeve of cups. "You look tired."

Kitty had a pile of candy googly eyes in her hand as she leaned across the counter to assess Lizzy. "Really tired."

Lizzy glared at both of them. "You two can go home now, you know. The morning rush is over."

"Why don't you go home?" Jane suggested.

"Because I never go home."

Jane shrugged. "Well, it's about time things started changing around here, then, don't you think?"

Lizzy could read the meaning behind Jane's words, mostly because Jane was also giving her a less-than-subtle look that drove it home. This was a family bakery; it was time they all started acting like it.

"Does that mean someone else is going to clean the bathroom?" Mary asked, standing up with a wad of paper towel in her hand.

Lizzy laughed. "No."

Mary frowned. "Fascists."

"Here," Kitty said, reaching over to hand her a black cupcake. "Have a mold spore."

Mary accepted and took a huge bite.

"Seriously, though, what's wrong with you?" Lydia asked Lizzy, her arms splayed across the table and her chin resting in her hand.

"Nothing's wrong with me," Lizzy replied.

"God, you're the world's worst liar." Lydia snorted out a laugh.

Suddenly, Lizzy was aware that all her sisters were staring at her, waiting. She had hoped that if she continued to deny it, kept pretending she was okay, people would stop caring enough to ask. But she hadn't considered how that wouldn't work here. Her sisters would never stop caring. They would annoy her and berate her until she finally opened up because here, with them, she mattered.

Her heart ached with the realization. And while she knew she didn't have the strength to reveal all the details about Will, she suddenly knew she had to tell them about Columbia.

"Okay," Lizzy said, releasing a long breath. "Promise you won't freak out."

Kitty perked up. "Who's freaking out?"

"No one," Mary said around a mouthful of cupcake.

"Well, maybe Lizzy," Lydia added.

"Everyone stop talking!" Jane demanded in her best first-grade-teacher voice.

Lizzy smiled. "I just . . . I think I'm ready for grad school. I'm going to get my master's."

A moment, then the room exploded with screams.

"Finally!" Jane exclaimed. "You were talking about it last year, but then you just dropped it after everything happened with Dad!"

"It's about time!" Kitty threw her arms around her. "Have you applied anywhere? Are you sticking with foreign affairs journalism, or thinking about something else?"

Even Mary was smiling. "You could do an investigative piece on Long Island's lack of recycling centers!"

"Oh my God, you should do celebrity reporting!" Lydia squealed. "You could work at TMZ!"

The five of them were dancing around now, jumping up and down, laughing and hugging so much that Lizzy didn't know why she hadn't told them before. Suddenly, everything was on the tip of her tongue—her acceptance to Columbia, the lingering hope of starting in January—but she was interrupted by the sound of the bell ringing out from the bakery's front door.

"Excuse me." A deep voice interrupted them.

The sisters turned around in unison to see Charlie Pierce in the middle of the room, his hands in his jeans' pockets.

"Hi," he said meekly.

Jane inhaled sharply, Kitty and Lydia glared at him, and Mary picked up her squeegee like it was a weapon. Meanwhile, Lizzy looked to see if he was alone.

He was.

"Hello," Jane responded after a moment.

Silence descended on the room. No one moved. Lizzy wasn't even sure if they breathed.

Then the front door swung open again and Mrs. Bennet fell into the shop, her neon-green leggings blinding. "Guess what! Donna just called and said that Hank called Tristan to thank him for repaying everything, and Tristan didn't know what he was talking about! And then Barb said that someone saw Charlie Pierce in town and now everyone thinks he—"

Her gaze found Charlie and she froze like a deer in headlights, her eyes wide and purse still precariously balanced over her arm.

"It's nice to see you again, Mrs. Bennet," he said with a small smile.

Mrs. Bennet blinked, as if to reset her brain. "Oh! I didn't know you were here, Charlie! How lovely." She moved sideways to the front table and slowly set her purse down, her eyes clocking each person, then lowered herself into a chair, as if all she needed was some popcorn to watch the show.

Charlie's gaze was locked on Jane's.

The room fell silent again until Lydia finally spoke. "Did you need something, or what?"

Charlie cleared his throat. "Right. Yes. Well, I just wanted to stop by. I haven't seen you in a while, so I thought I'd see how you were doing . . ."

Jane opened her mouth, but Kitty spoke first. "You mean, after you left without an explanation?"

"And tried to pull the slow fade afterward?" Lydia said, head tilted to the side.

Mary continued, "And then you—"

"You came back after possibly saving our town's biggest event after Mary's little episode!" Mrs. Bennet responded quickly, shooting them all a pointed look.

Charlie's expression contorted in confusion. "I'm sorry?"

"The money you paid to reimburse HamptonFest," Mrs. Bennet clarified.

"Oh," Charlie said. "Well, that sounds very generous, but that wasn't me."

Mrs. Bennet's wide grin fell and she turned back to her daughters. "What were you saying?"

Mary opened her mouth to continue where she left off, but Jane interrupted.

"It's okay. I think we get the gist of it." Then she turned to Charlie. "Is there anything we can help you with?"

He hesitated. "I just . . . wanted to see you. Say hello."

"That's . . . very nice of you," Jane replied softly. "But you can't come here after all this time to just say hello."

His face blanched, even as he nodded. "I know. But I wanted . . . I had to make sure you were okay."

"I am now." Tears began to line Jane's eyes. "But I wasn't. Not for a long time. Because I fell in love with someone who just . . . disappeared." Her voice cracked as Mrs. Bennet gasped. Lizzy, Mary, Kitty, and Lydia watched, mouths hanging open.

Charlie's expression softened. "You fell in love with me?"

Jane nodded. "And you left before I could tell you. Before I could apologize and explain."

"Jane—" he whispered.

"You gave up so easily, Charlie," Jane said. "You can't just walk in here and expect to pick up where we left off."

Charlie's gaze dropped to the floor as he nodded. "You're right. I'm sorry."

"I'm sorry, too," Jane replied. Silence fell again, and it was another minute before Jane continued, "I just don't know what to do now."

He looked up, meeting her gaze. "We start over."

He turned around and left the bakery, the bell above the door the only sound in the room until a stunned Mrs. Bennet jumped up from her chair.

"What is happening!" she cried.

Before Jane could answer, the door to the bakery opened again. Charlie stood on the threshold and cleared his throat, then he walked by a gawking Mrs. Bennet, Kitty, Lydia, Mary, and Lizzy to stop in front of Jane.

"Hello." He held out his hand to Jane. "I'm Charlie."

A smile tugged at the corner of Jane's mouth as she tentatively placed her palm in his. "Hi. I'm Jane."

"It's a pleasure," he said softly. "I'm new to town and heard there was a really nice bar nearby. Donato Lodge?"

Lydia scoffed under her breath. "Really nice?"

Lizzy elbowed her.

"I was hoping you might like to grab a drink with me sometime," Charlie continued.

Jane's smile broadened. "I'd like that."

"Really?" Charlie replied, as if genuinely surprised. "That's great!"

"You should go now!" Mrs. Bennet smiled brightly, her hands clasped together like she was watching the end of her favorite romantic comedy.

Jane laughed and shook her head. "I don't finish here until five."

Charlie smiled. "Okay. I'll be back to pick you up at five." Their gaze remained locked on one another, then he turned to the rest of them. "Nice to see you all."

They nodded, barely able to wave goodbye as he walked out the door and disappeared down the sidewalk.

A moment of pure stillness passed before the room erupted in chaos again. Laughter and screaming and smiles. Lizzy joined in, too, her heart practically bursting for her sister. But she couldn't help how her eyes traveled back to the window, just to make sure Will didn't suddenly appear.

He didn't.

CHAPTER 35

He pulled her against his hard armor. The spell he cast over the room made time stop, suspending them in the dark shadows of the curse. Her dragonbone dagger crashed to the cold ground as she reached up to touch his face. His skin felt like fire and sin. His emerald eyes danced over her shimmering skin right before he—

Lizzy's eyes blurred at the words in front of her. She couldn't focus on a High Fae's bastard heir right now. She couldn't focus on anything. The euphoria from Charlie's visit to the bakery earlier had worn off, and she felt restless.

She slammed the book closed and turned to stare out her bedroom window, the stolen Columbia sweatshirt warm and loose around her body. It had rained earlier, leaving her usual spot on the roof too wet to enjoy, so she just watched the trees from her bed, their leaves just beginning to turn red and yellow.

It was late, well past ten o'clock, and the Bennet household was beginning to settle. Down the hall, Lydia and Kitty were laughing as they got ready for bed. Mary was probably still at the kitchen table, finishing up her research on how to shut down offshore wind projects on the East Coast. And judging from the lack of noise in the dining room, Mrs. Bennet had finally powered down her industrial-sized bedazzler. Apparently, the Luxe Leggings winter collection was done.

And Jane was still out with Charlie. True to his word, he had waited until her shift ended, then they had disappeared with barely a glance back as they left the bakery. Lizzy doubted she would see them before tomorrow.

She was happy for her sister. She really was. But there was still an inkling of loss, too. Something final about the fact that Charlie came alone when all summer Will had been a permanent fixture at his side.

Enough, she thought. She could analyze it all day, but it wouldn't change the fact that he wasn't there. She had told him to let her go, and now she would have to be the one to admit she wanted him back. That would mean facing the pity she'd seen in his eyes before she left, though, and she didn't think she had the strength for that. Not tonight. So instead, she picked up her phone and unlocked it, ready to scroll through her email and social media, anything to turn off her brain.

But then she saw a new message waiting in her inbox. And there, in the center of the subject line: Columbia University Graduate School of Journalism.

Lizzy's pulse stuttered. "Oh my God."

She stood, fumbling with the screen. Finally the message opened, and she was barely able to concentrate, as her eyes skimmed over the words: *Welcome back . . . Spring semester . . . Partial scholarship*.

There were documents attached, instructions for registration, but Lizzy couldn't focus on that right now. All that mattered was that she was going back.

She was going to get her master's.

And she had to tell her dad.

Her stomach fell. She should be smiling ear to ear. Instead it felt like she had set something irreversible into motion, and she wasn't sure why that scared her so much.

Lizzy headed downstairs and out the front door to her father's boat. It was late, but she knew he would still be there, probably finishing up for the night.

"Permission to board?" she yelled up, noticing the ladder was now painted with a shiny white finish.

"Granted," her dad yelled back.

She made her way up the ladder and found him on the deck, sorting through his toolbox. She sat down across from him, but it was a minute before he looked up and noticed her expression.

"What's wrong?" he asked.

"I need to talk to you."

He leaned back against the railing. "Did someone else get arrested?"

She let out a meager laugh. "No." Then the words faltered, and she had to take a deep breath before she continued, "Remember last year when I was thinking about grad school?"

He nodded.

"Well, I ended up applying to Columbia. Their school of journalism is one of the best in the country, and it was a long shot. I didn't even think I would get in, so I didn't tell anyone about it . . . but I did." She tried to smile, to make her voice sound celebratory, but it only came out flat.

His brow furrowed. "When did you find out?"

Her eyes darted down to where she fumbled with the edge of her T-shirt. "A few days before your stroke."

Her father stared back at her, his expression stoic.

"I wasn't trying to keep it a secret," she continued quickly. "I was just . . . trying to figure out how to tell you. Work out the financials and everything so you wouldn't worry. And then everything happened, and your doctors made it sound so . . ." Her voice cracked. "I deferred enrollment until I knew you were better and we all had a plan. Columbia gave me a semester, and it seemed like so much time. But after a while I realized that we were never really going to have a plan because . . . it's us. So everything just fell into the same pattern, and going to Columbia, becoming a journalist—it started to feel so far away. Like it was a dream I had no business dreaming."

She dared to look up and meet her father's gaze again. He had barely moved. "Did you let the deadline pass?"

"No. I wrote them last week. They're letting me enroll in the spring."

A long moment. Then her father let out a long sigh. "Well, thank the good Lord for that."

Lizzy blinked. "What?"

"You've been dreaming of being a journalist and traveling the world since you were old enough to hold a pencil, Lizzy. Do you have any idea how pissed I'd be if you let that deadline come and go?"

"Really?"

"Really. I'm proud of you, kiddo." He smiled, one side still a little higher than the other.

A familiar pang of guilt hit her in the gut. "I can come back on the weekends. Or maybe try to go part-time at the bakery, and—"

"Lizzy, the bakery was never your dream," he cut in. "Hell, it was never my dream. But it keeps us going. Makes enough for us to live, for you girls to go to school. Get bailed out of jail once or twice." He shrugged. "At the end of the day, it's there to work for us, not the other way around. Got it?"

She nodded, trying to keep her emotions in check. Still, a few tears filled the corners of her eyes. "I think you're going to miss my scones, though."

"Probably." He let out a hoarse chuckle. "But baking has never been the issue."

Another stab of concern hit Lizzy's chest. He was right, the bakery was great, but it was everything else that seemed to trip them up. The website, the bookkeeping . . . her worries must have been written across her face, because when her father looked up at her again, his expression softened. "Jesus, Lizzy. Stop worrying about us. It's not your problem anymore. I'll figure it out."

She smiled. Then an idea struck her. "What about Kitty?"

"What about her?"

"She studied business management. She could help."

He shook his head. "I don't think she'd be interested."

"Are you serious? Dad, she spends every waking hour coming up with ideas for the bakery. She's even spent the past year working on some top secret business plan. And, yes, she's not great at the actual baking part, but we can make up for that. When it comes to numbers and marketing plans and all that? She's perfect."

"Kitty, huh. I thought she wanted to be an influencer."

Lizzy threw him a sardonic glare. "That's Lydia."

The corner of his mouth turned up again as he seemed to consider. "Right, right."

The sound of a car pulling up the driveway grabbed their attention. Lizzy's eyebrows knitted together as she listened to the engine die, a car door open and close, and footsteps walk up the porch.

Her father glanced down at his watch. "Who the hell is coming by at ten thirty?"

Lizzy shrugged and the two of them stood, peeking their heads over the deck to see a black Mercedes sedan parked nearby. There was a thin silhouette of a woman standing at the front door, her blond hair pulled back in a tight ponytail and a bouclé jacket hanging off her shoulders.

Crap. Birdie Carrington.

The doorbell echoed out from the house, and Lizzy could hear chaos erupt inside.

"Get the door!"

"It's probably just Jane!" Lydia yelled back.

"Or one of your jilted lovers finally tracked you down!" Kitty cackled.

"Shut up!"

Then the bellows became a disjointed racket as Mrs. Bennet opened the door, her bathrobe barely covering her worn cotton nightgown.

"I should go," Lizzy said, already scrambling toward the ladder.

She made it to the porch to find her mother already rambling, and Birdie's red lips pursed.

"Oh, here she is!" her mother said, looking almost relieved. "Lizzy, this is Birdie Carrington. She just wanted to have a word with you."

Mrs. Bennet stared at her daughter, her smile skewed by utter confusion.

"Elizabeth," Birdie said, adjusting her fitted blazer. "Apologies for the late hour, but if you have a moment, perhaps we can talk. In private."

Lydia, Kitty, and Mary were all in their pajamas and crowded around their mother, waiting for Lizzy to answer.

"Okay." Lizzy looked around the yard, trying to decide how much privacy Birdie was looking for. She couldn't see Will's aunt climbing the ladder to the boat, and the garage—

"Why don't we go for a ride," Birdie said, as if reading her mind.

Lizzy nodded, following the woman past her father, who was now standing in the middle of the yard looking as confused as Lizzy felt.

With a loud chirp from her key fob, Birdie unlocked the doors to her sleek Mercedes and slid into the driver's seat.

"Have fun!" Lydia called out as Lizzy climbed into the passenger's side.

Lizzy shot her a look, then shut the car door, sealing them inside. The street was dark as they pulled out, the car's headlights illuminating small gnats that flew frantically in front of the bright beams.

After a moment, Birdie spoke. "Your family seems . . . nice."

Lizzy nodded. "Thanks."

"You know, just because I didn't grow up out here like you doesn't mean I don't appreciate how special it is. I love the history of this area."

Lizzy didn't know how to respond, so she kept her eyes locked straight ahead as Birdie pulled out onto Main Street, heading toward town.

"But change is inevitable," Birdie continued. "We should embrace that fact, see it as an opportunity."

"I'm sorry, Birdie, but I'm not sure I know what you're talking about."

Birdie's lips pursed. "Yes you do."

Lizzy waited, her eyebrows knitted together.

A sigh, like Birdie was growing impatient. "I was promised the Darcys' Montauk house by Will's father, John. He was my brother-in-law and he always said that when he was ready to sell it, I would be the broker."

Lizzy froze. Montauk. Will. She felt her stomach drop as her heart pounded against her ribs.

Birdie took a breath, then continued, "The loss of John and Claire was tragic. For me and for Will. But it's time to start moving on. Yes, Will was technically left the house, but his life is in the city, not here. It makes sense to sell."

Lizzy turned enough to narrow her eyes on Birdie. "I think that is up to Will, not you."

"And I think it's not your place to interfere."

"I haven't."

Birdie gave Lizzy a doubtful glance, then looked back at the road.

Lizzy shook her head. "I'm sorry, I don't—"

"We're both adults, so please don't placate me. I know there is something going on between you two. I can connect the dots. First, you tried to steer him away from selling the Montauk house when we were at the club having dinner. Am I supposed to think it's a coincidence that just a month later, he decided to stay out there for a week and comes back only to tell me he's not selling?"

Lizzy's pulse tripped. "He's not?"

"No! His receptionist said something, but I didn't believe her. That's why I insisted he call me himself. Then he waits until an ungodly hour tonight to finally get back to me? Unacceptable. He should know how rude it is to just ambush someone like that after hours." Lizzy was tempted to point out the irony of their current situation, but Birdie barreled on. "What's even worse is the fact that he barely said anything to me other than the house is going to remain in the Darcy trust and if I have questions, I should call his lawyers. Do you have any idea how much Page, Lefroy, and Brandon charge an hour to field my phone calls? It's ridiculous!"

Page, Lefroy, and Brandon. The name sounded familiar, but Lizzy couldn't place why. Her brain was spinning in too many directions. "Birdie, I didn't even know he had decided to keep the Montauk house until right now."

"Oh please," Birdie huffed. "You told him not to sell it."

"I told him to do what he wants."

"Well, clearly he wants what you want."

Something in Lizzy's chest tightened. "Is that what he said?"

"He didn't need to say anything," Birdie replied haughtily. "But I know how women like you see him. You love the bank account, the big houses—"

"Are you serious?" Lizzy replied, eyes wide.

Birdie turned to glare at her. "I'm always serious when it comes to real estate."

And just like that, Lizzy was done. "Pull over. I need to get out of this car."

"Don't be ridiculous. We're in the middle of nowhere."

"Let me out, Birdie."

Birdie huffed again, then swerved to the side of the road. The car had barely come to a stop before Lizzy flung the door open and stepped out.

"Will has been through so much!" Birdie cried, leaning across the passenger seat. "You can't manipulate him where he's most vulnerable just to get what you want!"

Lizzy stopped and turned around. "Neither can you."

Birdie's face blanched just as Lizzy slammed the car door shut.

The Mercedes sped forward, did a U-turn, then disappeared down the dark road, gravel and dirt swirling in its wake.

Lizzy looked down at her hands and realized they were shaking, adrenaline still coursing through her veins. Birdie's revelations were a jumbled mess in her head, but one fact remained clear: Will wasn't selling his house in Montauk. And he wasn't selling because of her. She hugged his stolen Columbia sweatshirt tightly around her, trying to tuck her nose into the soft material of the collar to inhale it. She missed his lips, his touch, and she wasn't going to deprive herself of him a second longer.

Her cell was tucked into the sweatshirt pocket, and she quickly reached for it. Birdie was probably calling Will right now, recounting their drive. Or maybe she was calling those lawyers of his at Page, Lefroy, and Brandon.

Wait.

She knew that law firm. The name had sounded familiar, nagging at her memory. Suddenly, Will's voicemail came back to her, the one when he told her to contact his lawyers for proof about Tristan. It was the same law firm that had witnessed Tristan's affidavit, the one that ensured Mary's release: Page, Lefroy, and Brandon.

Oh my God.

Will was the one who had saved Mary. He was probably the one who had repaid Hank as well. Her brain felt like it was going to explode.

She had to talk to him right now. And she had no idea how.

"Shit." She cursed as she stared down at the screen.

How had she left Montauk without getting his number? And when did she become one of the characters in her books that has no way to reach the guy she was swooning over?

Lizzy quickly dialed her sister.

"Hey," Jane answered sleepily. "Everything okay?"

"Yeah, are you with Charlie?"

"Yeah, we're staying at the Ocean Surf Inn tonight. Grand gesture, you know?" Jane said. Lizzy could hear the smile in her voice. Then she heard Charlie groan in the background. "And we're about to—"

"I don't want to know!" Lizzy said loudly.

"Watch a movie! Charlie's never seen *Attack of the Clones*." Jane laughed. "I would not have answered if we—"

"Okay. Right. Got it," Lizzy said, cutting her off. "So, ah, can you ask Charlie for Will's number?"

"Will Darcy's number?"

"Yeah."

Jane paused. "Why?"

"Well." Lizzy hesitated for a moment, then answered quickly, "I'm pretty sure I'm in love with him."

A long silence followed.

"You're joking," Jane finally said.

Lizzy cringed. "Not exactly the reaction I was hoping for."

"You're in love with Will? Will Darcy?"

There was a loud crash then, and Lizzy could hear Charlie yell something.

"Everything okay?" Lizzy asked, brow furrowed.

Jane sighed. "Hold on."

Her sister must have been covering the microphone because their voices became muffled. But Lizzy could make out a few of Charlie's words. *Ridiculous . . . Deserve each other . . . Point Break.*

Then Jane returned. "Okay, I have it."

"What's wrong with Charlie?"

"Something about Keanu Reeves, I think."

Lizzy was tempted to prod, but then her phone pinged with a text message.

"Just sent it to you," Jane said. "Call me later and tell me what exactly is going on?"

"Promise." Lizzy hung up and opened Will's contact information.

She saved it to her phone and started typing.

LIZZY

Hey. It's Lizzy. So, funny thing, I'm in love with you.

She immediately erased it and started again. Typing and typing, her head down and her focus on the screen, as she walked home.

> Hey. It's Lizzy. I hope you don't mind me texting you; I got your number from Jane. I should have gotten it sooner. I should have called as soon as I left Montauk and apologized for how I left things. I'm so used to doing everything myself that I don't know how to ask for help. Or how to accept it. You're maybe the only person I know who understands how that feels. Maybe that's why you did what you did for Mary. And I can never thank you enough, Will. But I can say I'm sorry. For the way I left. For not trusting you with all of this. For not telling you how I felt from the very beginning. You've always been honest with me, so I need to be honest with you. I've been falling for you since I saw you on the beach that first day in Montauk.

She had just reached the house when she finished typing. Staring down at the glowing screen, she pressed send before she could think better of it.

A half second later, she heard a ping. The sound of a text message being delivered.

She looked up, confused. It took her eyes a moment to adjust to the darkness, but when they did, her heart stumbled in her chest.

Will Darcy was standing in the middle of the road in front of her house, his head bent down as he read a text on his phone.

CHAPTER 36

Lizzy stopped, her feet planted in the pavement. "Will."

He raised his head to look at her. "Elizabeth."

She glanced up to her yard. The house was dark, everyone clearly in bed. Then she turned back to the man in front of her. His black sweater and jeans made him blend in with the night. Blond hair fell around his face, messy and unkempt like he'd been out for a late-night jog.

"What are you doing here?" she asked slowly.

"Currently, I'm reading."

Oh God.

"Listen," she said, squeezing her eyes closed to ward off the embarrassment. "I wasn't expecting to have to actually watch you read it, and to be honest, I don't even know what I wrote, it's so dark out—"

"Since Montauk?" he said, his voice low.

Her stomach dropped. "Um. Yeah. Yes."

He lifted his head to meet her gaze. "I've been falling for you a lot longer than that."

She stood frozen in place, questioning whether she'd heard him right.

He slipped his phone into his pocket and started toward her, stopping just inches away. A nearby streetlamp silhouetted his towering frame, highlighting every strand of his golden hair.

"Is that why you're here?" she breathed.

"I would have come sooner. I wanted to. But that would have meant admitting something to you—"

"You got Mary out of jail."

He released a deep sigh. "How did you know about that?"

"Your aunt was here. Just dropped me off about a mile down the road, actually."

"What?" His soft expression suddenly wavered between shock and anger.

"It's all right. I've never ridden in a Mercedes before."

Will cursed under his breath.

"She told me about the Montauk house," Lizzy continued. "That you're not going to sell. I think she blames me for that, like I'm the one who convinced you not to—"

"You were."

She swallowed around the lump in her throat and tried to smile. "I'm just glad you changed your mind."

He was staring at her from under the hard line of his brow, his eyes so intense she looked away, down at her Converse.

"She also mentioned your lawyers at Page, Lefroy, and Brandon," she said, and let out a shaky breath. "That's the same law firm you told me to call about what Tristan had done to your dad."

He nodded once.

"Those are the same lawyers that witnessed Tristan's affidavit that dropped all charges against Mary. And I bet if I looked at who paid back Hank, I'd find the names Page, Lefroy, and Brandon, too," she said.

He took a step closer and brushed a strand of her unruly red hair behind her ear, sending a shiver down her spine. "You weren't supposed to figure that out."

Tears were already forming in the corners of her eyes even as she smiled again. "Then you should have done a better job covering it up."

He smiled back, that same unpracticed grin she loved so much.

"You have no idea how much it means to my family," she whispered. "How much it means to this entire town."

He cocked his head to the side, as if picking his words carefully. "I didn't do it for them, Lizzy. I did it for you."

She shook her head. "But I just left. I barely said anything, and when I did, I was so angry and scared, I didn't—"

"Lizzy." His voice was deep, demanding. She looked up to meet his gaze. "It was all for you."

She could feel the tension radiating off his body, as if it was taking all his energy to hold himself back. Like he was waiting for her to tell him it was okay.

So she reached out and rested her hands on his chest.

He let out a long sigh, then ran his hands down her arms, pulling her closer to him. His face lingered close to hers, his breath hot on her skin until he moved to kiss her cheek, softly. Then he pulled back enough to look at her.

"I love you," he breathed.

Her heart was hammering in her chest as she studied his face, her gaze darting from his eyes to his mouth, then back up again. His hands drifted down to circle her waist, pulling her closer.

"I don't need you to say it back," he continued. "And I don't need you to feel the same way. But—"

"I love you, too," she whispered. "Of course I do."

He stared at her for a moment. His expression was like stone, but his eyes . . . there was a vulnerability there that was so intense it made her breath hitch.

His hand moved to cradle her face, his thumb gently tracing over her cheekbone until he tilted her head up toward his.

"Of course," he repeated. Then a small smile ticked up the corner of his mouth. "But I loved you first."

Time seemed to stop. It was only them. Her heart drummed against her chest while his lips hovered above hers. Then he drew her mouth to his. His lips were soft as he kissed her, his movements unhurried as she arched into him. She hummed into his mouth, the grip of his hands lacing through her hair sending shivers down her spine.

Standing on her toes, she fell against him, desperation taking hold. She wrapped her arms around his neck, burying her fingers in his hair. He groaned, his kiss deepening. Their hands were everywhere, grabbing at each other, pulling at one another's clothes, until Lizzy remembered where they were. "Where . . . can we . . . go?" she whispered between kisses.

"Lizzy. We're at your house."

"Can't go inside," she mumbled, licking at his full lips. "Whole family . . ."

"Right . . ."

"Your place?" she asked.

"I don't have a car," he panted, nipping her jaw.

She pulled back to look at him. "How did you get here?"

"I took a helicopter from the city, then walked from the airport. Marv said he had five other rides before me. So . . ."

"But it's after dark in a town that barely has working street-lights," she said, mimicking the same tone he had used with her outside the Fourth of July party.

He smiled. "Are you trying to convince me to get in your car?"

"It's a single cab truck. And currently blocked in by my mom."

"Damn it."

She leaned her head against his chest. "This is ridiculous."

"You don't have an old boathouse packed with surfboards nearby, do you?" he asked.

"No . . ." Then she lit up. "But I do have a boat."

She grabbed his hand and led him to the side of the house where her father's boat sat shrouded in darkness. The lights were off, and at this time of night there was no way her dad would be there, she was sure of it.

"Shit," Will said as he tripped on a rogue twig. "I can't see anything."

"Shhhh." Lizzy motioned to the windows of her parents' home.

The rickety wood ladder hung off the side like it was waiting for them. They barely made it up to the deck before Will grabbed her by the waist as she kicked off her sneakers, then followed suit, flinging his shoes off the side of the boat to the grass below. Together they stumbled backward toward the outdoor cushions, which immediately slid off the bench, landing with a smack on the wood deck.

"Damn it." He laughed, looking up at her from the ground.

"Oh! Right. The cushions aren't attached," she said, covering her mouth to suppress a laugh. He grabbed her hand and pulled her down.

Lizzy let out a shriek and landed on top of him.

"I thought we were supposed to keep the volume down," he murmured, holding her close so he could kiss her neck.

"I don't know if I can do that," she whispered.

"Try."

She gasped when he started to move his body against hers in a slow, addictive rhythm, as his fingers roamed to the base of her sweatshirt to lift it higher.

She stopped him and leaned back. "This way… bed… follow me."

Then she took his hand and snuck over to the steps, crouching down so as not to hit her head on anything. The cabin was narrow, barely big enough for one adult, but a full bed fit snugly in its berth. With only a small curtained window to let in any light, Lizzy waited for her eyes to adjust to the darkness.

"Watch your—"

Will smacked his head against the low doorframe. "Shit."

"Step."

"Where the hell is the light switch?" he murmured.

"No light switch," she whispered, crawling up onto the bed. "Just follow my voice." She lifted her hips, pulling off her jeans and kicking them to the floor, sinking back into the boat's threadbare quilt in only his Columbia sweatshirt and her underwear.

She could just make out his silhouette as he undressed down to his boxers before moving over her again. The bed creaked with his weight, and she felt his body at her side, his warm skin against hers. They were all shadows and figures moving in the dark, feeling their way toward each other.

"I feel like I've just snuck into my girlfriend's dorm room," he whispered, wrapping his arms around her body as they lay facing each other.

"Girlfriend?" she asked, running her fingers down his chest, his heart beating fast beneath her palms.

"Yes. And she has entirely too many clothes on."

His face was so close, but she could barely make out his expression. Still, she brushed her nose against his before kissing the side of his mouth and what felt like a smile.

"That's unfortunate," Lizzy replied, deftly lifting the sweatshirt over her head, then lying back down in just her bra and underwear. "How about now?"

"Let's see," he mumbled, his voice deep.

His fingers pushed her bra to the side so he could graze his thumb across her nipple. He pulled back, then clicked his tongue disapprovingly. "Can't have this."

He ran his fingers around her back, unfastening her bra. She helped remove it down her arms and threw it to the floor. He cupped her breast in one hand, then leaned forward to capture and lick the other one, teasing her nipple while her fingers threaded through his hair.

"Will," she whispered, sucking in a breath.

His hands moved to her thighs, skimming up to her right hip, hovering there until he finally traced his fingers along the lacy material of her underwear.

She whined softly, squeezing her legs together.

"Or this," he whispered in her ear.

His thumb hooked into the fabric and pulled it slowly down her legs until she had nothing on at all. She kicked the material to the floor as his hand continued its slow journey over her hip bone to her stomach, and up to her rib cage. His palm splayed across her body and stayed there.

"Fuck," he whispered. His breath was labored and hot against her skin.

She touched the elastic waist of his boxers. "What about these?"

He swore and yanked them off, pulling her against him once he was bare. She could feel him hard against her, but when she tried to move, he stilled.

"Don't stop," she whispered.

He began planting soft kisses down her neck. "I don't want to rush this."

She touched his forearms. "I know. But you're stuck with me. I'm not going anywhere."

She ran her fingers across his chest and felt him inhale sharply, as if it were killing him to hold back any longer.

"Neither am I." His hand grazed across her collarbone, sending chills down her spine, then his palm slid up her neck to cup her face. He traced her jawline with his finger as if he was trying to memorize her silhouette in the dark. Then he slowly tilted her chin up to meet his mouth and slowly, deliberately, pressed his lips against hers.

It was as if the darkness heightened all her other senses: the sweet smell of his skin—sandalwood and leather—mixing with the cool fall air, the taste of his lips as it melded with her lip balm, the light touch of his rough hands against her skin.

"More," she breathed.

"I'm trying to control myself," he murmured.

"Don't."

With that, he captured her mouth in a hard kiss, the restraint quickly replaced by a raw hunger. His arms wrapped around her frame, her legs circled his hips, and they sank into each other. She traced the taut roped muscles of his arms as he moved down her body, planting kisses down her abdomen before settling between her legs. Then his hands gripped her thighs. She could barely make out his movements in the dark, but she could feel *everything*. His mouth was on her, soft at first, teasing, tasting, until she felt the pressure building, untethering her from reality.

She drew in a breath, sucking her bottom lip between her teeth to stifle a cry. "Yes . . . right there . . ."

His tongue worked faster, her hips jerking up to chase the feeling that threatened to consume her. Her hand twisted into his hair, holding on to him as he sent her over the edge.

She shuddered as warmth and pleasure flooded through her entire body. She lay bare in front of him, her heart beating in her ears until suddenly he was next to her again, nuzzling into her neck and kissing her hot skin.

"I could watch you come undone all night."

"Okay," she responded breathlessly. "We can do that."

He let out a gravelly laugh.

Turning toward him, her hand moved down his abdomen. She traced the chiseled outline of his hip, threatening to go lower, feeling the restraint in his muscles, the tension in him. She wrapped her fingers around his hardness, thick and substantial, and squeezed gently, eliciting a groan from his lips. He kissed her fiercely, his tongue fighting for dominance as she moved her hand up and down again and again, stroking his considerable length.

"Fuck . . ." he groaned.

He moved her body, lifting her to straddle him as he lay back, the sounds of their labored breathing filling the small cabin. The ceiling was too low for her to sit up, so she hovered over him, using her knees for balance, and they locked eyes in the dark night.

"You okay?" he asked, his hands running down her thighs.

"Yeah," she breathed. "Promise."

A hint of that crooked smile, then she slowly sank down onto him, the stretch already addictive and familiar, and a moan escaped her throat.

She started to move slowly but deliberately, a steady pace to satisfy the need already building again deep within her core. His hands ran up over her chest, teasing her, then down her arms until he grabbed one of her hands. He held it, entwining his long fingers with hers.

"Lizzy . . ." he whispered, moving his other hand to her jaw to pull her over him and press his lips against hers.

Their rhythm picked up and then, suddenly, there was no way

she could be quiet. She gasped loudly, moaning and demanding more as her hand tightened around his.

"God, you're gorgeous," he growled. Then his arm was around her waist, flipping her onto her back. He grasped one of her thighs, hiking it over his hip, so the angle was deeper, and he was rewarded with a string of soft whimpers.

"Yes . . . *yes*," she moaned. "Will . . ."

It was all the coaxing he needed. He snapped his hips into her, a slowly building crescendo. Then his hand journeyed down her stomach, lower, and his thumb circled her, slowly applying pressure until something inside her exploded.

She cried out, waves of pleasure crashing over her as she shuddered underneath him. He watched, his gaze intense and movements offbeat and frenetic, until he finally threw his head back and came with a groan.

They were still for a long moment, clinging to each other, the sound of their ravaged breathing filling the small space until he finally fell beside her.

She exhaled, turning to look at his profile illuminated by the smallest sliver of moonlight streaming in through the cabin window. His eyes were closed as he reached over, wrapping his arm around her waist and bringing her back to his chest to cradle her body against his.

There were sure to be a million different problems to tackle tomorrow. She had to figure out logistics for Columbia, help her family adjust to running the bakery . . . But where anxiety usually rose to fill her chest, there was nothing but warmth and peace. Then Will sighed, his breath falling in her hair, and suddenly, every ounce of worry left in her body disappeared. She didn't need to face tomorrow alone. She never would. They would face it all together.

CHAPTER 37

The morning sun filtered through the small boat window, waking Will. He turned to his side, barely registering the lumpy mattress or the threadbare quilt. Then the memory of last night came rushing back and he opened his eyes. Elizabeth Bennet was asleep next to him, lying on her stomach with half the quilt draped low across her naked back. The second he shifted, she opened one eye, then closed it again with a groan.

"Morning," he whispered.

The corners of her mouth turned up, even as her eyes stayed closed.

"Hmmm," she said groggily. Her hair was fanned out across her pillow, a halo of crimson and copper and rust. He picked up a few strands and softly rubbed them between two fingers, entranced by how the color changed in the morning light.

He had flown out to East Hampton last night to tell her the truth, to admit that despite her wishes, he had intervened to help Mary. He hadn't expected Lizzy to forgive him, but he had to try. He loved her too much to give up now. So how had they ended up here? He was still trying to work it out in his head. In the meantime, though, he was going to take his damn time soaking in this beautiful woman he loved, and who, for some reason, actually loved him back.

"You're staring," she said, opening one eye to look at him.

"That all right?"

She sighed, stretching her arms above her head. "I'm used to it."

"Oh really?"

"Yup. You're very good at it. Probably one of the reasons I fell in love with you."

The words hit the same warm part of his chest as they had last night. "Is that so?"

She nodded, yawning.

"That's good. Because I love you, too," he murmured, tracing a finger up her arm, across her back.

"And you loved me *first*." She hummed, a soft smile on her lips. "Supposedly."

"Lizzy, I think I fell in love with you the minute you suggested that Charlie and I go to Donato Lodge."

She finally opened both eyes and turned to lie on her side, her dark eyes dancing with amusement. "How is that possible? I was so mean to you."

He smiled. "I deserved it."

"Is that why you invited me to dinner after I washed up on your beach in Montauk like a stalker?"

"Stalkers have to eat, too."

She laughed. "I can't imagine what you thought when I actually showed up that night."

The memory of Lizzy standing there at his front door, the rush of relief that had filled his body the moment he saw her face, came back to him in an instant. "It taught me to hope."

Her smile faded as she studied his face. "Yeah?"

He nodded, watching her expression as the revelation settled in her mind. Then she slowly leaned forward and kissed him.

It was soft and languid, and after a moment he shifted over her, caging her in. When his knee coaxed her thighs open, she instinctively wrapped her legs around his hips, her hands lacing through his hair. She breathed in, grasping the back of his head as he kissed her again.

But then she stilled, pulling back suddenly. She put a hand on his chest for him to stop.

"Did you hear that?" she asked abruptly.

"No?" he replied, caressing her collarbone with his lips softly.

She moved to sit up and he collapsed next to her, resting on one elbow.

"It's coming from outside," she whispered, pulling the sheet over her.

"I would hope so, considering how much space is left in here—"

"Shhhh," she hissed, her hand moving across his chest to quiet him.

The ladder creaked, hitting against the boat several times, like someone was about to make the climb. Then it stopped.

"Oh my God," Lizzy whispered. Will didn't seem to understand the urgency of the situation and just watched her with a half smile, unbothered. "Will! Hide or cover yourself, or something!"

"Lizzy?" Bob Bennet's deep voice called from outside. "That you?"

"Ah, yeah?" she called back.

There was silence, then her father continued, "Permission to board?"

She replied hesitantly, ". . . Not granted?"

"You left your shoes out here, in case you were wondering," he called back.

"Ah, thanks!" she yelled back, an octave too high. He didn't sound mad, he didn't sound worried, he sounded . . . like he might be amused.

"When you two are done up there, come in for breakfast. I'm making pancakes," he added.

Then his footsteps retreated.

"Oh, for fuck's sake," she exhaled, burying her face in her hands.

"He seemed . . . good," Will mused.

She gave him a look. "That's great. Meanwhile I'm going to go jump off a tall building."

"Come on. Get up. We're all adults here, and I don't know about you, but I'd love some pancakes."

"Will, my entire family is inside."

He moved to the foot of the bed and stood, his head almost touching the ceiling. He found his boxers and slipped them on, then extended his hand to her.

"I'm all in, Lizzy." He smiled. "You're stuck with me, too."

"Get ready for a shitshow," she muttered to him, then leaned up and put her hand in his.

A disjointed cacophony welcomed them when they entered the house. Laughing and yelling could be heard over the sound of a local commercial blaring on the television.

Lizzy hesitated in the foyer, looking up at Will with a crease of worry between her eyebrows.

"What?" he asked.

She let out a shaky breath. "What if they all just . . . freak out?"

"They won't."

"What if they bombard you with insane questions?"

"I'll probably answer them."

"What if they're so embarrassing I run into the woods screaming?"

He smiled. "Then I'll come find you and bring you back."

A smile of her own started to slowly turn up her lips. "Really?"

"Yes. After the pancakes. I'm hungry."

She laughed. The warmth of it was enough to run a slow current through his body. He wanted to kiss her suddenly, carry her back to the boat and delay the rest of the morning for a few hours, but he could already hear movement from the kitchen.

"Lizzy?" Mrs. Bennet called out. "Where have you been?"

"Come on," he whispered, leaning down to kiss away the frown line between her brows before leading her forward.

They entered the kitchen, but there was a delayed reaction to their arrival. Kitty and Lydia were at the kitchen table arguing, while Mary sat opposite them reading a book. Mrs. Bennet was standing at the kitchen sink, her phone to her ear as she ignored the pancakes on the stovetop, nodding and agreeing with whoever was on the other end.

Then she caught sight of Will.

Her mouth fell open as she took in his rumpled sweater, his matted hair, and his hand wrapped around her daughter's. That's all it took for her to lose muscle function and drop her phone to the floor.

"Oh my God, Mom!" Lydia yelled. She turned in her chair to continue chastising her, but her eyes locked on Will and Lizzy instead.

"What's wrong?" Kitty asked her twin.

Lydia let out a strangled whine.

Kitty turned to see them, too. Then Mary.

The kitchen was enveloped in silence.

All eyes followed Will as he walked to the coffeemaker, took two mugs off the shelf, and poured a cup for Lizzy and the other for himself. Then he leaned a hip against the counter as he took a sip. "Good morning."

"What . . . is . . . *happening*," Mrs. Bennet croaked.

Lizzy opened her mouth to reply, her cheeks so flushed it was almost comical, but no words came out. She looked up at Will for a lifeline.

He gave her one. "I'm in love with your daughter."

For a half second it looked like Mrs. Bennet was about to pass out. The girls at the table let out a collective gasp. And Lizzy . . . she was still looking up at him, but the apprehension was gone. Her dark eyes were clear and large, locked on him.

"What?" Mrs. Bennet whispered.

"He's in love with Lizzy," Mr. Bennet announced, entering the room. He walked to the pancakes and flipped them over. "Who wants pancakes?"

And just like that, the chaos started all over again—Mrs. Bennet berating her husband, the girls firing questions at Lizzy, who tried to wave them off while Will threw his arm over her shoulder, bringing her close as he took a sip of his coffee.

Then his phone pinged with a message, followed quickly by another. He set his mug down on the counter and pulled his phone from his back pocket to look at the illuminated screen.

GEORGE KNIGHTLEY

Hey, did you see this?

The second message was a link to an article from the *New York Times*. Will clicked on it and froze.

A picture of Tristan Cole filled his screen. But it wasn't the same cocky man he had seen in the city just a few days ago. This Tristan was in gray sweatpants and an ill-fitting T-shirt, like he had just been pulled out of bed by the two men in suits at his side. His hands were behind his back, and even with the black eye, Will could tell that he was crying.

LONG ISLAND PROMOTER ARRESTED
ON 3 COUNTS OF WIRE FRAUD

What the fuck?

Lizzy must have felt him start, because she looked up from where she was wedged at his side, concern on her face. "You okay?"

He turned his phone so she could see the screen.

Her eyes slowly widened as she read. "Oh my God."

"What?" Mrs. Bennet asked, looking at her daughter with a mixture of excitement and despair. "Are you pregnant?"

Lizzy ignored her. "Tristan Cole was arrested this morning."

Mrs. Bennet's mouth fell open in shock, while Mary let out a laugh.

"Finally," Lydia murmured. Then she leaned forward and gave Kitty a fist bump.

"Wait," Lizzy said, pointing between them. "What did you two do?"

"What do you mean?" Kitty asked. It almost sounded convincing, except she didn't look confused. In fact, she and Lydia seemed to share a moment, looking at each other with smug satisfaction.

Will picked up on it, too. "What's going on?"

"Nothing," Kitty and Lydia replied in unison.

Mrs. Bennet let out an impatient sigh. "I swear to God, if another one of you ends up in jail . . ."

"No one is going to jail," Lydia said, about to put a forkful of pancakes in her mouth. Then she paused. "Well, except for Tristan."

"I just helped Lydia with a . . . project," Kitty said carefully.

"What project?" Will asked.

Kitty shrugged. "Just a little investigation into criminal insurance fraud."

Lizzy stilled. "What?"

"It's honestly not that complicated," Lydia said as she finished chewing. "Remember that video of Mary destroying that huge modern art painting in Tristan's apartment?"

No one answered; they all just stared at her, waiting.

"Okay, fast-forward to the next day when Lizzy came home from Montauk," Lydia continued. "When we were all in the bakery freaking out? Well, this woman called looking for Lizzy, but Lizzy was too busy yelling at Mom—"

"I wasn't yelling at Mom."

Lydia rolled her eyes again and barreled on. "So, I took a message. Her name was Emma . . . something. I forget."

Will paused. "Emma Woodhouse?"

"Yeah, something like that." Then Lydia paused, taking a bite of her pancakes. "Is there any more maple syrup in the fridge?" she said around the food in her mouth.

Lizzy sighed. "Lydia, focus."

"Fine," Lydia said, chewing. "So anyway, this Emma woman said she knew Lizzy and that she had an art advisor emergency, or something. And *then* she told me that we needed to look into that painting on Tristan's wall because he technically shouldn't even have it since it was, like, stolen or something. Oh, and she said Mary shouldn't feel bad for ruining it because it was awful and—"

"Lydia," Lizzy seethed.

"OKAY!" Lydia said, dropping her fork and leaning back. "So, I got off the phone and went to tell you, but you were busy and, honestly, being kind of a bitch, so I went to Kitty and told her. And it turns out this Emma woman was right."

Lizzy turned to Kitty, exasperated. "What is she talking about?"

"The painting on Tristan's wall was reported stolen three years ago," Kitty explained. "The insurance company paid out hundreds of thousands of dollars on the claim."

"But it could have been a print. Or just a really good fake," Lizzy said.

"Except that on the police report after the party, where it asked

Tristan to list all his damaged property, he actually put the name of the painting. And its value."

Lizzy blinked. "Are you serious?"

"Yup," Kitty said. There was a satisfied smile on her lips.

"Which could have just been a mistake, right?" Lydia continued. "Like, if Tristan just bought the painting, how would he know? But if he was the one who submitted that insurance claim and got the payoff, all while he still had the painting on his wall, that's like a big deal. So I called Danny."

Will was trying to keep up and it was clear he wasn't the only one.

"And who the hell is Danny?" Lizzy asked, looking completely lost.

"You remember Danny," Lydia replied, as if Lizzy was being purposely obtuse. "The insurance guy with the Bentley? We've only been talking all summer."

"Oh, you showed me a picture of him!" Mrs. Bennet exclaimed, apparently excited to have knowledge of at least one thing they were discussing. "He's really cute."

Lydia nodded proudly.

"Okay," Lizzy said, throwing her arms out as if it would keep everyone on track. "So what did Danny say?"

"Well, he said *technically* private insurance claims are confidential, so as far as anybody is concerned, he never looked up the old claim to see whose name was on it. Which was Tristan's."

A ripple of shock went through the kitchen.

"So what did you do?" Will asked.

"I called the FBI," Lydia continued with a flourish of her fork. "Obviously."

A thousand questions began to spin in Will's head, but it was Lizzy who was able to articulate the first one.

"You can just . . . call the FBI?" she asked.

Lydia rolled her eyes again. "It's on their website. Duh."

Will opened his mouth, ready with further questions. He wanted to know the details, to organize the information in a way that made sense.

But then he closed it again. He didn't need to control this. All that mattered was that Tristan was in jail. And for now, that was enough.

So instead, he raised his mug to Lydia. "Well done."

Lydia smiled smugly. "Thank you."

Everyone watched, dumbfounded, as they clinked their coffee mugs together and gave each other a nod. Will took a sip of his, while Lydia paused to study him unabashedly.

Then her head cocked to the side. "Are you seriously a natural blond?"

The stillness was broken as the kitchen erupted in yelling again: Mrs. Bennet telling Lydia she was being inappropriate, Lydia telling her mother that it was a good question, and Kitty telling them both to stop yelling. To her credit, Mary kept her head down, still reading her book.

The sound was deafening, the scene chaotic. After a minute, Lizzy turned to Will and groaned. "This is chaos."

He smiled down at her. Jesus, he loved this woman. No caveats or disclaimers. No deadlines or half-life. And the realization slowly dissolved the knot of tension in his chest.

"That's all right," he said, leaning down to kiss the corner of her mouth. "Some people don't mind a mess."

EPILOGUE

Memorial Day weekend arrived in East Hampton the same way it had every year before. By Friday afternoon, a long line of cars stretched down Montauk Highway all the way back to New York City, the beaches were crowded with Manhattanites, and the businesses along Main Street were bustling. Still, by eight p.m. the town had settled into its normal pace, and a sense of calm lay over everything.

Well, except for the party currently raging on the field outside the Village Hall.

"I LOVE THIS SONG!" Mrs. Bennet yelled over the guitar solo of the Friday night headliner, the Eazy E Street Band, a Bruce Springsteen and NWA cover group.

To the surprise of everyone, except maybe Hank Donato, the inaugural HamptonFest was a roaring success. Some of the initial plans had to be scaled back, of course—Marv refused to revise the village's noise ordinances so no acts were allowed to play past nine p.m., and Taylor Swift was unavailable to headline this year. But thanks to a sizable anonymous donation, a few generous sponsors, and partnerships with various local businesses whose tables now lined the periphery of the field, HamptonFest was kicking off with almost the entire town in attendance.

Lizzy stood to the side of the stage, sipping her beer as the band's guitar solo led to a DJ scratch, then the opening licks of "Born in the U.S.A." The crowd cheered, with Mrs. Bennet and Donna Donato front and center, screaming at the lead singer. Even Lizzy had to admit that he looked strikingly like Bruce Springsteen himself, except for the thick gold chain and L.A. Dodgers baseball cap. Her mother didn't seem to notice a difference, though. In fact, the way her hands were flailing behind her back now could only mean one thing . . .

Beside Lizzy, Jane winced. "Is she going to throw her bra onstage?"

"Let her have this," Lizzy said, patting Jane's arm. "She's earned it."

Jane smiled.

"Do you think anyone here realizes that this song is actually about the futility of war and a scathing critique of the country's treatment of veterans and the working class under Reagan?" Mary murmured from where she stood a few feet away. Her hair was a deep shade of green now. It matched her *There Is No Planet B* T-shirt.

Lizzy's head tilted to the side, watching as a very drunk Marv tried to balance his ex-wife on his shoulders so she could see the stage.

"Nope," she replied.

Mary snorted a laugh.

After her arrest last year, and the subsequent fallout, the truth about Tristan's lack of effort toward securing Gretna Island slowly came out—helped by Tristan's very public trial for felony insurance fraud and tax evasion. And while he was currently serving five years in prison, Hank begrudgingly gave up his dream of holding HamptonFest on the island.

Oddly enough, that motivated Green Justice to become one of the main sponsors of the revamped festival, securing the space around Village Hall and ensuring that all food waste was composted.

Where exactly Green Justice got the money to support such a festival was one of the worst-kept secrets in East Hampton.

Lizzy wasn't sure if it was out of boredom, spite, or actual altruism that made Vivienne Pierce write a personal check to Green Justice. Her ex-husband had finally been forced to honor their prenup, and Vivienne was awarded their Midtown penthouse and their French bulldog, Sha-Diamond, in the settlement. Afterward, she promptly sold the apartment and everything in it—except the dog, who never left her side—and donated a portion of the profits to the one organization she knew her oil tycoon ex-husband would hate: Mary's ecoterrorist organization. Now she was in Zermatt with Rainer, a Swiss-German ski instructor. Apparently, he saved her life after she slipped getting off a chairlift this past winter. They'd been inseparable ever since.

Hank also lifted his restraining order on Mary, after gaining the promise that she wouldn't get within fifteen feet of him during the festivities.

As if on cue, Mary craned her neck, looking down the edge of the crowd.

"See him?" Jane asked.

"No, but I think Lizzy's man is coming over. That, or he's about to do a runner."

Lizzy followed her gaze to where Will was walking along the periphery of the crowd, beer in hand. His face was grim, watching the scene with a mixture of confusion and aloofness.

She watched him approach, the lights from the stage flashing across his face as he came to a stop at her side.

"It's rude to stare, you know," he murmured.

She smiled. "Mary thinks you're a flight risk."

His brow furrowed. "Why?"

"Because you look miserable."

"Of course I'm miserable. Do you know what this song is about?"

Jane laughed as Mary rolled her eyes. "*Thank* you."

He let a crooked smile turn up the corner of his lips, then he raised his arm, the way he always did, inviting Lizzy into his side. She accepted, stepping forward and wrapping her arms around him.

Even after nine months, she couldn't get enough of his smell. That distinctive mix of sandalwood and leather, which she now knew was his body wash. She turned to press her nose against his shirt and inhaled. Then she looked up, her chin resting on his chest.

"Hello, Mr. Darcy."

"Hello, Ms. Bennet. Having a good time?"

She nodded, taking a deep sniff of his shirt again.

"You're not going to steal this one, too, are you?"

"Maybe."

He chuckled.

Mary groaned. "You two are gross."

Jane sighed, her eyes returning to the crowd. She had been looking for Charlie for the better part of an hour, and so far, no luck. Once the pair reunited last year, and Charlie decided the trip out to East Hampton from New York was much more pleasant in a car, he spent the weekends at his new beach house with Jane. Tonight marked their one-year anniversary of meeting, and she wanted to spend every second with him.

"Have you asked Freddie if he's seen Charlie?" Will suggested, pointing to the left side of the stage where Freddie Wentworth stood next to Birdie, casually sporting a look of restrained amusement on his face. Ever since he had decided to move back to the East Coast permanently, Birdie Carrington had been relentless in her pursuit to find Freddie the perfect turnkey apartment in the city. Unfortunately for Freddie, now a signed client, it seemed he would also receive the hard sell when it came to her quest to try to unload Marv's Lament as a summer rental yet again.

"He looks busy," Jane replied diplomatically.

"Do you think he's trying to see how long Birdie can go without taking a breath?" Lizzy mused.

"He might be there awhile," Will replied with a side glance.

Onstage, the DJ started looping the song, mixing "Born in the U.S.A." with "Straight Outta Compton," and the crowd began to oscillate between dancing and jumping, trying to find the over-riding beat. Lizzy didn't move, though, just relaxed against Will until Jane pointedly cleared her throat.

"Mary, eleven o'clock," she said in such a loud stage whisper that a few people nearby turned around.

Mary's head snapped in that direction, just in time to see Hank heading toward them, his face red and movements frantic. To anyone else, it would look like he was close to a heart attack, but Lizzy knew that the man had never been so stressed—and so happy—in his entire life.

"Right, I'm out," Mary said. "Text me when he's gone. I'll be over at Kitty's table."

Lizzy could see Kitty's table across the field. There was still a line in front of it, and the fact that people were willing to forgo tonight's headlining band to wait for their very own Kitty Cake was a testament to her sister's new business. After their father had approached her about taking a more active role at the bakery, Kitty had waited a whole twenty-four hours before presenting him with a detailed plan on not only how to modernize but grow. Within a month, they had a website capable of taking online orders, a new sign out front, and an automated voicemail system.

Then came the bigger surprise, the business plan Kitty had been working on for months: Kitty Cakes, a mail-order cake business that would send custom cakes anywhere in the country. It had been a harder sell to their father, but Kitty had anticipated as much. That's why she had first pitched the idea to Annabelle Pierce during Charlie's Fourth of July party. She became Kitty's first investor, and was the one to present Kitty Cakes in their meeting with other potential investors after their father finally agreed to secure the first round of funding. Now they were valued at over four million dollars, and were HamptonFest's number one sponsor.

"Grab me a piece of sour cherry cake," Will called out as Mary started away toward the Kitty Cakes table.

Mary gave a noncommittal wave. As much as she hated to admit it, she and Will had developed a unique friendship that seemed to revolve exclusively around a mutual love of land preservation and baked goods.

"Are you going to share?" Lizzy asked.

He sighed, heavy and dramatic. "We'll have to see. I'm very hungry."

She laughed and he smiled, and that wonderful warmth in her center glowed bright again.

Lizzy was surprised by how much she had been looking forward to HamptonFest. Her first semester at Columbia had kept her so busy that she felt she barely had a moment to breathe, let alone spend time with Will. Not that he made an issue out of it. The two of them split their time between Will's apartment in the city and the Montauk house.

As Hank got closer, Will leaned down and whispered in her ear, "Ready?"

She bit her lip and nodded.

Jane looked over at both of them, eyebrows knitted together. "Did I miss something?"

Lizzy was about to reply, but then Hank finally arrived.

"Lizzy! Jane! Oh, I'm so glad I found you both!" Then he gave a cursory nod to Will. "Hello, hello, hope you're enjoying yourself."

Will just nodded.

Lizzy still didn't know how he had managed to keep his HamptonFest donation a secret so even the organizer didn't know when he was talking to his benefactor, but she also knew it was exactly the way Will wanted it to be.

"Okay, it's time!" Hank said, already hurrying toward the stage. "Lizzy, give the signal!"

Why Lizzy had to be the one to cue Piper, she had no idea. But she still went up on her tiptoes, looking for her friend up in the wings offstage. The band was just finishing up their set when she caught sight of her standing next to her now-fiancée, Sasha, and a group of six-year-olds, waiting for her cue.

"What's going on?" Jane asked.

Lizzy ignored her and pulled out her phone, texting Piper:

LIZZY

GO TIME

Her friend saw the message a moment later. She looked up to find Lizzy in the crowd and gave her a thumbs-up. Then she leaned forward, whispering something to the band, who nodded in reply. For some reason, Sasha began to cheer, too, as if they had worked together to avert a global crisis.

The murmur of the crowd was silenced as the band's drummer started a drumroll. All eyes went to the center of the stage as Hank waltzed forward, smiling benevolently at the crowd.

"Hello, hello, hello! If I can have everyone's attention!" he announced. The crowd hushed. "Thank you all so much for being here for our first inaugural HamptonFest!" He paused for a splattering of claps and shouts. "I hope you're enjoying the music, courtesy of our sponsors, Donato Lodge, Green Justice, and Kitty Cakes!"

A lone *WAHOO* rang out from the front of the stage.

"Thank you, Lydia," Hank said, his smile looking strained. "Well, I know you think we're wrapping up for the first night of our three-day festival, but if you don't mind sticking around for another minute, there's one last surprise. So now, without further ado, straight from East Hampton Elementary, I would like to introduce Ms. Bennet's first-grade class!"

The crowd erupted in applause as a neat row of six-year-olds filed onstage, led by Piper and Sasha.

"What is going on?" Jane whispered, eyes wide.

Will's arms tightened around Lizzy's waist as she smiled.

Piper walked forward, bowing slightly to the crowd, then turned to the class and raised her arms. With a flick of her wrists, they began singing the opening verse of "God Only Knows," their small voices cracking and wobbling and creating such a perfect sound that Lizzy thought her heart would burst.

Next to her, it looked like Jane's had. Tears welled in her eyes as she watched her students struggle with the lyrics, trying desperately to hit the high notes and stay focused.

Then, just as they began the second verse, Charlie emerged onstage and walked to the microphone.

"Is Jane Bennet out there?" he asked, shielding his eyes from the lights shining on the stage.

Almost everyone in the crowd turned to where Jane stood beside Lizzy and Will.

Charlie smiled. "Jane, would you come up here for a minute?"

Applause broke out again as Jane walked forward, navigating the crowd in her light blue sundress. When she reached the steps up to the stage, Charlie leaned down and took her hand, helping her ascend until she stood in front of him.

"Jane, I have loved you since the first moment I set eyes on your TARDIS earrings. You are the best person I have ever known, and you make me happier than I could ever deserve. So, that's why I'm here. With a question."

The class was still humming the music as Charlie got down on one knee. Somewhere near the front of the stage there was a strangled cry, like Mrs. Bennet had just passed out.

"Jane Bennet, will you marry me?"

He barely had the words out before Jane was nodding, tears streaming down her face. And just like that, Charlie was up, taking her in his arms and spinning her around as the crowd lost their minds.

The band stepped forward again, and together with the class, began to play "God Only Knows" from the beginning. Jane and Charlie began to dance, laughing and spinning as the crowd began to pair off and do the same. Lizzy watched them, a look of such unabashed joy on her sister's face that her heart hurt.

Then Will's deep voice filled her ear. "Dance with me."

She turned to him, eyes narrowed. "You know how to dance?"

"No."

She laughed and took his hand, letting him lead her to the center of the crowd. He wrapped his arm firmly around her waist, pulling her close.

The field filled up with other couples then. Hank and Donna, Piper and Sasha, Mr. Bennet with his sobbing wife. Even Lydia and Kitty joined in, their exaggerated waltz cutting a line right through the space.

Lydia snorted, her drink sloshing over the rim of her cup as she twisted around Kitty, losing a grip on her hand so she almost landed on the Kitty Cakes table.

Kitty bent over, cackling. "So graceful!"

"I'm an angel!" Lydia cried, spinning back into her sister's arms.

Everyone was packed in tight, but Lizzy stayed tucked in Will's arms, leaning her forehead against his chest as the song slowly built.

Once it reached its crescendo, he leaned down and kissed the top of her head.

She looked up. His expression was exactly as it had always been, that hard line of his brow, the sharp line of his jaw. She wondered sometimes how she had gone so long only seeing that, never noticing the softness in his eyes, the earnestness there that revealed so much more than he could ever say.

She smiled, snuggling into him. It was funny—she had been running from this place for so long that she hadn't realized it was responsible for taking her where she needed to be. These people who had been with her since she was born, this town that had welcomed the two men who would change everything. No, it wasn't what she'd expected, but she knew now that she couldn't control it, either, and maybe it was okay to let go.

She closed her eyes, breathing in Will's scent again, and silently prayed to whoever might be listening: *Thank you for him. For this love that is so perfect I almost feel like I don't deserve it.*

Then she opened her eyes and looked up at Will again. "I love you, you know."

He grinned, that same unpracticed grin she had fallen for so many months before, then leaned down to whisper in her ear, "Yes, but I loved you first."

ACKNOWLEDGMENTS

Retelling a classic—especially one by Jane Austen—is an intimidating task. We cannot believe we've gotten the opportunity to do it again. *Pride and Prejudice* is one of our favorite books, and while writing *Emma of 83rd Street,* we gave Will Darcy a cameo, never thinking it would ever be more than a fun Easter egg for fellow Austenites. And now, here we are. Like so many of you, we have loved Elizabeth and Darcy for years (thank you, Colin Firth and Matthew Macfadyen)—all the movies, series, and adaptations have only added to their story and set the bar so high. And while we loved making it our own, we couldn't have even attempted this without our incredible team (and a lot of wine).

First off, thank you to the wonderful people of East Hampton and Springs, Long Island, who welcomed us so warmly—this book wouldn't exist without your insights, or your incredible farmers market.

Thank you to Joëlle Delbourgo, who is not only our agent but our biggest fan. None of this would have been possible without you! And thank you to our TV and film rights agent, Rich Green, as well as Ellen Goldsmith-Vein and the rest of the incredible team at the Gotham Group.

To our editor, Molly Gregory, who loves Will and Lizzy (and

Charlie!) almost as much as we do. Your notes and vision elevated their story beyond our wildest dreams—thank you. And thank you to our copy editor, Stacey Sakal, who ever so gently reminded us that fictional events still have to happen according to a real-life, human calendar. And to the entire team at Gallery Books—Jennifer Bergstrom, Jennifer Long, Aimée Bell, Sally Marvin, Lucy Nalen, Michelle Lecumberry, Caroline Pallotta, Emily Arzeno, Lisa Litwack, Matt Attanasio, and Christine Masters—as well as Anthea Bariamis and the team at Simon & Schuster Australia: we appreciate you all so much.

And thank you to everyone who has been there cheering us on from the sidelines since we started this crazy project. To Elizabeth Stoll Bellezza for all your support, positivity, and Hamptons' stories. To Whitney Tancred for helping us at every single turn. To Sam Bradford for all your enthusiasm and knowledge of life out east. To Molly Lyons, who was there with us from the start. To the wonderful Peter Robbins for being our gracious Hamptons tour guide and introducing us to the kindest community and the best sour cherry muffins we've ever tasted. To The Able Baker in Maplewood, NJ: thank you for not only educating us on the inner workings of a bakery, but also creating the greatest loaf of banana bread on the Eastern Seaboard. To Molly and Becca from *Pod and Prejudice*, for your support and shared love of all things Austen. And a big thank-you to our close friends Jenna Helwig, Nicole Page, Jessica Winchell Morsa, and Zoran Zgonc.

To Audrey's friends and family, thank you for embracing our first book so completely and already loving the second one! To my husband Mike for being my biggest supporter and always saying yes to every one of my ideas. To our boys, Bear and Dex, love you both. Thank you for announcing loudly that your "mom is an author" and people should "buy this book" whenever I drag you all to a new bookstore! I know your efforts helped our sales. I owe the Hamptons a shoutout and thank-you, as it is the location of my parents' meet-cute. In the summer of 1970, my mom and her girlfriends showed up to the wrong house party in the Hamptons and before anyone was the wiser, my dad had introduced himself. He got her phone number, they went on a few dates in the city, and they were married two years later. As they built their life together, they made sure my siblings and I took a few summer vacations out to Montauk to experience the beauty of it all. To my amazing mom, Elizabeth, the strongest, coolest best friend that I have been so lucky to have in my corner. Can you believe all this?! Only in our wildest dreams! To my dad, thank you for all the pep talks and support. To the sweetest, kindest sister ever, Veronica, and my brother-in-law, Mike G.; my super-cool and inspiring cousister, Diana; my wonderful brother, Philip, and sister-in-law, Yana: thank you all for always being there for me. To Ella and baby Meadow, love you. To the very best in-laws, Mary and Mike, and all the members of the Pierantozzi family, I'm very lucky. And to all my amazing friends, the outpouring of love and support for our books makes me emotional! Thank you, Whitney, for being family, and to Mason Pettit and Lindsay Fram—not sure what I'd do without your advice and support . . . daily. Katie S., Barbara W., Karen A., Amanda, Jake, Abby, Kerry P. Carolyn, Siu Ping, Amy, Allyson, Rachel, Marcia, Heather G. (or P. to me!), my Shangri-La girls, the *Office Ladies* podcast, Mountainside book club (twenty-five years and counting), the back road, [words] Bookstore, and SOMA—I appreciate you all so much. And of course, a huge thank-you to Tom, Poppy, and Henry—apologies for monopolizing all of Emily's time! To Emily, my bestie, I'd be a complete mess without you. Your friendship has meant everything. I can't wait to see what's next. Thank you for being there for me when I needed you most, for making work fun again, and for being the very best writing partner in the world.

To Emily's friends and family, thank you for your patience, your support, and your laughter. While being a writer is a dream come true, the process of writing can be daunting—all of you have made every second worth it. To my husband, Tom, who never lets a day go by without making me feel loved—Mr. Darcy has nothing on you. To Poppy and Henry, thanks for always cheering me on, even when it means I'm very busy and can't play Exploding Kittens. I love you forever and ever and always. To my parents, Kevin and Joan, for raising me in a house full of books and always supporting my love of writing. To my brother, Conor, my sister-in-law, Joowon, and to little Harper, for being the world's best cheerleaders, and to Melissa, for always knowing when a girl needs a good Taylor Swift video. To my transatlantic family, I am so grateful for each and every one of you! And to Audrey's family, Mike, Bear, and Dex: thank you for sharing Audrey with me so much over the past year. As you can see, we were actually writing a book and not just talking about odd pop culture milestones (although that happened a lot, too). And to my BFF, my sister from another mister, former prison cellmate, Audrey. Writing this book has meant the world to me, but getting to do it with you? It's like winning the lottery. Thank you for always being there, for listening, and for being my partner on this insane journey. Love you like Mary loves field slugs.

And finally, we want to thank all the readers out there who purchased, borrowed, or listened to our first book. Whether you're a Jane Austen fan or just wanted to read a sweet and steamy rom-com, we are so blown away by your support. Every post, mention, like, and addition to your TBR means the world to us. We never expected so much love for *Emma of 83rd Street*, and we hope *Elizabeth of East Hampton* hits the same chord with you. Thank you so much for spending your time with our book.

BOOK
CLUB
FAVORITES

READER'S
GUIDE

Elizabeth
of
East Hampton

AUDREY BELLEZZA
AND EMILY HARDING

This reading group guide for Elizabeth of East Hampton *includes an introduction, discussion questions, and ideas for enhancing your book club. The suggested questions are intended to help your reading group find new and interesting angles and topics for your discussion. We hope that these ideas will enrich your conversation and increase your enjoyment of the book.*

INTRODUCTION

This fresh and whip-smart modern retelling of Jane Austen's classic Pride and Prejudice—from the authors of the "great beach read" (*Bookreporter*) *Emma of 83rd Street*—transports you to summer in the Hamptons, where classes clash, rumors run wild, and love has a frustrating habit of popping up where you least expect it.

It's a truth universally acknowledged—well, by Elizabeth Bennet anyway—that there's nothing worse than summer in the Hamptons. She should know; she's lived out there her whole life. Every June, her hometown on the edge of Long Island is inundated with rich Manhattanites who party until dawn and then disappear come September. And after twenty-five years, Lizzy wants to leave, too.

But after putting her own dreams on hold to help save her family's struggling bakery, she's still surfing the same beach every morning and waiting for something, anything, to change. She's not holding her breath, though, not even when her sister starts flirting with the hot new bachelor in town, Charlie Pierce, and he introduces Lizzy to his even hotter friend.

Will Darcy is everything Lizzy Bennet is not. Aloof, arrogant . . . and rich. Of course, he's never cared about money. In fact, it's number one on his long list of things that only seem to complicate his life. Number two? His friend Charlie's insistence on setting him up with his new girlfriend's sharp-tongued sister. Lizzy Bennet is all wrong for him, from her embarrassingly chaotic family to her uncanny ability to speak to him as bluntly as he does to everyone else. But then, maybe that's why he can't stop thinking about her.

Lizzy is sure Will hates everybody. He thinks she enjoys being difficult. Yet just as they strike an uneasy truce, mistakes threaten Charlie and Jane's romance, with Will and Lizzy caught in the undertow. Between a hurricane and a hypocritical aunt, a drunken voicemail and a deceptive event promoter, the two must sift through the gossip and lies to protect the happiness of everyone they love—even if it means sacrificing their own. But when the truth also forces them to see each other in an entirely new light, they must swallow their pride to learn that love is a lot like surfing: sometimes the only way to survive is to let yourself fall.

TOPICS & QUESTIONS
FOR DISCUSSION

1. How did the authors modernize the characters from Jane Austen's *Pride and Prejudice*? Specifically, what traits, quirks, and details did they ascribe to each of the main characters (Lizzy, Jane, Kitty, Lydia, Mary, Darcy, Charlie)?

2. What did Will think of Lizzy when they first met at the bakery and vice versa?

3. How did the authors utilize the themes of *Pride and Prejudice* (e.g., class, family, integrity) to tell this modernized story?

4. How does the setting of *Elizabeth of East Hampton* lend itself to this retelling of the original work?

5. When do you think Lizzy started falling for Will and Will for Lizzy? Was there a particular moment or event? Do you think their personalities and lifestyles are compatible?

6. When Will and Charlie meet Jane and encounter Lizzy for the second time at Donato Lodge, why do you think Will sees Lizzy as "a mess"? Did you think she was a mess?

7. Discuss Mrs. Bennet's alleged involvement in multilevel marketing schemes, her leggings business, and her business strategies. How does it add to the picture of her overall character?

8. In Chapter 21, Jane tells Lizzy, "Being nice is easy. Anyone can pretend to be nice. But there's a difference between being nice and being kind." What do you think about this statement? Are there any characters who fit squarely in one bucket rather than the other? Are there any morally gray characters?

9. In chapter 18, Lizzy tells Will, "My courage always rises with every attempt to intimidate me." This line also appears in the original *Pride and Prejudice* novel. How do you think it translates to modern times? Where might Lizzy have previously experienced intimidation in both novels?

10. What did you think about Tristan when he was first introduced? How did your opinion of him change over the course of the book? Can you see his side of the story in his feud with Will?

11. Lizzy is an unwavering source of support for her family. Did you feel that this support was returned to her in any way by any particular character? How so?

12. Do you feel that Mr. and Mrs. Bennet fully appreciate the commitment of their daughters to the family business? Why do you think Mr. Bennet never spoke to Lizzy about pursuing journalism until she reveals her acceptance into Columbia's School of Journalism?

13. Discuss Piper and Mary. Did you feel these characters had any influence over Lizzy and her decisions and feelings? How so or how not?

ENHANCE YOUR BOOK CLUB

1. Discuss Lizzy and Will's story arc and then make a playlist for it, in chronological order.

2. Read *Pride and Prejudice* by Jane Austen, and discuss how the authors adjusted that story for the modern day in *Elizabeth of East Hampton*. What are the events in both this novel and *Pride and Prejudice* that set Lizzy and Will's story in motion, forcing them to interact with each other? Do a scene-for-scene comparison of these events.

3. Create a signature cocktail or mocktail for Charlie's Fourth of July party. Each ingredient should have some significance to the story and setting (e.g., sour cherries for the famous Bennet Bakery muffins).

4. If you were the casting director of a film version of *Elizabeth of East Hampton*, who would you cast in each role?

5. On any given Friday night at Donato Lodge, you could find a mash-up cover band playing a set, such as Here Comes the Sandman (The Beatles x Metallica) and Korndogg (Korn x Snoop Dogg). Create a list of mash-up bands you'd like to hear if you were a regular at Donato's.